The Night Belongs to the Maquis is a powerful and profound story of the ravages of war and the courage of ordinary people who rise to face the evil in their midst. Set in the harsh beauty of the foothills of the Pyrénées during the Nazi occupation of France, the narrative explores with both sensitivity and stark honesty the devastating choices facing the inhabitants of the tiny village of Foix. Not only does *The Night Belongs to the Maquis* take readers on a dramatic, suspenseful journey with a band of Resistance fighters shepherding Allied pilots and Jewish refugees to safety across the mountains, it also delves with acute perception into the darkness of the soul, the fears and imperfections that haunt its characters as they confront the loss of all they cherish.

A beautifully written, complex and layered story that both challenges our understanding of what it means to be human and offers hope that the seeds of goodness will prevail.

— LINDA CARDILLO, AWARD-WINNING AUTHOR OF *LOVE THAT MOVES THE SUN* AND THE FIRST LIGHT SERIES

The Night Belongs to the Maquis is both a highly imaginative and exhaustively researched historical novel that kept this reader glued to its pages, hooked by its page-turning suspense and rooting for its dynamic characters. Carolyn Kay Brancato has done a great honor to the real-life men and women who inspired this book and given all of us an important story of resistance and grace.

— CHRISTOPHER CASTELLANI, AUTHOR OF *LEADING MEN*

The *Night Belongs to the Maquis* is a riveting book that pulls the reader into the throes of what it might have been like to live during this incredibly challenging and horrific period in our existence. It brings to the fore a time when people risked their lives to save others. This is a

story of love and of staying true to one's beliefs. The bravery and truly heroic actions of the maquisards, who aided in the escape of downed Allied airmen, Jews and others pursued by the Nazis, is a part of our human history that is retold here and brought to life through the fictional characters of Sylvie and Hélène. A must-read!

— Anastasia Stanmeyer, Editor-in-Chief, *Berkshire Magazine*

Carolyn Kay Brancato, an expert in corporate governance, applies her forensic investigative skills to create a thoroughly researched and graphic depiction of French resistance to Nazi occupation. *The Night of the Maquis* describes how ordinary people handle ambiguous emotions to act with conviction. The novel is a timely reminder of the need to stand up to tyranny in the face of violence and intimidation.

—Andrew Tank, Executive Director,
The Conference Board Europe, Brussels

THE
NIGHT
BELONGS
TO THE
MAQUIS

A WWII Novel

CAROLYN KAY BRANCATO

STATION
SQUARE
═ MEDIA ═
NEW YORK, NEW YORK

THE NIGHT BELONGS TO THE MAQUIS: A WWII Novel
Copyright © 2021 by Carolyn Kay Brancato
Published by Station Square Media
115 East 23rd Street, 3rd Floor
New York, NY 10010

Editorial: Diane O'Connell, Write to Sell Your Book, LLC
Copyeditor: James King
Cover and Layout Design: Steven Plummer/SP Book Design
Production Management: Janet Spencer King, Book Development Group

Printed in the United States of America for Worldwide Distribution

ISBN: 978-1-7336380-3-6

Electronic editions:
          Mobi ISBN: 978-1-7336380-4-3
          EPUB ISBN: 978-1-7336380-5-0

First Edition

DEDICATION

To Howard

...and to all those courageous enough to fight fascism...
past and present

CHAPTER ONE

The Pyrénées, France. Mid-September 1939

SHOTGUN IN HAND, Sylvie Laget bounds down the ridge to her ramshackle farmhouse. Bracing against the biting wind, she heaves her leather pouch onto the cleaning table, then drags out a ring-necked pheasant and sets to work plucking. Now, there will be food for the table when Jean Galliard comes to Sunday supper, as he always does.

Sylvie pauses her work to watch the sun climb and illuminate the rugged contours of the saw-tooth Pyrénées surrounding her. The darkness that shrouds the jagged limestone cliffs gradually gives way to the light, infusing her with a sense of joyous rebirth each morning. This is something she can count on, even as the world lurches out of control with the advancing war.

Back to the task at hand, she pauses to admire the pheasant's crown of iridescent turquoise that travels around its red feathers and down onto its neck. Tracing this exquisite blue, though, she's pained to see it vanish underneath a thick white ring around its neck as if someone had strangled the color out of it, just there. She's further drawn to the blood-red circle of feathers around the bird's dead eye. She shudders, trying to shake off the increasing dread she's felt since Hitler invaded Czechoslovakia and then Poland, prompting the British and French to declare war.

Jean insists the fighting will be over in a flash. Sylvie both loves and hates that he's so protective, like an older brother, although they're both twenty years old. Imagining him not coming back, she feels a sharp pain as if she's been shot through, like the still warm, beautiful creature she holds in her hands. If he never returns, she'll be devastated, not only because they've struggled together for years to keep their neighboring farms going, but because she's finally ready to admit her yearning for him. Yearning for more than what they shared growing up together, her father teaching them both to hunt. Yearning for more than their bonding to amicably divide their game in the leather pouches slung over their shoulders.

In wanting more, however, a deep-seated fear surfaces—she'd be cornered, like a pheasant in the scrabbled underbrush, with a choking white-collared ring around its neck. Caught in a marriage she's been dreaming of, aching for, but one that could rob her of her independence—if she were to put a man, even Jean whom she trusts like no other, in charge of her farmhouse, her shotgun, her fate.

Sylvie hates acknowledging any vulnerability, so she rushes to finish her work and briskly enters the farmhouse to soak the birds before hanging them to cure. Tossing her jacket and leather cap onto hooks by the door, she strides to the large stone fireplace, stirs the embers, and throws on a small chuck of wood, sending fiery ashes flying. Étienne, her pale and skinny younger brother, scrambles up from his homework, spread over the large oak kitchen table where generations of their family have gathered. In addition to his school books, various political pamphlets are also scattered about.

Stirring the fire, she barks, "You can't even keep this going?" Her anger flares—she's had to run the farm and take care of Étienne since their parents died nearly two years ago. Claude, their father's brother, came to live with them and help out, but he spends most of his time in the village with the old soldiers from the Great War.

Étienne whips off his wire-rimmed glasses. "Sylvie, I want to go."

"I won't sign. Thirteen's too young."

He grabs a pamphlet. All angles and looming over her, he thrusts it in her face. "We've got to fight for the common good. A more perfect world. Where everyone—"

"Don't preach that communist rot to me. See what good it did in Spain."

"But it says here—"

"I told Uncle Claude not to give you those." Damn her Uncle for filling her brother's already bookish and impractical head with nothing but lost political causes.

He purses his lips and tramps back to the table.

Feeling the weight of never-ending chores around the farm, Sylvie exhales sharply. Cooking a meal, even their daily supper, is immensely satisfying, with its tangible and controllable outcome. It also provides an antidote to her mounting anxiety over the impending war. She reaches up to the wrought-iron ring in the ceiling and takes down one of her late mother's ceramic pots, its deep crimson clay identifiable as the well-known signature of their tiny village of Foix. Filled with a calming sense of control, she runs her hands around the smooth solidity of the pot, enjoying its flare of crimson in the light. Still, she struggles to dissipate her anger at her brother's latest, cavalier demand to enlist, as he's never once shown appreciation for all she's done to keep their family afloat. As Sylvie chops the potatoes, vegetables, and rabbit meat for the evening's stew, her work is interrupted by the frenzied screeching of crows outside. She catches sight of them through the window, flying towards the outcrop of brambles on the distant rocky ledge. A flock—a murder—of black crows.

Unsettled, she gazes down the valley at her beloved village of Foix. Its quaint red-tiled roofs and narrow cobbled lanes were laid out centuries ago in a confusing maze—a tangled labyrinth to protect the villagers from medieval invaders. She shudders as she imagines the Nazis overrunning Foix, her neighbors screaming as they flee—not from the bloody broadswords of old but from the efficient machine guns of the Wehrmacht.

She stands frozen, waiting for this latest feeling of dread to pass, then turns back to preparing the food.

Étienne warbles, "I'll get Uncle Claude to sign."

She calls over her shoulder, "Your voice hasn't even changed."

"Uncle Claude's dying to go."

"He's fifty years old, for heaven's sake. And you're too young." She makes the sign of the cross. "I thank God you'll both be out of danger."

They work in angry silence. After a while, she turns to him. "I'm sorry, Étienne." She adds, with exaggerated bravado, "Anyway, the war's not going to reach us way up here."

"Nothing reaches us way up here. The war's gonna be over before I'm old enough."

"There'll always be another war. Then you won't need my permission to get yourself killed."

"You just don't want Jean to go. I see the way you look at him." He mimics a big sloppy kiss.

Sylvie reddens as if she'd been slapped. With the war virtually inevitable, her feelings for Jean, which had been growing for some time, have significantly intensified.

As if reading her thoughts, Étienne chirps, "He doesn't want to marry you. You're an old maid." He slams his notebook shut. "Besides, you look like a man with your stupid trousers and that old cap."

She's appalled at his taunt—her father's hunting cap means the world to her. "If you'd taken your nose out of your books long enough to come hunting with us, he might have given it to you."

"Your precious Jean is teaching me how to hunt."

"How's that going?"

He opens his mouth but quickly closes it and adjusts his glasses.

"Not so well?"

"Maybe you can shoot straight. But that's all he sees in you."

"You're a jealous, hateful—" *Merde... another sin for the confessional.* "Étienne, let's not fight. We're all we have."

Étienne shrugs and returns to his books, sneaking glances at the political pamphlets on the table.

Sylvie heaves the makings of the stew into the pot, then hangs it on the wrought-iron bar over the fire. She wipes her forehead with her sleeve, crosses herself, and murmurs a silent prayer for God to give her strength.

CHAPTER TWO

The Village of Foix. Mid-September 1939

J EAN GALLIARD MUSCLES his way through the throng of villagers, trying to get close enough to read the long lists posted outside the Town Hall. After checking those lists, some men appear jubilant while others are downhearted. Frantic to get closer, he pushes past a clutch of women wiping tears from their eyes, and lurches to the top step. Through the chaos of arms jutting from the crowd, he finds his name on the list for immediate mobilization. Elated, he disentangles himself, shouting and whooping. He heartily pounds some of his fellow villagers on the back. Suddenly, as villagers rush around him, he sinks to the bottom step, immobilized by a rash of conflicting emotions.

This is his chance to prove them all wrong—his whole life, boys yelling "coward's son." How many bruising fights? The old priest pulling him off the same boys he'd pummeled for the fifth time. Detention. The helpless look of his mother reading note after note the teachers sent home. Sylvie and her father were the only ones to always take his side. Never judging. Now, his decision is all the more important. She's got to be the one waiting for him when he returns triumphant from the war. He'll regale her with his daring exploits. Someone steps over him, jolting him. *Sylvie…how does she feel about me? Am I more to her than the brother I've always been? Damn, if only I had more time to sort things out with her.*

Jean jumps up and swiftly heads to the far side of the plaza. He raps sharply on the side door of the Church of St. Volusien. Not a believer in archaic Catholic rituals, he still admires this stalwart medieval building that towers over the tiny village of Foix.

Coiled and ready to spring, Jean waits at the ancient carved stone portico for the priest to open the door. Father Michel, dressed in his long black soutane, has a tall, slender sturdiness coupled with powerful hands that speak of the kind of manual farm work Jean admires. In his early thirties, the priest grew up on his family's farm in the next valley, his father and Jean's, distant cousins.

Father Michel's dark eyes widen as he greets Jean, kissing him on both cheeks. "To what do I owe the honor of this infrequent visit?" The priest's swarthy complexion, so common in this part of southern France, contrasts with the pure white of his collar. He looks past Jean into the square. "I was about to go to the Town Hall, right after I finished my sermon for Sunday Mass."

Jean bounds into the church. "Forget Sunday Mass."

"You usually do." Smirking, the priest motions for Jean to enter, even though he's already well inside.

"Please no sermons today, Michel." Jean paces the ancient floor, its stone slabs smoothed by the footsteps of centuries of parishioners. "I haven't much time."

"Then you'd better come into my office." The priest smiles broadly as he leads the way, then installs himself behind a rickety desk that looks a hundred years old. He motions Jean towards a chair which he refuses, continuing to sprint from one end of the small office to the other.

As the priest calmly waits, Jean frowns then nods as if arguing with himself. At last, he blurts out, "I'm being called up."

Father Michel knits his thick eyebrows. "I gathered."

"This is my chance."

The priest shakes his head. "You don't have anything to prove. You didn't—"

Jean slams his palms on the desk. "Coward's son?" His eyes water as he recalls a lifetime of humiliation. No one in the village ever let him forget that this father, gassed in the trenches of No Man's Land during the Great War, was discharged suffering from war neurosis. He hated his father for his weakness, even though at times and in the privacy of their home, he felt truly sorry for him. He saw up close how his father's catatonic state was punctuated by horrific night sweats and terrors, which ultimately drove him to put a gun in his mouth. Rage surges as Jean relives finding his father's body.

Father Michel speaks softly. "And you think this will make up—"

"You know damn well it will." Jean walks a few paces, struggling to get control of himself.

"Like taking all those chances smuggling supplies into Spain?"

"That was just practice. Besides, the Republican forces were in the right. And I made enough money to keep my farm—and Sylvie's—afloat."

"I see," says the priest, with a doubtful look. "Just practice for this war?"

"Everybody knew the Nazis were supporting Franco with all their new weapons. I wanted to see some close-up."

"Jean, you don't have to convince me."

"All right. Sorry, Michel." He softly adds, "But there's more. I want to get married. Right away."

"You haven't gotten some poor girl—?"

"No!" Jean strides to the window to avoid the priest's inquiring gaze. "I came down to the village for some errands." He turns back, beaming. "Then I planned to meet her to propose."

"I see."

"I figured after we got engaged, we'd have a few months."

"No one expected the mobilization to happen so fast."

"Then we'd get married before I was called up." Jean's smile vanishes. "But I'm being mobilized...right away. I leave tonight."

Father Michel nods, then slowly picks up a large gold-leafed book and opens a page. "You want to be married in the church? I'll need to waive the reading of the banns for the next three Sundays. Under the circumstances, I suppose..." He leans forward encouragingly. "This woman is different, I gather."

Jean looks out the window into the garden where vines of red and white roses wind through trellises that line the small stone courtyard. His farm and Sylvie's lie side by side on the mountain above. Trekking with her, they'd laugh together in their easy way, with no artifice. A capable woman, courageous in grieving for her late parents and worthy of sharing a life. Not some shrill, vain girl from the village.

"You both don't want to wait. I can understand—"

"I don't want to wait." Jean smiles sheepishly. "She doesn't know...yet."

Father Michel laughs outright. "Not even the engagement part?"

"I'm—"

"A bit presumptuous, no? Jean, I've never seen you smitten. Who is this fortunate girl?"

Jean flashes the priest a proud smile. "Sylvie Laget."

Father Michel leans back, aghast. "You're more like brother and sister."

"In a way. I certainly owe her father my life." He quickly adds, "But he'd approve of me marrying her. I'm sure of it. Well, I'm reasonably sure."

"She doesn't seem your type." The priest smirks. "You've had your pick."

A mischievous grin from Jean. "Michel...you could say that."

"And?"

Jean's tone turns deadly earnest. "You're right. I'd never thought of her that way before. But these last months, sorting through who'd manage things for me when I got called up." Jean swallows hard. "Michel, I've wasted a lot of time. Not realizing how deeply I feel about—"

"She's a devout young woman. Quite independent, I'll grant you, but deeply religious. After her parents died...she's well...she's more vulnerable than she seems." The priest shuts his book with a loud clap. "I won't see her taken advantage of. If this is some whim—"

"Michel, I give my word."

"She'd take care of your place if you asked. Why marriage?"

"I don't have to prove things to her. She's not vain. Or manipulative." Jean looks intently at the priest. "I've only recently realized how deeply...I...I love her."

Father Michel gets up and wraps a consoling arm around Jean. "This is sudden." He holds Jean's gaze. "Why not wait until you get back?" He makes the sign of the cross over Jean. "Of course you will return, pray God."

"Damn certain. Sorry, Michel."

As shouts are heard outside the church, Jean says, "The men are getting ready out there." He adds, a sincere plea in this voice, "If I bring her here, will you marry us?"

Father Michel claps his hands together in the gesture of prayer. "*D'accord*. If I'm convinced you're sincere. And she thinks you're worthy."

"I'm sure she'll say yes. At least I think she will."

More shouts from outside.

Father Michel says, "Sounds like you'd better hurry."

On his way out, Jean grabs the priest and kisses him on both cheeks. "Stay right where you are."

CHAPTER THREE

Toulouse, France. Mid-September 1939

HÉLÈNE CALMETTE DODGES the frenzied traffic in the Avenue de Grande Bretagne, one of the busiest streets in Toulouse. It teems with cars, bicycles, and people scurrying in all directions, carrying all manner of suitcases, satchels, valises, and makeshift bags. Lugging a large suitcase in one hand and gripping a heavy sack of groceries in the other, she just manages to jump aside as a heavy-set woman on a bicycle nearly runs her over.

Hélène mutters under her breath, "Almost as chaotic as the surgery." A nurse in her late twenties, she's used to handling the unexpected—treating a knife wound in the emergency clinic or helping deliver an expectant mother a month early. Today, however, she's so distraught she's barely able to function. Her nurse's cap, normally sitting squarely on her tight waves of blonde hair, has slid to the side; she ducks into a shop entrance to secure it. She's drenched with perspiration, despite the cool autumn air and the profuse shade offered by the ancient, gnarled plane trees on the avenue.

Hélène hurries off the main road and down a narrow cobbled

street, finally reaching the black lacquered front door of her modest apartment. She enters and slams the door, shutting out the boisterous noises of the street. She wishes she could also shut out the piercing images of a war rapidly encroaching on her life and happiness. Her kitchen is minuscule, but she feels a momentary lift in her spirits as bright sunlight from the window filters through the profusion of green leaves in her myriad cache pots—containers for her cherished, healing herbs that occupy every square inch of every flat surface.

Forcing a cheerful lilt in her voice, Hélène calls, "Gérard darling, I found some food for the train." Triumphant, she rushes to the narrow sideboard and lays out a loaf of coarse black bread, a block of hard cheese, and a brown paper packet of sliced meat. She looks up and stifles a laugh as she catches an image in the mirrored glass of the kitchen hutch: Gérard Calmette, a huge, burly man, emerges from the bathroom, large clumps of shaving cream clinging to what remains of his thick, black beard. She watches him playfully creep up behind her, marveling that this large man can take such soft steps—like a circus bear dressed as a ballerina, tip-toeing towards her. As he reaches her, he lets out a mischievous growl and grabs her, easily lifting her off the floor.

"Gérard, put me down," she mock-protests. She's warmed to her core by his good nature and unbounded joy, which, for years now, have enabled her to tolerate so many exceedingly grim times at the hospital. Constrained by the tiny kitchen, he swings her in a tight circle, and she plays at resisting, kicking her feet like a little girl. Alongside her slender, tall frame, he's immense—massive but muscular and fit. As he propels her around, she feels her angular cheekbones soften and meld into a warm smile that expands into her typical silken giggle. She closes her eyes, finally relaxing into his embrace.

Having left her family in the mountain village of Foix to study nursing in Toulouse, Hélène thanks God every day that she met this rough-looking man with a sunny disposition, who drove the medical supply truck from Avignon to her hospital. He's always been able to gently coax her out of her seriousness, but today especially, she clutches him to her, trying not to think about the war. Gérard is being mobilized, and the usual methodical and calm façade she employs at the hospital is deserting her. Her intense familiarity with blood and death is fraying her nerves, compounding her fear.

Gérard sets her down on the kitchen table and kisses her. Lumps of shaving cream rub off his broad chin, smearing her white porcelain skin. He raises her skirt and helps her as she eagerly unfastens her garters and wriggles out of her panties. A warm ache rises within her as her stockings fall over her sturdy lace-up heels. He bends his head between her legs, and she braces her feet against the opposing wall.

Hélène suddenly stops him. "No, please, Gérard," she whispers. "Let's try one last time. Maybe we'll be lucky." She moves to unbutton his trousers. "Hurry, darling."

He inclines his head with a silent question. She loves that he's always so careful, a man of his size, searching her soft blue eyes for permission. She breaks into a warm, expectant smile as he works his buttons with one hand and positions her, carefully and protectively, with the other. She draws him close, hard, and their synchronized movements reflect their time-honored passion and deep trust.

Immediately after their climax, their words overflow.

"Gérard, I don't want you to go."

"It won't take long. We'll crush them—"

She stops him with a desperate kiss. Gérard returns her urgency with a hug that nearly suffocates her. For a time they remain in that position—Hélène afraid to let go, feeling him equally unwilling to budge. Finally, she pulls back, gasping for breath.

"My Hélène, I'm sorry. I forget—"

"Your own strength. I know." She sets her resolve, whispering, "We must go."

His reluctant nod nearly brings her to tears. He buttons up and bends to help her, but she waves him off. "Go get ready, darling." She motions towards the suitcase she carried in from the street. "Some extra things for you. *Mon Dieu,* do you know how far I had to walk? The world's gone crazy."

Gérard disappears into the bathroom, calling back, "Your mother will be happy to have you back home."

As she often does in the emergency clinic, Hélène takes up some immediate tasks to focus on, to keep her fears in check. She straightens up her clothes, then tries to freshen up in the bathroom as they dodge each other in the small space. He finishes shaving then goes into the bedroom to pack while she fixes her disheveled hair, setting it back into tight curls.

Two narrow doors open from their bedroom onto a neatly tended, bricked-in garden. The afternoon sun shines directly onto a stone patio brimming with more of her precious healing herbs in colored earthenware pots. She darts into the garden and clips masses of greenery, separating them into piles to wrap in brown paper: one for Gérard—a talisman to protect her beloved husband—and the rest to use in her nursing when she arrives back home in Foix.

Gérard follows her into the kitchen and reaches down to envelop her in his burly embrace. "I'll think of you all the time."

She shudders. "You must come back to me."

He nods and squeezes her hard.

They kiss once more, then break apart. As they gather their things, she turns to Gérard. Her voice, usually soft but clear, breaks. "You've made me so happy." She blinks back tears and forces a smile. "I can feel it. We'll be lucky, I'm sure of it. We'll get to come back right here and resume our lives." With a resolve she desperately tries to maintain, Hélène ushers Gérard out into the noisy, chaotic street, then firmly closes the black lacquered door behind them.

CHAPTER FOUR

The Pyrénées, France. Mid-September 1939

NOT WANTING TO continue to fight with her brother over enlisting, Sylvie checks the stew on the fire and takes the scraps from her cooking to the mulch bin on the far side of the kitchen.

Claude Laget bursts in, clumping his boots, as always, on the wide-planked wooden floor. With his barrel chest coming to an abrupt taper at his waist and his short, stocky legs, her uncle has always reminded her of a sturdy mountain goat. Bushy tufts of white hair sprout around his bald spot, topping off his usual jovial, boisterous presence.

She calls over her shoulder, "Back so soon, Uncle Claude?"

Claude rushes up to Sylvie, blinking back tears. "I'm sorry. I—"

Étienne interrupts, "Uncle Claude, can't I go?"

Claude calls back to him, "We've been through this, Étienne, my boy." He turns back to her, his round face covered with sweat. "I just saw Jean down in the village. Sylvie—"

She grabs his thick forearms. "What's wrong?"

"They've called him up."

She stiffens. "We've got months yet."

"Everyone thought so. But his train leaves tonight."

"That can't be."

"He said to meet up on the mountain. Right now. Said you'd know the place." He squeezes her hands. "I'm sorry, Sylvie."

Étienne's high-pitched voice sears through the farmhouse. "What about me?"

She ignores her brother, runs to the door, and grabs her jacket and cap. *He can't be called up so soon.*

Étienne hurls his notebook to the floor. "Wait!"

Claude heads towards his room at the back of the farmhouse, calling to her, "I need my reservist uniform. Sign in the men as they leave." He pumps up his robust chest. "At least they're letting me do that." His eyes mist. "I'll see you both at the train station."

Sylvie wrenches the back door open and flies up the rocky slope. The late morning sun, now full over the mountains, forces her to squint as she scrambles up the steep terrain. She pants heavily as she climbs higher, knocking loose a spray of pebbles that skitter wildly down the valley. Struggling upwards through dense clumps of burnished red undergrowth, she hears a gruesome screeching. She flinches to see the angry crows she'd seen earlier from her farmhouse window, now dive-bombing each other, fighting over the last of the dried berries on the windswept mountainside below. Distracted, she catches her trouser leg on a low-lying bramble, which spins her around. She thrusts her right arm towards the spidery branch and grabs hold to avoid skidding back down, head over heels. As she swings herself back to safety, a thorn pierces her palm. She lands hard on the ground and sits there, sucking in sharp painful breaths, as she digs it out.

She feverishly scours the soaring firs, looking up towards the entrance to the cave for traces of Jean's wiry frame. She scans the newly harvested fields below, with their peaked stacks of hay laying golden and proud in the sun—the lifeblood for all the farmers in the valley. She imagines German invaders, the *Boches*, ruthlessly scattering them to the wind. The trees on the valley floor are a riot of scarlet and orange as if Nazi occupiers had already set fire to the ravine. The air, sharp and frigid, catches in her lungs, and as she looks up to the final ridge ahead, fear roots her in place. Her boots weigh a hundred kilos each. This could be the last time she and Jean might be together. Her stomach turns to acid. Two million Frenchmen died in the Great War. More than 300,000 at Verdun alone, buried in mass graves with no markers for their women to pray over. *Mon Dieu, not again!*

Another raucous cawing of crows snaps her back to reality. Sylvie propels herself ahead, up to the mass of shrubbery at the entrance to the cave. Their special place. Hiding there as children. Later, staging their hunts and dividing their quarry from there. She thrusts the bramble bushes aside and calls to Jean. Only an echo returns. She backs away from the cave and collapses onto a log in the small clearing outside. A shaft of sunlight pierces the forest, shining down on her before it's obscured by threatening dark clouds.

Suddenly, two strong hands clamp onto her shoulders. She whirls around and rises to face Jean, smiling broadly, his olive skin weathered, like hers, from the harsh mountain wind and sun. His dark brown eyes are close together, deep-set with the glaring intensity of a peregrine falcon. Indeed, hunting for pheasant and fox with him, she's lately begun to fantasize the two of them as falcons, clinging to rocky ledges, soaring in aerial courtship...she shakes her head back to reality.

"Jean...Uncle Claude said—"

"I know. We don't have much time. Come."

His arms are muscular, surprisingly outsized for his lean frame. He holds out his hand for her. This surprises her as he doesn't normally reach for her like that. At first, she draws back, confused. Then, as he's leaving so soon, she decides to slip her hand into his. He brushes aside the brambles and leads them into the cave.

With dappled sunlight from the opening to light the way, they pass under the arched and rocky entrance. Sylvie glances up to see the familiar vaulted ceiling. She's always found comfort in this church made by natural forces. Virtually a cathedral, it always amazes her, with its thirty-foot-high ceiling and its towering sides, slick with willowy cascades of water that shine turquoise in the slender shafts of light from the opening.

Jean carefully leads her beside an indigo lake that stretches into the depths of the cave and eventually disappears through a narrow crevice. Farther in, a large limestone room is crowded with a rich array of stalactites in various thicknesses and shapes. The relatively even cave floor is punctuated by a raft of stalagmites scattered about in clumps. Jean brings her towards a smooth boulder. In front is a circle of the charred remains of decades of fires lit by countless pairs of lovers. He takes some of the wood everyone knows to replenish and strikes a flint.

She struggles to suppress the yearning she feels for him. Wanting him to be her lover. Now more acutely than ever. Jean slowly takes her shoulders in his firm grip, the brotherly stance he's always maintained with her. She's devastated. *This is all I'll ever mean to him…a sister.* She sighs deeply, resigning herself to having no more than their past relationship.

But then, he takes off her cap, allowing her long thicket of hair to fall around her face. She holds her breath as he gently moves her tresses aside to stroke her cheek, then leans down and plants a deeply earnest kiss. Warmth spreads through her like fire. Terrified to open her emotional flood gates, she breaks away from him, urgently wanting him to pursue her and even more urgently fearing he won't.

Taller than she, Jean more than matches her stride, reaches around, and takes both her hands in his. Carefully, protectively, he leads her up and onto the smooth flat rock. Her pulse stops as he lays her back and strokes her hair into thick spokes leading away from her face like streams of water. Having dreamt of being loved by him, richly and unconditionally, she closes her eyes and breathes him in. For a moment, they lay absolutely still, suspended in time in a cave carved by millennia of rushing water. He leans down to kiss her, and then, like a torrent, the dyke breaks for her—she rises up and kisses him back with a furious hunger.

She revels in this kiss, but all of a sudden, it becomes too much for her. She bolts up. "I prayed you wouldn't have to go."

"It's a matter of honor."

"Honor. Then I should be going too." She sneers, "Why is it only men who get to go? Women can shoot." His eyes flicker. He opens his mouth to speak, but she cuts him off. "You know I'm a better shot."

He kisses her on one cheek. "You're more patient." He kisses her on the other cheek. "And more ruthless." He pulls her into his arms. "Of course you're capable." Then he adds, mischievously, "But we won't be hunting pheasant."

"*Merde.*"

She struggles against his embrace, but, laughing, he refuses to let go. A serious look spreads across his face. "Stop…please…I'm trying to get this out…I…I love you."

"What did you say?"

"I love you. I want…I want you to marry me."

She lets out a soft gasp.

"Father Michel's waived the reading of the banns. He's waiting right now. At St. Volusien… to…to marry us."

She opens her mouth to say something, but her throat closes up. Startled, she feels like she's looking down, hovering above them in the cool, damp air, as the sounds of water drip haphazardly from myriad stone outcrops.

"Sylvie?" His tone is urgent, defensive. "You don't want to marry me?"

"Waiting at St. Volusien?"

"I asked you here to propose. I thought we'd have a few months to be engaged. Then we could get married before I was called up."

She shakes her head in disbelief.

"But now we need to get married right away." He cups her oval face in his hands. "I love you." He kisses her deeply then whispers, "Will you say yes?"

She hesitates, trying to process how their relationship could have changed so abruptly.

He seems to read her hesitation. "Sylvie..." His voice trails off, his jaw clenched, his face taut in genuine distress.

Her world comes to a halt. Drips of water pause in midair, suspended on the tips of ancient stalactites. The soft lapping of the lake also ceases. Jean's proposal is tangible proof that he loves her. At the same time, a familiar terror wells up. True, he's long been part of their extended family, so of course she could trust that he wouldn't...what? Relegate her to the second-class citizenship of married women whose men dictate their every move? Jean's never been like that, so why would he start after they're married? There's so little time to sort this out.

He leans her back on the smooth stone. She allows his arms to envelop her as she gives in to a long, languorous kiss, closing her eyes as they explore each other's mouths. She is lost, dizzy as she climbs into realms of feelings she's only imagined.

Gently disengaging, he presses her face against his chest. She burrows in, reveling not only in the feeling of safety but also with a passion that surprises her.

He gently raises her chin. "We can't now. We've got to get to the Church."

She never wants to move from this smooth stone. She looks into his chiseled face, into his dark brown eyes, filled with golden flakes reflected from the fire. "I...Jean...I don't understand."

"I'm sorry. There's only enough time to get married—"

"Before you catch your train?" Abruptly, she slides away. Looking up to the vaulted cathedral ceiling of the cave, she closes her eyes and says a prayer. Then she decides—laughing at how absurdly impetuous it is for her, the careful one, when he's always been the reckless one. In the face of his leaving, all that matters is the desire that's been building within her. She wants to be loved by this man—but she's got to do it her way. Forcefully, she draws him close.

He smiles his impish smile. "So you'll marry me?"

"We have enough time to get married, but not enough before your train leaves for us to—" She stammers, "For us...to...to consummate the marriage?"

"I guess...when you put it that way."

"I don't care about the ceremony."

"I don't understand."

"Jean, I want us to make love. To seal our bond. Here and now."

He flinches as if absorbing a blow. "What are you saying?"

"Just your asking means all the world. It says we've forged our life's bond together. Isn't that what marriage means to you?"

"I'm not a practicing Catholic like you. But...I guess so." She gives him a questioning look, then he firmly adds, "Yes, it is."

"Making love will bind us more closely than any ceremony ever could."

His close-set eyes narrow. "What about the church?"

"It's been my salvation. Especially after my parents—" Her voice gathers strength. "But I'm secure in my faith. And right now, our love is my faith." She takes a deep breath. "We don't need some words Father Michel mumbles."

"Sylvie—are you sure?"

"More certain than I've ever been about anything."

"You won't regret it when I'm gone?"

She shakes her head emphatically. As she sees the hint of a smile appear in the corners of his mouth, a feeling of affirmation engulfs her. They lie back and she moves to unbutton her trousers. Jean slows her down, feeling her ample breasts through the muslin blouse under her jacket. Reverently, he circles his fingers, pressing her hardening nipples. His cheek nudges her neck, his heavy beard deliciously scratching. Her skin prickles and her heart races. As he helps her slip off her trousers, she feels a flush between her legs and laughs softly. Nervously. Involuntarily. She's imagined this moment, again and again. The moment she'll remember her whole life. The consummation of another person's love for her—Jean's love the very best of all.

They kiss sweetly, gently. Then an explosive current ignites, flowing between them. As he enters her, she feels a jolt of pain. He freezes, but she wraps her legs around him, pushing him deeper. He rasps, "Is it all right?"

She whispers coarsely, "Yes." The pain, over in an instant, fades then mingles with intense pleasure that swamps the terror attempting to flood back into her. Terror that all the people she loves will leave her. Terror that she will lose herself in another person and lose her independence. She trembles, which he seems to take as a sign of her increasing desire, so he moves faster, deeper. Finally, he arches himself one last time, and together they shudder, then relax, their bodies entwined. She breathes heavily for a long moment. Her shoulders heave slightly underneath him as she sobs, gently at first, then it builds. She has no idea why she's crying, only that she feels a torrent of emotion—happiness, relief, dread—but mostly love.

He rises onto one elbow and searches her face. This prompts even more tears, which he gently brushes away, kissing each of her eyes in turn. A rumble makes its way up to her throat, and she laughs deeply. Sylvie loves that he stops to look at her with great concern, which allows her to relax and laugh some more. Then he laughs too. Together, their mounting peals of laughter build into a chorus of joy that echoes throughout the cave.

CHAPTER FIVE

The Pyrénées, France. Mid-September 1939

SYLVIE PUSHES HER battered Citroën to its groaning limit as she races down the mountain towards the village of Foix. Her whole world is being yanked into the vortex of a storm. She speeds by barren hemp fields, turned over in the recent fall harvest. As the tight curves in the narrow road open out, snatches of sunlight turn the valley into vivid flashes of glorious fall color. And wasn't it glorious to make love to Jean only an hour ago? To have him hold her. Have him inside of her. *Stop it... concentrate on the road ahead. Get him to the station before his train departs.* But, she laments—the faster she drives, the sooner he'll be leaving her.

Jean sits motionless beside her, except for an occasional deep breath. She thinks he's probably keeping a tight lid on his feelings, just as she's coiled hers taut inside. Surely she made the right decision. She's already rehearsing her arguments before a disapproving Father Michel. *Jean loved me enough to ask me to marry him. That makes it all right, doesn't it?*

He squints hard. "If I don't return, I want you to have my farm. I should probably write it down."

Mon Dieu! He must return. Especially now that they've... She's elated for him to think of her this way but shocked at the prospect that he might not return. She grabs the steering wheel even more tightly, her knuckles turning white. She barks, "If you don't come back, the damned *Boches* will have won. And no one will have a farm to call their own." She immediately regrets her outburst. *Another sin for the confessional. To add to the monumental one I just committed in the cave.*

He casts a long, serious look at her. "Anyway, Father Michel knew we were to be married."

A knot forms in her throat. She glances at him, inadvertently swerving the car.

"Careful, I'll end up in a ditch before ever seeing a damned *Boche.*"

They laugh the forced laughter of people trying to keep their unspeakable fear in check.

As they round the last sharp turn, the narrow lane opens up, and the tiny village of Foix appears. She drives under the south stone gate that forms part of the ancient walls splaying around the town's central, high point—the Château des Comptes. In the Middle Ages, troubadours heralded the Château's impenetrability against a relentless, thousand-year succession of brutal marauders—French, Spanish, Moorish. Sylvie prays that the Château and her village will again prove impenetrable. The sharp wind whistles through the tunneled opening, shaking the car with its force. Sylvie has the strange sensation of wanting the car to move but not wanting to make progress towards their destination—so they might remain forever stationary and together.

Inside the village gate, rows of two- and three-story houses built of stucco are painted various shades of cream and tan. Each house has shutters that boast a different color—golden-yellow, forest-green, turquoise, or reddish-brown. She's comforted by the familiar clusters of bright red geraniums in the window boxes. The flowers converge into a virtual, continuous garden row, skipping horizontally from house to house in the narrow alleys.

In a few blocks, however, her calm fades as she confronts a mad-house of people, cars, and horse-drawn carts. The constricted streets of the small village are jammed as people race to the far side of Foix and towards the train station, which is across the river and only reachable by one twin-arched bridge over the river Ariège.

Sylvie jockeys the clutch, trying to avoid hitting anyone in the crowd. She jerks the car forward, making her way to the end of the Rue des Chapéliers that opens out onto the main plaza that is the heart of the village. The plaza is dominated by her beloved church of St. Volusien. It has always filled her with reverence, especially after Father Michel gave her such wise counsel following the death of her parents. On the plaza outside the church stands the finely wrought-iron canopy that shelters the Monday farmers' market, always a joy for her to attend and mingle with her neighbors. And then, of course, there are the three metal *pissoires* that discretely occupy the far corner of the plaza, just behind the town's two cafés and its tabac.

The fierce wind, somewhat suppressed as they navigate the narrow streets, slams full force into the plaza. It whips people about, causing the men to press their berets in place and the women to grab hold of their skirts. Sylvie is unnerved by the chaotic scene before her. An elderly woman stumbles, spilling fruit from a paper sack. Two boys dash to help her, but most of the fruit skitters erratically across the plaza, smashes into gutters, and bruised and dented, is lost down the sewer.

As Sylvie eases the car forward, the ancient cobblestones in the plaza refract the still remaining daylight, maddening her as the glare further slows her already glacial pace. As she progresses around the village plaza, the sunlight catches in the shop windows, gleaming with delicate lace linens and glazed crimson earthenware—two of her village's signature crafts. She feels a rush of pain, imagining how the impending war might devastate their traditional way of life. But then, a momentary joy seizes her as she pulls within sight of the village's dueling cafés. They face each other, with their delicate, filigreed wrought-iron tables and chairs

Jean nods towards the statues. "We did it last time."

"Pray we do so again," Sylvie says. Looking down at the plaque, she crosses herself. "With less loss of life."

Father Michel stops and turns to them. "I have to call upon Madame Alain in this rue. I'll leave you both to make your way to the station." His eyes are red-rimmed as he kisses Jean on both cheeks, giving him a robust, parting embrace. "God be with you." He kisses her as well then makes the sign of the cross over both of them.

She whispers, "Thank you, Father."

Jean and Sylvie continue on. As they approach the railway station, she's stunned to see the platform crushed beneath men carrying duffels. Women and children hang onto the men until the last minute when they're told to board. Older men in reservist uniforms are stationed at various points along the platform, shouting orders, even as they're barely able to cling onto the crowded space themselves. As they call for the departing men to queue up to be checked in, the crowd surges back and forth, parting to allow a man to board, then closing up again as loved ones smother those left with hugs and tears.

Searching for her Uncle Claude, Sylvie finally spots him in the reservist group. His uniform buttons strain against a few recently added pounds, and his round face is red from shouting. Although she'd prefer him to be a bit more help around the farm, she's proud that he brings a commanding presence to the scene as he directs the men to say their last goodbyes and board the train.

She grabs Jean's hand and pulls him through the crowd to her uncle. He puts his clipboard under his arm, takes Jean by the shoulders, and fiercely kisses him on both cheeks. In return, Jean pounds Claude hard on the back. Now more than ever, she's immensely grateful that Claude treats him as part of the family.

Claude's voice cracks, "Well, Jean, I guess it's time."

"I'll make you proud."

"I expect nothing less. *Bon courage*, my boy." Then he puts his arm around Jean's shoulder, turns him slightly to the side, and whispers. "It's outrageous they didn't call me up. Took three-quarters of my old unit. I don't mind telling you—" Sylvie taps him on the shoulder. "Ah…I'm being told not to make a fuss. Well, Jean, ah…you come back in one piece. That's an order."

Jean stands erect and salutes him. *"Viva La France!"* Jean looks lovingly at Sylvie. "Take care of everything here."

"Bien sûr," Claude adds. "I will. I will."

Jean salutes again. "For my family's honor. And don't forget to look after Sylvie and Étienne."

She looks around. "Where is Étienne?"

Claude shakes his head. *"Merde.* The boy tried to enlist."

A twist of fear grips her. As much as they're often at odds, she'd never forgive herself if he came to harm.

Jean turns to Claude. "What did that young fool do?"

He smirks. "Don't worry. Everyone knows he's only thirteen. He went to Louis then to François. Combed his hair differently. Tried to deepen his voice. They turned him down." He leans in to whisper, "Wouldn't risk Sylvie's anger."

Jean laughs out loud. "Smart men!"

Just then, another reservist down the platform shouts to Claude to keep the line moving.

"I'm sorry, Jean." A tear trickles down Claude's cheek.

A surge of people nearly shoves them off the platform. Jean grabs Sylvie by the waist, and Claude pulls them both back to safety. She feels dizzy with fear for Jean. Even with the Maginot Line, he could be in for a long, brutal fight. She resolves to light a candle every day. Surely Father Michel will forgive what they've done, so her prayers for Jean will be heard.

Jean and Sylvie come together in a hard, fast embrace. After a long moment, they split apart. Neither says a word. Sylvie watches the man she loves turn and resolutely board the train.

CHAPTER SIX

Foix. February 1940

AFTER HÉLÈNE'S HUSBAND leaves for the front, she returns home to her mother's house in Foix, where she takes up a position as the nurse for Dr. Duchamps, the sole doctor in the village. More than five months after Gérard's departure, most mornings when she awakes, she still forgets he isn't by her side. She rolls over expecting to be wrapped in his burly arms and filled with his immense, jovial warmth. This morning, in her narrow childhood bed, she closes her eyes, and in her dreamlike state, pictures them lying together on their wedding night in this very bed. She hugs her pillow to her chest and laughs softly, recalling him turning towards her. In a passionate moment, he slipped off her small bed, flailing about like a playful otter and landing with a gigantic thump on the wooden floor. And she tried, without success, to suppress her laughter so as not to wake her parents.

Her moment of remembered joy passes quickly. She hates to think of him facing intolerable misery and pulls up the heavily quilted covers as if to warm both Gérard and herself. She's struggled to fight the feeling of dread that relentlessly blankets her these days. It's been the worst winter France has known in decades. Gérard wrote, from God knows where, that the soldiers were freezing, bivouacked in little more than tents. When it warmed even a little, the ice turned to slush then mud, before it froze again, their wet boots icing over.

Reading between military-censored lines, Hélène gathers that younger recruits like her husband are mixed in with older reservists. They train together, then the reservists are moved elsewhere, a new set of older men replace them, and their joint training begins again. Rumors of boredom, frustration, and poor morale widely circulate. The press refers to the situation as the "phony war," but Hélène doesn't care what they call it—her Gérard is in danger. The Germans boldly invaded Poland, and their Panzers already menace the small and ill-equipped countries of Holland and Belgium. The British publicly proclaim their intention to resolve things peacefully. Even some within the government in Paris talk of making peace with Hitler. Hélène fears that it's only a matter of time before the German *blitzkrieg*, the lightning-swift attack mode they used to overrun Poland, will descend upon the French army and her husband.

Unable to further justify lingering in bed, Hélène casts the covers aside and pulls herself up. Her limbs feel stiff and achy as if she were an old woman with advanced arthritis. She throws on a heavy woolen robe and walks to the windowsill to tend to her assorted healing herbs in their little clay pots. Every surface in her bedroom is taken up with cache pots of small herbal plants in various stages of germination.

Using herbs to heal is her way to put her stamp onto her nursing. Although she admires the doctors she works with, she's always believed there are additional ways to heal. Sometimes the body, as well as the mind, needs to be grounded in the remedies of the earth. She takes a great deal of pride in what she does but is annoyed at having to hide it from the narrow-minded medical profession. She's seen it in her patients over and over—an emotional calm from a mixture of chamomile and hemp and a physical relaxation from a fusion of mint and lavender. If only she'd been a man, she might have been a doctor instead of a nurse. She sighs—no good looking back. Maybe she does more good as a nurse with her unorthodox healing.

She exhales a warm circle of breath on the icy windowpane, rubs her fist around, and peers out onto the tangle of medieval streets below. Snow has steadily fallen for days, and it's desolately cold outside. Poor, dear Gérard. She prays that the packages of warm clothes she's sent have actually reached him. A brief smile flickers across her face—it's a good thing he's got all that burly hair.

The house is so cold that Hélène finds only frigid water in the white ceramic pitcher that stands on the bureau in the corner. She sighs heavily and pours the water into a large bowl to perform her morning toilet. Even as she shivers, she considers herself fortunate to be able to wash at all—in contrast with the deprivation the troops at the front are likely experiencing. She slips on her nurse's uniform—heavy white muslin blouse and dark blue mid-calf woolen skirt.

There's a small mirror on a stand behind the pitcher and bowl. Growing up, it was positioned at a height so she could see herself clearly. Since she's grown so much from her childhood years, however, she has to bend to catch her reflection. She leans down and arranges her short blonde hair in her usual close waves, neatly flattening them against her head, then fixing her nurse's cap in place.

Hélène picks up her gold nursing pin and reverently fastens it onto her blouse. As she does, she glances more fully at herself in the mirror. Startled, she looks away and dismisses unsettling thoughts of how much she's aged in so few months—creases have appeared at the corners of her soft blue eyes, and a number of lines around her mouth have emerged against her porcelain skin.

Hélène tiptoes quietly across the squeaking floorboards and looks in on her mother. Wearing her lace nightcap, her mother is still asleep in the same bed her parents shared for more than fifty years. Since her father died several years ago, her mother has never slept lying down—every night, she props herself up on the pillows to read and wait for him, then falls asleep in that upright position. *If Gérard is killed, will this be how I will sleep? Propped up in bed, forever awaiting his return?*

Hélène tries to clear her mind of these somber thoughts as she softly creeps down the stairs to make a cup of tea. As in her bedroom, she's also planted medicinal herbs all around her mother's kitchen. She snips some leaves from the little pots, wraps them in brown paper, and gently places them in her satchel to take to the medical office. The cupboards are rather sparsely stocked, as so much of the village's food has been requisitioned for the soldiers at the front. Fortunately, the region is rich with farms, and last fall, fearing war would soon be upon them, the town collective harvested and preserved considerable stocks. Even so, Hélène feels a twinge of guilt over her ample cache of oats and bread. Deciding, however, that she needs all her strength to care for her patients, she makes some porridge and eats some anyway. She frequently feels the need for an extra reserve of strength, as Dr. Duchamps is often called away to set broken limbs, deliver babies, and even help with sick livestock, which leaves her solely in charge of the office.

Still in a melancholy daze, she layers on two sweaters, her coat, woolen hat over her nurse's cap, and boots, then braces herself for the cold as she steps knee-deep into the snow that overnight has drifted up against her front step. The sky is a downhearted gray, clouded over as the snow continues to fall in big, fat flakes that Hélène would have found cheerful, but for the overarching gloom enshrouding her. The village streets are too narrow for the snow to be cleared by piling it up along the sides, so it must be carted away. While the street sweepers usually come through with their lorries early in the morning, now that gasoline is in short supply and most of the men are at the front, the remaining very young and very old sweepers use only wheelbarrows, which takes them considerably longer to make their rounds. This leaves the village with massive drifts, pure and untouched, beautiful but almost impassable.

She slogs to the end of the Rue des Chapéliers, which leads to the town's main plaza where the going is easier. Crossing the plaza, she enters the narrow lane, where Dr. Duchamps has his office. Here, despite her long legs, the drifts are daunting and nearly insurmountable.

Marcel, the elderly shopkeeper, calls to her, "Good morning Madame Hélène." She appreciates his indomitable spirit as each morning he unlocks his tailor shop two doors down. Fiercely bundled, he bangs the lock against the gate to dislodge chunks of ice. How horrible for old men like Marcel who must struggle to make a living instead of being at home by a warm fire, leaving their sons to run their businesses.

She reaches Dr. Duchamps's office, knocks away the ice, and opens her own frozen lock. Entering, she hears a reassuring tinkle from above—the little shop bell that provides a much valued welcome—a sign that a world gone mad still contains a few chimes of goodwill. She stamps the snow from her boots and lights a fire.

The office has become another home for her and a place to minister to those in need. People ask how she can tolerate being a nurse, with all the blood and more unsavory aspects. In truth, she feels supremely satisfied nursing, blessed even, to use her methodical practicality, strength, and health to heal another person—she experiences a feeling of joy every time she bestows the ultimate gift of caring onto another living being. Not especially religious, healing is her form of religion. Hélène also knows that the herbs, which she's worked so hard to cultivate over the years, have considerable benefit—they aid digestion, open clogged sinuses, drain phlegm from the lungs and take away some of her patients' anxiety and pain.

Hélène looks forward to seeing patients today. Brightening from her earlier melancholy, she hums softly in her silken voice as she goes to the shelving and carefully moves aside several green beakers and some cobalt blue jars of tincture. She takes the packets of herbs from her satchel and distributes the leaves among various porcelain jars at the back, hiding them behind stacks of bandages and gauze. She knows that Dr. Duchamps doesn't favor her "medieval potions," so after the doctor has sewn up a wound or splinted a broken limb, she surreptitiously rubs a mixture of herbal paste onto the patient before she applies the bandages. She might also dissolve some herbs in a glass of water, then step back to wait for the patient's pain to lessen and a look of calm to come over them.

Hélène straightens up the doctor's desk and finds a note that he apparently left early this morning before she arrived—he's gone to Tarascon to deliver Madame Rousseau's fifth child. Her fifth! How can anyone bring a child into this world of senseless destruction? Still, a child would be an amazing blessing. *If only Gérard and I could have finally conceived before he left.*

An elderly woman appears at the door, urgently tapping her black cane on the glass. Hélène jerks the door open, the little bell above swinging furiously. Madame Rumeau hobbles in. Petite and stout, she still dresses in her widow's black all these years after her husband's death. Her face, deeply lined in gullies of wrinkles, is now scarlet. Seeing the woman gasping for breath, Hélène quickly leads her to a wooden bench in front of the fire and brushes clumps of snow from her threadbare woolen coat. "Sit down, please, Madame."

Madame Rumeau blurts out, "I'm sorry. I know you must be busy." She fights for intakes of air. "But my grandson, Albert. Only eighteen. Dead in a training accident." She shakes violently. "His father...my son...died in the Great War. My grandson was all I had left."

Hélène looks down at this terrified woman whom she knows so well. Madame Rumeau and Hélène's mother used to make intricate lace tablecloths much sought after in the Monday farmers' market. The poor dear lady. Such a senseless death. In a training accident, no less. And such a young man.

With a profound sense of sorrow, Hélène pulls some herbs from one of the jars at the back of the shelf. She dissolves them in a glass of water and hands it to Madame Rumeau, who, unable to speak, nods her gratitude. Her liver-spotted, deeply veined hands tremble as she sips, then she pulls out one of her delicate hand-made lace handker-chiefs to wipe her mouth. As she does, Hélène quietly reaches back to the jar for some herbs of her own, dissolves them in her glass, and drinks them down in one swift swallow.

CHAPTER SEVEN

Toulouse. Early May 1940

SOBEL IS A bundle of nerves awaiting her performance. She sits on an upholstered chair in the green room of the recital hall of Temple Emmanuel of Toulouse. At fourteen, she's enormously proud to be giving her second annual recital. The whole congregation will be in attendance, not only her parents, Dr. and Mrs. Solomon Goldschmidt, but more importantly, her beloved Aunt Sylvie, who's taking the train from Foix just to hear her play.

Isobel opens a small black leather case and gazes lovingly at the three bright silver sections of her flute, nestled in luxuriant blue satin folds. Trying to fortify her courage, she smiles broadly at her reflection, which bends concave in the shaft of the largest piece of her flute. She's pleased to see her pale blue eyes flashing back at her, flanked by a thicket of auburn curls that cascades to her waist. If only her translucent white skin were not so densely freckled!

As she leans forward to take up the pieces of her flute and assemble them, she abruptly stops to discretely hike up the bodice of her dress. She curses under her breath—her dress keeps sliding down her tall, willowy frame. Another girl, clutching her oboe, plops down beside Isobel. She whispers, none too softly, "That's quite a dress you're almost wearing, Isobel." The girl sneers, then sucks on her reed.

Tossing her curls, Isobel smirks nonchalantly, but it's only for show. She's thoroughly chagrinned—she should have listened to her mother and worn something more conservative, something that would at least stay in place during her performance. But she absolutely, positively had to have this enchanting scarlet dress. She fell in love with it months ago at the dressmaker's, despite its utter impracticality. Not only is the dress strapless, but the fabric is velvet and much too warm for the lovely spring weather they're enjoying in Toulouse. And the dress being floor-length, she shudders at the very real prospect that she'll trip up the steps to the stage. All this on top of her usual, paralyzing stage fright.

Isobel's long, elegant fingers tremble as she picks up each of the flute's three pieces and polishes them to a gleaming shine. Next, trying to calm herself, she focuses on fitting the sections together, lining up the keys, the open holes, and the mouthpiece. Such a simple thing, but so rewarding, like fitting in place the pieces of her childhood wooden puzzles.

The stage manager, a volunteer member of the congregation, makes an announcement. "Ladies and gentlemen, our first chair." All the musicians rise and applaud as a short, squat man bounds into the green room, violin and bow in hand. He bounces to the piano and strikes a single note, precipitating a profusion of orchestral blurts, trills, and other sounds that fill the room.

Isobel anxiously looks around at her fellow students, as well as the professional musicians hired once a year to accompany them. She shakes out her hands, trying to relax them. Once again, she hikes up her dress, then raises her arms, rolls her tongue over her lips, and places them onto her flute, her upper lip extending beyond her lower, in a perfect embouchure. She takes a deep breath and is immensely relieved to find her dress remaining in place. Hearing her own sweet melodious tones, she feels considerably calmer.

During the warm-up, an occasional sour note shrieks out, causing the students to laugh and twitter. Glancing around the room, Isobel fastens on Joshua Milberg, who, she's happy to note, is awkwardly staring at her, his violin lodged under his chin and his bow frozen in mid-air. He's a year older, wears large, black-rimmed glasses, and looks even more painfully thin than usual, in a suit several sizes too large. He's regarded by the teachers, however, as the finest musician in their student orchestra. So, of course, she feels compelled to bring him under her spell. Lowering her flute, she shoots him a bright smile, to which he responds by blushing the color of her scarlet dress and jerking his gaze away to attack his violin. Isobel allows herself a small triumphant snear at his reaction, although she'd much prefer him to pursue her on his own, without their mothers constantly throwing them at each other.

The warm-up ended, the orchestra members file onto the stage, with Isobel and Joshua and four other students taking their places as soloists in the front row. Isobel produces one of her glittering smiles to enchant everyone around her, especially Joshua. She does this out of habit, even though she's inwardly terrified by her stage fright.

As the audience applauds their entrance, Isobel searches the room, not just for her parents but especially for her Aunt Sylvie. Isobel adores her aunt because she's always treated her like an adult and never tried to control her, like her domineering mother Louisa, Sylvie's older sister. She prays her aunt will arrive in time, despite how almost impossible train travel has become, with supplies being rushed to the front, and all of France on edge, waiting for the Germans to attack. Isobel giggles to herself, recalling how much everyone says she resembles her dear aunt in temperment if not in appearance—both are undeniably quick-witted as well as impossibly headstrong. Also, unlike her aunt, she's mastered the art of flirtation. Tonight she's going to forget all about the stupid war people say is coming and revel in being her usual center of attention. Just then, however, another wave of stage fright washes over her, and she swallows hard to tamp down her rising nausea.

The conductor arrives to further applause. Isobel proudly looks around the concert hall, which is oak-paneled, the benches cushioned, the ceiling carved in simple but graceful curlicues of beige plaster. The Temple Emmanuel is one of the most affluent in the South of France, attracting Jews not merely from their city but from well beyond. Although not as strict as an Orthodox sect, the men nevertheless sit separately in the synagogue proper. Today, though, everyone sits together in this adjoining recital hall, which serves as an auditorium, lecture space, theatre, and general community gathering place.

Isobel breathes a great sigh of relief as she sees her Aunt Sylvie slip into the seat next to her mother, Louisa. Her mother is older than her aunt by some thirteen years. When their parents died, Louisa was already married and taking care of baby Isobel while assisting her husband's growing medical practice. It was agreed that they would help financially as best they could but that Uncle Claude would move to Foix to look after Sylvie and her brother.

Isobel looks between her mother and her aunt, both diminutive in height, sturdy in frame, and with olive skin and thick black hair—virtually exact copies of each other. She's relieved to see her aunt wearing a presentable high-necked muslin dress instead of her usual trousers and cap. Next, she fixes on her mother's outfit. It is stylish but not nearly as decked out with lace, silk finery, and the long strands of pearls that the wealthier women of the congregation wear. Isobel's father, several years older than her mother, wears a discrete, well-tailored, light-weight gray woolen suit with a vest and gold watch chain draped across his ample frame. She's always been slightly embarrassed that his yarmulke doesn't entirely cover the comb-over on his balding head. But she loves him dearly and is proud to be the object of his constant praise and affection, even though she wishes he would charge his patients more so they could join the upper echelons of fashionable Temple society.

When the music begins, Isobel is transported. Ever practicing diligently, she's technically proficient enough to give in and enjoy the rich tones that she and the others—well, most of them anyway—produce. The concert over, Isobel gaily traipses through the crowd in the reception hall, where all the parents are kissing all their children and raving about all their performances.

"What a success!"

"Aren't our children talented?"

"However did maestro Schultz get everyone to play so well together?"

"And in tune—"

"Well, for the most part."

With her stage fright behind her, Isobel feels certain she's distinguished herself. And indeed, she's greeted with enthusiastic clapping and big hugs by her mother and aunt.

"You were wonderful," Louisa declares, squeezing Isobel so hard she has to grab the sides of her dress to keep it up.

Sylvie smiles and stands on tiptoe to kiss Isobel on both cheeks. "My darling, you've improved so much from last year." Looking down at her beloved aunt, Isobel feels the heat of her ginger-red freckles flush over her face.

Isobel then turns to her father. He clears this throat, strokes his reddish-brown goatee, and launches into his critique. "My dear, the legato in the Bach was a bit slow, and the Shubert was somewhat labored. However, you put a good deal of passion into them." Isobel gently swings her foot back and forth like a child, awaiting his final verdict. He continues, "That is indeed the mark of a true professional. To make the most of your own part, even when the conductor is off. In short—"

The girl smiles as she catches her mother giving her father a *get on with it* look, to which he abruptly responds, "Ahem. Yes... well, my dear... you were magnificent!"

Isobel screams and jumps up and down, trouncing the hem of her gown. Her father clears his throat, embarrassed at the emotion he's elicited. He brings his willowy daughter into a fiercely proud embrace, and Isobel feels him catch his breath as if stifling a sob.

Isobel notices, over her father's shoulder, that her mother is signaling to Joshua's mother, Sophie Milberg, to join them. She's pleased to witness her power over Joshua as she sees him fumbling with his violin case while his mother marches him over. Everyone earnestly congratulates the young man, and Isobel is forced to admit he really was very good. *All the more reason to conquer him!*

Still, Isobel inwardly groans, deeply embarrassed by her mother who has cornered Mrs. Milberg, and in an exaggerated and all-knowing voice, says, "They play so well together, don't they?" Before Joshua can escape, Louisa blurts out a question that is more a command, "Will you join us for tea? We're having a little reception for my daughter, and we've plenty of cakes." To Isobel's utter horror, Louisa whispers loudly to Joshua's mother, "He could stand a little fattening up."

Oblivious to Isobel's embarrassment—she wants to make this conquest all on her own—her mother ushers the adults ahead. Louisa nods to Joshua's mother, indicating that they should leave the two young people to walk behind them, properly chaperoned but able to "get to know" each other. Leaving the Temple, Isobel is relieved to have Louisa wrap her in a light shawl, so she can take a deep breath without fear of her dress falling. *It's glorious to finally relax from the stress of having to play so perfectly!* And now that Joshua is safely ensnared in her web, she happily gazes around to enjoy the delicate green foliage in the stately plane trees rustling in the gentle spring breeze.

Ambling along the boulevard with Joshua, Isobel chatters on about the players, the guest musicians, and the conductor. Finally, confused, she notices Joshua's lean, normally intense face grow even tauter than usual.

He snaps at her, "We shouldn't be celebrating like this, with the war coming."

Isobel is taken aback. She pouts, annoyed that he would ruin her otherwise triumphant day. "They've been saying it's coming for half a year now. I'm tired of all the clothing drives and gasoline rationing." She stamps her foot. "There's barely enough petrol to drive into Centre Ville for shopping. And everyone says, if the Germans break through, there won't be any petrol at all."

"If the Germans break through, that won't be the half of it."

"We'll beat them straight off. That's what Papa says." She pauses, then frowns. "Although I suppose Mama's much more worried."

"Pardon me, but your mother isn't Jewish, is she?"

"Not by birth. She and my Aunt Sylvie were raised Catholic." She quickly adds, "But, of course, my mother was converted when she married Papa."

As dusk descends on the boulevard, the shops and awnings of the cafés on one side of the street are bathed in violet shadows, while on the other side, they glow orange in the setting sun. Joshua abruptly stops in front of a confectioner's shop with its red and white striped awning that says: *Rubenstein's Cakes and Pastries.* Isobel steals a greedy glimpse at the multi-tiered cake stands, heavily laden with brightly decorated confections and candies. Sensing Joshua's aggravation, however, she turns back to him.

Joshua's eyeglasses reflect the light of the setting sun, as his gaunt face flames with anger. "Isobel, the *Boches* are doing unconscionable things. If we were in Deutschland, this shop would already be destroyed. You've heard of *Kristallnacht*? The night of broken glass?"

Isobel shakes her head, making sure that her curls land back in place. "I think I've heard something about it. But it's so far away."

Joshua's voice rises, "November 1938? A year and a half ago? You don't know about the violence against the Jews in Nazi Germany? Worse still, it wasn't only the Brownshirt thugs, but Gentiles…Christians… who took part. The police looked on but didn't do a thing. People were killed…thousands of Jews arrested and taken away." He pauses to take a deep breath that turns into a desolate sigh. "We never heard from my

Uncle Herman or his entire family. They were just…just gone. The whole family…" His voice trails off to a whisper, "Disappeared."

"That could never happen in France," Isobel retorts. "The Jews here get along fine."

He steps close, saying directly to her, "Isobel, what does your father think? Did he have family in Sudetenland? How many were killed or never heard from when the Germans occupied Czechoslovakia? Poland?"

She backs up a step. "I…I don't know, Joshua."

"Four of our cousins from Poland and their children now live with us. They had to leave everything behind."

Isobel opens her mouth to speak but pauses, thinking maybe she should find out more about the situation before offering a further opinion. As she turns from Joshua's accusatory gaze, she catches her reflection in the window, in her beautiful dress. She stares at all the cakes and pushes these awful thoughts about war from her mind.

"Joshua, I'm sure you must be right. I will ask my Papa. *Je promets,* I will. But for now, please, we need to hurry home, or we'll miss the celebration."

He exhales sharply.

She takes his arm and hurries them along, stealing a last, longing glance at the sugar cakes in the window.

CHAPTER EIGHT

SYLVIE AND THE rest of the concert-goers repair to the Gold-schmidt home. She proudly watches her sister, Louisa, float into the drawing-room carrying a silver tray of champagne flutes filled with sparkling liquid. The glasses glitter in the light of the candles in the chandelier above.

Dr. Goldschmidt raises his glass. "A toast, everyone! To a splendid concert—and to Isobel!!"

Louisa adds, "And to Joshua! Didn't they play well together!"

Isobel turns towards her aunt and rolls her eyes while Sylvie enjoys this private moment between them. Sylvie watches Joshua sullenly sip his champagne while Isobel sniffs at her glass, giggles as the bubbles tickle her nose, and drinks hers down. Sylvie admires her niece for being capable, warm, and loving, if a bit spoiled. But she wonders what Isobel sees in Joshua. Obviously an accomplished musician, he's certainly not as robust and capable as she'd prefer for her niece. His major redeeming feature appears to be standing up to Isobel—she's watched her niece outrageously flirt with, then walk right over, most boys her age.

As they all lift their glasses, Sylvie's gaze shifts to the lovely tapestries and paintings that hang on every wall, heirlooms that have been in the doctor's family for generations. She loves the hand-embroidered curtains gracing the ceiling-to-floor windows—her sister has certainly made the most of her relatively modest decorating budget. Chinese lamps glow on side tables, and the mantle dazzles with trinket boxes made of enamel and porcelain. Although she's always been impressed by the finery in her sister's home, especially compared with the rough-hewn furnishings in her own farmhouse, Sylvie most admires Dr. Goldschmidt's collection of leather-bound volumes, cherished and standing stalwart behind glass doors in polished walnut bookcases. She'd love to have time to browse through his library instead of having to work so hard on the farm. But she loves her sister and wouldn't begrudge her the life she's made with her husband or her conversion to Judaism, which seems to suit her well. And she's grateful to Louisa for the financial contribution she and her husband continue to make to keep Sylvie's farm afloat, even as the doctor's practice has never been all that flush since he only charges his patients what they can afford to pay.

Louisa insists that Isobel and Joshua play a flute and violin duet. Isobel tosses her head, trying to get out of it, but Sylvie knows there's no dissuading her stubborn sister—they have stubbornness in common—when Louisa's in high matchmaking mode.

"See how talented my daughter is!" Louisa loudly whispers, over and over to anyone within earshot. Sylvie pats her sister's hand, partly to agree with her and partly to hush her and minimize Isobel's embarrassment.

As everyone applauds, Sylvie is startled by a loud, urgent banging of the knocker on the front door. The butler, an elderly man from the Temple whom the doctor and his wife hire out of charity, shuffles across the hallway to answer the door. He shuffles back to whisper something to the doctor, who breaks into an outright run to the door. Jerking it wide open, he cries, "Rachel, my dear sister! Good heavens, Rachel. Come in—all of you."

In the drawing-room, the laughter and applause abruptly stop as everyone turns to the front hallway, where five disheveled people trudge inside. Sylvie is stunned. She knows Rachel Epstein to be a few years younger than Dr. Goldschmidt, but this woman looks more like the doctor's mother than his sister, with her unwashed gray hair wound in a haphazard chignon, ends straggling from under her once stylish black felt hat. Her shawl and overcoat drape on the floor as she bends to assist her husband, Abraham, who coughs in horrific fits, rattling phlegm in his sunken chest. Sylvie is horrified to see that his ordinarily sparse frame is now emaciated and weighed down by a long black woolen coat, much too warm for the season.

The Epstein's two teenage sons, Joel and Ezekiel, are slender like their father, with light, scraggly, reddish-brown beards. Neither looks as if he's washed in days. They both carry valises in each hand, and smaller leather satchels clutched under their arms, which they drop to the floor with great relief. Louisa, dumbfounded, is temporarily immobilized on her chair. Isobel, her nose already turned up against the guests' foul odor, can only stare open-mouthed, clearly appalled at her relatives.

Sylvie snaps out of her shock, and as the doctor escorts everyone into the drawing-room, she quickly helps Louisa and the butler get extra chairs and cushions. The boys sink into an exhausted heap on the carpet. The doctor helps his brother-in-law to a chair, and although he and Rachel ease him down carefully, the movement sets off another spate of agonized coughing.

As these alarming family events unfold, Joshua and his mother hastily bid everyone good evening. Sylvie is surprised to catch Joshua giving Isobel a decidedly annoyed glance, which the girl pretends to ignore, smiling coquettishly and thanking him for coming.

Meanwhile, the doctor asks the butler for brandy for Abraham, then adds, "And some for my sister and for this man." He turns to his sister for an introduction. "Ah...Rachael?"

Rachael makes several attempts to respond, then gives up and simply lets her head fall into her hands, her frail and bony shoulders silently heaving. Finally, she gasps, "Solomon, you can't imagine the refugees pouring out of Poland and Belgium." Rachel's voice is unsteady and hoarse. "Miles and miles and miles of them. We got one of the last trains out of Poland into Belgium. Then Alastair," pointing to the stranger, "this incredible man here, helped us bribe a lorry driver. After that, we walked and walked. Then he got us into a wagon." She closes her rheumy eyes against the images she describes. "It was raining. The wagon got stuck in the mud, but Alastair...he... Abraham would have died if it hadn't been for—" Rachel motions to Alastair, then weeps without restraint.

Sylvie eyes Alastair with suspicion. He appears to be in his late twenties, towering over his companions, broad-shouldered but lean. When he removes his dark blue beret, he reveals a thick head of dark blonde hair. He also wears a mustache that once might have been dapper but has grown erratically, topping off at least a week's growth of blondish-brown beard. Despite his outer clothes, a pair of worn overalls and scuffed-up boots, he's clearly not a Frenchman. Whereas he was slouching and shuffling his feet when he entered, he's now straightened up as he strides over to the doctor and firmly shakes his hand. Finally, she's astonished to hear him speak excellent French, but with an accent she can't quite place.

"Doctor Goldschmidt, your sister speaks very highly of you. I am sorry to ah," he hesitates, "meet you under these circumstances."

The doctor looks askance. "And you are—"

"Sir, please just call me, Alastair."

Sylvie interjects, "British?"

Alastair nods.

The doctor adds, "Please, tell us what happened."

"You must appreciate, I am not at liberty to disclose any military details." He pauses, and Sylvie surmises he's considering how much, if anything, to divulge. "But I can tell you I was shot down during a bombing run over Northern Belgium."

The doctor volunteers, "We heard the British were trying to head off the Germans in Belgium." He looks around for the butler and calls into the next room, "Georges, where is that brandy?"

"Were you a pilot?" Isobel bursts out. "What happened to your crew?"

Louisa jumps in, "Isobel, please. Perhaps he doesn't want to—"

"It's all right," Alastair softly adds.

Louisa turns to him, "I apologize. Where are my manners? Please, have a seat."

The butler enters, stooping under the weight of a tray with large snifters of brandy, which he passes around.

Alastair settles in with a great sigh of relief. Sylvie can't imagine what he must have gone through as he stares into his glass, not really seeing anything. Finally, he takes a swig which he relishes for a long and grateful moment, then says, "Our mission was to knock out the bridges near Maastricht, to impede the German advance." He looks directly at Isobel with no hint of condensation. "To answer your question, Mademoiselle, I am indeed a pilot. Our bombing run was...well...cut short, if you take my meaning." As Alastair grips the brandy snifter, his knuckles turning white, Sylvie expects it to shatter in his hands. His voice wavers, "We took flak. One minute we were in the air. The next, my bombardier and navigator were—"

Louisa breaks in, "How terrible."

Sylvie whispers, "What happened then?"

Alastair takes another swig of brandy. "If there is no other option, our orders are to..." He struggles to form the words, then spits them out. "I headed for the nearest priority target and bailed out."

Everyone is silent for a moment. They stare at the carpet, the curtains, the piano—anywhere to avoid looking at Alastair. Sylvie shudders, picturing those men in the bomber, entombed in a burst of flames with no one to grant them last rites. *Mon Dieu, how horrible!* She crosses herself. "How did you make it here?"

"A Belgian farmer helped me bury my parachute. Gave me these overalls and boots. I couldn't head to the coast because of the enemy patrols. So, I started walking south. I simply folded myself into the endless stream of refugees." He looks over at Rachel and Abraham.

Rachel laments, "Solomon, you should have seen all those wretched people. Old men and women, they could hardly walk," she is barely able to go on. "With their candle sticks, bird cages, mattresses, anything they could carry. Pushing baby carriages, wheelbarrows. Pulling toy wagons." She gulps her brandy. "It was awful. Young women covered themselves in dirt…and mustard…so the *Boches* wouldn't rape them."

The doctor kneels beside his sister, gently takes the empty snifter from her shaking hand, and gives her his, which she also swigs as if it were water. Gasping, Rachel continues, "Along the road, the *Boches* strafed us. Can you imagine? We had to fling ourselves into a ditch. They shot at us while we were running away—why would they do that?"

Alastair swills back what's left of his brandy. "I did see French troops. Some heading towards Belgium. Others were heading south. No one seemed in charge, and I couldn't risk telling anyone who I was. My crew will have been reported shot down and missing, so their families will have been informed." He pauses to clear his throat before he finds the voice to start again. "I don't have a family to worry whether I'm dead or alive, so I decided not to attempt to report in, even if I could find the proper channel in all the chaos." He stares off towards nowhere in particular. "And you see, by that time, I simply couldn't leave Abraham, Rachel, and the boys."

The doctor nods gravely. "We are eternally grateful to you, sir."

Sylvie keenly watches Alastair's face as he appears lost in a terrible vision. Abruptly, he speaks in a gruff whisper, "There are hundreds of thousands of refugees heading towards the South of France, fleeing the bastards…" He nods to Louisa. "Pardon me, Madame."

Louisa goes white with rage. "The French won't let the *Boches* through. What about the Maginot Line?"

"Everyone hopes you are right, Madame. As for now—"

Letting out a soft gasp, Sylvie thinks of Jean somewhere in Northern France, perhaps close to the Maginot Line that he so fervently maintained was impenetrable. She feels a desperate urge to get on a train and go to the front line to join the fighting herself, even as she's furious to admit how impossible that would be. But with Alastair sitting right in front of her, expressing his severest reservations, she's enraged. A burning spreads through her throat as if someone had plunged a hot coal deep into her mouth. Now more than ever, she fears for Jean and the entire French line. She's suddenly determined to help Alastair as best she can, as if helping him would ensure that someone, somewhere, might help Jean if he were ever in need. She leans forward and softly asks Alastair, "Where do you go from here? And what can we do to help?"

"Afraid I've bent the rules by not reporting in. They'll be cheesed at me, to say the least. Some might even call me a deserter."

The doctor stands, his ample frame shaking. "That is absolutely ridiculous. I will vouch for you to any authority you wish."

"I hope I won't need your intervention, sir, but I thank you. If I can get over the border to Spain, the RAF has a line of communication in Barcelona. It would be better if I turned up in person to argue my case."

Abraham is racked with another coughing spasm.

The doctor says, "Alastair...Sylvie...please help me get my brother-in-law into my office."

The doctor leads the way as Sylvie and the Englishman carry the slumping man between them. She glances over at Alastair and whispers, "I can help you."

Sylvie sees a puzzled look cross his face. She takes a deep breath, then confidently adds, "Where I come from, we know the mountains. I can get you across the border and into Spain."

CHAPTER NINE

SYLVIE LUMBERS INTO the kitchen, weary from a poor night's sleep, fraught with hellish nightmares of bombardments, flak-littered skies, and aeroplanes being shot down. Alastair's news of British bombers staging raids on German targets buoys her spirits, yet last night he laid out the most horrific first-hand picture of the casualties of war. She's changed from her concert-going dress into her usual trousers and cap and stands in the kitchen, back to the door, putting food together.

Alastair, now clean-shaven, enters the kitchen. His clothes have been exchanged for a cleaner version of French work clothes similar to those he wore when he arrived last night. He stops short. "Morning, my good man."

Sylvie slowly turns to face him, thoroughly enjoying how he squints at her, not sure what he's seeing. Then she laughs outright, a deep rolling melody, even as she tries to suppress her hearty tones so as not to wake the household.

He says, "Ah. Oh. Terribly sorry—"

"It's happened before."

As Alastair smiles sheepishly, she feels a measure of sincere warmth shining through his proper British reserve. She turns back to her work.

He jumps to, "May I help?"

She shakes her head, then abruptly stops her preparations and looks directly up at him. "Alastair, I'm terribly worried about Jean. He's my, ah—"

Alastair nods, encouraging her to speak frankly.

"Do you know anything about the French troops in the north? I have no idea where Jean might be. Only that the uncensored parts of his letters mention a dreadfully cold winter, recently given way to a spring knee-deep in mud." She shrugs apologetically. "That's not much to go on."

He steps to the counter next to her, his erect bearing indicative of the RAF officer he claims to be. She's pleasantly surprised as he helps her wrap some slices of cheese in the brown paper she's laid out.

"The RAF isn't privy to how well-equipped the French are. Sorry to say, rumor has it, they've damned few units with well enough trained men and supplies."

"The French haven't let on."

"I expect not. Seems you chaps are counting on the Maginot." He pauses, cheese slice in mid-air. Then he puts the food down and turns directly to her. "For the life of me, Mademoiselle—"

"My name is Sylvie."

"Sylvie, I cannot think why they didn't fortify all the way north . . . to the coast."

She feels a crushing dread, having thought of this herself but not wanting to argue with Jean about it. She makes a valiant effort to be positive. "Well . . . yes . . . anyway . . . Jean says they can't wait to attack. Everyone's so bored." Seeing Alastair's extremely doubtful look, she rapidly scoops up some of the bread and cheese. "Thank you. I can finish this." She puts his sandwich together, then takes some fruit and slides it all into her rucksack. She sets her jaw. "We should be off."

While she gathers the rest of her belongings, he laces up his shabby work boots. She glances at them, frowning.

He smiles wanly. "The doctor offered to find me a new pair, but I declined. These are already worn enough to be credible—a newer pair would just attract attention. Besides, they've brought miraculous good luck to get me this far. I wouldn't part with them on any account."

He pauses, looks around, clearly checking to make sure no one is within earshot.

He whispers, "Look here, Sylvie, if I'm discovered traveling with you, I could endanger you."

Feeling protective of him, she's about to object when he interjects, "The French army still theoretically controls the country. But it's chaos out there. And German spies could easily have infiltrated the masses of refugees making their way south, just as I did. I'm at risk of being arrested by either French or British troops as a deserter."

"But—"

"It could implicate you. You might be arrested for aiding a deserter."

Despite his warning, she feels an excitement she hasn't known since Jean left for the front. She's already made up her mind to help Alastair as her way to contribute to the war effort—to do something, anything, even if it doesn't directly protect Jean. "I won't hear of you going alone. I know this country, and I intend to escort you to my village. From there, we can get you over the mountains and into Spain."

He opens his mouth to object, but she cuts him off. "You'll find out soon enough how headstrong I am."

Without his scraggly beard, his face looks quite boyish to her.

He smiles and says, "I'm quite looking forward to it."

They quietly gather their things so that they won't disturb the sleeping household and head for the train station. Once outside her sister's house, Sylvie is pleased to see him taking up his shuffling walk and slouching posture so as not to call attention to his innate military bearing. They've concocted their cover story. Although his French is quite good, he does have a slight accent, so they agree that he should be Belgian and trying to reach his elderly mother, who is ill and living with French relatives in Foix. She insists on doing the talking to buy their tickets. So he—as a proper Englishman—insists she use the money the doctor gave him for getting his sister's family to Toulouse.

They get off the SNCF train in Foix, but do so separately and head in separate directions. Sylvie has instructed him to walk to the church of St. Volusien, enter by the side door, light a votive candle, and wait for her in the chapel of the Virgin Mary. Since he isn't Catholic, she's also familiarized him with the appropriate rituals—to cross himself with holy water when entering the church and kneel and cross himself again before sliding into a pew.

Returning to Foix from the bigger, more urban Toulouse always fills her with a sense of elation. The fresh mountain air fills the village with a blizzard of delicate pink blossoms from the apple trees in the orchards up the hill, across from the train tracks. The church stands across the Ariège River from the station. Its steeple is sharply etched against a brilliant cerulean sky, with the lofty Château rising directly behind. These are the landmarks of her heart. She turns to take in swaying fields of lavender beyond the town and the sharp mountain peaks she loves so well to the south. She keenly watches Alastair, the airman she will help escape France, as he shuffles across the bridge, the river below, running full and swift with the melting spring snow. He turns right and heads around the sharp bend, then uphill on the narrow cobbled street towards the church. Alastair is now her connection to Jean, her first in so many months, and she will not let him down.

Sylvie waits a couple of minutes, then crosses the bridge and turns sharply left, hurrying along the stone quay that borders the riverbank in the other direction from Alastair. She's so excited that she's barely able to keep her boots on the cobblestones as she doubles back through a tangled mass of alleys to the main square, where she hopes to locate her Uncle Claude.

Not finding Claude in either of the two cafés on the plaza, Sylvie climbs the stairs to the Town Hall. It's an imposing structure with impressive—perhaps overly so for such a tiny village—Corinthian columns holding up the portico. A large French tricolor hangs between the central columns. She shoves open the heavy front door, strides along the cool marble floor, and swiftly reaches the Army office. Sure enough, she finds Claude in a small, densely smoke-filled office cluttered with maps, papers, and files. Dressed in his tight-fitting reservist uniform, his jacket unbuttoned for comfort, he's arguing with his two closest friends. They are also elderly reservists: Louis, short, barrel-chested, and built like a diminutive bull; and François, very tall and broad with sagging jowls and a long black bushy mustache. They are all bent over a large sector map on a massive oak table as a radio blares in the background.

Louis shouts in a high, shrill tone, "Those damned *Boches* could never get through the Ardennes. It's absolutely, utterly, completely impenetrable, I tell you. Everyone says so."

François takes a long, slow drag on a Gauloises, then exhales a voluminous cloud of smoke. He speaks deliberately in a deep basso voice. "But what if they did?"

Her anxiety rises, recalling Alastair's belief that the German plan of attack could well circumvent the Maginot Line by going north around it through the Ardennes. Lost in their argument, they fail to notice her.

Claude booms, "They've invaded Holland and Belgium, damn them."

Louis pounds the map with his fist. "The Brits will cut them off on the coast, and we'll cut them off along the Maginot. Not even Rommel's Panzers can get through the Ardennes." He pummels the map some more. "We've spent two decades fortifying the hell out of the border with Germany. From the Ardennes, which is absolutely impenetrable, all the way down to Switzerland. *Mon Dieu,* it'll be over before Bastille Day."

François calmly, stubbornly continues to press his point. "They have mechanized vehicles, light infantry, maneuverable Panzers. Why wouldn't they surprise us by going through the Ardennes?"

"They're not... I tell you... they're not," Louis sputters, his face flushing crimson. "They're not going to get themselves snarled in that dense forest. They want to go in straight lines. That's what Germans do. Go in straight lines."

Sylvie is comforted to hear Claude calmly add, "We'll just have to see, and pray, they try to go through the Maginot—our strongest defense."

In the brief silence that greets Claude's remark, she clears her throat. The three immediately turn towards her.

Claude rushes to kiss her on both cheeks. "How was your visit? Did Isobel play well?"

"She's lovely, Uncle Claude. So talented."

François bends down, his face close to hers. "My dear, any word from Jean?" For such a large, gruff-looking man, she's always known him to be a sweet and extraordinarily tender man.

"Not since the Nazis invaded Belgium." She puts on as good a face as she can. "Last I heard, Jean was tired of sitting around. He's itching for a fight."

"We know how he feels, don't we?" Louis adds, practically screeching, "They don't know how useful seasoned soldiers like us can be. I don't mean we'd be any good crawling through the mud, but—"

Claude interrupts, a sparkle in his eye, "Speak for yourself, Louis."

Ignoring him, Louis quips, "God knows we did enough of that last time."

Cigarette dangling, François slowly, methodically says, "I want to know what was so great about the Great War?"

Sylvie marvels at Louis's tenacity, as he's clearly determined to have the last word. He adds, "We know a thing or two about formations, keeping men in line, that sort of thing. Don't we?"

François takes a final drag and tamps his cigarette out in a battered metal ashtray, which looks as if it's been through the last war with him. Gray ashes scatter onto his sleeve as well as the map. Annoyed, Louis blows them off then brushes them to the floor. Sylvie laughs as she catches Claude rolling his eyes at his two comrades, who are always on each other's nerves.

She leans into her uncle and whispers, "Uncle Claude, may I have a word?"

"Anything wrong, my dear?"

"I'll tell you outside."

A few minutes with his niece under the Town Hall portico and Claude is brimming with his own, barely contained excitement at the prospect of ushering the Brit over the mountains into Spain. He shifts into high gear. "We can use the old watermill as a staging area. Hide him there." He pauses, then quickly adds, "Let him rest, of course. While we gather supplies and food for the journey."

"That sounds workable."

"Does he have a weapon?"

"I didn't see one, but that doesn't mean he doesn't have one."

"We'll need a couple of rifles, just in case. I haven't heard of any *Boche* patrols along the border yet. But those Nazis bastards supported Franco. And the Pyrénées are strategically valuable. Wouldn't surprise me if they're already bringing troops into Spain and—"

"I'm going too. I know these mountains better than you. "

"Sylvie, my dear, I know you want to get into the fight. I could be gone some time, and Étienne's still too young to leave alone."

"I'm tired of hearing I have to stay at the farm and take care of him."

Claude only needs to raise his bushy white eyebrows to get across his objection.

"I suppose you're right," she says. He's too impulsive to be left on his own. I wouldn't want him sneaking off to enlist down in Toulouse." She squares her shoulders. "But you can't go by yourself."

He locks eyes with her, then looks away. "All right, I'll ask Louis.

He's bursting for a fight. It'll do him good to put all that pent-up energy into helping the Brit."

Sylvie longs for any reason to escort Alastair up into the mountains. As she starts to lodge another objection, Claude puts his large, beefy hand on her shoulder. "They'll be other times. Who knows? Maybe other soldiers as well."

She sighs, knowing he's probably right. Reluctantly she takes his arm as they briskly cross the plaza and step inside the church, into the antechamber behind the transept. She breathes deeply, filling her lungs with the familiar, serenely comforting smell of incense and burning votive candles.

As they start to enter the nave of the church, Claude grabs her hand and pulls her to a halt. "Are you sure you trust him?"

"If you'd seen how grateful Rachel was."

"How do we know he's who he says he is?"

"I don't care. He saved Abraham, Rachel, and the boys." She struggles not to raise her voice in the hallowed church. "He deserves all the help we can give him."

Claude holds her gaze for a moment, then nods his approval, and they turn to look for Alastair. They enter the main nave of the church, with its thick walls and soaring gothic arches, which surround the transept and meet in a point high over the altar. The main body of the ninth-century church was destroyed by fire and rebuilt in the seventeenth century—even so, it remains an imposing edifice steeped in times past. Two tiers of windows circle all the way around the nave. The upper tiered windows, which rise into gothic arches, are positioned in a staggered pattern over and between the lower tier, with its more square and compact windows.

Sylvie prays here every day for Jean. She loves coming here not only because of her feelings for this sacred place but also because the vaulted stone arches remind her of the cave where she and Jean made love. Each time she dips her fingers into the holy water font, she's transported back to the underground lake. But now, as intense feelings of love and passion flood her, she draws back her hand, overtaken by confusion and shame.

Claude whispers, "What's wrong?"

She smiles weakly at her uncle, annoyed she'd allowed her intense feelings to rise so obviously to the surface. She proceeds to the Chapel of the Virgin Mary. Not surprisingly, it is dominated by a large statue of the Virgin, wearing a gold crown and a long, gold and white robe. The Virgin's hands are held high and together in prayer, and her fingers are draped with rosary beads which, in the slanted light from the gothic windows, resemble large dangling pearls. The statue is flanked by two smaller, white-robed cherubs who look up at the Virgin in awe and delight. Sylvie's always thought that this pose was how the sculptor placed the Virgin to capture the moment she received the blessing of child from the Holy Ghost.

As she stares at the Virgin, a symbol of love, Sylvie again envisions being in the cave with Jean. Her head swims with memories of making love to him. She wonders what might have happened if she'd gotten pregnant. If she were carrying Jean's child. Oh, the shame of it but oh, the deliriously happy prospect of holding Jean's child in her arms. Protecting it even as she cannot protect Jean.

She turns to see Claude quizzically staring at her again, then snaps to and searches the chapel. She spots Alastair kneeling in a pew, his head bowed. Approaching, she discovers him sound asleep. *I may not be able to usher Jean to safety, but here's someone I can help find his way home.* She gently taps his shoulder.

Alastair starts awake. His fine, patrician features dissolve into a sheepish grin. "Sorry, Sylvie."

She playfully shakes her head as if he were a truant schoolboy, then turns to Claude. "This is my uncle. We can trust him."

Claude looks around, then whispers, "I understand we need to get you out of Foix."

She instructs them both to wait a moment, then follow her through the far side door and around the rear cloister to the garden. She slips quietly into the garden, with its cobblestone paths ringed with boxwood shrubs. All along the perimeter, wrought-iron trellises are covered with roses, deep claret and white in color, which climb up and over the high Greystone walls. Their sweet fragrance nearly overwhelms her.

At the front of the garden, an ornately carved wooden gate leads to a back alleyway that in turn leads into the village. She looks through one of the slats in the gate to make sure the alley is clear, then quickly heads to the rear of the garden. As Claude and Alastair emerge from the church, she pushes aside a rose-laden, wrought-iron trellis that completely hides a smaller iron gate at the back of the garden. Sylvie smiles triumphantly. "Father Michel showed me." She holds open the small back garden gate for them to pass. This leads to a flight of shadowy, moss-covered stone stairs, then to an ancient passageway underneath the church and along the Ariège River. "If you turn left, this path connects to the Château. Centuries ago, they used this secret passage to bring in food when they were under siege. We'll go right, which takes us out and into a field beyond the village."

She leads them along the narrow, moist stone quay, as the river, constricted in this narrow spot, storms by in loud torrents. She's mesmerized by the velocity of the river, as it runs so fast and close to the quay that rivulets splash them, making their footing slick. After a kilometer of treacherous progress, they enter a tunnel and then, in another third of a kilometer, emerge into the blinding sunlight of a verdant field, where the riverbank is covered with waves of giant sunflowers, large enough to hide the three from view.

Alastair shields his eyes against the glare. "This is top drawer."

Claude turns towards her. "I never knew this was here."

"Isn't it remarkable? Come, let's get to the watermill."

Sylvie is in her element now. They push through the sunflowers until the riverbank gives way to a small tributary of another stream, which they follow as it rises steeply up into the forested mountainside. It is cool, and the ground is covered with dense lichen and moss. She stops to show them a waterfall surging down, nearly on top of them. A crumbling stone structure is visible on the bank above. She hasn't felt this exhilarated since Jean left. She guides them as they scramble up, pointing out a maze of tree roots to help them climb. After an hour, they make it to the top and a small clearing bathed in sunlight.

Flushed with exertion, Sylvie shows them around. "Alastair, this watermill was used to grind wheat and barley. After the villagers built a dam just outside Foix, it was abandoned." She helps Claude push aside the dusty semblance of a front door, and they enter into a crumbling mass of wooden beams, stone ovens, and rough-hewn tables. The roof has caved in at the far end, but there is shelter closest to the waterfall that thunders past. They scrape aside the thick dust and rest on some rickety wooden chairs.

Alastair is breathing heavily. As he sits and crosses his long legs, he straightens his back and lapses into his upright, military posture. Claude is hardly winded, although his broad forehead is bathed in sweat, and tufts of white hair around his bald spot stick up every which way. Sylvie feels her olive skin redden with exertion, and her eyes flicker with gaiety. She playfully cuffs Claude on the arm and turns to Alastair with a broad smile. "My uncle's a mountain goat."

Alastair wipes away large beads of sweat. "I can see that, old chap."

"OLD chap?" Claude laughs a boisterous laugh. "Alastair, you wait here. I'll be back with supplies and one of my men. We head for Spain at dawn."

She shakes her head. "*Merde,* I should be going."

"You'll get your chance, my dear." Claude turns to leave. "If there are others shot down, we may be following this route, more than once."

Sylvie sighs. "I suppose you're right. Who knows how many airmen we'll need to get out of France?"

CHAPTER TEN

Foix. 1 June 1940

ÉLÈNE IS ON a mission to collect clothing for the refugees who've come south to escape the advancing Germans. She makes the rounds visiting the elderly women of Foix, many of whom are widows who've kept their late husbands' clothing for decades. One of them, Madame Champignon, with her pure white hair elegantly piled high on her head, brings a pair of trousers down to her parlor.

She blinks back tears. "I buried my husband in his one suit. I kept these trousers of his. I...I don't know why." She holds them out with small, gnarled hands that are, nevertheless, impeccably manicured. "I suppose my daughter's husband might have worn them. But I never could bring myself to take them from our bedroom armoire."

Hélène hugs the old woman. "*Merci*, Madame. Your husband would be proud to know these will help a poor refugee family." She quietly lifts the trousers over her arm, even as she feels a stab of pain, imagining herself similarly reluctant to part with her husband Gérard's clothes that now hang in the spare upstairs closet in her mother's house in Foix.

Later, arms piled high with garments, Hélène makes her way to the plaza. Barely able to see behind her tower of clothes, she nearly runs into Father Michel, who has a similar, albeit smaller, bundle. She says, "I see we've been on the same errand."

"But you've been more persuasive." His smile is mischievous. "I should have you pass the plate on Sundays."

Hélène admires the young priest's down-to-earth manner, although every Sunday, her mother is careful to remind her that she still prefers the old priest who retired several years ago. Hélène is a woman inclined more towards science than religion, but finds Father Michel's welcoming manner tempting. "I wish I could assist during Mass, but it seems we're going to be swamped with refugees every day from now on."

Last month, the Germans swept through Holland and Belgium, sending thousands of refugees on an exodus from Northern France to the south. Then, on the thirteenth of May, the Germans did what few had expected: Rommel went north around the top of the famed forti-fied Maginot line and breached the French line, punching through the Ardennes Forest into Sedan. The French government did its best to squelch the terrible news, but reports from the front splashed over the newspapers. Since the generals had considered the Ardennes impene-trable, Sedan was one of the least well-defended areas, with the greatest number of older reservists mingled with new recruits, most of whom were poorly trained and ill-equipped.

Hélène quickly adds, "But of course, I'll find time to come and pray for Gérard."

"Not on any lists, my dear?" Lists of those killed, captured, or missing in action are posted in all the villages throughout France. Every day, Hélène joins the droves of anxious women gathering to check the notice boards.

"No, Father." The uncertainty is excruciating—she has no way of knowing where her husband was when the Germans broke through. Putting together news accounts and his letters about being stationed with so many reservists, however, she assumes he's in the thick of it.

For weeks now, she's stood rigid alongside the other villagers reading the postings, furious to learn that German Stuka dive bombers paved the way for the attack, their shrieking for hours on end unnerving the French troops. The Wehrmacht infantry, motorized vehicles, and Panzer tanks swiftly maneuvered in a "blitzkrieg" or "lightning war." They surged through the dense Ardennes Forest, around and through the deep chasms. The German Jaeger, the light infantry, determined in their assault, took large casualties on the front lines as they built rafts over the Meuse River for the Panzers to cross. Hélène and the other women wept to read that the French could have picked most of them off from their positions high on the sides of the steep terrain, but there were too many Germans and not enough French equipment and ammunition. Worst of all, there were reports that there was no French or British air cover. Reading the last, Hélène stormed away in disgust—outrageous there were no planes in the air to shield the French troops from German air and ground attacks.

Now, as she and the priest walk to deliver the clothes, his normally uplifting tone turns funereal. "It's been utter chaos."

Hélène vigorously nods in agreement, then adjusts her stack of clothes to prevent it from toppling. She's still plagued by what Claude told her—information from his army channels not reported in the news. Large numbers of French troops had been ordered to rush into the breach, while others had been ordered to retreat. But those who fell back found the Panzers had already reached the back of their line, where they were supposed to be regrouping. In complete confusion, some—whether from fear, desperation, or both—abandoned their posts. Others even posed as Belgian or Northern French citizens and joined the terrified refugees on their miserable journey south. Could Gérard be among them?

Hélène tries to dampen her fear by turning her attention to the practical problem at hand. "Father, do we have any idea how many refugees are coming?"

The priest stops for a moment to steady his pile of clothing, then continues his walk with Hélène. "I'm sure it will be more than we can imagine."

Petrified French citizens from the north have joined fleeing Belgian and Dutch refugees, leaving their homes in Rheims, Soissons, and Compiegne. In a matter of weeks, eight million people are swept up in the collective exodus south. Now, at the end of May, the population of one Southern French city, Toulouse, has swollen from two hundred thousand to one million. Those arriving in Toulouse, finding it too crowded, push further south into the mountains to smaller villages like Foix, hoping to reach more amenable conditions.

The priest and Hélène arrive at the tables under the wrought-iron canopy in the plaza where a group of village matrons accepts, then sorts the garments. After they relinquish their donations, they turn to the farther side of the plaza to see groups of refugees arriving in a steady stream—something that would have been unimaginable only a few weeks ago. After the refugees arrive and before they can be processed and given shelter in an abandoned warehouse that the French government has hastily opened, they're forced to camp out. Huddled against the church in the plaza, they sleep wherever they can find space, many on straw pallets the townspeople have put out for them.

"So many, Father."

"The Lord has put these poor souls into our care."

Hélène whispers, with as much fear as anger, "I'm not sure we're up to the task." Immediately she blanches, her porcelain skin turning even whiter.

Father Michel whispers, "We have no other choice. Do we?"

No matter how many days Hélène watches the refugees pour into Foix, she is continually horrified to see the desperate state of each new group—forlorn women, children, the elderly, and even some younger men, most in shock and hardly aware of what's going on around them. She's deeply grieved to see these souls, many barely limping along, pushing battered bicycles, or pulling wagons or makeshift carts, loaded with meager possessions—cooking pots, heirloom framed pictures, and even a hatbox or two. She searches every group for Gérard. They wear all manner of filthy clothing—shawls and sweaters layered over shirts and blouses, skirts inching out from beneath other skirts. They seem to have thrown everything they could onto their backs, and worn these clothes for weeks on end—it makes Hélène's skin crawl. Everyone, even the very old and feeble, desperately cling to battered cloth bags, leather satchels, or suitcases, tied together with fraying string. She shudders, flashing back to her own desperate search, in the chaos of Toulouse, for any kind of suitcase to give Gérard before he left for the front.

Hélène looks beyond the plaza to a group Claude is escorting up from the riverbank. One middle-aged man wrestles with a wheelbarrow filled with straw. As they come closer, Hélène gasps to see he's wheeling an ancient woman, frail as a sparrow and dressed in black, her eyes vacant, her legs sticking out on either side of the wheelbarrow. She looks as if she'll die at any moment. In an instant, Hélène is back at her hospital in Toulouse, nursing hundreds of people in their final stages of life. She feels a depth of sorrow for these refugees that she'd never known before—at least then her patients died in clean beds, surrounded by their loved ones. These forlorn souls have seen their loved ones die, then be discarded by the side of the road, never to know a peaceful end to life. Hélène is plagued by conflicting emotions—sickened at their appalling state, relieved she's not among them, but most of all, frustrated she can't immediately do more to help them.

Claude's fellow reservists, François and Louis, are stationed at tables under the canopy, trying to keep order as they move people into line so they can be registered and processed. Most joining the line try to remain calm, but Hélène notices spurts of fear and tempers flaring. Dozens are scattered about the plaza, many of which are huddled against the church. Responding to the order to queue up, they slowly rise, one by one, as if from the dead, gathering their meager possessions and stumbling forward in a daze—a slow-motion herd of people with vacant eyes.

"We should move along, Father." Hélène girds herself to the task before her—they will shortly encounter this very herd of refugees on an individual basis when they interview them for placement. The warehouse is filling rapidly, and the French government, under enormous pressure, has hastily begun to reopen camps along the border formerly used to house Spanish refugees fleeing Franco. As Mussolini has now sided with Hitler, hundreds of French children are arriving in the Pyrénées, sent by parents living throughout Southern France, all the way to the border with Italy. Hélène despairs that she will need additional facilities, preferably in private homes, to keep these children safe.

With her orderly and practical mind, it's almost too much for Hélène to process. And the progress of the fighting is not going well either. The next line of defense, Claude tells the others, is the Somme/Aisne line, but if that is breached, the Nazis will be free to storm Paris in a matter of weeks, most probably by the middle of June. Hélène clings to the desperate hope that Gérard has somehow managed to escape and is regrouping with army units further back to protect Paris. It's utterly unthinkable that Paris could fall into German hands!

Hélène and the priest leave the plaza and head down a narrow street to the medical office of Dr. Duchamps, where the doctor is positioning some small tables outside. In his sixties, the doctor is a small dark man with a thick, neat mustache and delicate hands. He wears over his suit a long smock that bulges slightly against his gently protruding belly. Sylvie emerges from his office carting a wooden bench, aided by a young woman, Giselle, who doesn't appear to be more than sixteen and seems fragile as a twig. The doctor speaks softly but authoritatively. "Ladies, Father, now that we are opening the new camp, we need a better system for checking in the refugees. Too many are coming in with lice."

Noticing Giselle cringe at the mention of lice, Hélène hopes the girl will not be too squeamish to be of help.

Dr. Duchamps continues. "So, we can't give them any new clothes until they've been treated and checked for medical conditions that need immediate attention. Or even quarantine."

"Doctor," Hélène offers, "We should feed them something as soon as possible. So many are starving and dehydrated."

The doctor nods and turns to Sylvie. "When you get them up to the camp, please instruct the workers to give them small amounts of water and a bit of gruel." He raises his voice slightly for emphasis. "But be careful not to feed them too much all at once. They'll only get sick."

While Hélène is assigned to be in charge of processing the newly arrived refugees, Sylvie and Dr. Duchamps go ahead up to the camp. Immediately after they leave, however, Hélène feels an overwhelming sense of panic. How can she possibly deal with so many anguished people all at once? Sometimes the hospital intake was quite busy, but it was always orderly. She can't recall a time when they were as swamped with so many people in such misery. She fingers her nurse's pin on her blouse, murmuring to herself: *Just fall back on my triage training all those years ago. Take one family at a time. Try not to think about the hundreds in line behind.*

Hélène signals to Claude to send along the first group from the plaza. The work is heartbreaking, as she tries to determine where they're from and if their families are together. Many have died along the way from illness, pure exhaustion, or the Luftwaffe's strafing. It's a miracle that some of the elderly have made it at all—she admires their indomitable spirit, certain she'd never have been able to endure such misery.

After a couple of hours, a large, heavyset woman, cradling a baby, motions for two children to present themselves to Hélène's table, then rapidly separates herself from the children and goes to Giselle's table. Hélène surmises the children are alone—a boy about ten years old and a girl a little younger, wearing a kerchief to hold back her unwashed, tangled brown hair. Hélène tries mightily not to cry as she watches them meekly approach, holding hands.

She turns to the boy. "And what's your name?"

"My name is Elias, and this is my sister, Deborah. Please, Madame, do you have anything to eat?"

The boy speaks in a formal but halting way, in French with a heavy Belgian accent. Despite their orders not to feed them anything but bits of gruel and water when they get up to the camp, Hélène can't bear to see them so hungry. She calls the two of them around to her side of the table, ostensibly to have them write something down. She reaches into her pocket for her luncheon—she keeps her food handy as there's never time to take a formal break. Twisting around to hid her actions, she divides her bread and cheese and slips some to each. As she does, she motions for them to keep their heads down and eat slowly, while pretending to give them directions as they eat.

But when they finish, the girl falls to the ground at her feet. Hélène is shot through with fear, terrified that she's done them harm by violating procedure. The boy, however, quickly picks up the girl in his little arms and stands her upright.

"Madame, please, Deborah...she is just weak. She will be good." Hélène sees him agonize as he searches her eyes. Finally, he says, "We are not supposed to tell."

How this boy Elias protects his sister! Hélène nods for him that it's all right to continue. He leans into her, takes a deep breath, and whispers, "We are Jewish."

CHAPTER ELEVEN

Refugee Camp, Pyrénées. 1 June 1940

SYLVIE HOPES THAT keeping her brother Étienne busy driving the refugees up to the camp will assuage his ire at not being allowed to enlist. Her brother is an intense and bookish boy, quick to anger and not at all socially mature or, for that matter, manually dexterous. She decides to allow him to drive the severely overburdened lorry filled with refugees up to the camp, trying to remain calm as he coaxes the vehicle up the steep mountain road. It's been raining, and the furrows are deep, with rivulets of water still streaming through the mist on the sheer side of the cliff and across the gravel road in front of them. On the slippery road, her need for control takes over. Seeing a deep crevice up ahead, she shouts at Étienne, "Watch out for that rut."

"I am," he shoots back, jerking left. Since the vehicle is carrying far too much weight for its size, the motion tips the left rear wheel high off the ground. From the back, screams and wails pierce the mountain air.

"You're going to kill these poor people," she chides. "Stop and let me drive."

"I can handle this, Sylvie. We're almost there."

"We should get out and calm them down."

"That'll only make it worse. Just let me get them there."

She reluctantly agrees, and they continue another ten kilometers, making slow progress on the narrow, muddy road. Mercifully, the fog lifts as they climb higher. Finally, Étienne stops outside a group of one-story concrete buildings, scarred and overgrown with vines, which the French government has hastily repurposed into a refugee camp.

As she surveys the flat, open plateau, Sylvie feels the welcome warmth of the bright sun. Smelling the wildflowers, she thinks this could be a lovely place for a fine mountain picnic, but for the large swaths of rusted barbed wire fencing that lie in clumps around the perimeter of the camp. As she scans the vista, she fixes on the barely erect wooden front gate, with its sign hastily nailed up: "Camp Darcet."

Some two years earlier, this very camp was used to house Spanish refugees fleeing Franco. Sylvie's mother, ministering to those refugees, caught the typhus that killed her and her father shortly after. Sylvie crosses herself, then sits for a moment in silent prayer as she relives those traumatic days, never imagining she'd be back here, where a new group of wretched refugees would be housed.

Sylvie jumps down from the cab and whispers to Étienne, "Ghastly. First Spanish refugees. Now Polish, Belgian, and even French. When will it ever stop?"

While the camp is in sad disrepair, she musters as much optimism as she can—it's at least a larger space than the dark warehouse they were using for the refugees down in Foix. And with magnificent rocky peaks surrounding them, the fresh mountain air is sure to heal the spirits and bodies of these desolate people. She's invigorated by drawing deep breaths of pure, sweet air. Sylvie and Étienne pull aside the canvas tarpaulin that shelters two rows of people who sit on rough benches fastened to the sides. They are mostly elderly men and women, but with some younger women and children of various ages, including an infant suckling at its mother's withered breast.

The refugees blink against blinding shafts of sunlight. Although Étienne signals for them to disembark, they remain frozen, dazed as they huddle together, refusing to move.

A plaintive voice rises from a frail and elderly woman in the rear, "Where are we?"

Another woman, wearing a dark-colored dress covered with mud, rises from her bench and wraps the old woman's shawl more tightly around her. She turns to Sylvie, "Is it all right?"

"You're safe here. We have food and places for you to sleep."

Étienne nods encouragingly as he reaches out to the woman with the infant. "Let me help you down, Madame." Sylvie is surprised to see her usually sullen brother be so congenial. Not all the people in the truck fully understand what's going on, but Sylvie is relieved that the group starts to move. They gingerly walk to the rear end of the lorry, their hands shaking as they lower their meager belongings, then disembark. A thin old man starts to whimper, and the woman next to him strokes his sleeve, murmuring something Sylvie doesn't understand but seems to be comforting.

Although encouraged that she's delivered these people to a safe place in her beloved mountains, Sylvie is still unnerved. She worries that having put their lives in her hands, they are now her responsibility. She prays she won't violate their trust.

Movement in the far side of the camp catches her attention, and she glances over to see a group of children playing in the field just inside the camp gates. These are among the first group of refugees the volunteers brought up earlier that morning. She's pleased that the children are enjoying the open space after being cooped up in the warehouse and is heartened at the resilience of some of the young boys who chase after a well-worn soccer ball. Farther on, some girls jump rope in the field just past the open-air jumble of boards that serves as the temporary latrine. But there is also a line of mothers sitting on some nearby benches, listless and unresponsive, watching dazed as their older children play. Sadly, some small children cling tightly to their mothers' skirts and appear too terrified to move, much less join in the play.

Sylvie turns back to the children in the lorry. "Come, there are other children already here. Maybe some of your friends from the village." Several young boys tentatively start towards Étienne, who lifts them off. She's astonished to see her brother laughing as he swings them to the ground. It's been almost impossible to be both sister and mother to him—balancing firmness with affection but always seeming to provoke nothing but his resentment. At least Uncle Claude has been somewhat of a good influence, even though she wishes he wouldn't fill the boy's head with his political rot.

A few months back, Claude gave Étienne a series of pamphlets from the *FTP, the Francs-Tireurs et Partisans,* named for the guerrilla fighters in the Franco-Prussian war of 1870. The FTP is the clandestine action group of the French Communist Party, based in the north of France, which started to publish in secret. The masthead for the *Voix du Nord*, the "voice of the north," is a line of factories, cranes, farm buildings, and windmills silhouetted against billowing clouds of smoke. *Liberté, égalité, fraternité* is inscribed along the left-hand side of these pamphlets that urge the French to resist the Germans by becoming Marxists and joining with communist labor groups springing up all across France. This idealistic message has resonated deeply with Étienne. But Jean's experience smuggling supplies to the communists in Spain—who turned into fascists themselves—convinces her that her brother is naïve to believe their propaganda about a "better" communist world.

When she voiced her skepticism about how collectivism might not work so well in practice, her brother turned nasty, vehemently defending his newly adopted position. "It's about a place where each man contributes according to his ability," he shouted at her. "Where people don't make fun of you just because you read a lot and aren't good with tools."

She wishes Jean were here to temper her uncle's influence—Claude's exuberance leads him to embrace any new political stream of thought.

And with Jean gone, her uncle holds considerable sway over the boy, which is especially difficult to counteract since Claude is the senior reservist and holds a position of authority in the village. Overwhelmed by caring for the refugees, she hardly has the energy to argue against her uncle's communist-leaning rants, so she tends to keep her opinions to herself—not an easy task.

In any event, Sylvie is delighted to see Étienne put aside his seriousness and romp with the children. She laughs to see her tall, gawky brother pick up the children. They giggle as he hoists one onto his narrow shoulders, then picks one under each arm like a sack of potatoes. The rest follow after him, as he pretends to be a giant, carrying some of them and leading the rest towards the gate. "Fee-fi-fo-fum!" He sits them down on benches just inside the entrance, then plops down beside them, playfully dusting them off, tickling them in the process.

Sylvie and the small volunteer group from Foix work to get the camp in shape, establishing a kitchen, an infirmary, and sleeping quarters for families. She and Hélène have already agreed that the adults are too overwhelmed with caring for their own children and elderly parents to look after the orphaned children. Until these children can be placed with local families, they will be housed in separate sleeping arrangements in the camp, with designated caregivers like Giselle to watch over them.

Sylvie, inclined to taking charge, soon discovers Hélène has the same bent. But, since her work with the refugees brings back such traumatic memories of her parents, she's extremely grateful to Hélène for her calm, pragmatic take-charge manner and her nursing and organizational skills. After seeing to the refugees she's brought up from the village, she checks the section of the building cordoned off as an infirmary.

Hélène has just arrived after her shift registering the refugees. She and the doctor help an infirm woman who expels short, hard staccato coughs that reverberate in her narrow, bird-like chest. An elderly man, Sylvie assumes the woman's husband, coaxes her to remove her blouse to allow the doctor to examine her. Dr. Duchamps motions for them all to wait. He then takes some twine and laces it through holes he punches in a tarpaulin drop. Hélène helps him hoist it to make a curtain, then ushers the woman behind it. The doctor smiles sagely. "We need to provide our Orthodox Jewish patients with an acceptably private facility."

As the doctor finishes with his patient, Sylvie whispers to him, "It's criminal what's going on in the East. What could this poor elderly couple possibly have done?"

"That madman wants to eradicate us all."

Sylvie looks at the doctor curiously. She grew up in Foix with him as their family physician and never once thought about whether he was Jewish. She murmurs a prayer: God willing, he and the others will be safe up here in the mountains.

She and Étienne make one final trip back down to Foix. As the day progresses, she notices that her brother comes to Hélène's assistance more and more, helping her move things in the dispensary and sort out shelving for supplies and the like. After she and Hélène finish straightening up Dr. Duchamps's makeshift office, they trudge to a bench outside to get some air.

Étienne immediately rushes up to Hélène. "Would you like something from the canteen?" Almost as an afterthought, he asks his sister, "Sylvie?"

Hélène pushes a stray blonde curl back behind her ear and smiles at the boy. "If they have the kettle up, I would love a cup of tea, Étienne."

He's halfway to the canteen when Sylvie calls to him, "Nothing for me, but thanks anyway."

As they settle on the bench, Hélène turns to Sylvie. "You've done a remarkable job raising him."

"He's got a mind of his own."

"You wouldn't want it any other way."

Sylvie leans against the concrete wall and sighs. "No, but sometimes, I'd like him to look before he leaps."

"He's young. And sincere. He'll sort it out."

"I wish Jean were here to give him more direction." Her eyes mist. "I miss him. I suppose as much as you miss Gérard."

Sylvie is surprised to see the usually stalwart and pragmatic Hélène tremble as she whispers, "I miss Gérard holding me at night."

Sylvie flashes back to the memory of lying entwined with Jean in the cave, making love. She feels her cheeks flushing.

Hélène shifts uncomfortably on the bench. "I'm sorry. I'd forgotten you and Jean weren't married."

"No, but we shared a...a great deal." A wave of guilt prevents her from saying more. "And I loved him very much."

They sit for a moment in their shared, silent grief. Sylvie notices Hélène quietly wipe her eyes as she pretends to smooth her blonde curls.

Hélène takes a deep breath and abruptly stands. "Moping won't solve anything."

Sylvie suddenly stands as well. "I don't see how you do it."

"What?"

"Deal with all these people. I get so...involved with every one of them."

"Sylvie, I feel for them too. As much as you." Hélène, much taller than Sylvie, reaches down to take her hand. "Working in the emergency clinic for so many years, I've learned the only way to function is to tend to the one patient right in front of me."

Sylvie jerks away. "That's what I try to do. But these people have lost everything. We can barely offer them a change of clothes." She shudders then wraps her arms around herself. "I can't turn my mind off. I think about one person's distress, on top of the next person's and—"

"We can only do what we can," Hélène says, her voice calm and resolved.

"Once the Lord has put them into our charge, I feel they're my responsibility."

"Forgive me. I don't have your strong faith in God. But isn't it God's responsibility, not yours?"

Sylvie abruptly steps back and starts to say something. Just then, Étienne arrives with a mug of steaming tea. He approaches Hélène like a puppy, proud to bring his owner a bone.

Hélène appears relieved to end the conversation. As she takes the tea, she whispers to Sylvie, "You did a fine job with this one. Try not to agonize over things we can't control."

Sylvie whispers back, "You're right. I've got to try. And yes, isn't this young man remarkable? He's one of the reasons I have so much faith in God."

CHAPTER TWELVE

Foix. 4 June 1940

HÉLÈNE WAKES WITH a start from yet another dream about Gérard. This time he's captured, lined up against a crumbling blood-spattered wall in a northern French village, and shot. She shivers, even though a dazzling, early summer sun streams through her tiny bedroom window. She allows herself only a few minutes to recover, then dresses quickly, knowing the sooner she puts her troubled sleep behind her, the faster she can get to the refugee camp.

Despite her calm and unflappable exterior, Hélène is constantly anxious about her husband. Now, on top of that she worries about the people and especially the children in the refugee camp—in particular the two orphaned Jewish children, Elias and Deborah. While she works in the infirmary, she arranges for the young woman who helped at check-in, Giselle, to pay special attention to them. Hélène slips them extra bedding, brings Deborah a doll from her childhood bedroom, and asks Étienne to carve a toy for Elias.

Horrifying rumors reach them of Nazi brutality in Germany and Poland, directed at civilians and especially Jews. Untold numbers of people are said to have disappeared, apparently shipped east to some sort of labor camps. Hélène determines to do more to protect the children before something untoward happens. She goes to the railway station, where Father Michel normally waits for the trains arranged by the French government that bring the continuing stream of refugees up to Foix from Toulouse.

As Hélène approaches the priest, she sees him balling up his fists as if preparing to take on an invisible adversary. "Father? Something troubling you?"

He shakes out his hands and turns to her with a weary smile. "I used to enjoy coming to the station to greet visitors who came to hear our beautiful organ at St. Volusien. Now I dread each train because it holds such misery."

"Not only misery here, Father. You've heard what they say is going on in the East?"

He swallows hard. "It's hard to believe such rumors."

She looks down the track, holding her hand up to shield her eyes from the bright sun. It should be one of those lovely days in the mountains, fresh with the promise of summer—but for her, it's not. "I'm extremely worried about the Jewish people in the camp. The children in particular. I want to find homes to place them in case…well, just in case." She searches his dark eyes for any sign of disagreement; seeing none, she presses her case. "I'm especially concerned about Elias and Deborah. I would take them in myself—Gérard and I always wanted children—but it's impossible with my work at the camp."

Father Michel gently shakes his head. "No one's blaming you."

"I appreciate that, Father." Hélène's soft blue eyes brighten as she zeros in on the priest. "I have a thought, but I'll need your help." She pauses, then, since he hasn't said no, quickly adds, "And the loan of the parish auto—and it would be best if you came with me and drove."

Father Michel rubs his hands together in a gesture of anticipation and smiles mischievously. "I'm sure I'm going to regret this."

Hélène and Father Michel arrive at the camp and go straight to the children's dormitory. The windows have been boarded over, as they lack glass to repair them. Volunteers have tried to make the darkened rooms more inviting by plastering gaily-colored posters onto the pocked and scarred concrete walls. In addition, Hélène found remnants of fabric from her rounds in the village to hang in sections to provide some semblance of privacy.

As Hélène sits on Deborah's cot, wrapping the girl in her arms, Elias stands watch, ever protective of his little sister. Hélène keeps her voice exaggeratedly light. "And how are my big children today? Did you have a shower last night?" They nod vigorously. "Good. Let me see if you washed behind your ears." She hugs each one in turn, looks behind their ears, and kisses them there, tickling them as they giggle.

Father Michel bends down to kiss each child on both cheeks and says, "Would you like to go for a ride in the country?"

Deborah squeals, "Oh yes, please!"

Elias, wary of any new situation, pushes back. "If you please, where are we going?"

Hélène quickly reassures him. "To visit a dear lady, Madame Rumeau. She and my mother used to make the most beautiful lace tablecloths in the Ariège." Hélène thinks back to the sad day last winter when Madame Rumeau came to the doctor's office in Foix, distraught after learning that her grandson Albert had been killed in a training accident. Afterward, her grandson's young fiancée, Noëlle, came to live in the mountains with the elderly lady and help take care of her farm.

As they leave the camp, Hélène worries that her plan to place the children with Madame Rumeau won't succeed, and she'll only have to bring them back, but she's intent on trying anyway. The church vehicle is an old Renault with small windows. Deborah happily climbs into the back seat and jumps around inside. Even the normally guarded

Elias appears excited. Their faces fill one window, then another, as they check all possible views. Father Michel shifts the vehicle into gear, and it sputters and coughs as they drive off.

Hélène admonishes them. "Now children. Sit back." But they immediately plaster themselves against the side windows.

Climbing the steep mountain road, they pass under arches carved into the granite of the mountainside. Higher up, they enter a series of mini-tunnels.

Elias squeals, "We're going into a tunnel. Deborah, do not be afraid. I'm not."

For a glorious moment, Hélène is caught up in the children's delight. Laughing, she asks Elias, "Why not?"

Elias looks at her with a solemn expression. "Because we will come out the other side. Wait. You'll see."

Father Michel laughs as he calls to Elias in the back seat. "Aren't you the clever one?"

Every curve presents a new reason for the children to stare wide-eyed out the windows until, all of a sudden, Deborah turns pale.

"I'm going to be sick," she whimpers.

"No you're not." Elias leans over to her side, rolls down her window, and motions for her to take a breath.

"Good girl, Deborah," Hélène says. She turns to Elias. "Where did you learn that?"

Hélène has tried to get the children to speak of their parents, but they've never uttered a word. She's never wanted to press them, although she's ached to know what they'd endured before arriving, all alone, at Foix. Perhaps now is her chance to learn more.

"My Papa had a car. It was new and black and shiny." Elias smiles proudly. "He and Mama used to take us into the country. It was very hilly but not as much as here." He looks kindly at his sister and continues. "Deborah sometimes feels sick, but Papa stops and rolls down the window. He tells her to breathe. And she wouldn't be sick anymore."

"That's very good, Elias. Tell me more about your Papa," Hélène cautiously adds.

Elias beams. "Mama always smelled good. Like soap."

Deborah starts to cry. "I miss my Mama."

Hélène asks the priest to find a place to pull over. She climbs into the back seat and takes Deborah in her lap. But Elias seems upset as he slides away and looks out the other window.

Hélène coos to the girl, "It's all right. You can cry." She turns to the boy. "Elias, it's all right if your sister cries. You too, if you want."

Deborah sobs, hiccups, and sobs some more.

Suddenly Elias shouts at Hélène, "No we can't! The train is crowded, and we are hiding. Papa says not to cry, no matter what."

The priest turns sharply around and opens his mouth to speak, but Hélène motions for him to stay silent.

Deborah wails, "But I was *ascared*. I'm sorry. I was ascared." She buries her head in Hélène's lap.

"It was dark and hard to breathe," Elias shouts. He shoves Hélène away and urgently grabs his sister, pulling her close to him. "I'm supposed to protect you. That's what Papa said. Before they dragged him away."

Hélène asks, "Where was this, Elias? Tell me."

"I saw it out the keyhole in the closet. In the train."

"Elias, what did you see from the closet?"

Elias suddenly stops talking, and Hélène decides not to force the issue. She allows Elias to keep hold of Deborah, who finally stops crying, then she climbs back into the front seat, and they drive on. Their progress is slow as the road steepens with narrow and precipitous drop-offs. But the sky is cerulean, and the air is fresh and clear, so Hélène allows herself a few moments of joy—a respite from the burdens of the camp. She glances back every now and then at the children to make sure Deborah isn't getting car sick and to reassure Elias. After a while, the priest starts to sing a song with verses for children to sing along. Deborah slowly joins in, singing off-key and a bit out of sync, while Elias seems frozen, not moving or looking at any of them.

After a while, the road levels out, and they approach a small, tidy farmhouse by a rushing brook. Mist rises from the cool water as it hits the warmer, thin mountain air. A young lamb grazes in patches of grass among the rocks. Father Michel honks his horn to announce their arrival, and Madame Rumeau, dressed as always in her mourning black but sporting an apron, lopes out of her farmhouse, leaning on her black cane. Hélène adores the feisty old woman and bends down to kiss her on both plump cheeks. Madame Rumeau chuckles as she reaches up to steady the enormous pile of gray hair wound around the top of her head.

Father Michel opens the car door for the children and motions them out. As he approaches the elderly lady, she twitters and smooths her apron, shifts her cane to the other hand, and smooths her apron some more. Thrilled to have company, her tiny eyes emerge from her round face, twinkling as she watches the children cautiously get out of the car. Hélène waves the children over for Madame Rumeau to fawn over them. She is so short that she hardly needs to bend down to meet them at eye level.

Madame calls back into the house, "Noëlle, come dear, we have guests."

Hélène hasn't felt this exuberant since she and Gérard were together before he left for the front. She watches as Deborah, her eyes soft and wide, peeks out from Madame's apron and spies the lamb. Hélène says, "Madame, is it all right if Deborah pets the lamb?" Madame Rumeau nods, and the girl patters towards the animal, although Elias gets there first, as usual, to protect his sister.

Hélène turns to Madame Rumeau. "You are such a warm and generous woman." She feels a combination of genuine sincerity, guilt, and trepidation over what she's about to ask. Before she can continue, a young woman emerges from the farmhouse, dusting flour from her hands. She is thin and brittle and moves slowly, wearing a heavy cloak of sadness. She gently kisses Hélène on both cheeks and makes a slight bow to the priest.

Hélène, shocked at the girl's melancholy demeanor, nevertheless tries to engage the girl. "Noëlle, you must be a great comfort to Madame Rumeau. The mountain air seems to agree with you."

"Madame Hélène, I'm coping. Really, that's all I've done since Albert died." She turns to the priest. "Father, you were to have married us this month." Her thin shoulders droop as she retrieves a handkerchief from her apron pocket and dabs her nose.

The priest says, "It's all so terribly sad." Turning to Madame Rumeau, he adds, "Shocking that your only grandson should be killed in a training accident, of all things."

Hélène volunteers, "Still, he was a hero."

With a forced cheerfulness Madame Rumeau says, "Yes, I know he was. But now, I couldn't manage alone up here on the farm without this young lady. She's been a Godsend." She twitters, "If you'll pardon the expression, Father."

The priest waves a kindly, dismissive hand.

Just then, Noëlle notices the children, and like a magnet, is drawn right to them. She kneels and shows them how to stroke the lamb under its chin. Soon they're all giggling.

Hélène watches Noëlle, then musters her courage and turns to Madame Rumeau. "Actually, Madame, the children are really very well behaved. And…ah…very bright."

The elderly lady looks between Hélène and the priest, then back to the children. Hélène sees her assessing the situation, praying things will turn out as she plans. The old woman nods, then cocks an eyebrow. "What are their names?"

Hélène steals a glance at the priest, then takes a deep breath before replying, "Elias and Deborah."

Madame Rumeau leans on her cane, straightening her short, plump frame. "Jewish children, are they?" Frowning, she looks over at them.

Hélène quickly adds, "Of course we'll continue to try to locate their parents."

Madame Rumeau stares a long moment at the children. "We are practicing Catholics here." She turns to the priest for support. "They should be raised with their...ah...their own kind. What I mean is, so they can appreciate their own heritage."

Father Michel jumps in, "But their *own kind*, as you say, Madame, are fleeing the Nazis. We teach our children in the convent to respect other religions."

The old woman casts a questioning glance at the priest, who takes her small, gnarled hands in his.

Hélène senses her cue to provide additional ammunition. "And when the fighting's over, we promise to look for their relatives. Or, if we can't find any, perhaps we can find some Jewish people who'd like to raise them. Meanwhile, Madame, they're all alone."

Madame Rumeau again looks over at the children, murmuring, "All alone." Her voice trails off. "Like my Noëlle and me."

The priest pats Madame Rumeau's hands encouragingly.

She smiles weakly at Hélène. "You were always so good at helping others. Since you were a little girl. Your mother was so proud when you became a nurse."

The priest softly adds, "Madame, there are so many refugees. They've lost everything. The children are innocent lambs."

Hélène adds, "Especially these two."

The children and Noëlle break into peals of laughter as they leave off patting the lamb and start stroking each other under their chins. Madame Rumeau turns from the priest and stares intently at them. She brushes her hand across her crinkled brow as if to banish an unwanted thought, then sets her stout shoulders. "I haven't heard Noëlle laugh like that since my grandson died." She pauses, then simply states, "Of course they can stay."

Hélène sucks in a sharp, relieved breath, then bends down and gives the old woman a fierce hug. While she and the priest exchange congratulatory smiles, Madame Rumeau, tapping her cane on the soft grass, lumbers over to Noëlle and whispers in her ear. At first, the young woman seems not to comprehend, but then her eyes brighten, and she thrusts out her thin arms, embracing Madame Rumeau and the children.

Hélène stands with Father Michel, watching Madame Rumeau and Noëlle play with the children. She feels a rare moment of pure joy—and a sliver of optimism that the world may not be such a horrible place after all.

CHAPTER THIRTEEN

Toulouse. 10 June 1940

SYLVIE HASTENS INTO the hospital ward with Étienne fast on her heels. They've taken the train down from Foix to visit Gabriel, Étienne's schoolmate, who was wounded on the front, then transferred to the major hospital closest to his hometown. As head of the reservists in Foix, Claude has arrived before them and stands at the foot of the last bed on the left, waving to get their attention.

Sylvie takes a few steps into the ward then abruptly freezes, coming face to face with the devastation of the war. Two solid rows of wounded soldiers. Bandages everywhere. Arms and legs missing or, if they're there at all, immobilized in plaster or slings. Blood oozing through gauze-wrapped head wounds. Each bed a fresh horror. A new stench.

Nausea slams into Sylvie. She wants to turn and sprint out of the hospital, but she forces herself to stay, holding herself together for Étienne's sake. Taking quick short breaths to avoid retching, she waves back at Uncle Claude, then she and Étienne slowly inch towards him, as if stepping on fractured glass.

Nearing the hospital bed, she says to her brother, "This may be a shock." Claude stands outside a drawn curtain, anxiously twisting his beret in his hands.

Étienne's says, with shaky voice, "Uncle Claude said he would...I mean...he's going to be all right, isn't he?"

"You mustn't let Gabriel know if he doesn't look very good. Don't say anything to upset him."

"I'm not dumb, Sylvie."

She looks around her. "I don't see his mother on the ward. I'm sure Uncle Claude let her know first thing."

"Maybe she's already here. Behind the curtain."

As they approach, Claude gingerly steps over to them, kisses them on both cheeks, and says, reassuringly, "The nurse is with him."

Just then, a nun with a small-sized white Whipple—more suitable for nursing than the usual full-sized convent version—emerges from behind the curtain carrying a pan covered with a bloody cloth. She efficiently draws the curtain back and swings around, nearly running into Claude. She gives him a pained smile.

For a fleeting moment, Sylvie hopes the nun will forbid visitors, which would spare her and Étienne the agony of seeing his friend. Instead, the nun turns to Sylvie, her tone flat and business-like. "You may see him now. Don't stay too long."

Claude motions Étienne towards the bed. A large young boy with a cherubic face sits propped up, his right arm resting on a mound of pillows. The boyish muscular arm ends at his elbow. Gauze bandages, with blotches of blood oozing through, cover the stump of what had been his right forearm and hand. The other arm is in a sling, and his puffy, bruised forehead is bandaged. On the bed itself, there is only a flat space underneath a blanket—where his left leg should have been. Sylvie's heart wrenches, seeing his adolescent blue eyes sunken into his round face, staring out and beyond the ward.

Étienne tentatively steps forward. "Gabriel, we came to—" He seems to want to say more but is only able to stare at Gabriel's missing hand. Finally, his voice cracks, "I mean, we heard—" Then he freezes.

Sylvie picks up the conversation, trying to muster a brave face. "Gabriel, we came as soon as we heard. We're very sorry, aren't we, Étienne?"

She catches a quiver in Gabriel's lower lip as he appears desperate to avoid crying. Even so, a tear trickles down his baby face, and he slowly turns his head away to face the wall.

Claude exaggerates a reassuring tone for the benefit of all. "Our Gabriel here has been getting the royal treatment. He's a real hero, aren't you, my boy?"

Trying to be as non-accusatory as possible, Sylvie says, "Your mother was worried sick. Then we found out you'd enlisted and—"

Étienne breaks in, "Gabriel, I wanted to go too. Remember we talked about going together? But Sylvie wouldn't sign."

Gabriel sluggishly turns his head back towards them, wincing in pain. "My mother wouldn't sign either. That's why I ran away. They didn't question me."

Sylvie assumes because the boy is so big, that he was able to pass for an adult and enlist. She looks over at her slender brother and says a silent prayer that the reservists found him out before he could sign up as well—he might very well have been the one in that bed.

Gabriel adds, "And now—" He violently dry heaves, and Claude grabs a pan from the foot of the bed for him to throw up in, but nothing comes. Gabriel moans loudly and coughs, flinching in pain, then slowly settles back down. A final shudder racks his beefy frame as he rests his head back on his pillow.

Sylvie reaches her hand out to comfort him but immediately pulls back, realizing with a dreadful shock that she doesn't know where to touch him, given his lost and wounded limbs.

Gabriel leans slightly forward, his eyes raised hopefully towards Sylvie. "Would you talk to my mother? She's going to be mad at me."

Claude booms, "Nonsense, my boy. You only did what you thought was the right—"

Sylvie casts a furious look at her uncle and jerks her head towards Étienne, her eyes flaring angrily, which causes Claude to abruptly stop talking. She quickly adds with extravagant kindness, "Your mother will understand. I'm sure she'll be along. You can tell her yourself."

Gabriel leans back, lets out a relieved sigh, then shrinks back into himself. At that moment, and despite his size, he looks to Sylvie more like a boy of ten rather than Étienne's classmate.

Claude waits for him to settle, then gently nudges the boy. "Gabriel. You brought something for Mademoiselle Sylvie, didn't you?"

Gabriel squeezes his eyes tightly shut. She can see rapid, pained movement behind his eyelids as though he were envisioning a ghastly, violent scene.

Claude goes to the cabinet by the bed and picks up a package of wrinkled brown paper, snugly wrapped in a large amount of twine.

Étienne lights up. "More pamphlets, Uncle Claude? I'm only just finishing the ones you—"

Claude cuts Étienne off with a rapid shake of his head. Claude's eyes mist over while Gabriel looks on—by now, tears are streaming down his face.

Claude tries to get the words out. "My boy. Sylvie—" Claude slowly brings the package around and holds it, like an evil talisman, straight in front of him towards Sylvie.

"What's wrong?" She senses something awful. "Uncle Claude? Gabriel?" She turns from the package Claude holds to Gabriel in the bed—then back and forth between the two.

Gabriel's whisper sounds desperate, coming as it does in halting fits and starts. "He gave me his jacket. Wound it around my leg to stop the bleeding." Gabriel swallows hard, trying to get the rest out. "Said if he didn't make it back, I should tell you how much he...he—" Gabriel shoots a pleading glance at Claude.

Claude turns to Sylvie. "Gabriel had it with him when the medics brought him in. He asked one of the nurses to clean it up. He knew you'd want to have it."

Sylvie stares at the package for a long moment. A fierce revulsion rises in her as she shakes her head, almost imperceptibly, in disbelief. She ejects a raspy, "No." Her hands fly over her mouth. Her devastation is total. She's in the cave now, falling into the lake, floating lifeless until she reaches the far end where she's dragged under by the rushing water and propelled into the darkness.

Startled, Étienne asks, "What is it, Sylvie?" He stares at Claude, who stands immobile, the package in his outstretched hands.

Sylvie looks at Étienne, her eyes weighted with misery. He doesn't understand what's going on. That her life is now over. Gone. She can no longer build a life with the one person whom she loved. And who loved her. Truly loved her for who she was.

Claude struggles to find the words to explain to Étienne. "They believe that Jean...ah...they are listing Jean...as...well..." He bursts out, "Jean was killed in a tank attack in the Ardennes." He stops to catch his breath, then slowly, reverently, unwraps the package and smooths out the heavy woolen olive-colored fabric with its patches of faded blood. Claude's hands shake as he tries, with his large fingers, to weave the fabric back together in several torn places.

Étienne stares at the jacket as if in a trance. Slowly and mechanically, he says, "Jean can't have been killed. The Maginot Line. All the fortifications..." The boy rambles on.

"Étienne—" Claude tries to get his attention.

But Étienne carries on, his voice thinning and rising. "The Ardennes? That's in the forest. Jean could never get killed in a forest. He knows all about that kind of terrain."

Again, Claude tries to interrupt. "Étienne, please—"

In extreme slow motion, Sylvie watches her uncle attempt to get through to her brother. She floats outside herself, trying to comprehend the situation, all the while, her eyes fastened on the blood stains in the fabric of the jacket.

Étienne continues, his words coming faster, his pitch higher and higher. "He was teaching me to hunt. He never minded I had a hard time keeping up. He never criticized me." Étienne stares daggers at Sylvie. "Like everyone else does." He stomps several feet around the ward, his arms flailing, his clenched fists pounding against his sides.

Sylvie watches her brother from a distant place within herself. She's slowly infused with anger, as she hovers over the ward, looking down at her brother and uncle.

Claude tries to quiet the boy, but Étienne won't be silenced. "He's not like everybody who makes fun of me. He told me: never let them stop you from your reading. They're just jealous." He shoots another vicious, accusatory glance at his sister.

Étienne's tone slices through her, causing her to snap back into reality. She looks around for an instant and realizes she's back down, standing on the floor of the ward. She tries to muzzle herself, but her extreme pain and anger force her to shoot back: "I never wanted you to stop reading. I just wanted you to get your head out of the clouds." She catches herself, takes a deep breath, and softly adds, "I'm sorry, Étienne. I don't mean to be critical. Especially now."

Claude's tone is somber as he hands Étienne the jacket. "My boy, give it to Sylvie."

Étienne slowly turns to give the dreaded parcel to her.

But instead of taking it, she shrieks. "NO!!! Take it away."

The nuns in the ward stop to look in their direction. The general murmuring stops, although not the groaning and intermittent calls in pain from the rows of patients.

Sylvie is oblivious to what's going on around her. Shoving the jacket back at her brother, she desperately searches for a valid excuse not to take it. Finally, she stammers, "Jean...he would have wanted you to have it."

Étienne stares at the jacket, then at her. "You mean it? You don't want it?"

"It's not that I don't want it." She doubles over, holding her stomach as if she'd been punched in the gut.

Claude puts his arm around her shoulders and brings her up and into an embrace. He interprets for Étienne, "If your sister doesn't take it, she doesn't have to acknowledge he's dead, isn't that so, Sylvie?" He kisses the top of her head and strokes her heaving back.

The acid that rises in her throat prevents her from speaking.

Étienne, confused, looks between his uncle and sister. "And if I want it?"

"It's yours," she rasps.

Claude wipes back his tears, now running without restraint down his ruddy face. Suddenly, Sylvie sees anger rise in Étienne's face as he fits the jacket up to his chest. Although the sleeves are clearly too short for his long, spindly arms, he straightens his back and lets out a ferocious groan. "This settles it, Sylvie—you've got to let me go now."

She breaks away from Claude's embrace, flushing a deep red. "This settles nothing. In fact, it's all the more reason you can't go." Her eyes dart towards Gabriel. "Do you want to end up like—" She stops short just as Gabriel jerks his head in her direction, and she realizes the true horror of her words.

"You can't keep me now," Étienne screams. He storms out of the ward, clutching Jean's jacket.

Sylvie stands at Gabriel's bedside, dazed, her mind buried in what feels like a mound of bloody gauze. After a moment, Claude says to Gabriel, "Thank you, my boy. For salvaging his jacket."

Gabriel looks up sheepishly. "I hope I did right."

Claude nods to him, offers Sylvie his arm, and starts to lead her out of the ward.

She stops, glances back at Gabriel, and rallies for the poor boy's benefit as best she can. "You did a good thing." Her voice trails off, "To bring us ..."

Gabriel manages a forlorn smile.

Sylvie hangs on to her uncle's arm as she tries to walk. Tries to put one foot in front of the other. Tries to enter the rest of her life without Jean.

CHAPTER FOURTEEN

"WHAT IS THAT dreadful knocking?" Isobel shouts to no one in particular. Annoyed to hear a fierce rapping on the front door, she calls for the butler, who doesn't respond. *He's probably flirting with the next-door maid.* She rolls her eyes, looks around her comfortable parlor, then returns her focus to the sheets of music she's carefully lined up on her mahogany music stand, which has been polished to a high gloss and richly carved with a G clef and notes. As the knocking persists, she carefully places her flute down, then marches to the front door and yanks it open. A tall, skinny boy stands there, holding a length of olive green fabric in one hand, his other arm in midair, about to lift the knocker again. Under his thick wire-rimmed eyeglasses, his face is streaked with dried tears, and strands of his bushy black hair are plastered chaotically onto his forehead.

Recoiling at the sight of him, Isobel stamps her foot. "Boy, deliveries go around the side to the kitchen." She points to a sign on the elaborate, wrought-iron fence outside her house. "Can't you read?"

How dare some delivery boy interrupt her practice! She turns on her heel and is about to slam the door when Étienne whimpers, "Cousin Isobel? I'm Étienne. Sylvie's brother."

She whirls back and peers into his face, then takes in his lanky frame. "Cousin Étienne? Ah. We weren't expecting you." Although he's Sylvie's brother and technically her uncle, the family has always referred to him as a "cousin" to Isobel since they are so close in age. She peers out the door to check the sidewalk. "Is Aunt Sylvie with you?" Seeing no one outside, she turns back to see Étienne staring at her.

He stammers, "You're so…so dressed up. Am I disturbing something?"

Enjoying his fluster, she flounces her frilly dress of lavender and beige silk and gives a little coquettish shake of her auburn hair, piled high except for some longer, strategically placed curls. "This dress?" She smooths it with one hand, and with the other, winds a curl around her finger. Even if he is her cousin, it's Isobel's long-held custom to dazzle any boy with whom she comes in contact. After she's posed sufficiently to leave him dumbfounded and silent, she shrugs and motions him inside.

Étienne gingerly enters, clutching Jean's jacket, then turns sideways, attempting to hide it behind him. Her eyes immediately zero in on something that could be a gift for her.

"What have you got there, Cousin Étienne?"

"Nothing. Really. Why don't I…I'll just leave it here, next to the door." He bunches up the jacket and moves to place it on the entryway table, but then stops. "Maybe I should go. We were just visiting the hospital. And ah, I don't think Sylvie planned to pay you a visit today."

"And why not? Aunt Sylvie knows I always love to see her." Isobel eyes the fabric. "But Mama says she's been busy with all those dreadful refugees. I hear you've been inundated with them up in Foix. They are absolutely taking over Toulouse." Isobel maintains her focus on the fabric while she continues. "Mama and Papa don't let me walk alone on the street anymore. There are so many of them. All so filthy. And Mama says you don't know if they're going to steal something—"

Isobel's curiosity finally gets the best of her, and she goes for the fabric. "What's this? A jacket of some kind?"

Before Étienne can grab it away, she opens the jacket wide and twists it around to get a good look. Spotting the faded blood stains, she drops it, shrieking, "What is that—?"

Mon Dieu! Isobel darts back several quick paces, her hand fanning her mouth as she tries to catch her breath. She opens her eyes wide as she watches Étienne bend to pick it up and reverently smooth it out.

"It was Jean's." Then he snaps, "But you wouldn't know about bravery and such things. You've always been a spoiled brat." Isobel winces like she'd been slapped in the face, actually rubbing her cheek as if it stung. She stares at Étienne for a moment, then turns and briskly walks back into the parlor, not quite sure what she intends to do. She's certainly too flustered to continue her flute practice.

Louisa rushes in from the kitchen. "Isobel? I heard a noise. What's going on?"

Not even caring to look in his direction, Isobel sullenly points to Étienne, still planted in the entryway, smoothing out the jacket. "Cousin Étienne just showed up...he's got something quite disgusting."

Louisa rapidly shifts her focus to the boy, then spies the dried blood on the jacket. "Étienne? What are you doing here? Where's Sylvie? Are you hurt?" She opens her arms and the boy rushes into them, breathing hard.

"Aunt Louisa, I'm sorry. I just ran out of the ward. I didn't know where else to go. Sylvie didn't want Jean's jacket. My friend Gabriel brought it back from the front."

Isobel watches Étienne's emotional display with disgust until she sees her mother becoming alarmed and wonders if something dreadful has actually occurred.

Louisa says, "Jean? At the front? What's happened?"

Étienne gasps, "Jean's dead. My friend Gabriel knew he wanted Sylvie to have his jacket. But then she didn't want it, so she gave it to me." He backs up to show her the jacket. "They tried to clean it up. See?"

Louisa stammers, "J...Jean? You s...said Jean is..." Her voice trails off.

Étienne bursts into tears. Louisa folds him into an embrace and reaches up to bring his face down to cradle in the crook of her neck. She rubs circles of breath into his back. She whispers, "Is Sylvie coming here?"

Between gasps of breath, the boy manages to say, "I just ran out. I didn't want Gabriel or Uncle Claude to see me cry."

Isobel increasingly realizes that she should be ashamed of how she's acted towards Étienne, especially because Jean means everything to her Aunt Sylvie. "Mama, I'm sorry. I didn't understand."

As the front door swings open, Louisa and Étienne break apart while Sylvie, Claude, and Louisa's husband, Dr. Goldschmidt, pile into the parlor. The street outside is filled with horns honking, banging pots, and screams as people race chaotically along the boulevard.

Claude shouts, "Those Nazis. *Merde*. We're *foutus*... totally fucked!"

Isobel knows that no one ever speaks in that tone in her household, so she becomes alarmed and looks helplessly at her parents for some clue about what's going on.

Dr. Goldschmidt tries to remain calm but blurts out, "Louisa, the worst has happened." The doctor's pale skin has turned the deep rust color of his beard. "The wireless. We've got to turn on the wireless." He races to the radio and twists the dials at the sides of the mesh screen. They all huddle close, staring intently at the brown velvet in the main arch of the radio, as if an announcer were about to pop out and report the news.

Isobel hears a man's voice but isn't sure what it means. Through the static he says, "...as far as the eye can see...German soldiers...down the Champs-Élysées...around the Arc de Triomphe...up and down the twelve avenues spoking out from the monument...coal shuttle helmets...misery on the faces of the Parisians...the Huns have surrounded the Arc de Triomphe built to honor Napoleon..."

Claude pounds the top of the piano. "*Merde*...Those Nazi bastards...pardon me, Louisa."

"*Merde* indeed," Louisa says. "My sentiments exactly."

By this time, the radio announcer is shrieking almost incoherently. "They're ripping down the tricolors. Hoisting...*Mon Dieu*... red flags with swastikas. They must be ten meters long. All down the Champs-Élysées..."

Isobel imagines the horrific scene described on the radio. She looks to her father for guidance on what to say, but he's just standing there, dazed.

Sylvie collapses into a chair and holds her head in her hands.

Isobel darts to Sylvie's side, kneels on the carpet and hugs her aunt's knees. "Aunt Sylvie, I'm so sorry about Jean."

Louisa rushes to sit on the arm of her sister's chair, squeezing her shoulder. The group falls silent as they continue to listen to the distraught announcer provide more details.

Isobel, trembling, looks up from her position on the carpet next to her aunt and surveys the room. Étienne clutches Jean's jacket, unable to move or speak, while Claude continues to swear and pound the top of the piano. Her father mulls about in a complete stupor, muttering to himself. It's all so confusing, but it's clear this is the most horrible thing that's ever happened to her family.

Isobel starts to sob as she fiercely clings to Sylvie, who, in her own dazed state, has begun to weep softly. It slowly dawns on Isobel that Joshua was right—things are going to change a great deal for the worse.

CHAPTER FIFTEEN

The Ardennes, Northern France. 10 June 1940

HE JOLTS AWAKE. Takes in a short, violent breath. Snaps open his eyes. A slender reed of light floats diffusely above him. *Mon Dieu.* He's in some kind of room with a stone ceiling, maybe a meter above his head. *Lift my head. Simple. Tuck chin... push forehead up. God help me, I can't move.* Gray ash drifts down through the thin light. Flecks settle on his lips. *ACCHHH... searing my lips...* He desperately tries to spit the ashes off. Agonizing pain. Hot coals. Blistering. He licks his tongue to clean off his lips but succeeds only in moving the ash around, not away. Now his tongue is scalding as well.

He wills himself to raise his right arm, but something blocks it. His left as well. Pinned, he squirms. Every limb in his body weighs a thousand kilos, like an anchor sunk deep into every cell. He notices a smell. Foul beyond belief. *I'm going to vomit.* But no, if he vomits, he'll choke. *I will not die that way. Calm down.* He wrenches his head, twists it as much as he can, which is ever so slightly. Large flattened tubes lay all around, crisscrossed. Thick and misshaped cloth tubes. Haphazardly, strewn across his torso, his legs, and one across his forehead. That's why he can't move.

Thank God, I can still see the space above my head. But ashes start to drift into his eyes. He blinks, desperate to tear up enough to keep his eyes clear. He can see up to the stone ceiling a meter above. Large and small stones. Not uniform. *But they're not structured like a stone roof. Haphazard, too, just like the tubes.* It's harder and harder to breathe. Too much ash in the air around him. Falling everywhere. Filling up the space between him and the ceiling. All over the tubes. He can see them more clearly now. Just make them out. Rough cloth of some kind. Dark red streaks bleeding through the fabric.

He sees something sticking out of one of the tubes. Is that...a finger? *Harder to breathe.* Is that...a hand? With no thumb? *Ash filling up...fast. Mon Dieu. Non, non, non...tell me it's not true.* That's when he realizes he's in a grave. With other soldiers. Their bodies scattered about, some with severed limbs. A mass grave covered with stones and lye. That's when Jean starts to scream.

CHAPTER SIXTEEN

Foix. 25 June 1940

THE SUMMER AIR in the tiny village is hot and still. Even the clouds are mere wisps, and there is no wind to whip about the narrow streets to muffle the increasingly horrific sounds. Sylvie shudders as the rumbling grows louder. It threatens to shake loose the cobblestones, wedged for centuries deep in the ancient, winding streets of Foix. She gasps as she catches her first sight of the press of tanks and armored vehicles. The German occupiers are rolling into town.

Shop doors are shuttered, as are the tall windows in the floors above. While flower boxes still overflow with bright red summer geraniums, the vines in the boxes seem to twist inward, away from the streets, as if seeking refuge at the back of the finely wrought-iron balconies. An occasional movement, a crack in the shutter, then a quick closure, indicates anxious people within. Along the narrow streets, the wizened faces of old men and women are frozen in masks of dread. A lone baby starts to cry, and its mother anxiously carries it to a back alley, trying to quiet it by offering her breast.

Sylvie tastes a bitterness in her mouth as she turns towards an alleyway behind the church, where she sees a few young boys goose-stepping in mockery—until their mothers grab them and pull them close. Many of the women, dressed in their everyday full skirts and muslin blouses, have pulled their kerchiefs low on their foreheads—both to hide their faces from the *Boche* invaders and make a show of their disrespect. Sylvie, dressed in her typical trousers, has pulled her cap way down as well. She channels her anger by digging the heel of her boot into a loose cobblestone as she forces herself to stand and watch the parade of conquerors stream by in their spotless verdigris uniforms and polished jackboots. They are smug, victorious in the brutal battles fought in the Ardennes and Sedan, culminating in their march into the City of Light on the fourteenth of June. Following this, the French Republic President Reynaud resigned, and the next day, the hero of the Great War, Marshal Philippe Pétain, became Prime Minister. At half-past noon, on the seventeenth of June, he addressed the nation over the radio, saying he had a heavy heart as he urged the French to cease fighting. Then, on the twenty-second of June, France signed the armistice in the very same railroad car in which the French had forced the Germans to sign a similar armistice at the end of the last war.

Sylvie is grieved beyond words. The whole country seems to have imploded. Given up. Now Foix, her very own beloved village, is being occupied. Ever since the Spanish Civil war, the Germans have viewed the Ariège Region of France as prized territory. A strategic route over the Pyrénées into Spain, it is a key stronghold the Germans now claim. She clenches her fists so tightly her nails dig crescents into her palms. She watches in angry silence as fair-haired, broad-faced German boys sprout from the center of tanks and stare at the villagers. Solemn and self-important, they condescendingly scrutinize the collective, trembling populace. Rows of neat soldiers, sitting upright, line the benches of a stream of lorries and cast smug glances at the crowd. Other half-track vehicles with open pens contain dogs that viciously bark and pull at their chains. Shiny black motorcycles, sidecars mounted with machine guns, rev loudly. Their haughty riders flaunt their presence, even as they have to hold back so they don't outpace the slower rumbling entourage.

Bull horns screech orders in Germanic-accented French. "Stay calm and no one will be hurt."

Sylvie thanks God Jean isn't here to see them overrun their village. Deep within her, however, she still refuses to acknowledge that he's dead and talks to him constantly, asking what he would do in all kinds of situations. She's heard ghastly stories of atrocities: the *Boches* shooting French prisoners of war outright or else forcing them on grueling marches to prisoner of war camps. She was deeply saddened to learn that Hélène's husband Gérard was taken prisoner—no one knows if he was wounded or where they took him—and again wonders if it's possible that Jean was reported killed but is instead a prisoner somewhere. She knows Jean would rather die on the battlefield than be caged like an animal—but she never, for one moment, believes he would ever give up.

Out of a morbid sense of curiosity, Sylvie weaves in and out of the crowd of villagers, wanting to keep up with the head of the column: a General, driven in an open vehicle flying red, emblem-emblazoned Nazi flags from each side of the windshield. The seated General appears to be so tall and broad-shouldered that he barely fits in the vehicle. She smirks as she watches him hanging on tightly, trying to look nonchalant, as he's bounced hard over the bumpy, medieval cobbles. His rows of medals flap up and down unceremoniously as they glint erratically in the bright sunlight.

She's drawn along with the *Boches*' advance, passing the round thick-stoned fountain in the center of the main plaza. Sylvie glances up with pride at the trio of bronzed French soldiers, the village's monument to bravery in the Great War. *How horrible for them to have to stand there, frozen in time, forced to watch the plaza fill with their most bitter enemies!*

As she stares up at the statue, Sylvie nearly runs into Father Michel. She's pained to see him as disheveled as she is. Dust from the vehicles

THE NIGHT BELONGS TO THE MAQUIS

coats not only his boots but the hem of his long black soutane as well. Smudges mar his normally brilliant white collar as beads of sweat collect on his slender face.

He smirks, "How long before the *Boches* use that statue for target practice?"

As the German victory parade winds through town, several soldiers brazenly move forward, rifles held across their chests. They clear the crowd as the General's car comes to a halt in front of the fountain, just across from the Town Hall. The General barks an order to his driver, who passes it to one of the foot soldiers who had been running alongside his vehicle.

Father Michel winces as he looks in the direction of the Town Hall. "A welcoming party...of sorts."

She sees them right away. The first is the mayor, a slight, elderly man. His beret is perched on the side of his mound of gray wavy hair, and his face, normally creased with wrinkles, is pulled tight with anxiety. Wearing a red, white, and blue sash fitted diagonally across his thin, concave chest, he gingerly steps down the wide stairs, clearly mustering all his resolve to approach the Germans in the plaza below. On either side of him are two of the other town elders. Watching them, Sylvie has a sinking feeling as it appears they're reluctantly being dragged down the steps by an invisible, taut thread. The General pries himself out of his vehicle, and with disgusted grunts, takes his time dusting himself off. The mayor discreetly wipes his sweating palm on his trousers, then offers it to the general, who sniffs at the hand, and nearly hitting the Mayor in the chin on his way up, snaps his arm high into the air. "*Heil Hitler.*"

A German soldier jerks his head, and dozens of soldiers disembark from their lorries to form a perfectly curved line around the circular fountain, facing the villagers in the plaza. Sylvie is horrified to see them raise their right arms in unison, and as if lead by a symphony conductor, taunt the villagers, chanting, "*Sieg Heil! Sieg Heil!*

Sieg Heil!" They continue to chant, louder and louder, waiting for the villagers to take up the salute.

The General whips around expectantly, but when he doesn't see any of the townspeople responding, he looks down into the diminutive Mayor's face and angrily snarls something. The Mayor quakes and nods his head. With sad resignation, he makes a weak *Sieg Heil* salute with his right arm. As he does, he circles his left arm, palm upwards, as if to encourage, then virtually plead for his townspeople to do the same. The elders standing next to him make even larger gestures, imploring the crowd to salute.

Sylvie sneers to the priest, "I'd rather cut off my arm."

Frowning, Father Michel's face pinches inwards. "We need to choose our battles—this isn't one of them." He raises his right arm slightly, a barely perceptible *Sieg Heil*. It might even be the start of a blessing. It's a gesture hardly big enough to satisfy but small enough to register disdain. He mouths something but, with the noise of the soldiers, Sylvie can't make it out, even though she's standing next to him.

Sylvie steals a look at the slender priest. He's much tougher than he appears. She admires his calm patience, in contrast to her tendency to immediately fly off the handle when angered. She swallows the lump of acid collecting at the back of her throat, makes a spiritual leap of faith, and manages a slight replica of his movement. The mayor looks over at the two of them, profound relief spreading across his wizened face. Slowly, the half-hearted *Sieg Heil* gesture circulates through the crowd. Sylvie struggles mightily to contain her disgust at having to acquiesce—this time. She swears, under her breath, that she will indeed find a way to resist.

CHAPTER SEVENTEEN

A s the Germans march into Foix, Hélène feverishly searches the crowd for Dr. Duchamps. She convinces him to slip away and drive straight up the mountain to the camp, to protect the refugees as best they can. It's a brilliant summer day, with the sun high above the sharp peaks surrounding them. Would that she and the doctor were merely on one of their lovely picnic outings with a few of his elderly patients, whom they sometimes drive to take in the mountain air. This trip, she fears, will not be anything so pleasant.

As they approach the entrance to the camp, Hélène spies one of the young girls, Esther. Athletically slender like a runner, she's apparently been posted at the gate as a lookout. Her yellow kerchief, normally holding back her thick ringlets of dark brown hair, is askew, and her dark eyes are rimmed red from crying.

Esther races up to Hélène, gasping, "Madame Hélène, my grandfather must speak to you at once. They're all in the kitchen."

"Of course. Certainly."

Esther pulls Hélène's hand while the doctor follows. When they arrive, Hélène sees a group of refugees, including Isaiah, an elderly man whose black tangled beard reaches halfway down his chest. Three older women and a dozen children are there as well, holding bundles of clothing. They are arguing with the kitchen staff.

Isaiah rants in broken French, "All we need. Three day food." His tirade is directed at a heavyset village woman in an apron who stands guard in front of the larder.

Hélène steps between them. "What's going on, Isaiah?"

The village woman on the kitchen staff shouts more at Isaiah than Hélène. "If we give them all these supplies, everyone will want more too. We won't have anything left."

Hélène sees the veins in Isaiah's forehead pump blue against his pale white skin.

He shouts, "We need to leave right now. They will set up patrols. Close the border."

Hélène surveys the terrified group. She desperately wants to protect them but their plan seems deeply flawed. "Over the mountains into Spain? You can't possibly make it over such steep terrain." The women are sturdy but are all well past fifty; two of the children are under five, and Isaiah is over seventy.

Isaiah counters, "My daughter. Other women walk here. Now, they walk over mountain."

"I can carry my little brother," pleads Esther.

The girl is no more than twelve, and Hélène knows that she's physically fit from watching her play soccer with the boys. In fact, Hélène has marveled at the fights Esther's had with them, garnering her more than one black eye before they finally accepted the girl on the field.

Hélène bends down and tries to tame the girl's tangled hair back under her yellow kerchief. "Esther, that's very good of you, but—"

"Madame Hélène, you know I can run really fast."

"Running's not the issue. The mountains are very steep dear, even for grownups."

Isaiah jumps in. "Better than stay here. Rest of family in Poland. They shoot all."

Hélène turns to the doctor. His shoulders slump dejectedly as he says, almost to himself but just loudly enough for Hélène to hear, "I would go with them myself. If I were not needed here." He pauses, then straightens up with defiance. "Hélène, we must let them go before it's too late. And anyone else who wants to leave. They should have our blessing and what meager supplies they can carry."

Hélène stares in disbelief that the doctor would allow such a dangerous journey. She opens her mouth to object but is struck through with uncertainty. This is no emergency in the clinic where they can fall back on their training and reserves of medical supplies. This is a life and death situation of an entirely different sort. She looks between the desperate family and the doctor, then finally nods in resigned agreement. As she helps them pack, she hears a car and looks out of the kitchen window to see a German field vehicle pull up to the front gate.

She turns to the group. "Hurry! You must leave right now."

The family races to collect what they can while she gives them directions. "Go through the backfield behind the camp. Follow the stream up. It leads to a path. Be careful." Hélène kisses Esther goodbye. "I'll keep them busy while you get away."

The doctor starts towards the German at the gate, but, like a mother fiercely protecting her cub, Hélène motions him back. "Dr. Duchamps, it's not that you obviously look Jewish. But until we know more, you must wait in the infirmary."

His eyes mist over. He clears his throat, takes off his glasses, quickly cleans them, and nods.

Hélène strides defiantly to the front gate, straightening her nurse's cap. She glances down to her blouse, to her nurse's pin—her protective talisman. She'll have to make this up as she goes, but she'll not give an inch, as she vows to shield these people from the *Boches*.

A reed-slender German officer rapidly extracts himself from his field vehicle and smartly walks to meet her, whisking his hat off and bracing it under his arm as he approaches. His hair is a darker brown than most of the blonde soldiers who occupied the village earlier that day. Her eyes are drawn to the insignia on his chest—an eagle with outstretched beveled wings, its talons gripping a circular wreath with a swastika in the center. Never having seen this emblem up close, she shudders at this malevolent symbol of Nazi domination over the world.

Hélène is transfixed, gazing in horror at the eagle, until two lorries divert her attention. A dozen Wehrmacht field soldiers carrying rifles jump down from the first vehicle and take positions along the front of the camp. Another dozen from the second unload huge concertina-bundled rolls of barbed wire. A crowd of refugees gathers, and two soldiers step forward, menacingly blocking them from approaching too close.

Hélène struggles to keep her voice even. "Major…it is major, isn't it?"

"*Ja*, Major Spitzer." He makes a slight bow and clicks his heels—a sharp retort echoes like a rifle shot in the thin mountain air.

"Major, what is the meaning of this? These people are not prisoners. They're refugees who've had to flee their homes. Lost everything."

He stares at her, unblinking, then smiles a thin smile as if having to force his lips into this uncomfortable position. In a thick German accent, he speaks to her in French. "Who is in charge here?"

Without waiting for her answer, he takes a few brisk steps to the front of the camp, but she darts ahead to block his way. Out of the corner of her eye, she sees movement in the distant backfield—Isaiah and his family. She motions him away from their direction, towards the gate, as if to give him a tour. Forcing a smile, she says, "I am the nurse here. I'd be happy to show you our facilities. They're quite sanitary, I can assure you. We do have a doctor too, but he's presently in the infirmary."

The major takes his hat from under his arm, his fingers neatly spinning the brim in a precise circle. His cap has the same insignia as his uniform—an eagle clutching the globe in its sharp talons. Hélène imagines herself in the grasp of those talons, being spun around, then carried off to God knows where. She shivers, despite the heat of the summer's day.

Hélène anxiously glances at the soldiers who've begun to fasten barbed wire to the front gate. Mechanical puppets, they move in unison with amazing efficiency. She is mesmerized—in minutes, they have the barbed wire wrapped around the entire right front of the camp. She looks up and into the major's gray eyes, willing her voice to be steady. "How does a well-trained soldier like yourself merit this assignment, if I may ask? These people are destitute. What could you possibly want with them?"

Spitzer's eyes bore into her, his eyelids never shutting as his mouth forces itself into a wry grin. "I am an administrator. A servant of the Wehrmacht."

"An administrator? But you carry a pistol."

"In case we encounter trouble. But, I have never had to use it."

Hélène can't tell if he's toying with her—a cat sizing up a mouse it has cornered—or whether he might even be flirting. *Let me see if I can get more with honey than vinegar.* She shoots him a forced smile. "I'm sure you won't have to use it here either, Major. That being said, why are your men putting up this barbed wire?"

"Let's just say…to avoid trouble." He scans the crowd of ragged elderly men, women, and children. "You will bring me their papers."

"Meaning no disrespect, Major, but these people fled across the border. Most are without papers."

He stares at her hair under her nurse's cap. She knows that the bright sunlight lightens her normally light blond hair. Is he trying to determine her ancestry? Perhaps his darker brown hair indicates less than pure Aryan roots, and if so, would that mean he feels he must do more to prove himself?

"You like things in order, do you not, mademoiselle?"

"Madame Calmette. They call me, Madame Hélène."

"Of course. In order. Your medicines? Your clean sheets? Sanitary, you said."

Hélène has the sensation of driving a car that's heading for a brick wall, but she's unable to steer away.

The major says, in a low voice which is almost a growl, "You would not want them to become dirty, would you? Or maybe become removed altogether?"

"Certainly not," she says, trying to muster resolve, even as her knees start to buckle.

"I did not think so. Show me to the doctor. You said he was inside?"

"Well, yes. But he's examining patients right now." She fears for the Jewish doctor's safety, so, despite her revulsion, Hélène leans into the major. *Honey, not vinegar.* She smiles sweetly. "Can't I help you with whatever you would have discussed with him?"

Flaunting his power, he eyes her with an intense, unblinking stare that drills into her. "If you vouch for him, then I talk to you." As he nods, a lock of his dark brown hair falls onto his pale, colorless forehead. "So, I tell you how it will be, *ja?*" He motions to the men to hurry to fasten the barbed wire fence around the rest of the camp. "We will permit you to run the camp."

Hélène is relieved but tries not to let it show, lest he think he has the upper hand. Flatly, she says, "Thank you, Major."

"Under one condition."

Her heart sinks.

"You give these out." With his eyes fastened onto her face, he jerks his head towards a soldier who sprints over, bringing a box from his vehicle. The major snaps on his hat, takes the box with both hands, and opens it, holding it away and flinching as if expecting the smell of a dead rodent.

Aghast, Hélène stares at a pile of yellow fabric, each piece in the shape of a six-sided star. She steps back in confusion. He leans into her as if preparing to speak to her with the utmost confidence. His breath is warm on her neck. It takes all her willpower not to recoil sharply.

"The Jews must sew these onto their clothes. They must wear these at all times."

Her soft blue eyes widen, first in confusion, then in fear. "I…I don't understand."

Slowly, in a most affable manner, as if walking in the park on a sunny day, he says, "We must separate out the Jews. The others cannot be contaminated."

His matter-of-fact manner catches her off guard, and she blurts out, "That's absurd. Contaminated?" Hélène starts to shove the box away. "We don't even know who is Jewish and who is not. The French government never required us to collect that kind of information."

He shoots out his finely manicured, bloodless hands and shoves the open box back at her. In the process, several yellow fabric stars fall to the ground. He does not bend to pick them up, nor does she.

Blood flows into his pale face, turning it violet with rage. He snarls, "Pick them up, Madame."

Hélène stands inert. He shifts the box to his left hand, and with his right, pulls his Lugar from the side of his belt, clicks off the safety, and shoves it against her temple. She stays absolutely still, holding her breath. *I am a nurse. This cannot be happening to me.* After a terrifying moment that feels like an hour—and without looking at him—she slowly bends to pick up the yellow stars. He stretches out his arm, never lifting his gun from the side of her head until she has straightened up, put the stars into the box, and taken the box from him.

His face relaxes into a malevolent grin, as he slips on the safety and replaces the gun in his holster. "I told you. I have never had to use this. See how easy it is to do things right the first time."

Hélène strains to force her voice to become audible. "Yes, of course, Major. Much easier."

"Now go along and organize your—"

Hélène flinches as rifle shots are heard from the hillside beyond the camp. The refugees near the gate, who've been sullenly watching the soldiers unravel the barbed wire, turn toward the noise, jostling to see. Some of the women instinctively clutch their children. A look of terror comes over some while others close their eyes, resigned to learning a horrible truth.

A soldier runs up to the major, gives him a *Sieg Heil,* and points to the forest. He barks something in German that Hélène doesn't understand. She imagines herself running in the direction of the shots but finds she's unable to move. And even if she could muster the strength to run, the major has already put out his shiny leather boot to stop her.

"You will not wish to see what I assume has just taken place. Some of your people have tried to escape, *ja?*" He grabs her arm, pressing his long, manicured fingers into her delicate white skin. "I will make the excuse for you. This time, you did not know about this escape attempt. But, in the future—"

He savagely digs his fingertips into her arm, immediately raising several ugly welts. She does not move. *I refuse to give him the satisfaction of hearing me cry out!*

Another soldier jogs down from the hillside behind the camp, clutching a white handkerchief with something in it, which he shows to the major—Esther's yellow kerchief, stained with blood.

Hélène screams. It is a piercing sound. *How could they do this to a child? I should have done more to prevent them from leaving.* Her knees weaken, and she turns away from the kerchief, trying not to retch.

The major beams at the soldier and his offering of the kerchief—as if it were a piece of chocolate. He does not touch the bloody fabric but motions for the soldier to hand it to Hélène.

"ACH. How nice. More yellow cloth. Maybe you make a star out of this for yourself to wear, Madame? You can sew, *ja?*"

She takes a step backward. "A yellow star? But, Major..." She blanches. "I'm not Jewish."

He screams, "TAKE IT."

Hélène, on the brink of collapse, gingerly takes Esther's yellow kerchief by a corner, trying to avoid touching the bloody spots.

In a lighthearted tone, he finally blinks coyly and several times for effect. "But of course, you will have to wash it clean first? We want everything here to be absolutely sanitary, do we not?"

Hélène stares at the major, then at the fabric, then back at him. The most intense hatred she's ever felt coils up within her, threatening to explode. She pants in shallow breaths to slow the blood pounding in her temples. Finally, she takes the whole kerchief in her grip, blood streaking her hands. The image of little Esther flashes through her mind, the little girl sporting a black eye that earned her a place on the soccer field with the boys. She clutches the kerchief to her breast and stares with fury at the major. His unblinking eyes narrow to slits like a lizard's as he recoils at the sight of the red pooling on her nurse's white blouse and smearing over her nurse's pin. Hélène smiles a faint, pained smile as she continues to stare directly into his gray eyes—she now sees quite clearly the reservoir of evil behind their translucence. She resolves to do whatever she can to protect the rest of her refugees from this monster and all the others like him.

CHAPTER EIGHTEEN

The Ardennes. Late-June 1940

BARELY AWAKE, HE hears a soft snorting. A horse, maybe? The faint smell of something fresh—like hay? Suddenly an acute pain sears through the fog of his sleep. *Burning. On my lips. Now on my hands... they're blazing... on fire.* He tries to open his eyes, but he sees only blackness. *Mon Dieu, I'm blind.* In a panic, he tries to rub his eyes, but his hands are wrapped entirely with rough gauze.

"Don't. You'll only make it worse."

He tries to sit up but finds he's restrained, his body bound with rope, although his gauze-wrapped hands are free.

"Stay still, *s'il vous plaît.*" A voice. A woman. Kind but firm. Speaking French with a heavy German accent.

He tries to talk. To say, "Where am I?" But what comes out is only a muffled wad of sound he doesn't recognize. *Did someone cut out my tongue?* He grabs at his bindings, violently thrashing his head about. *Someone's cut out my tongue.*

"Be still. Don't try to speak." The voice is firmer now. "You had lye in your mouth. It burnt your tongue, but it will heal."

It will heal, she says. Thank God.

"It will be all right. I had some salve." She calls down, "He's awake."

He hears soft steps, like very small, light people coming up a ladder, maybe in a barn. *Dwarfs. I'm dreaming. Ridiculous.*

"Mama. Is he all right?" A tiny voice. Also speaking in French laced with a German accent. From a young girl?

"He's alive, dummy." His mind is still hazy, as if in a dream . . . no . . . a swirling whirlpool of nightmares. This other voice sounds like it belongs to a young boy—likely the girl's older brother, judging from his mocking tone.

The woman says, "Do not try to move. You were not in such good condition when my boy pulled you from that pit."

"Where am I?" He can't even recognize his own words, tumbling askew from his mouth.

The boy translates, "I think he wants to know where he is."

"At a farm. On the outskirts of the Ardennes. We are in Germany, along the French border."

"Germans? Panzers?" He desperately tries to get the words out of his burning mouth. "Explosions. I've got to get out of here." The effort completely exhausts him.

The woman is firm. "Lie back, and I tell you what happened."

He strains against the bindings, twisting some more. Finally, completely spent, he sinks back down.

"Can you hear me?"

He barely has the energy to nod.

She continues, "The Germans ram right through the forest. Build bridges for the tanks to cross the river then go straight on. Their soldiers collect the French prisoners. Start to march them off." Her voice trembles. "My boy says they open fire. Shove bodies together. Into one big grave. Cover it with lye and stones."

He shivers uncontrollably as the memory floods back into every pore in his body. *A tomb. Bodies on top. Got to get out.*

124

Her hand is on his arm, comforting him. "My boy here—"

The boy interrupts, "My mother said not to go. Stay in hiding in the root cellar. But I snuck out."

The girl chimes in, "Me too. I go with him."

The woman sighs deeply. "You could have been killed."

The boy is defiant. "We just want to see their tanks. We hide in the woods." He hears the boy pause, perhaps trying to suppress his own horrific memories. Finally, the boy blurts out, "It all happened so fast. We saw them dig a big hole. Throw the bodies in."

The girl starts to cry, "I couldn't look."

The boy says, "We were running away, but then I hear a noise. You are screaming. I pull you out."

"I helped too," the girl adds through her tears. "I did."

The memory shakes him violently. He lurches up as if to flee the horror of even thinking about it.

The woman says, "Calm down. I think you are safe here. They already search before my boy drags you here. He makes a sled—"

"Like we do for firewood," the boy adds.

The girl says, "Then the Germans go ahead. In a big hurry."

He takes some deep breaths, willing himself to say calm. *If I'm safe here, why am I tied up?* He holds up his hands.

The woman says, "I understand. We can untie you now." Her voice softens. "We were afraid you would wake. Try to climb down and fall." She continues with a more business-like tone. "I had to bandage your eyes. They were burned very bad from the lye. But you did have some movement underneath your—how you say—lid of the eye? Before I put on the salve and the bandage. I hope you will be able to see."

The boy adds, "Your hands were even worse."

He tries to ball up his fists, but the gauze and the pain prevent him.

"They were not so bad, Hans," the woman quickly adds. "You will get him upset again."

He hears a tiny voice, most probably from the girl. "Monsieur, you were very sick. But Mama made you better."

He does feel better, despite the terrible pain in his eyes, mouth, and hands. The boy has saved his life, and the mother, God willing, has saved his sight as well as the use of his hands.

CHAPTER NINETEEN

Foix. July 1940

S YLVIE IS STILL reeling from the shock of last month's occupation of her village by the *Boches*. Rumors are rife that, when the Germans broke through the French line in the Ardennes, they summarily executed large numbers of surrendering French soldiers—although it is said that some escaped in the mêlée. Still refusing to accept Jean's death, Sylvie seizes on these rumors as reason for hope. This energizes her to make plans to thwart the invaders any way she can.

To that end, in the early morning, with many of the tiny buildings in Foix still in shadow, she and Uncle Claude skirt the main plaza where the Germans have taken up the administration of the village in the Town Hall. They head down the maze of back alleys on their way to meet Monsieur le Mayor at a café behind the plaza. The owner wipes down the tiny tables in the back while his wife brews what now passes for coffee—a blend of roasted acorns, chicory, and beechnuts. The mayor is already seated, nervously smoking and sipping the thick sludge of coffee from a small cup.

Sylvie is shocked to see that, in the month since the occupation when he first had to deal with the Germans, the mayor has become quite frail, and his mass of curly gray hair has turned completely white. After the Germans took over, the other two town elders maintained they were too ill to perform their official duties and resigned rather than administer the village under occupation. Patrols of soldiers now regularly walk the village streets, and a curfew of nine at night is imposed.

The mayor has been threatening to resign as well, but Sylvie and Claude desperately need him to stay on to ensure their efforts develop unimpeded. Claude looks around to make sure no one can overhear, then says in a rather too loud, boisterous whisper, "Better to be in charge and steer things the right way. Can't let those damn *Boche* bastards run everything."

The mayor gulps the rest of his coffee, and despite the early hour, asks the owner's wife for an Armagnac, the local brandy, which he downs as well. He turns to Claude. "Why don't you take over?"

Sylvie opens her mouth to object but is relieved when Claude shakes his head. He leans in and puts his large puffy red hands on either side of the teetering café table, steadying it in his sizeable grasp. "Because I can be much more useful behind the scenes."

Sylvie is heartened that her uncle and his fellow elderly reservists, François and Louis, are making plans to get any and every British airmen out of the country—just as they did with Alastair. Undoubtedly fortified more by the Armagnac than coffee, the mayor meekly agrees to stay on. Visibly shaking, he gets up and heads towards the Town Hall. Sylvie and Claude follow.

Major Spitzer has ordered all the villagers to present themselves in the main plaza in front of the Church and Town Hall. Summer temperatures are at their height, although the humidity in the mountains is generally so low that it rarely feels uncomfortably warm. This morning, however, Sylvie is experiencing a full blast of heat from her anger at the *Boches* for occupying their village. She tries to rein in her temper as Father Michel keeps insisting they all must do, at least for now.

Many of the townsfolk are already sweating profusely—more from fear than the heat. The only villagers left are women, children, and elderly men like the mayor, although a few wounded French soldiers have been permitted to return home and sullenly join the crowd. The bulk of the remaining French troops have either been imprisoned in camps or detailed to factories to keep the German war machine running.

Standing next to Claude at the foot of the Town Hall steps, Sylvie sees Major Spitzer jump lithely from his army vehicle. His black boots, rising high on his reed-thin frame, gleam in the sunlight as he clacks up the stairs of the Town Hall. He gives a vigorous *Sieg Heil* to the mayor, who tightens his jaw and returns it, although much less emphatically. Spitzer breaks into a thin, forced smile as he turns to face the villagers. Some are shrunken and fearful, while others stand even more erect, projecting silent, rebellious anger.

In his reedy voice and heavily German-accented French, Spitzer calmly addresses the crowd. "We wish you no harm. The fighting is over. We want to live in peace with you." He takes a breath and continues with pride in his voice. "The food and supplies we require are for the honor of the Third Reich. You are doing your part as we unite all of Europe under our great Führer's guiding hand."

Although the elderly mayor looks relieved and many of the villagers visibly start to relax, Sylvie doesn't trust his benevolent tone. Claude steals a glance at her, nodding to confirm her wariness.

The major continues, "We wish to show you our goodwill and allow you to run your shops and businesses as autonomously as possible." His thin voice gradually broadens and becomes louder. "But, we fully expect you to return our generosity." Then, all traces of his affable demeanor disappear as he screeches, "And we will not tolerate any disobedience. Do you understand?"

He waits for the crowd to respond—no one coughs, no one takes a breath, no one moves. As frozen in place as the crowd, Sylvie clamps her hand down, like a vice, onto Claude's arm, wishing she were crushing Spitzer's head instead.

Spitzer takes a deep breath and manages to corral his voice back into submission. "I will explain it to you, then." He motions to two soldiers, who part the crowd, dragging a man of about sixty between them, his legs rubber, his face bruised and bloodied. Letting out a collective gasp, the crowd steps aside.

Sylvie turns to Claude, who motions for her to be still, which she finds nearly impossible. This elderly man, Monsieur Lafitte, is the town grocer whom she's known her whole life. He would slip some sweets for her and her brother into their parents' food orders. And with Jean's family in financial difficulty because of his father's war neurosis, he extended credit for years without once boasting of his generosity. Sylvie exclaims, louder than she intended, "Monsieur Lafitte!"

Spitzer, hearing a noise, whips his head around and stares unblinking at the crowd. After a moment, not finding the source of the outburst, he continues, "This man. You all know the grocer, Heir Lafitte, do you not?" He waits for a response, and when he fails to receive one, he yells, "DO YOU NOT?" Isolated nods and mutterings spread throughout the townspeople. Satisfied he has their attention, Spitzer barks, "This man tried to short his food delivery. We found hay in the bottom of his food requisition barrels."

Although the soldiers have his arms twisted back from his shoulders, Monsieur Lafitte struggles to lift his head. "I was only cushioning the food. I swear. It was all there. I swear on my mother's grave."

Several villagers quickly cross themselves. Outraged, Sylvie takes a step forward, but Claude grabs her elbow, holding her back.

Lafitte continues, his plea becoming more plaintive, "I gave them all the food you asked for—someone must have counted wrong!"

Spitzer jerks his head back, growling, "Are you accusing my soldiers of counting wrong? Like a child counts on his fingers and gets it wrong?"

Lafitte collapses into the soldiers' grasp, whimpering, "No, of course not. I must have made the mistake. My…my mistake. Please. I will give you the food and more."

Sylvie's stomach churns as she watches the corners of Spitzer's mouth curl, looking pleased to have secured this admission of guilt. "Yes, you will give us the food and more." He motions to the soldiers, who let Lafitte slip onto the cobblestones, where they repeatedly kick the old man. One cherubic-looking German soldier smiles broadly, as he raises his Lugar. Isolated screams and groans arise from the crowd, but no one moves a muscle. Thoroughly enjoying their terrified reaction, Spitzer nods to the soldier who turns the gun around, takes the butt end, and pistol whips Lafitte in the face. This time it's Sylvie's turn to hold Claude back as he simmers in fury.

Lafitte's wife runs up to shield him. She has difficulty making her old joints bend to protect her husband, by now a bloody ball curled into a fetal position. The soldiers kick her once or twice, then Spitzer waves his hand for them to stop.

Sylvie, breathing heavily, takes in every detail, imprinting the scene on her memory and vowing to take her revenge—to Hell with the teachings of the Church. She crosses herself, struggling to reconcile the "turn the other cheek" doctrine she was raised to believe with this monstrous aberration of humanity before her.

At last, glancing down with complete contempt for the elderly couple, Spitzer shakes his head, signaling the soldiers to withdraw. He then surveys the villagers. In his most pleasant tone, and with Lafitte's wife sobbing at the base of the steps, he says, "You see how easy it is to get along. Just do not make mistakes." He lifts his knee and stomps his foot along with his *Sieg Heil*, which the villagers now return with zeal.

The bile rises in Sylvie's throat as she watches him stride down the steps, making a show of disgust as he steps around Lafitte and his wife. The crowd, alternately stunned, angry, fearful, and numb, silently parts to let him pass. He jumps into his vehicle, and his driver speeds them out of the plaza.

Claude breaks into a run to follow Spitzer, but Sylvie races to block his way. "Uncle Claude. Stop. There's much we can do, but it's got to be in the background."

Claude snorts with disgust, then turns to the old man Lafitte, groaning and writhing on the cobblestones, blood from his nose and mouth staining them red. His wife's shawl is tattered, her dress filthy from the soldiers' boots. The villagers surround the couple and help them stagger home.

Sylvie turns to Claude. "I want to shoot him myself. But we can't expose ourselves."

As Sylvie and Claude turn to leave the plaza, a small woman in her fifties approaches them, clutching her shawl tight around her frail shoulders, despite the warmth of the day. She furtively checks around her, then motions for them to follow her down a narrow side street. When they are a few meters clear of the plaza, the woman whispers, "I don't know where to send them."

Claude takes her by the arm and ushers her into a doorway. "You're Madame Gisguard, aren't you? Your son Jacques was listed among the dead." He continues gently, "You remember, I came with Louis to give you the news. Again, *je suis désôle*, Madame."

The woman rises on her toes to speak to Claude—even so, he has to bend down to hear her. Sylvie senses the woman's distress—her right eye twitches, and she takes several short gasping breaths before she's able to proceed. "That's just it, Monsieur Claude. My boy Jacques— he's not dead." She brings her shawl up to cover her mouth as if to hide what she's about to say. "He escaped. And he's brought two other boys with him. I don't know what to do—"

Sylvie's heart races. "Which boys?" she whispers. "Jean Galliard? Was he with them?"

The woman shakes her head solemnly. "I am sorry, Mademoiselle Sylvie."

Sylvie hates to grasp at straws like that—having her hopes raised that Jean might still be alive, only to have them dashed again.

Just then, Claude notices a German patrol of two soldiers marching up the alley towards them. "We can't talk here. Please, Madame, come with us."

Claude quickly leads them into a side alley, where they slip into the back of François's carpentry shop. Sylvie tries to breathe as shallowly as possible since the shop is dense with cigarette smoke, ashtrays everywhere, piled precariously high with butts. She notices, oddly enough, that the wood behind the counter is meticulously sorted, cleaned, and stacked with extreme care.

Claude's ruddy face reddens with excitement. "You say some of them are back! I knew it was only a matter of time." In a surge of enthusiasm, he grabs the woman and kisses her on both cheeks. "Madame, you did right to come to us." He turns to Sylvie, adding, "We have a place to hide them. Like we did for Alastair."

Sylvie listens intently as the woman tells Claude how her son escaped, even though he was reported dead. Although the two of them talk animatedly less than two meters away, she can't hear what they are saying—she's so distracted by the flashes of memory searing through her. She knows Jean is dead. She's seen his name on that official document, scrawled in black-death ink, in an elaborate and florid hand. But if these boys, also listed as killed in action, have escaped, why couldn't Jean?

CHAPTER TWENTY

The Ardennes, France. July 1940

A S HE AWAKENS, Jean is plagued by the memory of burning debris accompanied by chaotic gunfire and blasts from the Panzers. But worse are his nightmares of being entombed, unable to move, dead bodies grotesquely strewn on top of him, and that ghastly, unimaginable smell—attended by the most dreadful burning in his eyes and mouth.

To steady his nerves, Jean clings to memories of his youth, growing up in the Pyrénées, on rocky farmland just outside his village of Foix. Over and over, he retraces his steps from his farm to Sylvie's for Sunday supper, when the family shares rich stews and stories of Claude's exploits in the Great War. *I must find a way to get back home.*

He's enormously grateful to the woman caring for him, whose name he learns is Suzanne. She's treated his wounds—he suffered quite a few about his torso and on his legs from flying shrapnel. His body seems to be healing rapidly, although the condition of his eyes continues to terrify him. He's itching to rip off the bandages and learn whether he'll be able to see again. Meanwhile, he's managed to regain enough strength to climb down the ladder and stumble around in the barn, although he detests having to feel his way like a blind man.

One morning, Suzanne comes to him. "It is time."

She brings over a stool and directs him to sit. Suddenly, he leans over, his hands on his knees, breathing heavily to avoid retching. Living like this, blind and piteously dependent, is not living at all. After a few moments, he regains his composure, sits up, and waits for her to cut off the bandages. He blinks tentatively. *Mon Dieu,* his pupils are covered with a misty film. He breaks out into a cold sweat.

"Be calm," she says.

He gasps and blinks some more. At last, although everything is masked in gray tones, he begins to make out shapes as well as light and dark. He's giddy with hope.

"To tell you the truth, I was not completely certain the salve would work," Suzanne says. "My husband used it on the horses." She laughs softly. "And of course, we never really knew how much they could see, except they didn't bump into anything big."

They both laugh, gently at first, then with abandon. Her gaiety nudges an ache inside of him. He's known that kind of laughter too, and someone with whom he shared that kind of joy.

Meanwhile, with his improving vision, Jean can make out Suzanne's strong Aryan features, blonde hair, and a broad forehead with a wide smile. Her children are Hans, nine years old, very big and exceptionally strong for his age, and Justine, round-faced and smiling, a five-year-old miniature version of Suzanne. With their white-blond hair, the children look characteristically German,

Over the next few days, his sight steadily improves. Although his hands are badly scarred from the burns, he's gained enough strength and dexterity to pick up tools. Despite his constant exhaustion, he forces himself to chop wood to earn his keep until he recovers enough to leave. But, given the merciless German incursions deep into France—information

Suzanne finally supplies after his incessant questions—he wonders where he can go, even when he's well enough to travel.

Suzanne tells him that this part of the Belgian Ardennes Forest was the prime route for the Panzer advance and is now in occupied German territory. The forest is especially dense, and he's relieved that she seems to have a sixth sense about when the German patrol will sometimes drop by—when she vehemently insists he remain quiet up in the hayloft. She hopes the dogs will be distracted by the smell of her broken-down mare, which the German army didn't want when they requisitioned the rest of her livestock. He especially admires her strategy to spread dung from the horse around the base of the ladder to throw the dogs off his scent. Not so nice to smell from the loft above but, he hopes, an effective deterrent. Why is she hiding him at such risk to herself and the children? He hates to dwell on this because he's immensely grateful for her lively spirit, her calm competence in nursing him, as well as the easy, loving way she has with her children. He shudders to think what would happen to all of them if the patrol discovered him.

This afternoon, he and Suzanne are in the barn. She feeds the horse while he strokes the old mare's swayback. The small clearing for her farmhouse and barn are the only areas where the sun penetrates the surrounding forest canopy. At the edge of the clearing, he notices that several trees have been cut down to make an elaborate treehouse for the children. He hasn't wanted to pry into her life and is relieved when, seeing him staring at the treehouse, she finally confides in him. "My husband was called to serve the Führer. Although they know I am Belgian, I give the patrols food. They don't bother me, out of respect for my late husband."

"Your late husband?"

"Killed in Poland."

"I'm sorry."

"He didn't believe in all this killing. Not to speak ill of the dead, but he was very stubborn." As she tugs at the horse's feed bag to remove it, the mare whinnies, so Suzanne relents, allowing the animal more to eat. "He was always arguing with the soldiers in his unit. He came home on leave that last time and I told him you must be quiet. Do not make your views known." She pauses. "I think maybe he was killed by one of his own. Some of them are so fanatical."

"Why do you live in such isolation here? Don't you have family to go to?"

"My parents were Belgian. They died some years ago. And why would I want to go to his people in Berlin? I will not let my children grow up with such hatred." She reddens. "But, all we talk about is me. Tell me, where are you from? Do you have a family?" He sees her glance at his bare wedding ring finger. Before he can respond, she quickly adds, "Just as well. The lye would have burned through it. You would have lost your finger."

He winces, recalling how much he wanted to marry Sylvie before he left. He's not sure how much of his previous life he should share with her in case they capture him. They've discussed that she might be able to claim that she thought he was German—with the lye having burned his mouth, perhaps she couldn't detect that he didn't speak German. He marvels that she seems entirely content and self-sufficient on her small farm in the thick woods. To show his gratitude, and with his sight getting closer to normal, he's begun to trap hares and other small animals, skinning them for her to cook.

"The children have not eaten so well in a long time." Suzanne smiles broadly. "Myself either." She teases him that he's so agile in the forest because he's so slender. She gave him some of her husband's old clothes, which hung so long and wide on him that she had to cut them way down.

He enjoys playing with the children and teaching them how to hunt by setting traps.

He proudly demonstrates to Hans how to locate tracks in the dense bushes. He takes a thin wire and makes a snare, so when the hare runs through, it snags its head, and as the animal struggles, it quickly chokes itself.

The boy says, "I don't really like to kill them." He pauses to think for a moment, then nods sagely. "But it means we eat better."

Justine is another matter, and of course, her brother enjoys making fun of her squeamishness.

Jean wonders if life can really be this simple: here, deep in the forest with Suzanne and the children. Although recovering, he's easily exhausted and is supremely frustrated that his eyesight hasn't recovered to a level even close to what it was before. He suffers night sweats and horrific dreams, and having seen what this did to his father, recoils at the thought that he's emotionally breaking down in exactly the same way. If and when he makes it home, he vows he'd never subject Sylvie to marriage with...with a coward. And as the days wear on, he doesn't know what frightens him more—that he will do everything he can to leave here and plunge back into the war or that he won't.

CHAPTER TWENTY-ONE

Foix. September 1940

SYLVIE ENTERS THE Church of St. Volusien. Breathing deeply, she's comforted by the smell of incense and votive candles that lingers in the air. The refugee situation in the camp brings her to new depths of despair over her powerlessness, although helping her uncle hide the three escaped French soldiers in the watermill somewhat tempers these feelings. Although having them there fills her with renewed energy and purpose, it causes her to obsess over Jean. She comes daily to the church to light a votive candle and pray for him. She's increasingly certain that, if those boys could have escaped, reports of his death are—must be—a terrible mistake.

She dips two fingers into the ancient, marble holy water fountain at the side entrance to the church. As she begins to make the sign of the cross, Jean's bloody jacket flashes before her eyes. Abruptly, she flings the droplets aside and backs up against the stone wall. Through her blurred veil of tears, she stares at the stone veil carved into the statue of the Virgin Mary in the side chapel. Sylvie isn't sure how long she remains standing there when she becomes aware of Father Michel standing beside her.

"Sylvie, my dear. Are you ill?"

She turns away, hastily using the sleeve of her jacket to wipe the moisture from her eyes.

"Sit for a moment." He motions her into a pew in the side chapel. "I was filling the votives with wax. We have the luxury of real wax for now, but who knows when we'll have to give that over as well." The priest lowers the box of candle wax onto his lap, then turns to her. "Sylvie, you look weak. You can't give all your food to the refugees. You must eat if you're going to help them."

"That's not it, Father." She feels an unbearable ache. "Jean—"

"Perhaps it's time you consider a proper funeral service."

Sylvie's normally deep and hearty voice rises to a shrill reed. "No! He must have gotten away." She stands and tries to climb past him to leave the pew. "You know how resourceful he is." The priest remains seated, blocking her way. He takes her small hand in his, seating her back down. After an awkward moment, he says, in hushed tones, "You haven't been to confession in—how long?"

She stiffens. "I…I don't know. Father…Jean and I…well—"

He looks around the church then whispers, "Sylvie, I believe I know." He pauses, then adds, "There's a priest in Toulouse. Some things may be too private to confess in your home church."

"There's more to it, Father." She turns away, stealing a quick glance up at the Virgin. "It was my idea to have relations with him. Since we didn't have time to—" She pauses then blurts out, "Consummate the marriage and have the ceremony too."

She searches the priest's dark brown eyes for his reaction. She knows what they did was a sin, but in truth, she doesn't see it that way. Their love bound them together as tightly as any vows in front of the altar. Yet, the church gives her solace, structure, a framework for her to carry on. She needs that, especially now that she's alone.

The ancient wooden pew creaks as Father Michel sits back. "I don't ordinarily advocate that kind of thing."

She stops breathing.

"But the war rips everything apart. All our institutions." He shifts uncomfortably. "Jean came to me, so I know he wanted to do the right thing by you. I see how sorry you—"

"I'm not sorry." She juts out her chin ever so slightly, more to convince herself than him. "I'm glad I have that to remember him by."

"That may be so, Sylvie. But I sense you long for some kind of absolution." Father Michel looks intently, sincerely at her. "Let me know how I can help."

Sylvie sighs. "I will. As soon as I know myself."

He adds softly, "Besides, who are we to judge? With so many deeply troubling things around us."

She raises her eyes to him. "There's something else." She hesitates, then quickly adds, "I've begun praying."

He looks genuinely surprised. "Is there something wrong with that?"

"No, I mean really praying. To shut everything out. But it's more an escape than a proper act of devotion. I feel guilty using my prayers to God in that way."

"Each of us does what we must. To salvage as much of our humanity as possible during this obscene occupation."

"Sometimes the camp—it's overwhelming." Then spitting out pure venom, she says, "These damned *Boches*."

Father Michel presses his eyes shut—Sylvie can't tell if in prayer or to restrain his hatred of them. She decides to continue anyway. "I try to help Hélène, but I can't understand how she remains so calm. I get uncontrollably angry when they march in and demand more food."

"And the supplies hidden along the river quay?"

"So far they remain hidden. But we can only take small amounts up to the camp." She glances around the church. "I'm worried someone might turn us in."

A shaft of brightness spills onto the statue of the Virgin Mary as someone opens the side door. The priest immediately breaks off, and Sylvie whips around to see who it is. A shadowy figure, slouching and faintly limping, slips inside the church. Sylvie notices something familiar about him as he crosses himself with holy water, then heads directly towards the chapel of the Virgin Mary, where she and the priest are sitting. Just before reaching it, however, he quickly turns and shuffles back towards the door.

Sylvie jumps up and walks rapidly to catch up to this suspicious person. "Monsieur, may we help you?"

The figure stops, slowly turns, and says in reasonably good French, "I'm sorry. I may be lost. I am looking for—"

"Alastair? Is that you?"

The Englishman whispers, "Sylvie, I was hoping to make contact. I saw the priest talking to someone, a man, I thought. I'd forgotten how you dress. How is everything here?"

"We're managing...barely. I don't understand." She looks back at the priest, nodding to him that things are all right. He takes his cue and moves on to fill the votives.

Sylvie brings Alastair around the stone column just inside the chapel. She's pleased to see him in much heartier shape than when he left. "Why did you come back? Didn't they believe you?"

He slightly straightens his frame, giving just a hint of his military bearing. "The RAF believed me so earnestly, they want me to help you and your uncle set up a permanent escape route through the Pyrénées."

"Tell me what's going on. The Vichy press is censored."

"The RAF flies aeroplanes. Halifaxes, to be precise. We bomb factories making equipment for the Wehrmacht. Our Hurricanes and Spitfires escort them. Shoot down the Luftwaffe's Messerschmitts."

Sylvie nods vigorously at this marvelous news.

"We've had some success in these raids. Even so, pilots and crews get shot down, and we need to get the survivors out."

She tries to process how he's changed. His hair is darker and longer, identifying him more clearly as a Frenchman. They've gone to a lot of trouble to send him back.

"A number of escape lines are being formed in the north of France, and we want to start sending our lads down here. Over the mountains and into Spain. Then to North Africa." He finishes with a modest smile. "That is, if you still want to help."

Sylvie tries to calm herself, afraid to feel the full force of the elation racing through her. "What would we do?"

"Exactly what we did before. Use the abandoned watermill as a way station."

Sylvie opens her mouth to tell him that they already have three returned French soldiers hiding there, but she decides instead to hear more from him.

"Your uncle acted as a guide to get me over the mountains. He's still available?" He smiles. "And the little, vibrant one?"

"Louis? He'll be ecstatic."

Just then, two German soldiers enter the church's main door, bless themselves at the holy water fountain, and head towards the altar. Sylvie swiftly takes Alastair by the elbow and leads him around the columns, out the back, and into the garden. Fall leaves are settling onto the cobblestones, and the rose bushes are bursting with red and white blossoms. It invigorates Sylvie to see the garden in such robust bloom. She opens the rear gate, and they descend the steps onto the quay by the rapidly running river.

Alastair straightens up fully now and shakes out the leg he was limping on. "I remember this passageway from last time. Still operational, I see."

"It's been here for centuries." Her smile is broad and relaxed. "It's at your disposal now."

"Good. Our unit back in London has given this quite a bit of thought. We'll provide a wireless, and I can teach you how to fix up an antenna to receive broadcasts." Sylvie paces the quay in front of the stone steps, barely able to contain her enthusiasm. Alastair continues. "We'll signal you when we intend to make a drop. Parachute in canisters of medical supplies, Sten guns, French francs, and false ration cards for your group to buy supplies. We'll need your people to set up a series of level landing fields high up, where drops can be made. I assume you can do that?"

"I know these mountains." Sylvie feels a surge of warmth, thinking back to the days when she, her father, and Jean explored the narrow trails and high pastures. Who would have thought those trips would become so immensely useful now!

"Excellent. We'll coordinate drops with the cycles of the moon, at the full. Your people will bury the parachutes and hide the supplies." He lowers his voice over the rushing river. "I must be firm. They might be tempted to take away the parachute silks, for undergarments and such. That would spell disaster for your entire circuit if they were found."

"Understood."

"Even more important, we need to establish a place in Foix for the airmen to make contact so you and your uncle can escort them up to the watermill and then over the mountains. I assume the watermill is still a secret?"

Sylvie hesitates, then plunges ahead. "We have three young French soldiers hiding there already. Local boys, from Foix and Tarascon. They escaped the march to Germany."

Alastair sinks down onto one of the stone steps. "That could complicate things."

Sylvie joins him, leaning in towards him. "Not at all. They know the area." She pauses, then swiftly adds, "They could even act as guides. My uncle and Louis aren't so young anymore." She feels his plan lifting her out of her despondency and anger. Helping him would bring meaning back to her life—she would be in the war at last.

Alastair turns to look directly at her. "I had to do quite a bit of convincing back home. We must work only with people who are absolutely trustworthy."

She meets his gaze. "I swear they are." She crosses herself for emphasis.

He searches her eyes, pauses for a moment, then says, "All right. I expect we'll have to take one or two things on faith."

She exhales. "What else do you need?"

"We'll send our airmen from the north down south. We plan to have them escorted by young volunteer French women who can speak for them. Couples attract less attention, and it's less dangerous than a man traveling alone—especially if he doesn't speak French." Alastair continues. "It's best they meet somewhere safe in Foix so the young women escorts can get back on the train as soon as possible."

Sylvie winces. "I don't know. These men can't be seen in the cafés in the plaza. There are patrols everywhere." Alastair furrows his brow. The roaring of the river sounds in her ears as she struggles to think of a solution. "The church garden here is the safest place. St. Volusien's tower can be seen from miles around. They can come from the train station, cross the bridge and follow the river bank. Slip into the side alley out back, then into the garden."

"What about the priest?" Alastair nods back at the church. "It'll put everyone here in a packet of danger."

"Give me a moment," she says as she rises and heads through the back garden gate and into the church.

The two German soldiers are deep in prayer in a pew near the altar. Sylvie approaches the priest, who stands before a bank of votive candles in a side chapel, filling the ones that aren't lit with wax. "Father Michel, I need to tell you something."

"I'm not so sure you should. I probably know too much about the food cache already."

"It's not about that. And we appreciate what you've done already." She hesitates, then plunges ahead. *He must agree—he must.* "I'm sorry, but I absolutely have to ask one thing more. Can we use the garden access to the passageway, like we did when the British pilot was here before? He's back and wants to bring airmen who've been shot down here to Foix. Then we can get them over the mountains. We just need a place for them to meet us."

The priest stiffens. "I'm sorry. I can't put the nuns and children at the school at such risk."

"We can't meet the airmen anywhere else in the village. The church is the only place."

Father Michel leans closer, angrily whispering, "We can't have these men wandering in. Who would be here to meet them? What if one of them was a spy?" He quickly turns to survey who else might be in the church. "Major Spitzer would have us all shot—if we were lucky."

"You're right, of course." *How can I make him see how important this is?* She feels a cold shiver, even though she's standing in front of so many flickering candles.

The priest twists around to look up to the vast arches in the nave as if to beseech the Lord. He looks back at her, sighing deeply. "I'm sorry." Then he turns to leave the chapel.

Sylvie desperately tries to think of something. Then she calls to him, "Wait, Father, I have an idea."

He stops and turns back towards her with a wry smile. "You always do."

Sylvie quickly checks on the German soldiers praying and is relieved to see them heading out. She takes the priest by the arm, pulling them both to kneel before the bank of votive candles, mumbling as if praying until the Germans pass and exit the church. She whispers, "This might sound crazy."

He smiles mischievously, saying between clenched teeth, "I'm sure it will."

"What if I were here to meet them? What if they were told to come only at dusk? To the alley behind the church." Her mind is working overtime. "If…if…they gave some signal only we both knew so I could let them into the garden. Then lead them down the passageway by the river."

"You can't live here, in the convent."

"Why not?"

"What about Étienne?"

"Uncle Claude can see to him. Besides, he's completely involved helping Hélène in the camp—she looks after him these days more than I ever did."

He takes his thumb and scratches some excess wax from the rim of a votive. "It would be suspicious to have a layperson living in the convent."

Sylvie thinks for a moment. "What if I weren't a layperson? What if I were a nun?"

The priest leans against the bronze offering bar, his dark eyes flashing with silent laughter—more merriment than she's seen from him in some time.

"Sylvie, that's preposterous. You just told me a host of things that make taking your vows completely impossible."

Sylvie feels her chance to help Alastair slipping away. "What if I didn't actually take my vows?" She nods towards the Germans. "They'd never know if I was really a nun. I could shield you and the others when the airmen came. Get them safely away."

Father Michel's dark complexion reddens. His tone turns angry, mixed with anguish, "Playacting as a nun. That's blasphemous!"

"You don't think God would understand? You just said we have to do what we must to keep our humanity in the midst of this obscene occupation."

He gets up, snorting, "I'm truly sorry, my dear. But look at you. You dress like a man in your"—he waves at her clothes—"you'd have to learn to walk. Carry yourself with humility. Not one of your strong suits."

Sylvie abruptly stands and stares a long moment at the priest. She steps back, takes a deep breath, and bursts into a mellow, full-throated laugh. Astonished, the priest steps back as well, then he too begins to laugh.

"I'm sorry, Father. I couldn't help myself. You're absolutely right."

"My dear, your lack of humility and stubbornness are legend." He pauses, then looks intensely at her. "That's why I'm going to put you in touch with Mother Superior in Toulouse. If she can't turn you into a nun, even a nun to outsmart the Nazis, then no one can."

Sylvie smiles broadly and throws her arms around the priest, kissing him on both cheeks.

Flustered, he smooths his cassock. He looks down and directly into her eyes, saying with a deep sigh, "I hope God will understand."

Sylvie bows her head, adopting an exaggeratedly penitent nun-like attitude. Then she sneaks a twinkling smile at the priest. "I'm sure you can convince Him."

CHAPTER TWENTY-TWO

Foix. September 1940

HÉLÈNE IS STILL filled with profound grief at her mother's passing. When any of her patients at the hospital in Toulouse died, she'd always been able to view their passing as a natural progression of life's order. But when her mother died last month—a virulent flu having taken her in a matter of days—the very foundation of her belief system was shaken to its core. Now, passing by her mother's empty bed every night reminds Hélène of her powerlessness in the face of all her nurse's training and herbal potions. Her malaise is compounded by the fact that she's had little word of her husband, Gérard. He was reported to be in a German prisoner of war camp, but she's had no news of his condition.

As the fall wears on, the brilliant, clear summer air in the mountains is increasingly enshrouded in a cold fog signaling the coming winter. So too, she feels herself walking about covered by a thick blanket of depression. Given the heavy weight of caring for the sick at the refugee camp, with increasingly limited medical and food supplies, her only joy is stealing away to spend time with Elias and Deborah at Madame Rumeau's farm.

It's difficult to make the trip because of the shortage of gasoline. The Germans now require all Jews to have their papers stamped *Jeuden*. The yellow star Major Spitzer has forced her to wear since their first acrimonious meeting also heightens her sense of foreboding. The escalating German animosity against the Jews convinces Hélène that she and Father Michel need to warn Madame Rumeau. They slip away, ostensibly to gather food from a neighboring farm collective, then they brave the icy road up to Madame Rumeau's. As they approach, they see cheerful smoke wafting from the chimney and hear laughter from inside the house.

Madame Rumeau uses her cane deftly to navigate her short, stout form outside to greet them. She receives Father Michel's blessing, then turns to Hélène and gives her a sympathetic hug. "My dear, your mother and I went back more years than either of us would care to admit. I'm so sorry. How are you?"

Hélène's emotional state is still raw, something she finds unnerving. She manages a thin smile. "Thank you. I keep busy with the refugees. How are things here?"

In a gleeful rush, Madame Rumeau says, "I can't tell you what a difference these children have made. Noëlle and I have never been happier."

Father Michel beams down on the old woman. "We are so pleased to hear that, Madame."

Hélène hands Madame Rumeau a basket containing extremely scarce foodstuffs: meats, cheeses, breads, and pickles.

"Mon Dieu! Merci bien." The old woman graciously accepts the gift, then turns to the priest. "Father, we've been reading from the Old Testament. To help them understand their heritage, you know. We're enjoying the wonderful stories. David and Gol—" She is interrupted as Noëlle, Elias, and Deborah bound out of the farmhouse.

Deborah squeals, "Madame Hélène," as she jumps into Hélène's arms.

Hélène swings the girl around and kisses her. Elias still seems reticent, but when Hélène puts Deborah down and opens her arms to him, he rushes in. She kneels down, pulling both children close. "Let me see, did you wash behind your ears?" Hélène checks their ears, then kisses them there and on their necks. They giggle and screech. Both now have color in their cheeks. Elias's sour reserve is virtually gone, and Deborah is even getting a bit plump—the girl's sunken cheeks have filled out, and Hélène is delighted to see her looking more and more like a happy little chipmunk. And Noëlle, flushed with excitement, also seems to have undergone a transformation. No longer thin, drawn, and brittle, she is ruddy-cheeked and flowering. As much as Hélène has missed the children, she's sure this was the right decision.

After a moment, Hélène bends down to the children. "Father Michel and I brought you each a toy. Would you like Mademoiselle Noëlle to show them to you? Maybe in the barn?"

Deborah chirps, "Oh yes, please," while Elias even manages a smile. Father Michel holds out a small sack, which Noëlle happily takes and leads them to the barn.

Madame Rumeau ushers them inside the farmhouse. "I'm sure you want some tea after your long drive." She speaks with a lilt in her voice Hélène hasn't heard in a long time. "Little Elias is a very diligent worker. He's taken to turning over the ground like he'd been raised on a farm. It's as if my grandson and Noëlle had their children after all."

Father Michel wraps an understanding arm around her shoulder as Hélène shifts uncomfortably.

With misting eyes, Madame Rumeau says, "Sometimes I can't believe our good fortune. They give us such hope." She serves the tea, offering them something dense that looks like cake. "We're short on yeast these days. So this might be a bit heavy."

The priest takes a bite and chews…and chews. "Wonderful, my dear Madame."

Hélène can't resist a smile, then straightens up, her voice turning serious. "Madame, we must tell you about some disturbing developments."

But Madame Rumeau refuses to allow the merriment of the moment to be destroyed. "I'm sorry for what I hear is happening down there, but it surely doesn't affect us. Who would care about our little farm way up here?" She folds her tiny, liver-spotted hands together and emphatically places them in front of her on the table, signaling an end to the conversation.

The priest gently puts his hand on top of hers. "Madame, the Nazis are clamping down on the refugee population. Sorting through papers and—"

Hélène breaks in, trying to keep her voice level. "First, they promised I could run the camp. Then they started to interfere. Major Spitzer insists on documenting all the Jewish people. He's made them wear these stars." She nervously fingers the yellow fabric on her blouse.

Wrinkles cascading down her plump face, Madame Rumeau frowns at the yellow star. "But you're not—"

"No, but the major has his own ideas about how to control the refugees…and the rest of us." Hélène feels the blood rising to her cheeks. "We don't know that anything, in particular, will happen. We just thought you should consider having the children play in the barn during the day."

The priest adds as nonchalantly as possible, "In case someone should wander by."

Madame Rumeau squints back and forth between them, tucking a stray gray hair into the high pile on the top of her head. Her vibrant smile is gone, her features turned to stone, as she pronounces in a strong, clear voice, "I will shoot them myself if they come for these beautiful children."

Astonished, Hélène feels a rush of admiration.

The priest says, "We're sure things won't come to that."

Hélène quickly adds, "And now that winter's setting in, the passes will be closed. It won't be easy for anyone to just to drop by." She draws a sharp intake of air, not fully believing what she's about to say. "I'm sure the situation will be much improved by the spring. The British will certainly take action by then."

Father Michel leans in conspiratorially. "You might even consider making a hiding place for them."

Madame Rumeau's eyes widen. "You mean like a trap door or something like that?"

The priest grimly nods.

As Madame Rumeau leans back, her rickety chair creaks alarmingly. She put her hands on her belly and laughs boisterously. "Father, we beat you to it. My husband was in the Great War. He was certain we might need to take refuge someday from one sort of invader or another. Like those damned fascists in Spain." Her smile broadens, crinkling up her entire plump face. "We have a place. With dry supplies already packed in. We can all hide there for a month."

A profound sense of relief washes over Hélène. She lets out a shocked laugh, then she and the priest toast Madame Rumeau with their teacups.

"I'm not so old and feeble as you think."

Father Michel smiles broadly. "Whoever said you were?"

Hélène marvels at the little but fearsome woman before her. Even so, as she and the priest leave, Hélène can't shake an unsettling feeling of distress. She's subjected them all to danger—the old woman, young Noëlle, and of course, her cherished Elias and Deborah. There doesn't seem to be an alternative, however, as the Germans continue their tight-fisted hold over the refugee camp and the village of Foix—as well as the entire Ariège region of France.

CHAPTER TWENTY-THREE

Foix. September 1940

As Sylvie, Claude, and Alastair climb the narrow path to the watermill, Sylvie marvels at how much better shape Alastair is in than the first time they made this trip. The late-summer water is low, softly flowing alongside the old overgrown trail before it plunges fifty feet into the steep crevice. They tread carefully on the dried fallen leaves and twigs, not only to avoid slipping but also to minimize crackling noises that might attract a German patrol. Suddenly, Sylvie hears a rustling in the trees up ahead, then is profoundly relieved to find them surrounded, not by the *Boches*, but by the three young escapees from the French army.

When Sylvie first saw the boys hiding in the shed behind Jacques's mother's farmhouse, her heart went out to them. They were all famished, extremely weak, and nursing various wounds. Jacques had a horrifically long gash down the side of his face, Ernst limped from shrapnel in his leg, and Marcel winced as he coughed, gravel rattling in his chest. Sylvie was even more distressed that not one of them could utter a coherent sentence.

With considerable coaxing, Claude managed to get them to tell him what happened, but only in small increments. Their platoon was captured, and the Germans forced them to plod for several kilometers, hands overhead, through the mud. Suddenly, the Germans began firing, brutally machine-gunning the French soldiers. The boys were lucky to have been at the edge of the forest. As the Germans focused on the main body of the platoon, the three dove under one of the French machine gun flatbed lorries, rolled off into the brush, then slipped away. They hid in farmhouses and slept in fields until Jacques managed to lead them back to Foix. His mother alerted Sylvie and Claude, who brought them up to the watermill, where the boys began to recover.

Now, the three young men escort Sylvie, Claude, and Alastair the rest of the way through the forest, the fresh, thin air foggy with the promise of a cold rain and possibly sleet that evening.

Claude's reservist comrade, Louis, greets Alastair—he reaches up to grab his face and furiously kisses him on both cheeks. *"Mon ami! What an adventure we had, n'est-ce pas?* Getting you over that final ridge into Spain." He turns to Sylvie, "We had to push his ass—"

"Great to see you too, Louis." Alastair jumps in, hoping to staunch Louis's florid description, while she turns away, trying to avoid laughing out loud.

Claude tosses Jacques a package. "From your mother. Don't eat it all at once."

Jacques has a large head and big hands, but the skinny body of a rapidly growing teenager whose torso hasn't caught up with the rest of him. Taunting the others with his superior height, he playfully holds the package above Marcel and Ernst, but they pounce on him, rip open the brown paper and start on the sweets. Marcel is short, dark, and spindly, missing several teeth, but not shy about eating voraciously with his mouth open. Ernst is stockier than the other two and more reserved, chewing and quietly groaning his appreciation. Sylvie is pleased to see the boys so animated, as the sweets disappear in no time.

She also admires their restraint, as Jacques solemnly takes the bread and cheese to a communal set of shelves near the old ovens in the mill.

Louis proudly shows Alastair what they've done to shore up the mill's collapsing walls. With the boys' help, they've cut tree branches and latticed them together, filling in the spaces with mud. A small campfire area has been cleared, permitting them to boil water for their ersatz coffee and prepare small meals—but only during the day when a fire would not likely be noticed by a German patrol.

Sylvie settles back to enjoy the falling dusk that brings deep purple shadows to her beloved mountains surrounding them. The setting sun refracts light from the bright fall trees, and a golden hue settles over the jagged, craggy peaks. Sitting there in the watermill, it's almost as if the war hasn't encroached in such horrific and unfathomable ways on her life.

Her respite, however, doesn't last long. The boys report in halting terms to Alastair, detailing how they escaped. Sylvie notices they become more emotionally withdrawn as they speak. She's grateful when Claude signals Alastair not to dwell too much on their traumatic experiences and sends the boys to collect firewood. He and Louis give Alastair some locally made Armagnac. Sylvie is amused to see that the Englishman, probably knowing what's coming from his previous visit, steels himself and knocks back the strong mixture, while the others watch, ready to laugh if he chokes—a pleasure Sylvie happily sees Alastair deny them.

Claude lifts his tin cup in a salute to Louis. "All of us...in the Great War...in the trenches. So caked in mud, I swear it's still under my fingernails. *Vive la France.*" He downs the rest, pours more from the jug, and turns to Sylvie. "Your father and I were there together. Rats in a maze. Months on end. Never saw daylight for the haze of the gunfire through the barbed wire above our heads." Claude continues morosely, "This time, it's Panzers and machine guns. All over in a flash. But our boys are just as shell shocked."

Louis refuses to succumb to Claude's melancholy—he jumps up, raising his tin cup. "To shell shock. It made us what we are today!"

As they drink and reminisce, Sylvie ambles outside to catch the last of the sunset. Swishing leaves in a circle with her boot, she recalls Father Michel's admonition: In order to make the church a safe meeting place, she'll have to live in the convent, and worse still, she'll have to learn to look and act like a demure nun. *Ridiculous! How could I ever adopt a humble demeanor?* She swears under her breath—isn't she adding to her sins by perpetrating such a farce, even in a good cause? She picks up a twig and hurls it into the crevice. *This is crazy—I'm going to get Father Michel, the nuns, and the school children all killed.* She collapses onto a rock, barely able to cross herself for her violently shaking hand.

She's unaware of Alastair's approach until he sits down beside her. "It's asking a lot of all of you."

She nods, dejectedly. Looking down, she notices his boots then laughs. "They couldn't get you a better pair? In all of England?"

"I didn't want a better pair. I told you before, these are my lucky boots. They got me home safely, thanks to you, your uncle, and that little madman Louis."

"Jacques and the boys look up to him. He motivates them."

"Good thing Claude can rein him in—"

"Most of the time." Sylvie turns to face Alastair. "Your hair. It's darker. You even look nicely unkempt, if you don't mind my saying."

"Part of the plan."

"Can I ask you something? If these boys could have escaped, why couldn't Jean?"

"Sylvie, if I understood, they were farther south. Not in the Ardennes, where I gather Jean was."

"But he helped a boy in his unit. Took his jacket off to use as a tourniquet. Mightn't he have run? They never did find his body—not that they would officially report."

Alastair reaches out to put a comforting hand on her shoulder.

She pulls away, livid. "Tell me why he couldn't have run! He was raised in the mountains. You see the kind of forest we have here. He'd know how to survive."

"Sylvie, the Panzers in that area pulverized everything in their path." He sets his jaw and continues, "The French simply listed most of them as dead without identifying individual remains."

She pounds her knee with her fist. "Damn it to Hell."

Through gritted teeth, he says, "Must be intolerable to have them crawling all over your village."

She gives him a despairing look.

"I'm sorry. I have to ask for more of you."

"What do you mean?" She sighs heavily, wondering what else they can do—they're already putting so many at risk.

"The mill. I remembered it as more substantial. They've done much to improve it." He pauses, then swiftly turns to her. "I'm sorry...it's too fragile a shelter for what we have in mind."

"I don't understand."

"We want to get the downed pilots out. Maybe some agents as well. But we also need to establish a network to disrupt the Nazi infrastructure. Blow up communications. Rail lines. That sort of thing."

"How will we do that?"

Alastair motions for them to get up and walk further down the path to talk more privately. They come to a sharp outcropping, still washed in the golden light of the setting sun. Flecks of water from the mountain stream cascading down the crevice splash up onto them.

Sylvie cups some translucent droplets in her hands and lifts them to her mouth. She laughs her deep melodious laugh. "It's like champagne." She sits on a tree stump while Alastair leans against a white birch, now a brilliant deep yellow in the setting sun. Suddenly, she turns toward him, sneering, "What am I saying? Champagne? There's no reason to celebrate anything anymore." She wipes her wet hands on her trousers, resolutely looking up at him. "What else do you need?"

He takes a breath and plunges in. "With the whole continent under Hitler's control, and bombings obliterating portions of London and the English countryside, civilization as we know it isn't...well, not to exaggerate—"

"I've never known a Brit to exaggerate."

"I have to be frank." Alastair pushes off the tree, pacing as he continues. "This is crucial for an eventual English invasion. We need a bigger, more secure place to shelter more like twenty-five to thirty men instead of five. And keep explosives dry."

Sylvie struggles to appreciate the scale of what he's asking. They've worked so hard just to hide three boys. And now she's agreed to turn her life inside out to live in the convent to receive whoever makes it to Foix. But he wants more. And more is certainly needed. She debates whether to divulge the cave's existence, with its underground lake, where she and Jean made love. She frequently goes there to commune with him, and renew their vows of love. Bringing men and equipment there would break their sacred bond. She'd be admitting that he was never coming back.

She raises her eyes to the shadows on the mountainside where she and Jean roamed so freely. Yet, in the flash of the setting sun on the birch trees in the distance, she realizes what Alastair is asking could be the very best way to avenge Jean's death. She slowly turns to Alastair. "A staging ground for a real resistance? Yes, I do know somewhere."

CHAPTER TWENTY-FOUR

Foix. September 1940

HÉLÈNE RETURNS HOME from visiting Madame Rumeau and the children with a bone-chilling sense of dread, despite the elderly woman's surprisingly zealous determination to protect the children. She builds a small fire to warm the house, makes herself a cup of herbal tea, and settles down to mull everything over. Feelings of powerlessness compete with her sense of optimism that the children will go unnoticed. Suddenly, the door knocker sounds sharply. It comes again, urgently. She gets up in a rush, spilling some tea on the side table next to her chair. She opens the door to find Major Spitzer standing before her.

"Major? I wasn't expecting anyone."

"I am sure you were not, Madame Hélène. But I know you will be pleased to do your part for the Fatherland." She stands staring at him, trying to comprehend what he means. His eyes are a clear gray, inscrutable, unblinking, betraying nothing but his version of the truth at hand. He waits to be let in, but when she doesn't offer, he snaps off his hat, tucks it under his arm, and brushes his slender frame past her, striding into her parlor.

"Ach, what a warm fire I see you have made. The house feels cold for such a blazing fire. Did you just get in?"

Hélène's voice cracks as her heart constricts. "It's not...not so big. The house, that is." She turns her back to him so he can't read her anxious face. Her hands tremble as she wipes up the spilled tea with one of her mother's lace doilies—which she would never have used had she been less flustered. She says, over her shoulder, "The house is old. It was my parents. It never warms up much at all."

The major nods. "Still, it is very charming here. I am going to be quite comfortable."

Hélène whips around, her stomach heaving. "What do you mean?"

The major flicks a perfectly manicured finger towards her chair, motioning for her to sit. He strides to the couch, brushes it off, and with a perfectly erect torso, eases himself down. He carefully places his hat beside him, the Wehrmacht eagle staring directly at her. Leaning slightly forward, he reaches inside his jacket and brings forth a paper, which he unfolds and thrusts towards her.

"My billeting orders. We are to be housed in the village, among the *native* population, so to speak." He smirks. "We will get to know everyone better that way. You will all come to realize we are not the monsters you might believe."

"Here? In—in—my house?" She does not reach for the paper, instead remains sitting frozen in disbelief.

The major bends his ram-rod upper body farther towards her, like a praying mantis. The slits of his eyes grow large with anger as he stabs the air with the paper. "You will please to examine this. You will see that everything...it is in order."

Hélène's blood thunders in her ears. She imagines yelling at the top of her lungs that he should leave that instant but manages to restrain herself. She isn't sure how to handle this ghastly development and considers how to buy herself some time. Her mind races as she sees him upstairs in her home. He will certainly insist on taking the larger bedroom her parents occupied, just across the hall from hers. The thought of a German officer in her parents' bed cuts through her like a knife. And what would he expect of her…physically? It's all too terrible to contemplate.

She forces her voice into a steady tone. "I don't doubt your word, Major. But, I had no idea I would be—ah—graced with your presence, so to speak." She nervously watches his reaction. He ponders for a moment, and it seems to her that he, too, is trying to feel his way through this awkward situation.

All at once, the major's chiseled face twists in anger, and he abruptly stands. She gasps, then watches him stomp to her chair. Looking directly down at her, he holds the paper just above her lap, then lets it go. She's cornered, obliged to grab for the paper or see it fall to the floor—surely a grave insult for which she might pay dearly.

Hélène manages to recover the paper and straightens it out. Panic rises as she looks around at her modestly decorated home. The drapes seem to have transformed themselves into a Wehrmacht bright red with black stripes. Her sofa throw is suddenly emblazoned with a swastika, while balls and claws appear on the fireplace tools, and a ferocious eagle perches on the andirons. She shakes her head to dispel these horrific images, then turns to mull over the official-looking Germanic type, marked with various brightly colored stamps. She can't read a word but decides to pretend to admire the authoritative nature of the communication, all the while trying to find some way to argue him out of his plan.

As she looks the paper over, he wanders the room, surreptitiously glancing back at her from time to time. She steals a look at him and notices him frowning at a speck of dust on a side table, which he wipes off with his finger. Then, not knowing what to do with the smudge on his finger, he bends down to caress a plant—like the rest of her house, every level space in her parlor is covered with her healing herbs in cachepots. He stealthily transfers the smudge to a leaf. Could he act any more outrageously in her home?

He says, "I see you are quite the indoor gardener. What are all these?"

"I grow plants. I use them for medicinal purposes."

The major cocks his head as if listening to a foreign language, yet he seems intrigued. "For medicines, you say?"

She's on the brink of exploding at his clumsy, insincere attempt at small talk but decides if she must endure his presence, this might be the only way to get along. Find a neutral subject to discuss. Perhaps he'd even allow her to give him some herbs, so he might sleep more soundly at night. If so, she might herself sleep with less fear of him intruding.

Hélène smiles as genuinely as she can force herself. "You would be surprised how calming herbs are at the end of the day." He shrugs, so she presses on. "I was just having herbal tea. Would you care to join me?"

His thin, forced smile broadens, and he nods curtly. "That is very kind of you."

Hélène sighs, returns the paper to him, then goes into the kitchen to put the kettle back on. She hears him walk the room, and when she brings the tea, finds him examining the pictures on the mantle.

Hélène stands next to him, tray in hand, as they stare at each other in the mirror over the fireplace. He gazes, unblinking, looking like he's fascinated by her gold spun hair in its tight nursing curls. She takes in his dark brown hair, slicked back, pomaded, and shining almost black in the firelight. She wonders again, as she did on the day they first met at the camp if his coloring—darker hair than the German ideal—compels him to go to greater lengths to prove himself, more than if he looked more Aryan. With the fire softly crackling, they take each other in, almost in a trance. He studies her nursing pin, shining in the glow of the fire. She notices that his eyes—instead of the typical Aryan brilliant-blue—are like watery gray pearls: a shield to wash over his thoughts, preventing observers from seeing the viciousness behind them.

Trying to maintain calm and find a neutral subject to discuss, she says, "Those photos are of my parents."

"I gather they passed away. I am sorry for your loss."

"My mother died only recently. I was glad I could spend her last days with her." She motions for him to sit, and he settles back down on the sofa while she pours the tea from a nearby chair.

"We have at home so many who have died for, as we say, *Family, Folk, and Fatherland.*" He pauses, trying to judge her reaction. She forces a sympathetic frown, although she does indeed feel bad for the terrible loss of innocent civilian life on both sides. He continues, "You and your husband used to live elsewhere?"

"In Toulouse. Near the hospital where I did my nursing training."

"He was captured?"

Through the fog of her misery at having him in her house, Hélène's eyes momentarily brighten. Perhaps he could find out about Gérard. Maybe he could even ease her husband's imprisonment. "Major, I would be most grateful if I could find out how he is. We've had no word following the initial news he'd been taken prisoner in the Ardennes."

The major thoughtfully sips his tea. She can plainly see a boastful broadening of his chest, even in his ramrod seated position.

"You are aware the French tried to wage the same kind of war as they did before. Because your generals succeeded then, they did not question their tactics this time."

Hélène's stomach curdles at his sharpened tone. The opportunity to help Gérard is slipping away. "I'm sure I don't know anything about combat tactics. Perhaps you can tell me what happened to all the men you captured?"

"Ah—combat tactics. Most crucial in war. You know what is positional warfare?"

"I'm sure you can enlighten me." She hopes she can swing the conversation back to the prisoners of war after he's had his boastful say.

"Yes. Well, where to begin? All the Maginot Line fortifications were...it was a long and highly fortified line, as you know. But stupidly, they all faced east. East! Your generals assumed the fighting would be all in one direction—from the east and head-on. But our generals were smarter. They decided not to wage this positional kind of war but a blitzkrieg. You know what this is?" He doesn't wait for her reply but charges forward in his own verbal blitzkrieg. "A fast-moving non-positional attack. And, of course—*ja!*—in the least anticipated area: the Ardennes."

"We understood your Panzers were extremely effective." *More honey than vinegar.*

"Unparalleled in modern wartime, Madame. Did you know the French actually had the superiority in one area?" He quickly answers his own question. "In their ground forces—their men and materiel." His voice takes on an almost religious fervor. "But our Panzers, and our armored car Pumas, were even more superior. We out-maneuvered your army, which was stuck in its position. Do you see?"

Hélène desperately wants to find a way to steer the conversation back to her husband but is acutely aware she must make admiring comments to feed his ego. "And somehow, no one really knows how we did not have the air power to combat your tanks as they crossed the Meuse River."

Spitzer puts down his tea, leans forward, and gesticulates with his graceful, tapered hands. "But that is the brilliance of our plan. To cross where no one thinks we would go. So, of course, there was no air power to prevent us from ramming straight through." He continues, his reedy voice rapidly rising. "Tanks are the most humane way to wage war, did you know? Fewer casualties on both sides. One battle in the Great War...two hundred thousand men lost. With our tanks? One-tenth that." He abruptly stops, looking surprised at his outburst. He clenches his jaw and shifts uncomfortably on the couch, trying to look nonchalant.

With all his talk of humanity, Hélène decides this is the time to press some demands upon him while he is under her roof. She starts out with a bit of sarcasm. "I have heard much about *humanity* from your side." Then tempers it with some honey. "But I am pleased to know you hold life in such high regard. Major, I'm sure you will agree that, while you are billeted here, we must observe the utmost decorum."

Startled, he clenches his fists. It's a small movement but one that tells her she's scored an important victory.

He abruptly stands and marches towards the door, flings it open, and signals a soldier to enter with some bags. He moves to the foot of the stairs. Barking as much to her as to the young soldier, he says, "Madame, you will show this soldier to my quarters."

Her heart plummets. "Of course." She swallows hard, turns to the soldier, then back to him so he can translate. "First room, top of the stairs on the right." The soldier carefully climbs the stairs, obviously trying not to drop anything. As he disappears into her parents' room, she grips the ball on the banister post—hard.

He turns to her, lightly adding, "I will be grateful for you to serve my breakfast in the morning. In the evening, I will eat with the officers. I need not trouble you for supper."

She turns away so he cannot see the color rise in her cheeks. "That's a relief, Major. I mean…in the village we don't have the type of food I'm sure you are accustomed to."

He bows slightly from the waist. "Of course, I wish to be unobtrusive. Not disrupt your work at the camp."

"I appreciate that."

The soldier clumps down the stairs and out of the house. Spitzer follows behind him, then casually turns back as if he'd remembered something trivial.

"Tonight, I will return after my supper. Ach, and of course, while we are discussing your work, I want you to know I do not wish to disturb your caring for the children. Elias and Deborah…those are their names?"

His thin smile straightens into a broad gash across his face. He snaps on his hat, clicks his heels, and gives her a *Sieg Heil*.

Hélène opens her mouth to make a parting remark, but no sound emerges.

CHAPTER TWENTY-FIVE

Foix. September 1940

L ate at night, Sylvie suffers bouts of insomnia accompanied by uncontrollable panic attacks even her most fervent prayers can't dispel. Tonight, she gets out of bed, goes to her armoire, and pulls out a paper with official-looking seals. She quietly pads into the kitchen, lights a candle, and reverently smooths the paper onto the table. Too anxious to read it again, she puts on the kettle and gazes out the window at the harvest moon, pale golden, luminously full, and resting lightly on the jagged silhouette of the surrounding cliffs. Aching to her core, she recalls when she and Jean would traipse down that mountain, leather pouches full of partridge, this special moon lighting their way.

Two months after the disastrous June battle in the Ardennes, Sylvie received Jean's official death notice. Now, she stares at the paper with its black-death ink, unable to purge her mind of the image Alastair planted—Jean, pulverized into nothingness by a blast from a Panzer. The newspapers reported that the French fired down on the German engineering corps as they scrambled to build bridges to ford their tanks across the Meuse River. *Étienne's right—this is exactly the kind of territory Jean knows best—surely he'd be able to escape.* As she toys with the paper, steam from the kettle shrieks into the kitchen, the sound piercing her very soul. Sylvie feels in her robe for the packet Hélène gave her—some herbs "to help you relax." She doesn't believe in Hélène's *hocus-pocus*, but her nerves are so frayed that she empties the herbs into her tea and drinks it down. Without actually reading it, because she knows all too well what it says, she returns the paper to her armoire. Sleep never comes that night.

Early the next morning, Sylvie climbs to the watermill, feeling Jean's presence beside her. She's decided she must show Alastair their cave, even if it breaks the spell of their special place. Even if it signals she's decided to admit that he's finally...No! Not yet! Just look at the boys who managed to escape—they made it back against all odds. She'll care for those boys and any downed pilots Alastair sends her way as practice for how she'll care for Jean when he finally returns.

Sylvie is pleased to see Jacques and Ernst up and about, although concerned that Marcel lies coughing on his makeshift bed. Jacques motions for her to be quiet, pointing to Alastair, whose lanky frame rests on a straw pallet against the far stone wall. His fine, patrician features show through the RAF's attempt to roughen his appearance in order to blend in with the French. And his calm reserve at times feels out of place among the passionate French, Basque, Spanish and Moorish temperaments in this part of the country.

Jacques makes her some ersatz coffee. The barley brew smell wafts through the mill, and Alastair slowly stretches, further elongating his long limbs. Then he flips over and goes back to sleep.

Jacques brings Marcel some coffee spiked with Claude's version of the local Armagnac. "This should help that cough." Marcel takes a sip, shivers, and is racked by another fit of coughing.

Sylvie registers alarm, whispering to Jacques, "I must get Hélène up here to see to that cough."

As Sylvie sips her coffee, she hears a noise overhead and looks up to see Ernst. Having climbed up to one of the rafters, he now hangs upside down by his knees, like an acrobat. She laughs. "Ernst, what in heaven's name are you doing?"

Ernst shows off for her. "Have to get rid of this limp. Exercising my knees. Got to get back in shape so we can run those *Boches* out of France."

Marcel puts his coffee down and sinks back. "I wish we still had our anti-aircraft gun. Ernst liked to crawl all over that gun—"

"I was cleaning it—"

"You were riding it," Jacques jokes. "Like a Yankee cowboy."

Marcel rises, suppressing a cough. "Like a man riding a—" He abruptly shuts up as he looks around to find Sylvie looking askance at him. He sips his coffee while absent-mindedly rubbing the wounds on his neck and arms. They are more diffuse than the frightening single lightning bolt down Jacque's face, but they are blotching angrily and oozing white pus.

Still, Marcel enjoys telling his stories. "Did you know, the hedges in Normandy are thick as stones? You can't part them like a bush." He rubs his arm. "I tried. You have to find a narrow passage into the next field and crawl through."

Sylvie feels a painful jolt, his comments taking her back to the brambles that cover the entrance to her cave. Soft laughter makes its way into her consciousness, causing her to glance up to see Ernst grinning as he makes his acrobatic way along the rafters above Alastair.

But Marcel, who wants to remain the center of Sylvie's attention, continues his story for her benefit. "In this one field, the farmer had left his cows. They hadn't been milked. So they were moaning."

Jacques, competing for her attention as well, interjects, "Marcel, what would you know about milking cows?" Then, to Sylvie, "This boy's from Paris. Up on that hill where the artists are."

"Montmartre, you dunce," Marcel calls out.

Jacques continues, "By the cafés where the whores come from. He used to empty the garbage to make some extra centimes, didn't you? And steal a look at their udders."

Jacques and Ernst giggle like schoolboys.

"Some of them looked pretty full to me." Marcel snorts. "I would have milked them if I could."

Ernst calls down from the rafter. "Back to the story. Those damned Normandy cows wouldn't let us close!" He dangles some rope on top of the sleeping Alastair, pulls it back up, then dangles it some more, swishing it just above Alastair's head.

Sylvie marvels at the resilience of the boy to carry off such a prank. Everyone holds his breath as Alastair, entirely in his sleep, waves away the bristle end of the rope, then swings at it when Ernst sends it back. Alastair finally sits up startled, and the boys break into gales of laughter.

After a while, Sylvie goes over to Alastair and whispers to him, after which they make their excuses and leave the mill. She leads him through the forest, up towards the jagged peaks. Drawing near her precious cave, Sylvie makes her peace with her decision to show it to him. Before the war, it was a place where lovers came for a tryst, but for obvious reasons, it's unlikely to have been used for that purpose in a long time. Now, her cave will be her personal sacrifice to the resistance. When they arrive, she sees the familiar brambles, buffeted by the wind, growing horizontally across the entrance. Was it only a year ago that she and Jean were here—the day he left—the day they slept together for the first and last time?

Alastair is shocked when he sees the thick, seemingly impenetrable brambles. "What's this?"

Standing in a patch of bright sunlight, Sylvie flashes back to when Jean took her by the hand, pushed aside the brambles, and led her into the cave. The memory so distresses her that she feels dizzy and needs to steady herself on the rocky entrance.

"Are you all right, Sylvie?"

"Just didn't sleep well last night." She takes a breath and briskly moves forward before she can change her mind. "Come, I'll show you."

She brushes the brambles aside and motions him in, anxious to see his reaction and whether, after all her agonizing, the cave is actually fit for his purpose.

Once inside, he walks around, turning slowly and craning his long neck to survey the vastness of the cave. An occasional drip of water from a nearby stalactite reverberates through the stillness. Sylvie silently creeps up to his side, part of her wanting him to like it and part of her praying he'll reject it. He nods curtly, which Sylvie takes to mean that the usually taciturn Brit likes it. He says, "A natural source of water too," as he suddenly takes off, loping across the rocky floor to the underground lake. She follows, pleased to see him so appreciative—mesmerized in fact—as he stares into the indigo lake that goes on to infinity.

She says quietly, reverently, "No one knows its source. The lake empties into an underground river somewhere between Foix and Tarascon."

They stand respectfully as if in a church, bathed in the mottled sunlight that breaks through the brambles at the entrance, providing a faint, natural source of illumination within.

Suddenly, Alastair grins boyishly and says, "This is remarkable, Sylvie. How did you ever find this place?"

"I...I grew up here around here."

He cocks an eyebrow. "I'm guessing you and Jean came here?"

Although she feels her eyes stinging, she manages to deflect his question. "Is the cave suitable?"

Alastair looks down into her misted eyes. "This place must mean a great deal to you. But what you're doing for your country and Jean? It's a sacrifice, but crucial."

"I know you're right. I just can't put him out of my head."

"Nor should you. He'll always be with you, especially here." He pauses, then adds softly, "I'm sure he'd approve of how you're honoring him."

Sylvie's intake of air is sharp, painful, searing. She stands motionless for a moment, staring up into Alastair's kind face with his intense but gentle smile. Then she adds, in a strong, clear voice that reverberates throughout the cave, "You're right. We need to avenge Jean's death. I only hope we do him justice."

CHAPTER TWENTY-SIX

Toulouse. October 1940

SYLVIE MUMBLES ONE curse after another as she tries to locate the entrance to the convent in Toulouse. The impenetrable configuration of ancient stone buildings towering around her is more complex than all the buildings in her little village of Foix put together. She looks through the lofty and menacing iron fence with its ornate, filigree spikes. She feels as if she were a prisoner—except she's on the outside looking in at the medieval church and can't find the way inside.

Are the spikes on the gate there to point the way to God? To protect the religious people inside? Or to taunt those like her, who would enter with a less-than-pure heart? But no, Father Michel has agreed to the ruse. She'll pretend to be a nun in order to live in the convent, wait for the airmen in the church garden, then escort them up to the cave. Uncle Claude and the others will take them over the mountains in convoys to Spain and safety. She and Father Michel will have to lie to the nuns at St. Volusien and everyone in Foix, but it will be a falsehood for the greater good. She crosses herself—God-willing no one will come to harm for this particular sin of hers.

After some hesitation, she chooses to go left and briskly walks alongside the fence, lightly brushing the bars with her hand. The image of a prison creeps back into her consciousness as she thinks about the nuns inside. With all their strictures and limitations, aren't the women who take the veil in a kind of prison? She shudders, imagining being pent up in a convent cell, unable to roam the mountains. Well, she's not really going to be a nun, so she'll be free, and anyway, it's only for as long as the war lasts. But how long will that be? She slows her pace, then stops, ostensibly to admire a rose bush but really to consider reconsidering. Perhaps it's a good thing she's worn her trousers after all, as the Mother Superior is likely to reject her out of hand. Then she won't have to perpetrate this blasphemous charade.

A deep voice, full of mirth, booms in her ear. "They're lovely this time of year, aren't they?"

Sylvie, enmeshed in her internal debate, ignores the voice. But it persists.

"We have many more in the cloister. Would you like to see them?"

Sylvie turns to see an exceedingly tall and stout nun, her heavy black rosary beads swinging jauntily from the woolen belt at her waist. She's dressed in a floor-length black habit with a starched white guimpe or "bib" covering her neck and shoulders. Her face and several chins are framed in a white coif around her head, with a black veil on top that cascades around her wide forehead and down past her shoulders. Her features are heavily creased with age, although she has two refreshingly youthful dimples, one on either side of a mouth that seems to be perpetually either smiling or talking in a generous and welcoming way. Sylvie is astonished by her warmth and informality.

The nun surveys Sylvie's trousers and cap then smiles broadly. "You like to wear comfortable clothes," she spouts. "You'd be surprised how comfortable these habits are. I always hated those infernal corsets. Talk about the circles of Hell." She crosses her hands in front of her, rocks back and guffaws, patting her ample middle as her beads swing up and down rhythmically. "But, tight as they were, they never reined me in." Suddenly, she thrusts her arms wide. "Not even an inch, if you know what I mean." The nun leans back, letting loose a boisterous laugh.

Sylvie decides this is a woman she'd like to know better. "Sister, I'd love to see the roses in the cloister. Another time?" She looks to the right and left along the iron fence. "I can't find my way in. Perhaps you can help me. I've come to talk to Mother Superior."

"Well, you've found her." Mother Superior chuckles, then takes on a serious tone. "You must be the young woman Father Michel wrote me about. He's a scrappy one, that village priest. He's got a lot of guts to agree to this. Come."

Mother Superior briskly leads Sylvie through a nearby gate, camouflaged in plain sight within the ornate iron fence. Sylvie is a fast walker, but she can barely keep up. They enter a corridor and pass several willowy, pale nuns in black, as well as some very young women Sylvie gathers are novices since they wear mid-calf-length gray skirts and short white veils. They twitter pleasantly and bow to Mother Superior. Farther along, they pass a chapel where three novices lie prostrate, face down, arms stretched out to the sides, their bodies in the shape of a cross. Sylvie knows this practice will be part of learning to be a nun, but she instinctively recoils.

Mother Superior doesn't break stride, although she lowers her voice, "I don't demand they do this for all the hours they choose. One hour, that's it. The rest is up to them."

Sylvie's questioning eyes find those of Mother Superior, which have become bright blue twinkles in the voluminous flesh of her face. The elderly nun stops short. "Something instituted way before I came. Personally, I think it's barbaric. And not especially sanitary, my dear."

Sylvie opens her eyes wide, trying to suppress a laugh as Mother Superior takes off again at high speed. In minutes, they traverse the length of the convent and arrive at Mother Superior's office. Her desk is a large mahogany affair, heaped with mountains of papers spilling every which way. She rummages through one stack, then another, finally pulling a letter from the middle of a third precariously towering pile.

"Father Michel says you want to perpetrate a fraud on the Church," Mother Superior reads, her eyes sparkling as they narrow on Sylvie. "We all admire him for his commitment to his flock. But he's also been known to bend the rules. And—on occasion—not to turn the other cheek."

"I suppose that's a good thing?" Sylvie says weakly. She steals a glance around, uncomfortably surveying the room. All the furniture is oversized—perhaps because Mother Superior is so large herself. Sylvie sits on the enormous chair in front of the nun's desk, feeling foolish as her feet dangle. She squirms as a spate of childhood transgressions floods her memory. Out of sheer force of habit, she reaches hands out to be rapped by some unseen ruler but catches herself just in time and transports herself back to adulthood and her present mission.

Mother Superior's shelves are laden with books in French, English, Spanish, Latin and Greek, both religious and secular. Sylvie is surprised that they include titles of current fiction. A small, faded picture in a modest oval frame is perched on the only level, unoccupied space on her desk. Sylvie makes out Mother Superior in the photo, apparently in earlier days before becoming a nun, together with a handsome man and a small sweet-looking boy wearing a cowboy hat.

"My late husband, Samuel, and my little boy, Jonas," she answers Sylvie's unspoken question. "I loved my husband very much. But God saw fit to take him. Much too early."

"He was American?"

"You're surprised?"

"I didn't expect…"

"My husband's family was from Toulouse. He immigrated to the United States when he was a boy, although he returned to fight for the French in the Great War. The war to end all wars. Rubbish!" Mother Superior grabs the photo and reverently cleans some non-existent smudges on the picture. "He even survived Verdun. I met him in Toulouse right after the war, and we lived in California for ten years. Some years ago, he had heart failure, and I came home. Took my vows."

"I'm sorry."

Mother Superior smiles sheepishly, then checks one or two drawers before finding one empty enough to accommodate the photo. "I'm not supposed to keep such photos here in the convent. We renounce our past, you know. But I'm not a stickler for the rules, as Father Michel knows. Or you wouldn't be here."

She turns back to Sylvie. "Yes, well…our son still lives in California. Oh! And I have five grandchildren!" She sighs deeply, heaving her large bosom. "But, when I lost my husband, well…I know the loss you're coping with, my dear. I also know how important it is to get those bastards out of our country."

Sylvie is startled, even pleased, to hear the nun's blunt language. Just as she's thinking this isn't going to be so difficult after all, Mother Superior lobs a stern warning. "You've got a dung heap of hard work to do before you can pass. But, after I'm done with you, no one—not even your own family—will suspect you're anything but a full-fledged nun."

Sylvie feels a sharp stab of regret. Her uncle, of course, has to be in on it, but she hadn't thought about having to lie to Étienne, to her sister Louisa, and especially to her niece Isobel. "I'm not very good at lying."

"Well, you're going to have to start. If you're concerned about not blabbing to your family, think of it as protecting them. What they don't know can't hurt them, and I mean that literally." Mother Superior chuckles at her joke, her enormous black veil bouncing up and down on her expansive white bib. The image of a grinning whale briefly crosses Sylvie's mind.

"My family might need protecting. My sister is married to a Jewish doctor."

"Things are getting bad for the Jews. There're already calls to limit the number of Jews in various professions. Law. Medicine. Even pharmacists." She leans forward, whispering something that can easily be heard in the next room, "If you ask me, the French go along with the Huns because too many see the Jews taking their jobs. And they want to be rid of them, especially the foreign Jews."

"My sister's husband isn't foreign. He was born in France. He was a doctor on the front in the Great War. Decorated for his valor."

"That's good. For now, Vichy's less concerned about French Jews. But we hear the distinction won't hold for long. Vichy wants to ingratiate itself with Hitler, who wants to rid the world of Jews. You know about the Jewish Statutes?"

"We heard something of them up in my village."

Mother Superior gets up abruptly and angrily paces—three of her long steps easily make it across the room. "Jews can't stand in ration lines. How are they supposed to get food? They can't make telephone calls from public booths. Absurd."

Sylvie is stunned to see such anger from a nun. Mother Superior continues her rant, "They have especially strict curfews. The *Milice*, those damned collaborator French gendarmes, are rounding up middle-aged men, hauling them off to synagogues and making them drop their pants. If they're circumcised, they take them away. No questions!"

"We hadn't heard any of that up in Foix."

"Does your sister have property? Art, that kind of thing?"

"Yes, they're very cultured."

"The Germans have a great affinity for paintings. Not degenerate stuff like the Impressionists." She flutters, "Picasso—whom I adore— he captures the inner essence of women, don't you think? All those interesting shapes and angles. Anyway, they're calling them *degenerates* and burning anything they don't like. Older, more valuable stuff? In Paris, they're carting it away by the truckload. Stocking the homes they just confiscated with the art they just stole from the very same Jews."

Sylvie squirms, unable to imagine anyone hating her sister's family so much they'd arrest them and confiscate their beautiful home and valued possessions.

"My sister isn't Jewish by birth. She converted when she married the doctor."

"She might be safe if she divorces him right away. Even so, any children will be considered Jewish." She shakes her head vigorously, her veil swishing. "Vichy goes and puts out some standards, then the local *Milice* bastards do something to one-up them. Make them stricter in order to cast a wider net. It's a race to the bottom. You must tell them to leave the country if they have anywhere to go."

Sylvie sucks in a sharp breath, overwhelmed by the thought of losing her family to such an unjust cause.

"Sylvie, I know this feels like a lot right now. I also know from Father Michel's letter, you've always had a strong faith in God. That will fortify you for what's to come. You understand?"

Mother Superior seems as strong as the iron fence outside and with just as many spikes. Sylvie nods, although she feels a stab of fear that she might not be up to the task.

"You'll have to put away those clothes, of course. And we all shear off our hair."

Sylvie slowly removes her cap. As her hair cascades down her back and around her shoulders, she whispers, "I hadn't thought of that."

"Well, my dear, you're not really taking your vows. So I suppose we can find a way to hide all that unruly hair inside your coif while you're here with me. But we can't let the others see. And when you leave, that kind of oversight could pose a serious risk if you come under suspicion."

A memory floods back—Jean stroking her hair, laying it out in spokes on the stone in the cave before they made love. Sylvie winces. "May I think about what to do about my hair, Mother?"

"Of course. One more thing. You must choose a name. You'll need to be Sister…what?"

Sylvie has given this some thought. She hops down from her chair and says, without hesitation, "Geneviève. I'll be Sister Geneviève."

"Who led the charge to expel the Huns from Paris? It was in the fifth century, something like that. They made her a saint."

"If I can accomplish even the smallest fraction of—"

"You will, my dear." Her clear blue eyes gleaming, Mother Superior claps Sylvie encouragingly on the back. "If I have anything to do with it."

Sylvie fastens her gaze onto Mother Superior, enormously grateful to come under her protection. Here is a knowledgeable ally who will help her deceive the Nazis. This woman understands what she's lost and how desperately she wants to succeed in her mission. Even more importantly, Mother Superior is someone Sylvie can turn to for spiritual guidance. Someone who will throw her a spiritual lifeline—which Sylvie feels certain she'll need to survive.

CHAPTER TWENTY-SEVEN

Foix. October 1940

H ÉLÈNE IS TOUCHED to see how proud Étienne is to show her the way up to the watermill. Fog drifts in curls down the mountainside as damp, chilled air envelopes them, making the path treacherously slick. Étienne is gallant, her champion, glued to her side as he insists on navigating her over the steeper patches, even as she's quite capable of managing them herself.

She and Gérard always wanted children. As a nurse, she was often assigned to surgery because she was so unflappable. But it was the natal unit that she gravitated towards. First the babies, then the children—the girls with their bright red hoops and the boys recklessly kicking their soccer balls. In a way, Étienne, awkward, serious, and headstrong, is becoming the son she never had.

When they arrive at the watermill, Étienne proudly enters as if he's in charge. While Marcel lies asleep in the corner under a pile of old blankets, Étienne introduces her to Jacques and Ernst. She immediately detects a not-so-subtle competition among the boys for her attention.

"I brought you our nurse to see to your wounds," Étienne boasts.

"I'm her assistant in the infirmary. I help her with the medicines and bandages."

Hélène is quite pleased that Étienne has learned a great deal, attending her every move in the camp. He anticipates what size strips of bandages she needs to treat each limb, and he cleans up and organizes her supplies to put into her large satchel. Hélène prefers to do the latter herself but doesn't have the heart to tell him. She's amazed that, at such a young age, the fourteen-year-old is so adept.

Jacques acknowledges Étienne then quickly says to Hélène, "Please, could you see to Marcel right away."

Resisting the urge to examine the lightning-strike wound down Jacques's face, Hélène catches the urgency in the boy's voice and asks where she can clean up. Jacques shows them the water spout they've rigged.

Jacques says to Étienne. "I remember you from school. I was four years ahead."

Étienne shrugs. "I...I don't recall."

"Always with your head in a book." Jacques surreptitiously winks at Hélène. "You must have learned a lot to be so helpful to Madame Hélène."

"Oh yes, now I remember you," Étienne says.

Hélène thinks how nice it is of Jacques to play the politician and put Étienne at ease. The last thing she wants is for the boys to quarrel over her.

After they wash, Hélène goes to Marcel and is immediately alarmed to see him shivering as well as sweating. She notices a red welt streaking from under his shirt up to his neck. She whispers to Jacques, "I thought he just had a cough. Help Étienne get his shirt off, quickly."

Hélène is horrified to see jagged red streaks on Marcel's torso. His face is severely blotched, and when they sit him up, he coughs so hard she thinks he might blow out a lung. He hardly seems aware of her when she says, "Marcel, I'm sorry we don't have any sulfa medication.

But my own remedies can be quite effective." She turns to Étienne. "Please, some poultice. Soak the bandages in it and bring it as fast as you can. And some of the strongest herb tea you can make. Then bring the kettle over so we can steam his lungs."

Jacques and Ernst wait anxiously for Hélène's prognosis. She tries to hide how alarmed she is at the seriousness of the situation. *This boy will most likely die because we haven't got proper medications.* She tries to spare the other boys her rage, instead offering a more leveled, professional response. "His cough probably indicates pneumonia. But I'm afraid he might have a touch of blood poisoning in that arm." What she does not tell them is that this has most likely spread to the rest of his body.

Ernst wails, "He was fine a day or two ago."

Jacques interjects, "He had a cough, but—"

"His cough lowered his resistance. It's not your fault." She chews her bottom lip rather than tell them the truth—blood poisoning comes on notoriously fast. He probably got the arm infected, and nothing can prevent it once it starts. Nothing except high doses of sulfa and even then...

Étienne helps Hélène wrap Marcel's arm and neck in the poultice. Marcel is limp and moans slightly, awakening just enough to swallow the tea. Hélène and Étienne then tend to the wounds Jacques and Ernst suffered. It's astonishing that Jacques's wound down his face is actually healing rather well, considering its severity. As Hélène and Étienne wash up, Alastair strides into the watermill, with Claude and Louis fast on his heels.

Red-faced from exertion, Claude makes the introductions. Hélène somberly approaches Alastair, kissing him on both cheeks. "I've heard a great deal about you, Alastair."

"And I of you." He turns to Étienne. "This must be Étienne. I admire your sister very much. I see you're doing your part here as well."

Claude claps his nephew on his slender back. "The boy's become invaluable, haven't you?" Claude turns to Jacques and Ernst. "Anyone hungry? Of course you are!"

Hélène smiles as Jacques and Ernst playfully grumble about how the food is so horrible, and there's never enough. But she hears an edge to Louis's voice as he challenges Alastair. "I wish you'd let us shoot some pheasant. Squirrels, at least. Trapping hares hardly brings enough food."

Alastair counters, "Gunfire would attract too much attention."

Claude jokes to Alastair, "Don't mind Louis here. He likes to shoot things up. Anything that moves. Or doesn't." He turns to Louis. "My friend, you know how sound carries in the thin mountain air."

After they say goodbye, Louis and Claude can be heard arguing softly as they head back down to the village.

Meanwhile, Alastair asks Hélène to speak with her outside. The fog is denser now, laying out in thick fingers across the valley floor. They walk a few meters down the misty path, alongside the waterfall.

She stops short, coarsely whispering, "I hear from Sylvie you've set quite a task for them. You must know they're just elderly men and boys."

Alastair gently counters, "They're up to it. We've all got to be up to it. The best way to defeat the Germans right now is to organize from within. To provide massive disruptions when the invasion comes."

"If it comes."

"It will. Eventually. And we've got to prepare. For the present, we can only bomb so many factories. That has some effect on the Nazi war machine but doesn't lessen the stranglehold they have over France and Belgium and—I needn't go on."

Hélène, feeling increasingly beleaguered, raises her voice. "We're doing as much as we can to take care of the refugees. And I can try to treat the airmen you intend to bring here. But we've no medicines." She balls her fists, struggling to control her temper. "What am I supposed to do with no medicines?" Looking around to ensure they're alone, she urgently whispers through gritted teeth, "That boy is going to die without them."

"There'll be parachute drops. Canisters of supplies. Guns. Medicines. Tell us what you need, and we'll have them dropped in."

"How soon?"

"Very soon. Around the full moon."

"That won't be soon enough for Marcel."

"I'm sorry, I am. It's the best we can do. Meanwhile, the watermill here remains a staging area, but we're moving this outpost further up. Claude, Louis, and I have just come from looking at a large cave. It has a fresh supply of water."

"A cave you say? For wounded men?"

"It's quite dry inside, actually. And they'll be squarely out of the elements. Not like here."

"A field hospital in a cave? That's absurd." She stomps a few paces down the path, nearly slipping on the fallen leaves. He grabs her arm to help her. She says, "I suppose we don't have a choice. I'll write up a list of medicines before I leave."

As she starts back towards the watermill, Alastair steps in front. "I'm sorry, but there's something more we need from you."

She's tall, almost his height, and stares directly at him, searching his face. The mist is thick, and she can feel light droplets landing on her high cheekbones. He makes a small movement with his hand as if to brush them away, then stops, apparently thinking better of it.

"We have to ask you something. It's a bit unsavory, you could say." He rapidly adds, "But I assure you, it's absolutely necessary."

She looks askance.

"Major Spitzer is billeted in your house?"

She nods slowly, uncertainly.

"How do I put this? We want you to get information from him. Troop reinforcements. Movements in Southern France. That sort of thing."

"He's not going to tell me that."

"Well, now, here's the point. We need you to get, ah, close enough

185

to him so he'll feel comfortable telling you." He gets the last words out in a rush, then pauses.

It gradually dawns on Hélène what he's asking. Involuntarily, she steps back a few feet, and he has to grab her hand, lest she slip onto the rocks and slide down into the crevice.

She snaps, "You want me to sleep with him?" She flings Alastair's hand away and hisses at him, "I'm a married woman. My husband is God knows where in some prisoner of war camp. Or on some hard labor duty. And you ask this of me?" She starts to run back to the watermill, slips and has to put her hands down into the mud to steady herself.

Alastair calls to her, "Wait. Please. Let me explain."

She turns to him, venom in her voice. "That man held a gun to my head. Made me bend down and pick up those damned yellow stars they make those wretched people wear—and I have to wear one as well."

He casts a glance at the yellow star sewed onto her jacket and winces.

"All the while his gun. At my temple." She struggles to breathe. "I'll never forget that for the rest of my life. Even now, when I hear a noise like a click, I imagine him cocking that gun, ready to blow my head off." She breaks into a cold sweat. "And I want to vomit." She takes a handkerchief from the pocket in her skirt and furiously tries to wipe the mud from her hands.

"I'm sorry for all you've gone through. This is asking too much."

"Yes, it is. I'm glad you realize that."

Alastair whispers, "Forget what I said."

Satisfied that he's dropped his request, she follows him back to the watermill to collect her things. She checks Marcel, who's still feverish, and gives Jacques orders to feed him as much herbal tea as he can drink and change his poultice every two hours. As she and Étienne prepare to leave, she says, "We'll come back tomorrow."

Étienne and Hélène start back down the slick and rocky path to Foix. They've only walked about fifteen minutes when Jacques and

Ernst catch up with them and call them back. When they arrive back at the watermill, Marcel has gone into convulsions. Hélène races to him, aghast to see white bubbles of foam rushing from his mouth, his body shaking uncontrollably.

Ernst paces while Jacques shouts, "What should we do?"

Hélène bends over the boy. "A clean cloth, Étienne."

Étienne, hands shaking, grabs a cloth from her satchel. She wipes foam from Marcel's mouth, trying to clear a passage for air. Cloth after cloth. She hardly has the foam under control when the bubbles stop.

Ernst is distraught. "He's dying, isn't he?"

Hélène shushes the boys. On her knees by his makeshift bed, she leans close into Marcel and whispers, "That's all right, my dear Marcel." She lovingly strokes his forehead with one hand and takes his hand in her other, even as his convulsions become greater, and his wheezing breath becomes sharp, fast, and agonized. Finally, his convulsions slow as Hélène continues to murmur over him.

She looks over at Étienne kneeling beside her, his eyes brimming. She knows what is coming but seeks to calm the boy by nodding to him. Then she turns back to Marcel and calmly, softly whispers, "You can let go. Your mother loves you, and you are her hero. Just let go." She can't tell whether Marcel has heard, but his eyelids flutter. He sits up, looks around, and gives a small wave to Jacques and Ernst.

Ernst is joyous. "He's going to make it." Jacques nods and claps Ernst on the back.

Marcel smiles at Hélène. Then his breath expels all at once, and his body falls back, going completely limp. Hélène keeps hold of his hand to comfort him as the last bit of life rushes from him.

Jacques shouts, *"Non, Mon Dieu....non..."* Ernst breaks down and cries. Étienne turns away, not wanting the others to see his tears amassing. Alastair takes off his beret in respect.

Hélène finally lets go of Marcel's hand and forces herself to get up and place his arms across his chest so he will stiffen in that beatific position. She presses his eyelids shut. She's coaxed many people to take their last breath, but rarely one so young and so recently as strong. If only the canister drops of medicines had already arrived, she might have saved him. Standing before Marcel, tears mist so heavily in her eyes that, when she turns to find Alastair among the others, she can barely make him out.

What he's asked of her is unthinkable. But the loss of this young man, for want of medicines, before he had the opportunity to enjoy his life and raise a family, is equally unthinkable. She looks over at Étienne, then Jacques and Ernst, all of them in tears, acting just like the young boys they are. They're already doing the unthinkable. Risking their lives to resist the *Boches*. She shudders, wondering if she has it in her to do what Alastair is asking. Once again, she recoils at the thought. Taking a deep breath, however, she makes a promise to herself that she will at least consider the unthinkable: to consider Alastair's horrific request in the name of the dead boy lying before her.

CHAPTER TWENTY-EIGHT

Toulouse. November 1940

SOBEL IS PRACTICING trills on her flute—and is especially happy to master a particularly difficult one—when she hears the knocker on the front door. Annoyed, she ignores it, assuming the butler will take care of it. But the intrusion has now interrupted her intense concentration, and her mind begins to wander, thinking about the war.

She's listened with increasing trepidation to her parents' horrific stories, as well as the distressing reports from Joshua about what's going on in Germany. While everyone says things are much worse in France's Occupied Zone, they also say it's only a matter of time before the Germans occupy the rest of the country as well. Then, they expect the same terrible things to befall her close-knit Jewish community in Toulouse. There's only one thing she can do—shut it all out, pick up her flute, and focus on her music.

She interrupts her technical practice to play a few bars of a Bach flute sonata she's been working on. A crackling fire does much to alleviate the wintry chill in their plush drawing-room. All is well. She continues, pleased with her clear tone, but then hears a loud murmuring in the front foyer. She stamps her foot. What is it now? As Isobel goes to see, the collar of her blue silk dress gently rustles against her long auburn curls. She hasn't ventured more than a meter towards the front door when she stops short at the sight of her Aunt Sylvie, dressed as a nun. *I must be hyperventilating. Hallucinating.* But no, it's Aunt Sylvie in person—in a long habit, with a small shoulder-length veil over a starched white collar of some sort that she wears close around her face. Isobel steps back in complete confusion, her ginger freckles reddening.

Sylvie smiles sheepishly. "Isobel, my darling, don't be shocked."

"Aunt Sylvie? Is that really you?"

"Yes. Let me explain—"

Isobel puts her flute down and struggles to say something polite, thinking of her mother's mantra: *if you can't say something nice...*"Yes, well, Aunt Sylvie, we knew you were upset to lose Jean, but we had no idea you were thinking of...of..."

"Taking the veil?" Sylvie gently says. "That's what they call becoming a nun."

Louisa comes into the parlor from the kitchen. "Isobel, the butler said we have a visitor." As Sylvie's back is towards her sister, Louisa stops short, flustered. "Sister, ah, may we help you?"

When Sylvie turns towards her sister, Louisa gasps, and Sylvie grins and says, "You really can call me sister now, dear Louisa."

Isobel stands looking down at her aunt and mother, wringing her hands as she waits for her mother's response. This is her beloved aunt, and she has no idea what this change will mean. They've never had a nun in their Jewish household before, and she's not sure if it's even allowed.

Meanwhile, Louisa stands immobile in the parlor, staring at the familiar face emerging from the folds of a nun's veil. Then she smiles broadly and takes Sylvie by the hands to sit on the sofa. "We've always known how religious you are, but this is indeed a surprise. I hope it's what you want."

Sylvie hugs Louisa. "Thank you for being so understanding."

Isobel interjects, a tear rolling down her face, "Does this mean we can't see you anymore, Aunt Sylvie?"

Sylvie shakes her head. "Not unless you don't want to see me. And I'm sure you think this long dress an improvement over my trousers, which I know you never liked."

Isobel sighs with relief. *My aunt doesn't seem so much changed after all.* She rushes to the couch and sits next to her, giving her a big hug.

Sylvie takes her niece in her arms. "Fortunately, they let me choose a small veil instead of that gigantic wimple the others usually wear. I would have felt like a spinning top in one of those."

With her aunt making light of the situation, Isobel feels more and more relieved.

Louisa's husband, Dr. Solomon, enters from his study, holding his glasses on their silk rope as if he'd been interrupted in his reading. He, too, appears stunned at Sylvie's transformation. "Well, now, ah, what have we here? Sylvie, is that you, my dear?"

"I'm to be known as Sister Geneviève now," she says, "if you can get used to that." She turns to Isobel with a smile. "But you can still call me aunt." Before any of them can say more, Sylvie quickly adds, "I know you have a million questions, but please, I've come for something very important. Something quite urgent."

Sylvie repeats Mother Superior's news about the new Jewish Statutes enacted by the Vichy French, as well as the German Ordinances against the Jews.

Louisa, clearly furious, says to her husband, "I knew this was going to happen."

Isobel doesn't fully understand, but she's alarmed—she's never seen her mother so angry.

The doctor is resolute. "This is not the Occupied Zone. We are still French here. No one in our community has ever been subject to the slightest religious discrimination."

Isobel flinches as her mother becomes even more enraged. "Solomon, can't you see the handwriting on the wall? We've talked about this before, but now it's different. We must make plans. Right away."

The doctor's voice is deep and firm. "And I've told you, they're not running us out of our home."

Isobel anxiously twirls a strand of hair around her delicate finger. She has no inkling who she should believe, as her parents have had so many recent arguments about whether or not to leave the country. But now, her mother's grave concerns are reinforced by her aunt. Her mother has nagged her father repeatedly about fleeing to England, where the doctor has some distant relatives. Isobel is horrified to see her mother get up from the couch, march right up to her husband, and reach up and grab him by the shoulders. "We have to go now. Right away, before they close all the borders. Through Marseilles."

Sylvie softly adds, "Louisa's right. It's only going to get more dangerous."

Isobel looks at her father; his red beard seems to flare, and his pale face appears on fire.

"Nonsense. We are French. Those Nazi bastards might arrest Polish Jews. Hungarian Jews. Russian Jews. But the French people aren't going to allow French Jews to be harmed. I was a doctor during the war. France gave me a medal." He is shouting now. "This is a civilized country."

Isobel has always believed every word her father ever uttered. Her mother has always deferred to him, as has everyone else in the family. He is the educated one—the one who treats patients and makes them well. He has special and enlightened knowledge and always encourages Isobel in everything she does. She is his daughter and has received, directly from him, his gift of superior intelligence. But now, her world is crumbling beneath her. *What if he's wrong and Mama's right? Maybe we should leave. But where would we go? And could I take all my music and my dresses with me?*

Suddenly, Isobel hears something she's never heard before. Her aunt is yelling at her father. "You may think no civilized society will tolerate it. But Vichy is complicit with the Nazis. And you know Hitler wants to rid the world of... well... they're already ordering roundups."

He yells back, "Of foreign Jews. Not French Jews. The world won't permit such treatment of people on their own sovereign soil."

Isobel's stomach grinds as her aunt becomes thoroughly exasperated. "It's the French who're doing the rounding up. They're not making any distinction. They've already set up camps outside Paris. They're not run by the Germans." Sylvie is shrieking now, "They're run by the French."

Isobel tries to imagine what it might mean to be in a camp. From the way her aunt speaks, it surely must be dreadful, not in the least the kind of camp she's been to where they played chamber music and learned composition. But what about the night her cousins came with her father's sister? They'd been driven out of Poland, carrying only what they were able, and her Uncle Jacob became deathly ill. People in the synagogue found them a tiny apartment in the back of the rabbi's house, but her uncle is still very sick. If that's what her mother expects to happen to them, maybe her father should reconsider—maybe they should leave right now. Plan it out as her father taught her to do with her studies. Organize, make outlines, and double-check. *Maybe we could ship some trunks ahead, leave with more of our possessions. But where would we go? I've only known this home. The synagogue. My music lessons...*Isobel pulls hard on one of her curls. *Would we be like my cousins and have to live on charity?*

Then Isobel considers something possibly even worse—if her father refuses to leave, what then? Would the Nazis be as brutal to them as people say? Torture and kill them? While her parents and aunt continue to argue, she slowly walks back to her music stand. She starts to hum her scales softly to herself. She imagines the fingering on her flute for the first movement of the Bach sonata she's learning as a surprise for her father. Anything...scales...a sonata...anything to shut it all out.

CHAPTER TWENTY-NINE

The Ardennes. November 1940

B Y NOW, JEAN'S head has stopped aching all the time, and images of roaming through the forest with Sylvie—olive-skinned, capable, and independent—fill him with warmth and a longing to get back home. But these remembrances are constantly spiked with horrific images of the fighting he saw during his time in the Ardennes. Scaling a forested rim. Stuka bombers shrieking. Firing down with what ammunition they had. New recruits and reservists terrified, scattering. The Germans, fording the river on pontoon boats, bringing their Panzers across. Where was the damn air-cover? Then blackness. Shivering. Retching in the night. *Mon Dieu! I've become my father—wretchedly immobile. How can I ever face Sylvie?*

He does his best to hide all this from Suzanne. He should leave before he humiliates himself before her and the children. And he hates himself doubly because he knows he's not strong enough right now to take off through the forest, with its dusting of snow marking the rapid onset of winter. It's unlikely he could make it home anyway, through what Suzanne says is German-controlled countryside. Meanwhile, she seems willing to have him share her bed, but he's filled with self-loathing at the thought: first of betraying Sylvie, then of being unworthy of Suzanne, who is risking everything to hide him from the German patrols. He demurs from her advances, saying they must observe decorum for the sake of the children.

To show his gratitude, however, Jean concentrates on caring for the children, teaching Hans to become an expert at trapping hares with the snare. This morning, he's amused to learn that Justine insists she wants to trap hares too, just like her big brother. Admiring the girl's pluck—she reminds him of Sylvie—he decides to take them both trapping, so he can supervise the boy and make sure he doesn't taunt or frighten his sister.

As he's rigging the snare, he whispers to Hans, "You are the older one. You have a responsibility to teach her things."

His white-blonde hair shines in the shafts of sunlight that penetrate the tall firs. The boy makes a face. "She's always messing things up."

Jean shakes his head. "I'll have none of that."

Justine grabs for the stick and the wire. "I want to do it. Show me how!"

"Shush," Jean gently says. "I'll show you. But we have to be quiet."

Jean finishes instructing them on how to set the snare when he hears Suzanne call. He immediately senses danger, as she's counseled him and the children never to make unnecessary noise, lest they attract the German patrol. Having already laid out several snares, he bends down to ask the children to hurry and help him gather their things. As he stands, he spies three German soldiers in the clearing, smoking and laughing, as they casually walk towards Suzanne's house. He quickly kneels and motions for the children to crouch down and be still. He holds his breath as he anxiously watches Suzanne greet the soldiers she—thankfully—seems to know. She laughs a bit with them, then disappears into the house, presumably to get them their usual supply of food. One of the soldiers leads a large shepherd dog on a leash. As the dog starts to whine and growl, the soldier yells at the animal to be quiet. Suzanne emerges with a basket of food and a bowl of water for the dog. She tries to pet the dog, but he barks at her, and she jumps back. The soldiers laugh and are just about to leave when a scream pierces the forest.

Justine starts to shriek, "Oh no...no...no...the hare."

Jean moves to put his hand over her mouth, but it's too late. He looks back a meter or so to where they had set the first of the snares and sees a hare, eyes bulging, neck nearly snapped in two by the wire. The hare is twisting violently, thumping its powerful hind legs and struggling to get free, which only tightens the wire around its neck, even more, slicing through and causing blood to spurt in a geyser.

The boy snarls at his sister, "Shut up, you idiot."

But there is no consoling Justine. She watches in horror as the animal thrashes wildly.

The three soldiers run towards the noise. Jean knows he should take off instantly and race into the forest, but he simply can't leave Justine shrieking like that—the soldiers will be angry and could very well do her and her brother harm. Two of the soldiers draw their rifles on him, while the third struggles to keep the dog from attacking the children. Justine is screaming hysterically now, and even Hans is howling. Suzanne runs around the men to swoop up the children. Heading back towards the house, she yells something in German at the soldiers, which he doesn't understand. The soldier with the dog pulls the animal back. Although she's carrying the children, the first soldier strikes her in the back of her head with his rifle butt, knocking her down and splaying the children out on the ground. She moans and holds her head while Hans grabs his sister, protectively shoving her behind him.

Meanwhile, the second soldier trains his rifle on Jean, indicating he should raise his hands or be shot. Jean feels a thundering of rage in his head but decides to comply for the sake of Suzanne and the children. He slowly raises his hands without speaking, hoping they won't realize he's French.

Suzanne, still on the ground, pleads with the German who hit her. Yelling at her, he puts his boot on her shoulder, pinning her. Angry, he shouts and motions to her and then to Jean. It must be that the soldier knew her husband and is furious to see another man with her at the farm. Hans takes a run at the soldier's boot to free his mother, but the soldier viciously kicks him, flinging him off and into the bushes. Justine, whimpering, hides her head while Suzanne screams and grabs the soldier's leg, trying to swing him off balance.

The soldier with the dog yells something, and everyone falls silent. Jean is now looking down the barrel of the rifle at the soldier who says something in German to him. Suzanne manages to sit up and tries to translate, so Jean can prove he's German too, but when Jean doesn't respond, the soldier breaks into a sadistic grin and says, "French?"

Jean makes no reply. Suzanne manages to yell something else to them, motioning in pantomime that he's deaf and can't understand. He catches on and puts his hands on his ears to confirm. By then, the soldier with the dog has crept around to his back. The soldier lets the dog loose a few steps on its leash. As the dog lunges, snarling savagely, Jean whips around at the sudden noise. The German holding the rifle on him steps back, laughing to have it so easily confirmed that Jean isn't deaf at all. Jean feels an agonizing pain shudder through him. Instinctively, he goes to tackle the soldier holding the rifle on him, but the other one comes up behind and knocks him on the head with his rifle butt. Jean doubles over, his rage now blinding him as he falls to the ground.

Two of the Germans tie Jean's hands in front of him, yank him up and force him to walk. He hurls an agonized yell back to Suzanne, "I'm sorry. Forgive me." As they march him off, the last he hears from behind him are the children wailing and Suzanne screaming, "*Nein... nein.*" Three gunshots ring out, piercing the dense forest. Jean collapses in agony.

CHAPTER THIRTY

Toulouse to Foix. November 1940

SYLVIE, DRESSED IN her habit and traveling cloak, anxiously plunges her hands inside her tunic, trying to keep them as still as any real nun would. She sits in the second class section of the railway car traveling from Toulouse back up to Foix, anxiously awaiting her return to the mountains. Despite the leaden and somewhat depressive winter sky, she becomes increasingly excited as the landscape gives way from its urban setting. She sees neatly squared meadows, bordered by hedges and delicate willows, terraces of gnarled barren vineyards, then as the train climbs higher, untamed forests of thick evergreens, spruce and fir, sprinkled with stands of white birch. As they pass through ever steeper terrain, a bright sun streaks through the clouds affording her the first sight of those craggy limestone mountains that always take her breath away, their peaks now covered with a fine crystalline powder from the winter's early snow.

Her new papers show her to be Sister Geneviève of the Order of Our Lady of Perpetual Help in Toulouse. But she desperately hopes to avoid attracting any kind of attention that might lead to the French police examining them. The train jostles and bounces as she nervously checks the rack above her to make sure the small, well-worn valise Mother Superior gave her remains secure. Inside, she's packed her trousers, jacket, and boots—clothes completely incongruous for a nun, which, if found, would surely lead to being taken in for questioning.

The train is crowded with German soldiers who make themselves comfortable, spreading out like they were on holiday. They converse animatedly and smoke, filling the carriage with a dense fog. The French in the car, mostly elderly men, women, and a few children, sit hunched and deadly silent on their benches. Watching the soldiers' arrogance, Sylvie clenches and unclenches her fists under her tunic. She turns her head towards the window, so her veil hides her face. She must avoid seeing someone from Foix who might recognize her and be surprised to see she's become a nun—that could arouse suspicion. The train makes several unannounced stops, which the other passengers seem to ignore, but Sylvie's anxiety surges lest the sudden jerking dislodge her valise—she doesn't want to call attention to herself by standing to secure it further.

Sylvie is relieved when the train finally pulls into her familiar station of Foix, only a little more than two hours behind schedule. She's elated that she's made the trip without incident. But then she sees a pair of German soldiers patrolling the station platform nearest the exit, their dogs sniffing passengers and luggage for anything suspicious. As the train lurches to a stop, her stomach pitches. She gingerly rises, smoothing her habit and cloak. Standing on tiptoe, she's reaching for her valise, when a slim German soldier, no more than twenty, quickly stands and blocks her way. She lets out a tiny gasp, then holds her breath.

He asks in heavily Germanic accented French, "Sister, you need some help for you?"

Her eyes widen as he lifts the suitcase and places it down. She moves to take hold of the valise, but he keeps it, gallantly motioning for her to pass ahead of him and exit the train. Rather than protest, she stays quiet, forcing herself to nod her head demurely. An inner fury rips through her—this humility is entirely foreign to her, having been encouraged by her father to stand tall and look everyone straight in the eye. She manages to calm herself as he smiles a handsome, broad smile and pantomimes that the suitcase is quite heavy for her to carry, but he can easily handle it.

She lifts her floor-length habit to climb down the carriage steps, briefly totters, then grips the rail. She swears under her breath, "Why didn't I practice more walking downstairs in this damned habit?" Realizing she's been muttering, she makes a small sign of the cross and mumbles a slightly louder prayer for the benefit of the soldier, as if she's relieved at having arrived.

Once on the platform, she turns to find the soldier descending closely behind her. With an expansively chivalrous flourish, he hands her the valise. Eyes still downcast, she meekly smiles and nods her gratitude. The soldier bows goodbye and joins his comrades. Out of the corner of her eye, she sees Father Michel holding back until the Germans surrounding her have dispersed. Her clumsiness with her habit on the train steps will likely occasion some teasing from the good-natured priest, but she's immensely grateful that he's meeting her. This is the first time she'll be greeting the villagers in Foix in her new guise, and she's thankful for his personal escort to the convent.

As he greets her with a broad smile, she's alarmed to see creases of worry on his face and pouches under his eyes. Things have obviously not gone well while she was away—all the more reason for her to pursue this perilous course.

He makes the sign of the cross to bless her. "Sylvie, it's good to have you back." After kissing her on both cheeks, his tone turns light and playful. "I trust you and Mother Superior got along?"

"Quite the character. Thanks for warning me." Rather than laughing out loud as she normally would, Sylvie forces herself to enjoy a quiet chuckle with him. She whispers, "You were right Father, she's a remarkable woman. I couldn't have made the transition without her guidance."

"I'm glad you took guidance from someone. Must be a new experience."

She drops her head to give him a smirk surreptitiously, then adds sincerely, "I appreciate all that you're doing, Father."

He steals a look at the German soldiers posted throughout the station and whispers, "The less we speak of it, the better." Then louder, "May I help with your luggage, Sister?"

They make it past the soldiers and the dogs without incident and head across the river into town. As they pass villagers she's known all her life, the priest deflects their inquisitive stares and responds to their questions.

"Sylvie? Is that you, my dear?" An elderly woman glances at her habit, at Father Michel, then back at Sylvie. "Forgive me...I...I didn't know that..." the woman's voice trails off. The priest readily acts his part. "Madame, this is Sister Geneviève now. We all wish her well in her new life with us here at St. Volusien."

Some express surprise at how suddenly Sylvie has made her decision and how quickly she was able to take her vows. The priest has an answer for this as well: "Mother Superior saw fit to expedite things so Sister can continue her important work with the refugees here in Foix."

Sylvie's story spreads rapidly, and people seem pleased for her. She's always been known as a good Catholic, and having lost parents not so many years ago as well as the man she was to marry, it seems logical for her to take her vows. But she feels a stab of guilt with each lie to each well-wisher.

When they arrive at St. Volusian, Father Michel takes her around to the entrance of the convent. They are met by Sister Paul, the convent administrator, a slender, brittle, and intense woman in her fifties.

Father Michel sets the valise down and takes Sylvie's two hands in his. "Sister Paul will show you to your quarters, Sylvie—ah! I mean, Sister Geneviève." He laughs. "I will see you at Vespers."

She looks directly at him, saying in a strong voice, "Thank you, Father." Then catching herself in front of Sister Paul, she casts her eyes modestly downward and murmurs, "I appreciate the escort from the train station."

As he starts to leave, he suddenly stops and turns back. "I almost forgot, Sister Geneviève, when you get to your cell, be sure to look at the beautiful roses."

Sylvie gives him a puzzled look but just nods.

Sister Paul leads the way to her cell, a moment she's been dreading. Sure enough, as Sister Paul opens the door, thick with heavy wooden planks and iron crossbars on top and bottom, Sylvie feels her knees weakening.

Sister Paul says briskly, "Sister Geneviève, let me know if there is anything else you need." She stands aside, waiting for Sylvie to enter.

As Sylvie walks into her cell, the enormity of the change in her life overcomes her. The small space, with its walls of thick stone, immediately closes in on her. There is a single iron bed with a crucifix above, a stark porcelain washbasin, a small trunk at the foot of the bed, and a *prie-dieu*—kneeling bench. A modest wooden table with a brass lamp on top serves as both bedside end table and desk. A tiny cloistered window, carved into the thick stone, with latticed iron bars across it, looks out onto the garden. Sylvie immediately rushes to the window, and with her back to Sister Paul, gulps down several deep breaths. Dizzy, she hangs onto the bars, desperately trying to keep herself upright. Her eyes come into focus as the afternoon sun casts a sparkling bright light on the roses that clamber over the trellises. *Thank the Lord for the roses in this beloved garden! Red and white glorious symbols of resilience!!* She feels a fervor that helps counter the swirl of doubt that's plagued her ever since she first embarked on this mission.

Sister Paul brings Sylvie up short, saying bitterly, "I gather you convinced Father Michel you deserved a window into the garden. I hope you appreciate it."

Sylvie turns, surprised. "I trust I'm not putting anyone out."

Sister Paul replies dryly, "We are trained not to take notice of such things."

"I'm sorry." Sylvie doesn't know what else to say—she doesn't want to make an enemy, but she's desperate to keep the windowed cell to counteract her surging claustrophobia. Clearing her thoughts, she realizes, of course, Father Michel has arranged for her to be assigned this cell because she needs to be able to look into the garden where the airmen will arrive.

Sister Paul quips, "No matter. Vespers in four hours, then supper. Tomorrow, Father Michel will assign your duties and chores." She turns to leave, managing a wan smile.

Sylvie quickly replies, "Thank you, Sister Pa—." Before she can get the rest out, Sister Paul has gone, the heavy solid door slamming behind her.

Sylvie is alone. A shock of panic courses through her. *What have I done? I'm an imposter, putting everyone here in danger.* She flings her traveling cloak onto the spartan bed. She wants to throw off her habit and run down the stone corridors to ask forgiveness of Sister Paul and Father Michel. But she stops to contain herself—she must see this through.

Sylvie paces the cell, counting the steps marking each side, then does it again just to make sure. From now on, this is her circumscribed space. As the damp cold from the thick stone walls seeps into her, she seeks the comfort of prayer and goes to the kneeling bench. Taking the rosary from her waist, she starts her first round of ten Hail Marys, desperately hoping prayer will bring warmth and solace. But when she closes her eyes, she sees Jean in the cave. Then the two of them, lying entwined, their passion at its peak. A warmth invades the dank cell, and, sighing deeply, she allows it to fill her despite her intent to use prayer for that purpose. She stands abruptly, the rosary falling to the stone floor with a clatter. How could she allow herself these blasphemous feelings in this reverent place?

Distraught, she turns to unpacking her belongings, transferring them to the trunk at the foot of her bed. She takes her father's cap from the valise and turns it around in her hands, longingly picturing herself roaming freely over the mountainside. Then she takes out a small picture of Jean in a silver oval frame. She knows she shouldn't be keeping this, but Mother Superior has a picture of her late husband. She didn't feel she had to renounce every aspect of her previous life, so why should she? As she stares at the picture, Sylvie feels strengthened, her resolve firm to avenge Jean's death. She knows the desire for revenge is inconsistent with her new identity as a nun, but she refuses to worry about that now—especially when she needs all the courage she can muster to follow her path.

She gently puts the picture into the trunk and kneels by the bed to pray for the strength to accomplish her mission. As she brings her hands together, she focuses on the slender gold band on her ring finger that serves to bind her to Christ as his bride. A voice screams within her, "I should have been Jean's bride, not Christ's." She crashes down on the stone floor, a low moan growing into a torrent of sobs. She pounds her hand on the stone floor, attempting to crack the gold band. She's bruising her hands, but she doesn't care—she just wants to fracture the ring. Finally, she curls up on the floor, silently howling, too wounded to allow any sound to escape.

She lies on her side for some time, breathing heavily, then manages to get up and walk to the window. As she stands there, streaks of the mid-afternoon sunlight fall onto one, then another of the rose bushes on the trestles. The roses! Sturdy in the face of harsh winters. Ever climbing upwards, seeking the sun. Never turning back down the trellis. That must be the message Father Michel was trying to send when he left her earlier. She slows her breathing and smooths her habit, then turns from the window to examine her ring. Relieved, she finds only a few scratches, although both her hands are bruised. She accepts this as penance for the sin of making love to Jean—but still, she would do it all over again—and over yet again.

Sylvie has to get out of that cell right now. She'll feel better about all of this when she sees her uncle, Alastair, and the others whose lives are depending on her. Looking up at the sun above the mountains, she calculates she can make it to the cave and back while it's still light. To Hell with the vespers and supper!

She hurriedly slips off her habit, dresses in her trousers and boots, and puts the habit back on. Mother Superior purposely had it made voluminously enough to hide her clothes beneath. Sylvie also kept her small knapsack for her cap and jacket, as well as for stowing her habit, when she is safely away from the church.

Now, how to get out? When Father Michel took his leave of her, he said something about the rose bushes. Sylvie hurries to the window and examines it. She discovers a latch where the window sill is attached that releases the iron bars. This enlarges the length of the window by about half a meter—just big enough for her to get through. She'll hide behind the trellises and escape through the concealed garden gate that she used before with Alastair. Now that she has a plan, she straightens up her cell—it's not nearly as confining as she'd first imagined. She opens the window, breathes in the sweet scent of the indomitable roses in the garden, and inches herself out.

CHAPTER THIRTY-ONE

Northern France. November 1940

JEAN IS ROUGHLY hefted to his feet as the shots killing Suzanne and the children reverberate in his skull. He howls and struggles, but the soldiers overpower him. He lets loose his anguish as they depart, leaving their bodies to rot without a proper burial. Jean pleads with them to let him dig their graves, but they pretend not to understand and shove him along. *I'm responsible for their deaths. Do I really deserve to survive?* He reasons he could fight back so hard they'd have no choice but to shoot him. That's all he can think about as they march him, hands tied in front, all day through the forest, then along back lanes. When to lunge at them? Could he survive attacking all three of them before the dog would shred him to pieces?

Downed electrical wires hang here and there across narrow roads with deep ruts. Every time he stumbles in the uneven furrows, they kick him along, shoving him dangerously close to some of the live wires. Perhaps he should just run into one of those wires. It would all be over so quickly—a better death than being mauled by the dog. *No...one more step...something might turn up...some way to escape.*

Just when he's certain his legs, rippling with spasms, will completely give out, they arrive at a farmhouse. In the dimming evening light, he sees that its beige stucco walls are pitted and cracked by dozens of bullet holes. As he gets closer, he makes out that the dark red smears on the walls are blood, presumably from firing squads. He's seen plenty of blood when he smuggled supplies to the anti-fascist Republicans in Spain, but he struggles to keep his anxiety in check, as he's never been taken prisoner and faced a firing squad wall himself.

Jean winces to see six French men, hands tied as well, huddled on the ground. Four are French soldiers, wearing filthy, tattered uniforms. The other two are elderly men in rough civilian clothing, most probably farmers who've done something to get arrested, maybe even hidden the French soldiers. Several German soldiers carrying rifles saunter back and forth in front of the prisoners, smoking and occasionally snickering. The soldiers who brought him throw him on the ground next to the others, none of whom acknowledge him in any way.

The weather has turned cold, with a chilling mist thickening the air and rain threatening to come in torrents. He has little hope they might be allowed some shelter when the downpour begins, but is determined to keep his anger in check and be as docile as the others appear, then wait for an opportunity to escape. As it darkens into night, a large uncovered lorry drives up, its low beamed lights barely penetrating the thick layer of fog rising over the wild forested landscape.

The French prisoners are forced to jump up into the back and are assigned places on the open benches behind two soldiers wearing oil-slickers. They take off, bumping furiously on the deeply pocked road and stopping every now and then to pick up more prisoners. The two soldiers at the front of the benches have poles, and when they come to fallen wires, they hold them up and yell. They duck down, motioning for the prisoners to do the same, lest the wire snaps someone's head off. Despite the jostling, some men give into their exhaustion, keeping their heads down as they sleep in that cramped position.

But Jean is wide awake, his mind still screaming over how he'd let Suzanne and the children down. His grief rises high and tight in his throat, nearly strangling him each time he snaps his head down to avoid the wires. He considers not even lowering his head—just allowing the wires to decapitate him, like that hapless hare. Throughout the rest of the night and the next day, every bump in the road pounds his anguish deeper into him, as he vehemently wishes he'd been shot instead of Suzanne and the children.

Prison Camp, The Vosges, France. November 1940

The lorry progresses along narrow roads as heavy rain during the night periodically soaks Jean and the prisoners, while the guards have slickers to keep them relatively dry. A foggy haze shrouds the mountainous horizon as the leaden sky begins to lighten. Jean strains to determine where they might be headed, but an oppressive canopy of firs obscures any glimpse of sun that might have indicated their direction. They traverse endless narrow roads with steep inclines, jostling them all day. Finally, a clearing appears, with two concrete posts serving as the entrance to a camp comprised of low concrete barracks on both sides and a towering smokestack in the distance, set against a steep mountainside.

A group of guards rushes out to meet them, shouting for the men to disembark. Hands still tied together in front, Jean jumps down and staggers a few steps, his balance precarious and legs cramped from sitting on the long journey. Suddenly, a truncheon strikes the back of his neck, sending a sharp pain searing through his head, spine, and down along the nerves in his legs and feet. The blow virtually paralyzes him, infuriating him, as he hasn't done anything to merit the attack. Even so, he has to marvel at the preciseness of the hit, producing the maximum result with a minimum of energy expended. Typical German efficiency, he notes bitterly, as the feeling in his legs starts to return and he is shuffled along.

As the other French prisoners scramble down, some appear to be randomly accosted by the guards, whom he can now see behind him dressed in black with red swastika insignias on their left arms. The blows don't seem to follow any pattern, most probably, he guesses, to instill a continuous state of fear, unassociated with any man's specific action.

Maybe he should object to the actions of the guards since he's technically a prisoner of war and entitled to humane treatment under the Geneva Accords. Then he thinks better of it since he might be considered a deserter because, after he awakened, he didn't actually try to contact his unit. Not that he was physically able to, or would have known how, given that the Germans were overrunning the north. He'll bide his time and see if any of the prisoners, wearing at least some remnant of their military uniforms, might be persuaded to argue the point.

In the dusk, Jean can barely make out the contours of the compound—a series of barracks surrounded by a tall barbed-wire fence with scrolls of wire on the top, leading to square observation towers in the corners. A large concrete smokestack is attached to a building on the left, while a flank of poplar trees lies beyond the barbed wire to the right, with distant mountains barely visible through the evening mist—not as high as those in the Pyrénées, and with softer, less jagged slopes. Jean guesses they might still be in France, more southeast, perhaps on the border with Germany. That might be a good sign, depending on how—or if—the French are still prosecuting the war.

Not having eaten or drunk anything since his arrest, Jean can barely swallow, as his mouth is so dry. Now that they've arrived, surely they'll be given food and water. But Jean's hopes for humane treatment abruptly end when the guards shuffle him down the length of the barracks and into a group of small cinderblock cells at the end, along a dank corridor with exposed light bulbs. The stench is savage, stinging his eyes. In Spain, he'd smelled the carcasses of dead horses, mutilated for their last scrap of meat along the River Ebro, and the gangrenous bandages of wounded men in makeshift tents in Zaragosa, but those odors, mercifully, were tempered by being outdoors. Here, the stink from the enclosed cells is putrid beyond anything he's ever experienced.

After untying his hands, the guards open one of the cell doors. Jean rubs the circulation back into his wrists and balls his hands into angry fists. He's stunned to see that four men, unshaven, unkempt, and filthy, already occupy the cell, sitting cramped tightly together on the damp floor, a space meant to hold two at most. There is only one small window high up in the airless cell. Groaning loudly, the others move aside as Jean is booted into the cell, followed by another man from his group.

The other arriving prisoner shouts to the guards as they turn to lock the cell door. "Food? When do we eat?"

The guard barks, "No more. *Appell. Appell.*" The new prisoner doesn't understand, so the guard screams, *"APPELL,"* while another guard strikes him in the head with his truncheon. The guards slam the metal cell door shut.

A short, emaciated man inside the cell, squashed next to the door, whispers in French, "He said, roll call. Tomorrow after roll call. We eat."

An older prisoner grimaces, his thick brown beard surrounding a toothy grin. Lumpy and bald with a massive chest, he good-naturedly nudges the smaller fellow. "You can't call it eating, my friend."

Having been booted by the guard to the back of the cell, and in the process, nearly tipping over a large bucket meant for defecation, Jean gets his bearings, sits up, and looks around. He eyes the single fold-down iron bunk along the right-hand side of the cell.

"Don't get any ideas, my friend," the large man barks. "I have survived in this cell the longest, so that's mine."

Jean holds his hands up. "No disrespect, my friend." Forcing a grin, he says to the men in the cell, *"Bonjour messieurs,"* as he positions himself next to the large man, hoping to find out what's going on in the prison camp.

Suddenly, a slot in the cell door opens, and two mess tins are flung inside. The large man motions to Jean and the newcomer to pick them up, saying, "Tomorrow morning, you get in line after us, clear?" Jean looks at the man and opens his mouth to say something but is interrupted by him. "Be careful. No talking in here. Spies everywhere." The large man surreptitiously looks around, growling under his breath and barely moving his mouth when he speaks. "Those guards. Guys in the black uniforms. SS. Elite guard. Nasty sons a' bitches." Jean nods. The man turns away from the cell door, whispering, "I'm Albert Morceau, seventy-first Infantry. Old soldiers, called out of reserve."

"Jean Galliard, fifty-fifth Infantry." He furtively looks around. *"Merde,* Panzers. Kept coming and coming." His whole body shakes, and his face reddens as if a noose were tightening around his neck.

"Easy, my friend."

"The *Boches* left me for dead. Buried me alive, but I was rescued months ago. In the Ardennes."

"For God's sake, don't tell them that. They'll take you for a resister."

"A what?"

"Like that poor kid." Albert motions to a young barefoot boy, no more than sixteen, sitting on the floor against the wall. The souls of his feet are covered with crimson and white lumps of skin, oozing pus. "Idiot. They caught him putting sugar in the gas tank of one of their jeeps. Damn waste of sugar."

Jean nods at the boy, acknowledging his bravery. The boy scowls and turns towards the wall, a far-away, utterly defeated look on his face.

"Yeah, well, they blowtorched his feet. Wanted to know who else was in his resistance unit." Albert shrugs. "He kept telling them it was just a prank. Acted alone. They didn't believe him."

"Animals."

"Keep your voice down. We're not supposed to talk in here. You'll get us solitary."

Jean throws Albert a questioning look.

A guard in the hall clanks past the cell, adjusting his grip on his rifle. Jean and Albert stop speaking but resume after the guard passes.

"Solitary...like in an upright coffin. Five days. No light. You can't stand up or sit. You stagger out bent over for a week."

"What about the Geneva Accords?"

Albert's face falls into a horrific pile of flesh. "Means nothing here."

A banging sounds in the corridor.

Albert says, "Get ready now. They'll throw in some pallets of straw and call for lights out. Move your ass. Find a place on the floor. As far away from the shitter as you can."

Jean feels blood pooling in his head, throbbing at his temples, as he imagines being so tightly confined all night in this small cell. He wheezes and starts to shake, remembering the horror of waking up in that pile of bodies.

"No good praying to God here. Just pray everyone shows up for *Appell*. Roll call." Albert sneaks a look at the guards passing in the corridor. He whispers, "They give you a number when you came in?" Jean nods, so Albert continues, "Roll call tomorrow morning. You line up, five deep. They count off. These *Boches*—they get off, counting off." His toothy smile turns into a grin, then muffled laughter at his own joke. In a moment, his expression darkens. "One guy isn't at roll call, they sound the alarm. Send the dogs. Better you die out there than they catch you, bring you back, and let the pack shred you to pieces."

The guard outside blows a whistle. The cell door opens, and filthy straw pallets are thrust inside. While the men grab at them, Albert lowers his bed on the wall.

"*Licht aus*," the guards are shouting down the corridor. "*Licht aus*."

"Lights out," Albert says, then whispers urgently, "Find a spot." He winces. "Try to find a clean butt in this place. *Bonne chance*."

Waves of anger crest over Jean, as he can barely believe the chaos surrounding him. He and the other new arrival seem to have upset any semblance of order on the cell floor. With their tufts of straw, the men rapidly mill about him to choose their space.

His fury surges as he takes up the whirling motion of the crazed men. *Even a God-damned dog gets to lie down in peace.* Diving for a spot on the floor under Albert's bunk, he splays his arms out, trying to expand the millimeters of space he's claimed around him. Is this his punishment for causing the death of Suzanne and the children? Desperately fighting for a last bit of room, he convulses in panic. *How in God's name will I get through even one night in this hellhole?*

CHAPTER THIRTY-TWO

Foix. November 1940

For Sylvie, life in the convent is much more confining than she'd imagined. She finds solace, however, in adhering to the structure of morning and evening prayers that help clear her mind of the hardships she witnesses daily at the refugee camp. Each day, although she has to go up to the camp to help Hélène and Étienne take care of the destitute, she has an overwhelming desire to stay behind and kneel in her cell, saying her rosary, in a pain-numbing trance. All that gives her any sense of hope is climbing the mountain to be with her Uncle Claude, Alastair, and the boys, Jacques and Ernst.

As the British bombing of German industrial sites becomes increasingly essential to disrupt the Nazi war machine, Alastair tells them that they need to help establish escape routes for a growing number of downed pilots and crews. A rudimentary line of escape is hastily assembled from Brussels, through Paris, and then south. More and more ordinary Belgian and French farmers are spontaneously rescuing airmen by hiding them in barns, as they first hid Alastair. Other French—often young women—volunteer to escort the airmen down the line. As it's unlikely an airman can speak French, which means he'll be arrested if stopped even for routine questioning, these young women are vital. As Alastair reminds them, a couple traveling together is less likely to attract attention than a man traveling alone. Various routes through Southern France are established, including one to the west coast and another to the port of Marseilles. Alastair has been ordered to temporarily base in Foix to help establish a third route over the Pyrénées, then down the east coast of Spain to Barcelona, where the RAF will transfer the airmen to the Free French and the British armies staging in North Africa.

In the event they're shot down, the RAF has given their pilots and bomber crews instructions to work with the various French circuits. For those coming down through Foix, they are to make their way at dusk—between six and eight in the evening—to the garden of the Church of St. Volusien, where they will be met by a nun. They are provided a coded phrase for Sylvie to recognize them, and she anxiously awaits receiving her first airman. She moves her kneeling bench under the window to keep watch, then each night, as dusk approaches, she finds various excuses to sweep up the garden. Her knapsack, with her trousers and boots, is at the ready by the rear gate, and she keeps careful track of the German patrol, which takes about an hour to make its rounds around the village, including through the alley that passes by the church garden.

One evening, after a light dusting of snow, Sylvie uses a sharp hoe to tend some soil in the church garden. The sun is beginning to set, slanting down on the roses, coloring the red ones a deep magenta and the white ones a lush orange. Russet-colored oak leaves flutter about the cobblestones in the chilly wind.

Sylvie hears a thud and turns towards the wooden garden gate leading to the alley. Through a slat, she sees a man stumble, then collapse, just outside the gate. This isn't the protocol she's expecting, as airmen are supposed to come inside the gate that she keeps unlocked for them only between six and eight. Perhaps he's injured and could only make it that far and not into the garden? On the other hand, what if he's a German spy? She can hardly chance endangering the entire resistance network before it's even up and running. She finally decides to creep into the alley, carrying the hoe. The patrol passed forty minutes ago, so she calculates that she has about twenty minutes to deal with the situation. She leans down to see if he needs help, reasoning she's not really risking exposing her circuit, since any nun would perform such an act of mercy.

He is stocky, dressed in corduroy trousers worn at the knees. His heavy woolen jacket is frayed and dirty. It's hard to tell if he's twenty or forty, given that his beret is drawn over his eyes, and he has several days' growth of a light brown beard. He slumps on the ground, breathing heavily and holding his right leg.

As she kneels, he roughly grabs her arm, bringing her down to his face. He whispers urgently, in broken French, "Sister, the red roses in your garden are hearty."

A shock courses through her as she recognizes the code phrase. She's been expecting this, but when the moment actually comes, she can't recall the agreed-upon response. A look of terror comes over the man. Weakened as he is, he struggles to rise up, then wraps his hand around her throat.

Choking, she grabs his hand in both of hers. In a flash, she remembers the coded phrase and coarsely whispers, "But the white ones are even heartier."

He nods and lets go of her neck, flinching and grabbing his leg in pain. Sylvie looks around, praying that the patrol hasn't doubled back to check on the noise in the alley. She gives him the hoe to help him walk, using it as a weapon, if necessary. She's anticipated she might need a hiding place even within the garden and has fashioned a sturdy trellis, thick with roses, right inside the gate.

Suddenly, Sylvie hears the sharp retort of jackboots at the end of the alley. She motions him inside the gate, indicating he should hide behind the trellis, while she flattens herself against the inside garden wall. Blood roars in her ears, the sound mixing with the onerous clacking coming right up to the gate. The patrol stops and she holds her breath, silently beseeching the airman not to collapse while the soldiers stand just outside. She hears one of them murmur something, then sees the small glowing tail end of a cigarette flung back into the alley behind them as the soldiers pass.

Her terror uncoils itself from her gut as she gingerly opens the trellis. He's leaning all his weight on the hoe, barely standing.

"My angel," he says in halting French.

"Hurry. Can you walk?"

"With your help," he says. Then adds, motioning to the hoe, "And if I lean on this."

She guides him to the back gate by the river, the hem of her habit sifting through dense piles of fallen leaves. She picks up the knapsack she'd hidden, and together, they struggle down the steps into the damp stone passageway. Several meters along the river, she motions for him to stop and rest. She turns from him, whisks off her habit with her trousers underneath, stuffs the habit into her knapsack, and throws on her jacket and cap. He looks terribly confused, and Sylvie enjoys his reaction as well as the fact that she's just pulled off her first encounter.

Since Alastair and Claude have moved the outpost from the watermill up to the cave, it takes Sylvie and the airman several hours and a number of stops along the rough mountainous trail to reach the cave. She resists asking him anything about himself—both because she's been ordered not to talk to arriving airmen and because he has barely enough energy to make the climb. He occasionally falls into a kind of stupor, muttering incomprehensible things, even as he forces himself to take one step, then another. When they finally arrive, Sylvie feels triumphant as she brushes aside the thorny bushes at the entrance to the cave. He manages a few steps inside then collapses. Sylvie is horrified. He can't have made it this far only to die! She calls for help from the men inside.

Alastair is the first to reach them, followed by Étienne, then Claude. They drag him to the small fire they've made farther back in the cave. Claude's reservist compatriot François unfolds his large frame and motions to the boys, Jacques and Ernst, to collect straw and blankets to ready a pallet for him.

Sylvie puts some extra blankets under his leg to elevate it. "He's wounded. His leg."

Alastair cuts away the airman's trousers. "Bloody hell."

Sylvie cringes—cloth soaked in blood is crisscrossed over the airman's calf and knee, then up along his thigh. She says to Étienne, "We've got to clean this right away. Get some bandages, will you." Étienne vanishes deep into the cave to fetch the medical supplies.

Alastair calls after him, "And get some of Hélène's salve."

As Sylvie and Étienne minister to the man, Claude whispers, "How did you ever make it up with him?"

His voice deep and gravelly, François asks, "Are you sure you weren't followed, my dear?"

Claude shoots him an annoyed look.

François shrugs. "I'm just asking."

Sylvie turns to Alastair. "It's a fair question. I made sure the patrol was well beyond the garden before I got him into the passageway." She wipes sweat from her brow with her forearm. "It was getting dark as we slipped out of town. He was walking better at first, but the trip up..."

While Jacques and Ernst tend the fire, Alastair, Sylvie, and her brother work on the airman's leg. It's bruised with black gashes in several places. Given the dark red, jagged holes, it looks to Sylvie like he dug the shrapnel out himself with a not-so-sharp knife.

Alastair says, "Probably treated himself. Can't think how the poor devil walked at all."

Étienne applies Hélène's salve and bandages up the leg as best he can. "He needs the doctor. Or at least Madame Hélène."

Sylvie says, "Too late tonight. I'll send her tomorrow, as early as possible."

The man slowly comes to, and Claude tips his head back to give him a sip of some Armagnac. He takes a swig, shakes his head, and seems to brighten. "Where am I? Some kind of cave?" He reaches out his hand to Sylvie. "My angel, am I dead?"

Alastair smiles, "Very alive, I assure you. I'm RAF."

The man leans up on one elbow, mustering all his strength to salute. In a raspy voice, he says, "Lieutenant Elliot Powers, RAF Bomber Command...sir. I presume I should call you sir?"

"At rest, Lieutenant." He introduces Claude and the others. "And these lads, Jacques and Ernst, escaped and made their way down here from Northern France."

Sylvie is amused to hear her ordinarily shy brother Étienne proudly speak up, "We're the *Maquis*."

Elliot says in broken French, "Hoped I'd run into you chaps."

Étienne continues, while Alastair translates, hardly able to keep up with the boy's exuberance. "*Maquisards*. The Resistance, you know—named for the tall grass they say we hide in." He stops, thinks for a moment, then adds, as if some deeply ingrained training compels him to blurt out the whole truth. "We use the name even though we don't really have tall grass up here in the mountains."

Sylvie laughs, wondering how her brother became so loquacious. In any event, she's overjoyed that she managed to get Elliot here. Saving even one life makes it all worthwhile—the effort to learn to pose as a nun, the fear of being found out by the *Boches* on the train, and the anxiety of spending so much time confined in her claustrophobic cell.

Elliot makes a weak salute all around that seems to exhaust him. "I never thought I'd actually reach you. So many helped me..." Elliot's voice trails off as he sinks back down.

Alastair says, "No need to tell us just now."

Elliot, although weakened, clearly wants to talk, so Alastair translates.

"I was shot down just nearing Calais. Flying back from dropping our load on a munitions factory in Essen." Claude offers him another swig, then Elliot continues, "God Damned Messerschmitts. Iron crosses on their bellies. Swastikas on their tails." He's sweating, his voice growing louder and more strident. "Gun muzzles poking out from the leading edges of their wings. Pumping the air full of—" He stops short.

Listening to Elliot's account, Sylvie feels not only the horror of what he's been through but a strange sense of exhilaration. Of accomplishment. This man dropped bombs on German targets, made his way to Foix, then put himself in her hands—and she got him this far.

Alastair motions toward Elliot's leg. "Someone relieved you of some hardware."

Elliot slams his eyes shut, as if trying to block out the memory.

Alastair pats his arm, "Get some rest. We'll tend some more to that leg tomorrow."

Elliot slouches down and immediately falls into a deep but troubled sleep.

Everyone huddles near the fire that crackles and throws flashes of warm light onto the stalactites and down into the lake. Alastair turns to Sylvie. "Before you arrived, we were just discussing. There's a drop tonight. Supplies, medicines. Not a moment too soon, if he's going to keep that leg."

"Tell me what I need to do."

"You performed a miracle getting him up here. I don't see why you can't finish the job by helping us pick up what else he needs at the drop." He turns to the group. "Let's go, everyone. Étienne, will you stay and watch him?"

Sylvie isn't surprised to see Étienne's usual stubbornness surface, as he says, "I want to go too."

Alastair raises his voice just a notch, but it's louder and angrier than Sylvie has ever heard. "That's an order, son."

The boy gives a sharp nod, but as the others gather their torches and digging gear, he takes a stick and roughly stirs the fire. Sparks fly and the flames flicker yellow and orange, like an indoor sunset, bouncing off the roof of the cave. Sylvie goes to him and moves to pat him on the shoulder, but he knocks her hand away. Even so, she looks up at her impetuous but earnest brother and whispers, "Thank you, Étienne, for watching over him. I'm sure Alastair will let you go next time." He turns away, shrugs and stares into the flames.

Leaving the cave, Sylvie looks through the tall trees to see the full moon shining. The forest is thick with wet dew, crystallizing into light snow. The air is so clear that, if they were to scale the nearest high peak, now completely covered in snow, she's certain they could see all the way to Spain. As she climbs, she aches with the sharp sense of loss, remembering going out on similar nights with Jean. Climbing and climbing, then eagerly gazing up at a million stars, with the craggy mountains silhouetted in angular purple masses against the cobalt night sky. The closer they get to the drop point, however, the more her sorrow is overshadowed by a mixture of intense excitement and anxiety. She's joining with her uncle, Alastair, and the others on their first mission to collect a vital drop of supplies.

They reach the clearing and wait under the trees until they hear a low and distant rumble. They quickly fan out onto the field, the boys carrying shovels and packs. Three of them form a straight line and turn on their torches, indicating the direction of the wind. Alastair stands at the far side of the line, blinking his torch in the pre-determined Morse code pattern so that the pilot can confirm the identity of the reception committee. Suddenly, white parachute silk flashes in the night sky, with even brighter patches reflecting as the silk catches the moonlight. Three black canisters float down like gliding coffins. They rush to receive the caskets of bounty from the sky. Ammunition. Supplies. And medicines Sylvie knows are vital, not only for this airman but for all those to come.

CHAPTER THIRTY-THREE

Foix. November 1940

HÉLÈNE STRUGGLES UP the slippery mountainside in the miserable rain. With the temperature falling, the wet is turning into sleet, and she grabs hold of tree branches to maintain her progress in mud that is freezing in slick patches. She swears into the dark, empty forest. On the lookout for her, Alastair meets her at the entrance to the cave.

Breathless, she says, "I'm sorry, I couldn't get away any sooner. The major paid a surprise visit to the camp and—"

"Just glad you made it up. Miserable evening."

She takes off her slicker and removes a small package from a secret pocket sewn inside. "How's the patient? I hear he's in desperate need."

"Barely holding his own." Ever the gallant Englishman, he brushes the freezing moisture from her slicker and hangs it on a small beech tree which the *Maquisards*, in jest, have fashioned as a "homey" coat rack at the entrance to the cave.

She removes her rain hat and pats her hair back in place. With her hectic life at the refugee camp and going back and forth to the cave, she's given up her neat, tight coils and grown her hair longer—it's now pinned up into a chignon, although strands trail haphazardly around her face. As Alastair leads her farther into the cave, her voice rings with excitement. "You said there'd be medicines in the drop. Did they come?"

Claude bends over the fire, stirring a bubbling pot of stew. He gets up to kiss her on both cheeks. When Étienne sees Hélène, he sets their metal serving bowls down and rushes to her. Because he's so young, she always forgets how tall he is until he's right up next to her. She's touched that the boy is obviously infatuated with her, although she subtly does all she can to discourage him. Even so, she can't avoid him as he bends down and hugs her tightly. He kisses her on both cheeks, lingering in his embrace quite a bit longer than necessary.

Hélène gives Étienne the package from her coat. "Please…dissolve these in boiling water right away. For the airman." She flashes him a smile. "You're a treasure."

His lanky frame seems to grow inches with her compliment. Determined and self-important, he springs back towards the fire and sets to work.

Hélène looks beyond Claude and waves to Ernst, who sits cross-legged by the fire cleaning a Sten gun. Nearby is François. His large frame overflows a small rough-hewn stool, as he organizes the supplies from the drop. Louis paces behind François, looking over his shoulder and offering a series of unwanted opinions. They remind Hélène of a large, silent, and heavy-jowled Saint Bernard, with a yappy terrier at his heels.

She asks Alastair, "Where's Jacques?"

"I'll tell you later. Come, see to Elliot."

The airman lies on the blanket nearest the fire. He struggles to rise, but Hélène motions him back down. Alastair brings a lantern, while François offers her his stool, which she draws close.

"I'm Madame Hélène, a nurse from Foix. How are you feeling, Lieutenant?" She takes his pulse, feels his head for a temperature, then gently unwraps the dressing from his leg. Her heart stops the moment she sees the maze of red and black marks. Before she touches his wounds, she sees him flinch and his face turn ashen, even as he manages a smile in an effort to make light of the pain.

Elliot says, in his halting French, "Another angel of mercy I see."

She calls to Étienne, "Is that broth ready yet?"

He brings a steaming cup and helps Elliot drink.

Hélène says, "This will make it easier for me to tend to your leg."

As he sips, Elliot makes a terrible face, and Claude offers him a flask. "Something to wash down that evil stuff."

Elliot smiles weakly. "Right. Damn bitter stuff."

Hélène tries to put him at ease. "But it'll put hair on your chest." She takes a deep breath and starts to ease open the biggest of the wounds to ascertain the depth of the infection. Elliot gasps and tries not to move.

Hélène says, "Alastair, you put the sulfa powder on last night?" He nods. "How many hours ago was that?"

"We got back just after midnight."

Étienne jumps in, "It's been about eighteen hours."

Having made her assessment, she speaks to Elliot slowly and carefully, as she would speak to her patients in the hospital in Toulouse. "Elliot, it's too early to tell if the antibiotic is taking effect. In any case, I need to do a better job cleaning out your wounds. You did this yourself?"

Elliot nods. She gives Alastair a quick, despairing side-glance then turns back to Elliot. "That must have taken some courage. Some of these shrapnel wounds are pretty deep."

Elliot says, "I've come this far. Do whatever you need."

"Take some more of that broth before we begin."

Elliot downs the broth, then Claude offers more Armagnac, which he guzzles.

She takes a scalpel from her bag, holds it into the fire, and pours steaming broth over it. Willing her hand not to shake, she wants to scream. *This should be done by a doctor, not me. And in a sanitary surgery, not in some God-awful cave in these God-awful mountains.* She turns away, using her sleeve to wipe moisture from her brow. Étienne shoots her a concerned look. Not wanting to unnerve the boy, who's shown great courage helping her, she forces herself back into the horrific reality of what she must do and sets to work digging out layers of pus. Alastair and Étienne hold Elliot's leg still. François discretely steps away, lights a Gauloises, and inhales some deep breaths while Louis, for once, sits immobile. Ernst gets up and quietly walks outside.

At first, Elliot moans, but the moans give way to screams. Still, Hélène forces herself to keep working until the pus is drained from the five wounds checker-boarding his leg. Finally, he passes out, and Hélène breathes a sigh of relief—this leaves her much freer to finish up the drainage and cauterize each wound with a hot knife. She hates having to rely on her memory of what she's seen the physicians do in Toulouse, although she's never actually seen anything like these types of wounds. She curses under her breath. Before the war, they had proper anesthetic, and they would have used ether for this kind of surgery, not put this poor man through such agony.

While she works, Étienne assists and even gets clean cloths to wipe her brow. When she's done with the wounds, he helps her apply more sulfa powder and bandage the leg. She thinks back to what she told Sylvie that day at the refugee camp. "I take it one patient at a time. That's how I don't get overwhelmed." But now she is overwhelmed. And shaking. Envisioning Sylvie in prayer, even the secular Hélène makes a silent plea with God that what she's done will save his leg, and, more importantly, his life. She smiles wanly at Étienne as he starts to clean up, readying the blood-soaked bandages to burn.

As she washes up, Claude quietly comes over. "I hope you'll stay and have some stew. I made it myself."

Étienne calls to her, "It'll put hair on your chest." The others howl with laughter as the boy looks around, puzzled, then he flushes at his inadvertent joke.

She gently laughs, then turns to Claude. "It smells wonderful, but I have to get back. I don't want the major to find out I didn't come home directly from the camp."

Étienne's face dissolves into anger. "I hate that man being in your house, Madame Hélène. You will tell us if he disrespects you?"

Hélène shoots Alastair and Claude a nervous glance, then says calmly, to allay the boy's fears, "He's been a perfect gentleman. Something about the honor of a German officer. I assure you, Étienne."

In fact, Hélène knows that Major Spitzer is attracted to her, although she senses he wants to win her favor rather than force himself upon her. Despite Alastair's prompting, she still hasn't been able to bring herself to become intimate with him to gain information. Instead, she sincerely hopes their forced but amiable conversations, over breakfast or when he returns in the evenings, will lead him to say something of use to the resistance without having to sleep with him.

She finishes up and asks Alastair to see her out. As he hands her the oil slicker, she asks, "So, where is Jacques? Is he well?"

Alastair whispers, "He's counting troop movements. Enlisted his younger sister and two cousins so they can take turns at the crossroads. They write down 'shopping' lists. Units of soldiers are sacks of potatoes. An anti-aircraft gun is a chicken. Various munitions are different kinds of vegetables." He shakes his head and says with a wry smile, "Makes me hungry just reading their reports."

"I won't ask how you transmit this information back."

His eyes shine. "I wouldn't tell you anyway." Then all levity leaves his face. "Seriously, Hélène, we must have more accurate information than these young people can glean, sitting night after night beside railway tracks."

She turns away. There must be another way. How can she betray her husband? She imagines the major's hands on her—she shudders.

He says, a bit louder to get her attention, "Just as soon as we figure out their pattern, we'll be sending Louis and some of the others down to Toulouse to set charges. Blow up tracks and derail troop trains. We'd better have the right information or—" He shoots a pained, accusatory glance in her direction.

"I hear you, Alastair," she says, her voice low and heavy with dread.

He helps her on with her slicker. She adjusts her rain hat and gives him a melancholy nod as he draws the brambles back from the entrance to the cave, and she steps out into the sleeting rain.

CHAPTER THIRTY-FOUR

Foix. November 1940

HÉLÈNE OPENS THE shutters in the dining room, taking in a deep, frosty breath of mountain air to calm herself before setting the table for Major Spitzer's breakfast. Looking out between the tiny houses surrounding hers, she catches a glimpse of the steep mountains far to the south, now blanketed with snow. Every morning, she wills the major to finish eating quickly, so she can get up to the camp and minister to the arriving refugees—she finds that caring for others helps her focus less on her own worries.

Would that the insidious nausea she feels each morning as she prepares his breakfast were because she was with Gérard's child rather than because Alastair has urged her to seduce Spitzer in order to obtain information. As a married woman, the mere thought provokes extreme feelings of anger, shame, even guilt, that she'd even contemplate such a thing. Insisting to herself that she will consider it, she always seems to put it off until later, hoping that he'll inadvertently divulge useful information and save her from this fate.

Hélène always sets one place at the table for the major, declining his repeated invitations to join him. Trying to appeal to the more humane side of him, she always demurs, citing her need to leave as early as possible to fulfill her responsibilities at the camp. She hears his boots hammering briskly down the stairs and rushes to the kitchen to finish up the coffee. He has access to the real thing, and it's always the first thing in the morning he offers to entice her to sit with him—but she will not permit herself any. The water boils in the kettle, and she pours it into the coffee press. The heavenly smell courses through her, and she sinks into a daydream—she's sitting at a café in Toulouse drinking coffee with Gérard as they plan a blissful outing in the mountains. She's smiling in the warmth of her husband's presence.

As the major comes into the kitchen, he says, "Well, now Madame Hélène. I see you are in a good mood this morning."

She quickly smooths her apron and tries to think of a suitable response. "Why yes, Major. It looks like a fine day that we should all enjoy. Before the snow reaches us and winter truly sets in."

His tone is bright, offhanded. "Perhaps you will join me for the coffee? I see you have it brewing."

She looks into the dining room with its single place setting. She imagines Alastair behind her, whispering how desperately they need information. She's tried to avoid this moment, but she thinks of the poor dead Marcel and of Jacques and his younger sister and cousins—children really—sitting in the cold at night, counting troop movements on the passing trains. She turns back to the major.

"Well, perhaps, just this once," she says, trying to control the quiver in her voice.

The major cocks his head as if he hasn't heard correctly, then fashions his thin lips into a wry smile. "Excellent. I have some extra minutes this morning before I must depart." He rapidly picks up additional silverware and a plate from the sideboard in the kitchen.

"I can do that, Major. Please, go and sit down."

"Surely I may help you?" He seems sincere as he takes the serving items and heads for the dining room.

She calls to him, "I appreciate that." As he disappears into the dining room, she shakes her wrists out, trying to expel her nervousness.

Entering the dining room, she stops short when she sees the table layout, barely able to control her panicked urge to run back into the kitchen. He has assumed his usual place at the head of the table, carefully setting her place on his right, where a wife would sit next to her husband. Alastair flashes through her mind as she proceeds with leaden steps to bring her tray and coffee press to the table.

He gallantly stands and gently taps the table, motioning for her to sit beside him. As she does, she perceives the curl of his lips straining to avoid a triumphant smile. She has a momentary change of heart and rushes back into the kitchen, calling over her shoulder, "I've forgotten the sausages." He also supplies her larder with ham, sausage, and eggs, which he acquires on the black market, although she takes defiant pride in avoiding eating these as well as drinking his coffee. She leans against the kitchen sink, her knees feeling about to buckle as her cowardice shames her. Then, taking up the platter of sausages warming in the oven, she squares her shoulders and marches to join him as if to a firing squad.

Later that morning, she turns over in her parents' bed—long since appropriated by Spitzer—and faces the wall, so he can't see her face streaked with tears. And he can't penetrate her eyes with his own, unnerving and merciless stare. Although he closed the shutters before taking her to bed, she can see slats of sunlight directly above, which means it's close to noon. He moves beside her, spoons her in his embrace, and traces his finger along the curve of her spine. It is only through the greatest of willpower that she avoids cringing under his touch.

"Such lovely white skin."

She is too choked up to respond, so she snuggles back up to him, squeezing his hand over her shoulder. He seems to accept her gesture as a positive response and squeezes back.

"I must go now, my dear Hélène." He leans over, kisses the side of her cheek, and affectionately ruffles her hair. "I will see you this evening, *Ja?*"

Unable to look at him, she pulls his hand around her shoulder and gently kisses it, whispering, "You have quite worn me out, Major. Of course, I will see you tonight."

Out of the corner of her eye, she sees him nodding with a full-blown smile of triumph. Dressing quickly, he rhythmically stomps down the stairs in his boots. It sounds like he's cheerfully marching to some inner military tune. As soon as she hears the front door close, Hélène runs to the bathroom, draws a bath, and scrubs herself raw.

CHAPTER THIRTY-FIVE

Prison Camp. November 1940

WHISTLES. CLANGING. A hare struggles in a trap. Suzanne shrieks. Shouting. Rifles firing. More Clanging. Sounds penetrating Jean's consciousness. At first, the cacophony seems faint and far away, but as it blares in his ears, Jean suddenly awakens on his thin straw pallet on the concrete floor, cheek to jowl with the other men in his cell. He starts up and hits his head on the bottom of Albert's bunk, realizing with a shot of dread, he's back among these filthy men, fighting for space. When the two SS guards come for him, he's actually relieved—he might be led to his death, but anything is better than the stench and dense packing of men. As they drag him away, he catches Albert mouthing, *"Bon courage."*

The guards bring him back along the corridor of small cells to another room in the main barracks. Through dusty warehouse windows and high barbed wire fencing, he can see a heavily forested area beyond. Despite being groggy from his nightmarish sleep, he surveys the surroundings, searching for cover if he were to attempt an escape. The sky is filled with dense gray clouds, and it appears to still be raining, although the windows are so caked with dirt, it's hard to tell. After the SS guards handcuff him to a gray metal chair, they step aside, leaving the single electric light bulb in the ceiling shining in his face.

Jean struggles to construct a story to tell them. Something plausible after he woke up in that death pit, so they'll believe he's a military man and not part of a brewing resistance in the countryside—which he knows nothing about. The soles of his feet burn, just thinking of that poor boy back in his cell.

A strapping man, dressed in a black SS uniform, strides in carrying a clipboard. Leaning against the wall, he whips out a pen and peers over his gold-rimmed spectacles. He speaks matter-of-factly as if he were bored. "I am Hauptsturmführer here. Kommandant, *Ja?*" The kommandant squints through his glasses, on guard for wrong information. "Name."

Jean takes a deep breath. "Jean Galliard. Private, 55th Infantry Division." Swallowing hard and willing himself to relax, he continues, "We were on the outskirts of the Ardennes. The last I remember, there were Panzers everywhere. Then I woke up in a lye pit, with maybe fifty dead bodies."

The kommandant draws back as if he'd taken a jab in the mouth. "That cannot be. We pushed through the Ardennes months ago. You would not lie to me?"

Panic. He looks at the kommandant, then at the guards. A hint of pleasure drifts over the face of one of the guards as he seems to have welcomed the lie.

Jean repeats, trying to keep his voice steady and believable. "That's the truth. I'm telling you all I remember. I woke up in a pit, on the edge of the Ardennes."

The kommandant strides to Jean's chair, leans down, and snarls, "The 55th was routed in the Ardennes. Where have you been since then?"

He quickly interjects, trying to speak in the most earnest tone possible. "I hit my head when they dumped me into that pit."

"You were hiding in the forest, *Ja?* Planning with others to sabotage us, *Ja?*"

"No. No. There was this woman. Her children got me out, well, her son, really. I was blind for a while, but she had this salve she used for horses—"

"Enough. We shall see." The kommandant pushes his glasses up on his long, boney nose and makes a sharp snap with his jaw towards the door. The SS guards double-time out and haul Albert in. The large burly man is all the two trim, well-muscled guards can manage as he drags his feet, resisting.

Albert yells at the guards, "Bastards. I didn't do anything."

The guards try to shove him onto the floor, but he stands his ground. Finally, one of them backs him up, while the other trips him, and Albert goes down hard on the concrete. Jean hears a bone crack in Albert's elbow, followed by a scream of pain and curses.

Albert rants, "You sons of bitches. I already told you everything I know. Now this new bastard comes in." He holds his elbow, looking up at the kommandant. "I don't know where he came from or what he's done since you *Boches* ran the hell over us."

"I didn't do anything," Jean yells. "So he can't know anything."

Walking over to Albert, the kommandant crouches down and sharply jabs his pen in the air, inches from Albert's eyes. "You have orders not to talk in your cell, *ja?*" The kommandant pauses, then cracks a broad smile showing an array of perfectly white teeth. "The rules, you know. *ja?*"

Albert is silent, his heavily bearded face closing into a sharp grimace.

"DON'T YOU?"

All Albert can do is nod, fury in his eyes.

The kommandant stands, replacing the pen in the clip board and nodding towards Albert. "Solitary. Five days."

Jean yells, "Wait, you can't. Please."

The guards pick Albert up by the arms, and for their amusement, jostle his broken elbow. Albert screams as they lead him out.

As Jean struggles against the restraints on his hands, the kommandant calmly walks to him, takes his Lugar out of his holster, and hits him hard across the face with the butt. Two new guards rush in and hit Jean repeatedly with their rifle butts, tearing gashes in his face, arms and legs.

Jean comes to, naked, in a bathtub of ice water. *Mon Dieu,* it actually feels good, clean, and numbing. But then the pain from his beating sharply courses through him. He jerks his head up and sees the kommandant and two guards standing over him.

The kommandant takes off his gold-rimmed glasses and pinches the bridge of his nose as if he were exasperated at a child's misbehaving. "You will tell us where you were hiding. What other evaders were there, and what sabotage you were planning."

"No others, I told you. Just this woman and her—"

The guards muscle him down. Ice water floods his lungs, freezing and burning at the same time. Drowning…gasping…plunging him into the water…drowning again. Finally, they bring him to the surface and hold him there as he gasps for enough breath to scream, "No one was planning anything."

The kommandant shakes his head slowly, sadly, then jerks towards the guards and leaves.

Jean yells, "You bastards. I'm not—" Into the water again.

They don't believe him or are intent on punishing him anyway. Finally, he loses consciousness and awakes in an empty cell on a stretcher. A male nurse comes in, puts some salve on his wounds, and throws him a blanket to cover his nakedness. Jean wonders why they are treating him. He realizes, with a lump of iron settling in his chest, that they probably want to keep him alive for more questioning.

Slowly and agonizingly, he moves his arms and legs, then tries to sit up. At first, he's too dizzy to move. Then he feels the searing pain— they've stuck sharp nails underneath each of his toenails. Pulling them out is torture. It's only his anger and hatred that keep him working to remove them, then gingerly but resolutely walking about the cell, muttering to himself, "One hundred paces. I will walk one hundred paces."

In the three days he estimates they keep him there, he manages, through sheer defiant willpower, to limp his one hundred paces a day, every step a torment. All the time, he recalls Albert's kindness to tell him what was going on when he arrived. He thinks constantly about the big man with the cracked elbow, pent up in solitary. Not only does he want out of this wretched hell-hole for himself, but now he's obsessed with getting vengeance for Albert as well.

CHAPTER THIRTY-SIX

WHEN THEY BRING Jean back from his torture, he is limping badly. Nevertheless, he struggles to help Albert recover from the agony of his time in solitary—the large man's back and legs are in constant spasm. At first, Albert refuses to have any more to do with Jean, which he fully understands. Jean blames himself for having made Albert suffer and vows to make it up to him. Although he's starving like everyone else, Jean manages to get back on Albert's good side by giving him part of his meager daily ration of bread and gruel. He cements their friendship by making light of his torture, saying he finally had a bath at the German's expense, which makes Albert laugh begrudgingly.

Their interrogations over, they are given thin overalls. Albert, being such a large man, barely fits into his. Jean wants to know what the red badge on the front symbolizes.

Albert says, "Political prisoner, whatever that means."

"So we can forget about the Geneva Convention."

Albert smiles his toothy smile. "Guess so, my friend. They want to disappear us all. Especially the yellow badges—Jews. Poles. Russians."

Jean finds himself staring at the high window above, visualizing

Sylvie in church, waiting for Father Michel to marry them. Inwardly he smiles, imagining her with a long bridal veil covering her thick black hair. Then he laughs to himself when, in his vision, he looks down and finds that she's wearing her trousers and boots!

He sucks in a deep breath and turns to Albert, his voice flat. "I don't suppose they're letting our families know we're here."

"I'm lucky I don't have a family. At least that I know about." As Albert boisterously laughs, their cellmates shush him.

Jean and Albert are moved to a larger work detail cell in the main barracks, although the space is still horrifically overcrowded with about a hundred men. The winter is savagely cold, with no heat and men coughing continuously and uncontrollably. The Germans reopen a nearby, long-dormant quarry, and the prisoners are drafted for the arduous work of breaking up stones. The men in his cell are joined by men in six or seven other cells, with work days lasting a grueling fourteen hours or more.

Each time their detail leaves the camp, Jean studies the terrain, memorizing key features and where they might hide if they got the chance to escape. But he thinks less of this idea after some of the guards, apparently out of boredom, stage phony escape traps for prisoners they want to get rid of: the guards capture them, chain them to posts in the yard, and let the dogs loose. The men in Jean's cell block can't see through the high windows, but the snarls and shrieks from the courtyard carry very well.

Work days are frigid. Down in the quarry, Jean tries to keep his spirits up. "Albert, did you notice it's warmer here than back in our cell."

Albert sneers. "*Mais oui!* With all your hot air, what do you expect?" He snorts, laughing at his bad joke. Most of the time on work detail, Jean coils his thoughts deep into his mind to shut himself off from the daily humiliations. Even so, he can't help keeping track of the deaths, calculating that in the first month of working in the quarry, twelve out of approximately one hundred men in their cell block have died. Albert gets the bright idea to run a lottery, with the men betting contraband food on the exact number of the dead each week.

After about two months at the quarry, Jean and a few other prisoners are ordered to break up icy ground within the camp. A high-ranking SS official comes to take measurements. The tall smoke stack Jean saw when he arrived at the camp anchors one end of a stone structure they're building, while at the other end, a large brick wall is erected, with a passageway between them. Narrow-guage tracks, which might be used to service cars in a coal mine, are laid to connect the stone structure with the brick wall.

Despite his perpetual exhaustion and attempts to numb himself against any feelings he might have, Jean becomes increasingly curious. He watches as the SS guards escort more officers into the complex, one of whom seems to be some kind of doctor—a plump man wearing a white lab coat with a stethoscope around his neck. Another officer, pale and slender, sweats profusely as he checks and rechecks documents on his clipboard, comparing them with engineering drawings spread out on a nearby table.

The doctor orders a group of men from various cells to line up and listens to them cough. The weaker ones are separated from the rest and housed in new barracks, together with hundreds of new prisoners who've recently arrived wearing yellow six-sided stars. Albert, always in the know, whispers, "Jews. They're bringing them in from somewhere called Drancy, near Paris. Foreign Jews, from what the guards were saying."

"Why are they putting them in with the sick men?"

Albert only shakes his head, but they're caught talking and called before the kommandant. He wipes his gold wire-rimmed spectacles on his handkerchief and sneers, "You are like two old ladies. Can't keep your mouth shut, can you, Albert?"

Albert quickly lifts up his face, and with a tinge of irony lost on the kommandant, says, "We were just talking about how we can be of service for the new construction, *Mein Herr Kommandant.*"

The kommandant peers over his glasses and down his long nose. "And you shall be. I shall have a count... keep count. I hear you are good at counting numbers of dead prisoners. Running a lottery?"

Jean exchanges a furtive glance with Albert but doesn't say anything as they're returned to their cell. The next morning, they're taken to what Jean can now see is a large oven structure next to the smoke stack. Under the direction of the pale engineer, some SS soldiers adjust the flue intake on the smoke stack. Another soldier paces off the distance between the brick wall and the room with the oven while the pale engineer argues with the kommandant.

Albert, who stands closest to the Germans and understands a bit of German, translates for Jean. "They're talking about another prison camp. They used bulldozers to make some kind of mass grave." He shakes his head in disbelief. "The high command there was furious— the mass grave polluted the water table for the prison as well as the nearby village." Albert steadies his gaze on the floor. "So now they're taking a new approach here. But our kommandant is angry because this new method costs so much more, and it'll reflect badly on his budget."

Then it begins. Fast. Relentless. The guards yelling and cursing. Dogs snarling as the first of the men are led to the brick wall—sick men from their camp, as well as the new Jewish arrivals from Drancy. They look dazed and shuffle in complete silence as the guards scream for them to hurry along.

The guards line the first group of about twelve men up against the brick wall, make them turn around to face it, and kneel. They shoot each of them in the back of his head. Another team of soldiers throws the bodies into a wheelbarrow-like small car on the train tracks and sends it rolling down to the oven. There, Jean sees a gurney, the exact height of the car, so that, when the car is tipped, the bodies can be rolled over onto the gurney and then slid into the oven. Jean, overcome with revulsion, just stands there, staring at the bodies in the wheelbarrow, until the kommandant yells, "Drag them out."

Jean turns around, confused, trying to understand what he's supposed to do. The kommandant tips the wheelbarrow, and bodies start to fall out onto the gurney. Jean hardly has time to notice the horror spreading across Albert's face as, just then, one of the bodies groans. Although the head on the body is partially blown off, and blood leaks from his neck, the man is not quite dead.

Another soldier stands guard with a snarling dog on a leash, which he allows to claw at Jean's leg. Jean tries to sidestep the ferocious animal but runs into another guard on his other side. Still, the kommandant screams, "Drag them out, *dummkopf.* Slide them in, then use *das hoe* to scrape out the remains." The kommandant picks up a hoe from the construction pile and hurls it at Jean. "Residue from furnace. For over there. On the scales."

As he weighs the hoe in his hands, Jean shakes with disgust. *I could take the bastard out with one swipe.* He slowly turns to stare at the bodies, bile rising in his throat.

The kommandant barks, "I said to work. Are you deaf *und* blind?" He motions to the other end of the passageway, to the brick wall. "Maybe you *wollen* join them over there."

Jean grips the hoe in his hands while the kommandant screams in his face. Jean thinks how odd it is that he can see the kommandant screaming—opening his mouth with his perfect white teeth, his gold-rimmed glasses rising and falling on his boney nose, as his mouth opens and shuts—but he can't hear a word. He can only feel a searing anger. Images of Suzanne and the children, with their white-blonde hair, flash through his mind. His hands tremble as he slowly raises the hoe, calmly eyeing the kommandant, wondering where exactly to strike in order to kill him instantly.

Jean casts a glance at Albert, who makes a small but violent shake of his head, imploring Jean not to act. Jean pauses for a moment as the sounds of the kommandant's screams and the dogs' barking finally reach him, dampened and delayed as if he were underwater. The blood drains entirely from Jean's face, and just as he feels he's about to lose consciousness, he snaps back into reality. He slowly puts the hoe aside, picks up one of the bodies, and drags it onto the gurney. The kommandant motions for another prisoner to help him load the gurney, so together they stack four or five bodies at a time.

The kommandant turns towards Albert. "*Compte.* Keep *compte, dummkopf.*"

When the gurney is full, another prisoner slides it into the furnace. Jean finds himself marveling, if just for a moment, at how efficiently the whole operation works—as the wheel barrel comes down the tracks, it tips at just the right height, so the bodies can easily be rolled over onto the gurney, which glides into the oven on newly greased wheels. Jean catches himself, his eyes glaze over, and his mind again recedes, shutting out all feeling as he mechanically sets to work. When the engineer, looking through a glass window in the door of the oven, makes a signal, the other prisoner slides the gurney out. Then Jean digs out the ash and bits of bone with the hoe and scrapes them onto the scales. The dogs, seeing the bones, unleash a torrent of snarling and barking.

It's all Jean can do to keep piling the bodies onto the gurney, especially since a few now and then move slightly, hissing and even groaning. He can't allow himself to notice too carefully, or he'll bring himself out of his self-imposed stupor—the only way he can manage to commit these atrocities.

Hours go by until the last of the bodies come down in the wheelbarrow. They are loaded into the oven, the ashes scraped onto the scales, and the kommandant yells, "HALT." He looks at his watch while several of the officers also mark time on their stop watches. He confers with the engineer, the doctor, and the others.

Albert again translates, "Only one bullet each? What is the production? The oven is more efficient if the bodies are still warm."

Then they ask Albert for the count.

Albert stammers, "Three hundred…ah…three hundred twelve, *Herr Kommandant*."

Jean stands motionless, sweating profusely in front of the blazing oven.

The pale engineer turns even whiter as he angrily, but very precisely, notes the calculations on his clipboard. He quickly makes some computations and shows the kommandant, who happens to look over and notices Jean and Albert staring at them.

"What are you doing, *idiotin*? Get out of here."

As Jean and Albert stagger back towards their cell, they hear the Germans violently arguing. Albert grunts. "Bastard says it's not fast enough. They expect to have too many bodies to dispose of. And one bullet each…they say it uses too much ammunition."

They've just turned the corner leading to the corridor and their cell when Jean hears the dogs barking in the distance and stops short, trembling, sweating, and shaking. He'll never hear a dog bark and not think of the horrors in the camp. Jean has forced himself to put aside all thoughts, all feelings, just to get through it, but now, triggered by the dogs barking, his mind races back to what just happened. His stomach recoils at the memory of smelling burning flesh. After what he's done today, he'll never be able to rejoin the civilized people he once knew. How could they ever forgive him? Sylvie and everyone he holds dear—they're dead to him now—like those corpses—gone forever. Jean stands immobile for a moment, then turns to the wall and retches his guts out.

CHAPTER THIRTY-SEVEN

Foix. Spring 1941

SYLVIE IS IMPATIENT to take up the battle once again, after a snowy and bitterly cold winter. The weather reduced the number of British bombing raids, as well as the number of downed airmen making their way south to Foix. She reveled in the success they enjoyed last fall. Before the weather closed the mountain passes, Alastair, Claude, and Louis managed to get the severely wounded Elliot and about a dozen more besides him over the mountains to an RAF safe house in Barcelona. In January, Sylvie was ecstatic to hear a coded message on BBC Radio London from Alastair, indicating that he, Elliot, and the other airmen had made it back to the U.K.

Pacing in her cell, which has become smaller and more confining over the winter, she laments that the Nazis have significantly tightened their grip over her village. Major Spitzer was promoted to the military side of operations, and a new kommandant took control over the refugee camp, after which the situation deteriorated alarmingly. To her horror, Sylvie now sees refugees whom she promised to protect become helpless prisoners of the Nazis. There was nothing she could do to prevent German soldiers from coming through the camp, extending the barbed wire perimeter and upending the meager barracks to reorganize them into so-called "pilots," or sections—one section for men and another for women and children. Additional primitive barracks were constructed, expanding the camp's capacity from hundreds to thousands. Refugees continue to pour into Foix, now arriving under armed guard by rail car from all over France.

In the camp, Sylvie continues her emotionally numbing work with Hélène and Dr. Duchamps, although even the most rudimentary medicines are denied them. One shipment contains boxes of thin men's overalls with various colored triangles emblazoned on the front. Sylvie is sickened to see the prisoners being roughly sorted into classifications, with the men and women designated as political prisoners made to wear the overalls with the red triangles. Jews from Belgium, Poland, and Holland, who fled to France during the early days of the war, are rounded up and sent either to her camp in Foix or other camps throughout Southern France. They are made to wear the same yellow stars Major Spitzer delivered when he first arrived, and all the Jews are separated into different barracks from the general prisoner population.

Each morning, all the blocks of prisoners are forced to shuffle in the yard along the barbed wire separations between the men's and women's pilots for a morning *"appell"* or roll call. Sylvie is heartsick to see the men, separated from their women and children, desperately searching for their loved ones. Then, if anyone in the family waves, a guard uses a truncheon on them—old or young, man or woman. Most soon stop waving, although a few defiant men continue until they are beaten senseless, their wives screaming across the yard for them to stop. If the count is off, showing a prisoner missing, all the prisoners are ordered to remain standing in the yard, even during the chilly spring rain, until the kommandant finds the runaway.

Sylvie is outraged that even the ill are made to stand, sometimes all day, without food or water. Hélène complains incessantly that her cases of pneumonia are increasing markedly under this inhuman regime. Moreover, the escapees, who are almost always found, are brought back, tied to a post in the yard for three days, frequently doused with cold water, and then shot. As a reprisal, another prisoner, randomly selected, joins the offenders to suffer the same fate.

The only bright spot in any of this is that Mother Superior manages to arrange for some of the international aid groups, such as the Quakers and the Red Cross, to drive up from Toulouse with supplies of rice, gruel, and powdered milk. A black market in food and cigarettes, however, soon springs up, fueled by the corrupt French collaborator lorry drivers, who divert considerable supplies destined for the camp.

This morning, Sylvie, dressed in her habit, stands with Hélène at a large sink in the kitchen, washing up in the camp's frigidly cold water. In addition to her work in the infirmary, Hélène is required to join Sylvie for a few hours each day to supervise the women prisoners designated as cooks. Two German guards arrogantly stroll about the kitchen, submachine guns slung on their shoulders. They watch carefully for contraband, making sure no one steals even the smallest scrap of food.

Just then, one of the women prisoners bends over, holding her head. Sylvie is shocked to see her slip a piece of bread into her apron pocket. One of the guards appears to notice as well, as he marches over, grabs the woman's hair, and brutally pulls her head back.

Sylvie, afraid he'll search the woman, shouts at the guard, "What's going on here? This woman is ill, can't you see?" Sylvie nods her alarm to Hélène, then strides over and puts the back of her hand on the woman's forehead. "She has a fever."

The guard reaches out to check the woman's forehead when Hélène calls to the guard from the sink, "You wouldn't want to catch what she has."

He jerks back and yells to the other guard, "Take her to infirmary."

The other guard, annoyed, moves towards the woman, but Sylvie steps in front of him and helps her stand upright. Eyes pleading, the woman looks directly at her. Sylvie feels a twist of pain, terrified that she'll be caught complicit, but nods, then the woman slips her the bread, which Sylvie stuffs into the pocket in the tunic of her habit. She watches the guard escort the woman out, and as the other guard turns to see them go, slips the bread back onto the pile of scraps. Trembling, she walks to the sink to join Hélène and continues washing up.

Sylvie whispers to Hélène, through gritted teeth, "These people are starving. Can't you ask Major Spitzer to do something?"

"I've asked him over and over." Hélène balls her fist in anger, her white knuckles turning even whiter. "He swears the camp isn't under his jurisdiction anymore. He's strictly military now. All the camps have been transferred to another branch of the Wehrmacht."

"When these poor people came, I promised to protect them." Sylvie leans down, pretending to wash some soap suds from the bottom of the sink. "I'm torn, Hélène. Claude wants me to tell the stronger prisoners to try to escape and join the *Maquis* in the mountains." She takes her thumb and vigorously works a perfectly clean spot on the bottom of the sink. "They even want to stage a raid to collect more men."

"That'll bring dreadful reprisals." Hélène rests her head on the metal front of the sink, then twists to the side to look at Sylvie. "What are you going to do?"

Sylvie's conflicting emotions race through her. Alastair has sent word they need to expand the resistance to prepare for a British invasion. But when? And at what cost to the miserable souls in the camp?

After a long pause, she hears Hélène's strained voice whispering through the veil of her confusion. "Sylvie… Sister… what are you going to do?"

Sylvie straightens up, makes the sign of the cross, and smiles weakly. "I have no idea. But… something. Something more."

CHAPTER THIRTY-EIGHT

Foix. Fall, 1941

HÉLÈNE IS IMMENSELY relieved that Major Spitzer hasn't taken any action against the children up at Madame Rumeau's farm. This is undoubtedly because, much to her humiliation and shame, she continues to sleep with him. The first time she and Spitzer went to bed, she couldn't bear to look at him, although she managed to conceal her revulsion. At least, he's a clean man who washes up before "inviting" her to "his" bed. And being extremely efficient in all things, he sees to it that their lovemaking is strictly utilitarian, which spares her the additional horror of having to pretend any passion towards him.

To insulate her feelings, she thinks of it as his need to clean a plugged drain pipe. When this image first came to her, she actually laughed out loud, and when it comes to her while they're in bed, she can barely keep from giggling. At least it takes the edge off her hatred of herself. Thankfully, he no longer requires her to wear the yellow star, perhaps because he doesn't wish to be associated with anything remotely Jewish. At first, she thought to wear it out of defiance, but then decided to accommodate him—honey rather than vinegar is always the better option.

Every now and then, however, sleeping with him pays off. One morning as she was clearing the table from his breakfast, he got up, stood behind her, and kissed her on the neck.

"My dear Hélène, I will not be joining you for dinner this evening."

She stays quite still. "I'm sorry to hear that. I shall miss you."

"I will return quite late. We are meeting a large shipment in Toulouse." He runs his fingers through her hair. "But of course, these things would not interest you."

She turns and strokes his cheek. "I am only worried for your safety. Your mission will not be dangerous?"

"We are just taking inventory of a shipment of tanks we've unloaded in Marseilles. *Ach*, I have to decide where to distribute them in the South. These idiots can not make such decisions on their own."

She kisses him. "Should I at least keep your plate warm?"

"*Nein. Danke.*"

"As you wish. Please be careful."

Other times he lets slip information about troop movements or Wehrmacht shipments to the Spanish military, which presumably keep the allegedly neutral Spain from straying too far from its tacit alliance with Germany. As soon as Spitzer leaves, Hélène gets word to Claude and the others. By now, they are stealing arms and equipment from transport trains and lorry convoys, and wherever possible, blowing up train tracks to disrupt their transport. She's careful to filter his information and not provide notice of every single train, so the major will not suspect her.

With all this, Hélène feels increasingly emotionally fractured, exhausted from treating an overwhelming number of patients at the refugee camp, as well as trying to obtain vital information from the major at home. Her usual outward calm belies this terrible strain—her lithe frame diminishes, and her high cheekbones become even more prominent over her gaunt cheeks. The major apparently notices because he encourages her to eat the plentiful German rations that he brings home. After dinner, he enjoys engaging her in philosophical discussions about the meaning of life, God, and good and evil.

At first, Hélène merely listens but then, quite gingerly, begins to express her opinion and is surprised that he appears to be interested in what she has to say. She's amazed to be treated as his intellectual equal, especially since she isn't nearly as widely read. Perhaps it's her experience with patients, of seeing life slip away, of knowing death first hand, that gives her views some credibility in his eyes. During these quiet evenings at home, he brings out his cognac, and she feels obliged to sit by the fire with him, like an old married couple. Too many evenings, however, she's on the verge of lashing out at him, deeply distressed that she has to play this role and doubly anguished that it isn't her beloved Gérard seated with her, warm and loving by the fire. Her stomach constantly fills with bitter acid, as she's always on her guard not to give away what she's doing and not to explode in rage. Her only respite is when she slips out to visit the children and allows herself precious moments of pure, unadulterated joy.

One day at the refugee camp, Hélène becomes incensed after Sylvie tells her what she's learned from Mother Superior—the Nazis have begun deporting foreign Jews being held in French refugee camps and taking them to work camps in Germany and the East. She becomes obsessed with the need to move Elias and Deborah to a safer place— most likely farther away—which nearly breaks her spirit.

She goes to Father Michel for advice. "I realize it's best for them, but I can't bear to see them leave." She holds her breath for a moment, hoping he'll agree, then adds, "And anyway, where would they go?"

He shuffles some books around on his desk. "Actually, Mother Superior says there's a Jewish aid organization. Mainly for orphaned Jewish children. They've secretly set up in Marseilles."

"Marseilles?"

"It's in unoccupied France, so the port is relatively open." Although no one can hear, he lowers his voice anyway. "Bribes can be made. And there's a place that will take them, not like what happened to that Jewish ship denied entry by so many countries."

"Where is this country?"

"I believe it's called Palestine."

"That's the end of the earth!" Hélène abruptly stands and walks to the window that looks out into the garden. Two brightly colored oak leaves, one bright red and the other a deeper orange, flutter by, then are snagged by a rose bush. Suddenly, the wind lifts them over the garden wall, and they're gone. She adds, "We can't just give them over to anybody."

"Hélène, I know this is upsetting. But it's their best chance for a good life. For any life at all." Father Michel gets up from behind his ancient, rickety desk, softly walks to the window, and stands behind her. "Don't you want that?"

"I wouldn't have put myself in danger all this time if I didn't."

He waits for a moment, starts to speak, but she cuts him off. "Not if they have to go so far away." Hélène's eyes brim with tears as she fights to control a sob, then breaks into wracking tearful gasps. Father Michel puts his arm around her shoulder. At first, she shrugs it off, then after a few moments, catches her breath and turns to him, giving him a quick, sharp nod. "You're right, of course." She pauses an agonized moment. "Will you help me get them to Marseilles?"

"Of course. I'll go to Toulouse tomorrow." He walks back to his desk. "Ask Mother Superior to get them identity cards. Their coloring is relatively fair, and they won't have *JUIF* stamped in red on the cards, so no one should suspect they're Jewish."

She watches him straighten out some papers, his lip quivering as he says, "Fortunately, they don't require photographs for... for children. I'll let you know when I have the cards, and we can make our plans from there."

Hélène whispers coarsely, "Thank you, Father."

"I'll drive you up to get them. I have some emergency gasoline ration coupons. Then we should take the three of you to the train, but not to the station in Foix." She nods as he continues, "If you leave from here, someone will ask questions."

Hélène sees that the priest is equally upset at the prospect of sending the children away. She takes the priest's hands in both of hers, squeezes them, and turns to leave.

Before she reaches the door, he smiles. "Don't think any of this absolves you from coming to confession. How long has it been?"

She musters a laugh, then shudders, picturing herself in bed with the major. She manages a weak smile of her own. "When things settle down, Father. I promise."

The trip to Madame Rumeau's is much worse than Hélène feared. The elderly lady becomes irate, puffing up her diminutive but stout frame and insisting she won't permit the children to be taken. She glances outside, where the children and Noëlle are playing. Her eyes fill with sorrow as she whispers, "This will kill Noëlle."

Hélène says, "We are so very sorry, Madame."

The priest quickly adds, "If there were any other way. We've heard such horrible things."

"I'm an old woman, but Noëlle...she's already like their mother. She would have raised them...seen to their education...talked to them about who they would marry." Madame Rumeau collapses onto her kitchen chair, sniffling bravely but refusing an outright sob. Suddenly, she grabs Hélène's hand. "You must promise they won't be separated."

"We've been assured, Madame." She casts a beseeching glance at the priest, who nods gravely in return.

Madame Rumeau asks Hélène to play with the children outside and send in Noëlle, so she and the priest can explain things to the young woman. Hélène is relieved to be able to spend some private moments with the children before their journey.

She scoops them up in her arms. As always, she looks behind their ears. "So when did my darlings last wash?" She kisses them, and they giggle wildly. "Have you been good for Madame Rumeau and Mademoiselle Noëlle?"

Hélène is pleased to see that Elias, although still serious and thoughtful, is not nearly as glum as when he first arrived in Foix. If she isn't truthful with him, however, she's certain that the progress he's made will be reversed, and he might never trust anyone again. She can hardly bear to tell him that he's to be taken away and entrusted to yet another strange group of adults. Elias has somehow managed to shield his sister Deborah from the worst of his fears. As a result, she has a sunnier and more open disposition. Hélène doesn't doubt that this lovable girl will be accepted by any family anywhere but worries that Elias will turn bitter and plunge into a downward cycle of mistrust and anger. She's been lying awake for nights trying to think how best to tell them.

"Elias, I have something I must tell you and Deborah." She gathers them tightly. "You are going away on a big ship. You are going across the sea to start a new life. Won't that be exciting?"

The children look at one another with blank faces, then stare at Hélène. Elias, in particular, struggles to gauge the situation.

He cries out, "Where will you be, Madame Hélène? And will Mademoiselle Noëlle be coming with us?"

Hélène swallows hard. "I'm afraid we can't go with you. Mademoiselle Noëlle must stay here to take care of Madame Rumeau. And I must care for all the patients in the camp. You remember how many of them there were?'

Deborah starts to wail, "But I don't want to leave here. Please, don't make us leave."

Elias is furious at Hélène. "You said we could stay here. Everyone keeps lying to us."

Hélène's voice cracks, "I am so sorry. I will be taking you to these wonderful people. Don't you want to go on a big ship?" She chucks Deborah gently under her chin. "Won't that be wonderful? You'll see the ocean. It's marvelously big and blue."

Elias grabs Deborah and pulls her away from Hélène, who strives to assure him. "Please, Elias." Hélène feels her heart sinking. "I love you both so much. Don't you believe that?"

Reluctantly, they nod their heads, even as they both start to sob. At their reaction, the low moan inside Hélène's head turns into a howling, yet she manages to keep her voice steady. "Come, you must give me a hug before we start our journey. I won't be able to survive unless I know that you love me."

At first, the children step gingerly towards Hélène, then all at once they rush to her and feverishly clutch onto her, refusing to let go.

Father Michel comes out of the house, bringing Noëlle and Madame Rumeau. Noëlle runs to the children, and they clasp onto her and weep. Madame Rumeau resolutely stands by. Hélène has never felt such anguish, but she admires how calm Noëlle becomes after her initial outburst, as she solemnly takes the children to collect their things.

Father Michel strains to keep control as well. He straightens up, smooths his soutane, and announces, "I should drive you to Marseilles rather than have you take the train. Now that I recall, Elias's parents disappeared while he was hiding in a closet on a train."

Hélène feels enormously grateful since she had become increasingly wary about this aspect of their journey. She was especially concerned that the boy would not be able to keep his terror under control—only a well-behaved boy and girl could hope to escape detection. There would be no chance of making it to Marseilles if he were to start to cry, likely setting off Deborah as well.

The drive to Marseilles is fraught with trouble, as the church's old vehicle suffers a flat tire, and they have to proceed on the spare. Also, they must make it before nightfall, as the car is not equipped with the blue filmed black-out headlight coverings required because of the Allied bombing of German targets in France. At last, they arrive at the meeting place Mother Superior has arranged. A kindly elderly woman, with dark hair laced with gray and thick spectacles, meets them and secretes them to a safe house near the waterfront to await boarding the ship.

When he sees the harbor full of colorful boats, Elias comes out of his sullen mood. He timidly asks the woman, "Are we going on one of those boats?"

"Yes, my dear. Only your boat is much, much bigger than all these little boats put together. And there will be hundreds of children aboard for you to make lots of new friends. I'm sure the Captain will let you sound the horn."

His eyes grow big as she describes their impending voyage. She prepares tea with some cheese and bread, then produces a sweet for each child. Deborah is quick to chew hers, and even Elias does not resist for long as he slips his into his mouth, although he turns it over and over in his cheek before starting to chew.

Hélène feels better as she observes the lady, but all the same struggles not to weep and break the hopeful mood of excitement. She earnestly wants to grab the children and run with them out of the safe house. Take them back to Foix and hide them...where? Where Major Spitzer can't get at them? No—this is the only way to save their lives.

At last, the woman stands, signaling it's time for Hélène and the priest to take their leave. Hélène resolutely gathers the children's things and hands them to the woman who smiles reassuringly. She kneels down and hugs the children. Before they have a chance to start crying, she gives Elias a small wooden ship she'd asked Étienne to carve and Deborah the last of her dolls from her childhood bedroom. Hélène turns and quickly follows the priest out. She prays the children will be sufficiently preoccupied with their new gifts and the excitement of their voyage to feel her same anguish.

CHAPTER THIRTY-NINE

Foix. Late March 1942

SYLVIE PACES IN her cell. For the hundredth time that evening, she looks through the bars of her cloistered window into the garden where the rose bushes are still gangly and bare. Thick, fat flakes of spring snow drift along the far wall onto the early blooming white azaleas, their spring blossoms blending into the gentle blanket of snow. She anxiously waits for the good weather in order to move into high gear. During the winter, bombing sorties were severely curtailed, resulting in few downed pilots reaching Foix. Meanwhile, her circuit has grown in number, and Claude and the others have continued their sabotage efforts with matériel dropped via canister. Alastair also had a radio dropped in for them to receive information, and Father Michel surreptitiously set up an antenna in the church spire.

Although Foix is technically not in the occupied zone, it might as well be, given the stringent control the Germans exert over the village. In other parts of France, the *Milice*, the French collaborationist police, carry out Vichy orders in local matters, which might as well be Nazi orders. But in Foix, the Germans themselves have taken charge of policing activities such as checking papers, monitoring rationing card distribution, and enforcing the nine o'clock curfew: this is not only because the village is a vital strategic location, positioned close to the Spanish border, but also because, in such a small and closely-knit town, it's been difficult to get what few village men there are around to collaborate and police their own citizenry. Sylvie feels considerable pride that mountain people like her, used to their fierce independence, are not so easily cowed.

A sharp rap on her cell door startles Sylvie. Sister Paul, appearing more sullen than usual, informs her that she has an urgent telephone call from Mother Superior in Toulouse. Sylvie takes the call in Father Michel's office as he nervously paces around his desk.

She slams down the phone. "They're rounding up the Jews in Toulouse. Not just the foreigners, but French Jews as well."

The priest's face pales as he makes the sign of the cross. "That can't be."

"My sister Louisa was desperate to leave last fall, but her husband insisted the government would never let the French Jews be arrested."

"What can we do?"

"Father, you're risking enough having me here in the convent."

His normally lighthearted eyes narrow defiantly. "It's never enough when innocents are involved."

Sylvie thinks for a moment, then blurts out, "We'll use the camp truck. Uncle Claude left it for me in the alleyway. Meet me there."

Father Michel stares at her questioningly, then nods. Sylvie hurries to her cell and slips on her trousers and boots underneath her habit. She throws on a warm cape and meets the priest at the truck. After securing the blackout film over the truck's headlights, she climbs into the passenger seat next to him.

The priest grips the steering wheel in the large truck. He turns to her, his lips thinning into a determined smile. "If anyone asks, we're visiting a parishioner in the hospital in Toulouse whose taken a turn for the worst."

In the darkening late afternoon, they drive off onto slushy roads. The road down from the mountainous Foix to Toulouse is slippery. There are uneven icy patches everywhere as the snow begins to freeze under the deep shadows cast by the steep mountains. The streets of Toulouse are virtually deserted, the cold having forced most people into their homes at sundown. As they near Sylvie's sister's house, Sylvie's jaw tightens as she sees a black Mercedes sedan and a large van, both parked askew outside.

"Hold up, Father. That's their house."

The priest pulls the truck to the kerb down the street. Sylvie gasps to see two German soldiers carrying out heaps of household objects, including a highly polished silver menorah and oil paintings in ornate gilded frames. They thrust them into the trunk of the car, then begin to fill the back seat. Sylvie lets out an enraged shout inside the truck as another pair of soldiers drags Louisa's husband, Dr. Goldschmidt, out of his house. They've got him under his arms. Furious and totally incredulous, he looks back and forth between the soldiers. The doctor wears a dressing gown and slippers as if he'd been sitting by the fire reading. His reddish-brown hair flies about as they pull him down the steps.

Even from several houses away, where the truck is stopped, Sylvie can hear the doctor's voice, loud and commanding, "I demand to know what you are doing. I am a French citizen."

The soldiers on either side of him merely tighten their grip and shout something in German.

Louisa emerges from the house, shrieking, "Why are you taking him?" Frantic, she runs down the steps after them carrying her husband's heavy fur coat and his shoes.

Shaking violently, Sylvie starts to leave the truck. "I've got to stop them."

The priest grabs her arm to prevent her from leaving. "Sylvie, there's nothing you can do."

Louisa begs hysterically, "At least let him dress warmly." She tosses the coat in the doctor's direction.

The soldiers sneer and stomp on the coat, grinding it into the slush, as they hustle the doctor onto the bottom step of the van. Louisa loses complete control—screeching, she runs up to the soldiers and starts pummeling them. They throw the doctor into the van, then turn around, lift her up and throw her in as well.

The priest backs the truck up and starts to leave, but Sylvie seizes the wheel.

"Drive around back. My niece is still inside."

He hesitates, then swings the truck around and into the alleyway behind the house.

Sylvie says, "Get close to that house there. Now, stop here."

She throws off her habit, and in her trousers, jumps out of the truck. She kneels by the rear doorstep to find the spare key hidden under a flowerpot, then opens the downstairs entrance to the servants' quarters.

Inside, she creeps up the back stairs to the kitchen and then into the drawing-room, trying to keep out of sight from the open front door. She can see Louisa, wild and screaming, trying to claw her way out of the van. Sylvie's heart is pounding so violently that it feels as if her chest were about to explode. But she wills herself to focus on finding the only one she can save—her niece. She tiptoes upstairs and looks into the master bedroom facing the street. Just then, a German soldier bolts out of the room, carrying a pile of clothes with a jewelry box on top. She swiftly flattens herself against the wall, barely in time to avoid detection.

She holds her breath as she sees the jewelry box start to slip from the pile of clothes—if it were to fall, that would mean sure detection. But he's able to steady it, swearing, *"Jeuden Schwein."* He hurries down the stairs, clutching his plunder.

Sylvie peels away from the wall and creeps back down the hall into Isobel's bedroom. Frenetically, she looks around then goes to the window where she sees the truck with the priest inside, parked and waiting just below. Snow is coming down harder now. Although desperate to find Isobel, she doesn't want to call out or make any noise, as the soldiers are still looting the entire house, piece by piece.

As silently as possible, Sylvie looks behind the heavily brocaded curtains, then opens the elaborately carved, mirrored armoire sitting in the corner of the room. Fearing she may be committing a fatal error and attract the Germans, she takes a chance and whispers, "Isobel, it's Aunt Sylvie."

She hears a sniffle coming from somewhere behind the armoire, then a weak knocking. She shifts the armoire slightly to gain access, taps on the rear, then along the sides, and finally comes to a latch that opens a false back. Isobel is hiding in a small, upright coffin-like space. The girl, in her thin lace nightgown, shakes uncontrollably. Her pale face with its red freckles has gone crimson with fright. Sylvie creeps back to the hall to make sure no one is there, then returns to help her niece out. At first, Isobel doesn't seem to recognize her aunt, as she shrinks like a frightened animal deeper into the confined space in the armoire. She shakes her head back and forth and softly moans. Sylvie reaches in and puts her hands on either side of Isobel's head, whispering directly into her face, "Isobel, You must come with me right now." Isobel opens her mouth to cry out, but Sylvie clamps her hand over the girl's mouth. "Be absolutely quiet. Hurry."

Isobel is shaking so badly that Sylvie can't be sure the girl has understood, but she must take a chance and move her. She pulls down one of the brocade curtains, wraps Isobel in it, and half carries, half drags her to the window. "Not a sound. Trust me."

Isobel's eyes are wide, her pupils dilated, but she manages to nod to her aunt. Sylvie suddenly picks up the girl and thrusts her out of the window, then jumps herself, praying they both land on the tarpaulin between the slats of the truck's frame. Sylvie positions Isobel's long graceful fingers to grip the slats. "Don't let go, whatever happens."

Father Michel turns on the ignition, then slowly starts off. At first, the priest drives slowly, as if he were hoping to be taken for a delivery man. One of the soldiers in the car outside the house, however, notices the truck coming out of the alley and yells. But, with so much loot on the ground waiting to be transferred to the black car and more strewn about the back seat, half in and half out, they're slow to organize it all. As soon as they do, they take off in pursuit.

Sylvie holds tightly onto the slats as Father Michel drives faster now, through back streets, and then out into the countryside. The road is more treacherous than it was earlier, with slick black ice almost impossible to avoid. As the truck swerves, Isobel nearly loses her grip, but Sylvie hoists her back onto the tarp.

When they're well out of the city, Sylvie's breathing slows as she assumes the worst might be over. Then she turns and sees the German black car in the distance behind them, roaring towards them. She yells down to the priest, "They're following us!"

He speeds up and takes a curve, hitting a patch of ice. The truck screeches and rolls over, throwing the women clear and into a deep snowdrift. Sylvie lands without hurting herself and is relieved that Isobel seems unharmed as well, although the breath has been knocked out of the girl.

Sylvie barks, "Isobel, crawl down the hillside and hide." Racing back to the truck, Sylvie sees Father Michel slumped over the steering wheel, blood streaming from his mouth, his eyes open and vacant. She shakes him to rouse him, but he doesn't respond. *Mon Dieu... not Father Michel!* She looks around and considers trying to call for help but sees the black car fast approaching. She sucks in a hard breath, reaches over, and presses his eyelids shut. Quickly whispering a prayer, she makes the sign of the cross over him.

The heavily laden patrol car, its chassis barely clearing the snow on the road, is coming closer. It careens and wobbles side to side as it barrels towards the truck under its heavy load. Sylvie reaches across the priest and grabs her habit and cloak from the front seat just as she realizes that petrol from the truck is leaking, the motor is still running hard, and the truck's wheels are spinning uncontrollably. She bounds down into the snow, whisking her cloak behind her to cover her tracks. She slides down the slope to join Isobel, who is hiding in a steep culvert.

Suddenly, the truck bursts into flames, lighting up the night and illuminating the two soldiers who've hastily parked and are running towards the truck. The explosion appears to catch them by surprise as Sylvie watches them duck to avoid flying debris. She turns to see Isobel, her chin quivering, the veins in her slender neck blue with the cold.

Sylvie throws her cloak over the girl. "I know you're cold. Stay still, dear. Please."

Sylvie peers above the culvert to see the soldiers stomping around the burning truck, searching for footprints in the snow. The temperature has dropped considerably, and the men slap their arms at their sides to keep warm. After a few minutes, one of them motions to the other to leave. They get back into the car and head back towards Toulouse, Sylvie bitterly assumes, to continue looting her sister's home.

And what of her sister and her husband? She vows to contact Mother Superior to see if anything can be done for them. And also to inform her of Father Michel's death. Sylvie is dazed, stunned at everything that just happened. She's barely able to process her grief at seeing her dear sister and her husband taken and at losing her trusted, beloved priest. Emotionally numb, she feels almost immune from the cold and everything else but then looks over to see Isobel shaking and crying. It hits her hard—they must get to a farmhouse before the girl succumbs to the cold. Sylvie looks into the field behind them, blanketed with a layer of soft spring snow. Thankfully it looks easier to navigate than if they had to contend with the more densely packed winter drifts. Lights flicker in the distance. Sylvie turns back to the burning truck and says a prayer for Father Michel. Taking Isobel's hand, she leads her niece towards the farmhouse, beseeching God for it to be somewhere safe.

CHAPTER FORTY

ISOBEL LEANS OVER and retches violently in the snow. Collapsing face down into a drift of snow, she's transported back to her armoire. She's panicking and twisting side to side. *Help me. I can't breathe.* She's dimly aware of someone—her aunt?—pulling some clothes on her then dragging her up.

"Let me sleep."

"If I let you sleep, you'll die." Sylvie yanks hard. "I'm not leaving you. Get up, or we'll both die—right here."

Isobel groans and reluctantly allows her aunt to lead her into drifts of soft wet snow and across the field. Her feet are horribly cut up, but once total numbness sets in, she finds it easier to walk. Dazed, she begins to make out the flickering light of a farmhouse ahead, and as her aunt picks up the pace, she manages to do so as well. Thoughts of a warm fire, a hot bath, and a soft down-covered bed propel her through the darkness towards the burnished light.

Seeing her aunt ahead of her, dragging her by her hand, she feels ashamed to have resisted. Aunt Sylvie is now her lifeline. But, her lifeline to what life? Her parents have been brutally taken away. Her house is in shambles, and her flute, her dresses—all of them gone—this can't be real. Surely she's imagined it all. This is just a terrible nightmare because she took an extra portion of ice cream at dinner. Of course! That's why she's so cold! She mutters to herself, "I'll wake up in my soft bed, and all this misery will have vanished."

Stumbling along in her daze, however, Isobel becomes aware that they're approaching a farmhouse. It is ramshackle, barely standing, made of a combination of stucco and logs. A pile of wood sits by a slanted front door that reminds Isobel of the nursery rhyme…the old woman who lived in a shoe. Maybe Hansel and Gretel. Even better, the Little Prince. Except there's no castle in sight. Her aunt is pulling her around to the back of the house, where a small light flickers. Sylvie raps urgently on the farmhouse door.

She hears her aunt whisper, "Damn, they're not opening up." Her aunt turns and looks around—no other houses are in sight. Desperately, Sylvie raps louder. "Please, Madame. We know someone's inside. We need help."

Isobel sees a light coming towards them, someone holding a small lantern. An elderly woman, with a thick plait of gray hair and a long thin nose, peers at them—first at her aunt, in her nun's habit soaked with wet snow, then at Isobel as she stands shivering. The door creaks open, just a sliver.

"We don't want any trouble," snaps the woman.

In her nearly comatose frozen state, Isobel sees the woman's wizened face morph into that of a troll, and she screams and backs up in terror. But Sylvie keeps a strong hold and cries out, "Madame. I'm Sister Geneviève from the Order of Our Lady of Perpetual Help in Toulouse."

"How do I know you're telling the truth?"

"Please, let us in. My niece will die. I promise we'll be gone in the morning."

Isobel can't quite understand what's going on. She sees the woman take her spectacles out of a pocket in her apron, put them on, and stare at her—first through them, then over them. The door rapidly opens, just enough for the woman to pull them through, then slam it.

Sylvie whispers, "We're so grateful."

When the woman takes a closer look at Isobel, she screeches, "My God, the child is a block of ice."

Isobel feels the woman grab at her with the great talons of some hideous monster. She goes limp with terror. The chipped crockery on the shelves spins around her. The last thing Isobel remembers is the rough wooden floor heaving up at her.

CHAPTER FORTY-ONE

SYLVIE IS ASTONISHED to see the old woman's sternness melt entirely when she sees Isobel faint. She actually brushes Sylvie aside to take charge, rubbing circulation back into the girl's hands and feet, helping Isobel out of her icy, wet clothes, giving Sylvie a clean muslin shift for the girl, and putting the girl's clothes by the wood stove to dry. The woman has a large, plump frame and walks on the flats of her feet as if every step were a chore, but she fairly scurries to make Isobel a bed by the stove. She lovingly covers the girl with all the ragged and tattered blankets she can round up in the farmhouse.

"My boy died some years ago, and his sons are...well...they were in the fighting, but we don't know where they are now."

Sylvie shakes her head slowly. "I am so very sorry, Madame." She warms her hands by the stove and spreads out the folds of her habit to dry.

"I saw flames across the field. Don't tell me what happened. I don't ask questions."

"We wouldn't expect you to. But I have one more favor to ask." Sylvie holds the woman's eyes in a pleading gaze. "May I make a phone call so someone can pick us up?"

As she considers this request, the woman bends down, shifts her long plait of grey hair aside, and stokes the stove with a small piece of wood from a meager pile. "If it is necessary."

"Thank you, Madame."

Sylvie calls Uncle Claude to come get them. With the curfew, it's daylight before he can drive down to Toulouse in the charcoal-adapted car—petrol being like gold—that he borrows from François. Unable to awaken Isobel, Claude carries her to the car and suggests they hide her in the trunk since he doesn't have papers for her. In light of the claustrophobic trauma the girl suffered, Sylvie adamantly refuses. They decide to put the sleeping girl in the back seat under a blanket and hope for the best. Claude gives Sylvie money to pay the woman for the blanket and her trouble.

The woman grimly smiles as she reaches out and presses the money back into Sylvie's hands. "Do not think I would take your money. I pray she will be all right."

Sylvie makes the sign of the cross. "And I pray your grandsons will be all right as well."

During the drive back to Foix, Sylvie feels a constant grinding in her gut, fearing they will be stopped and asked for their papers. When they finally arrive, she manages to wake Isobel and ushers the stumbling and dazed girl through the back alley, into the garden, and then into the girl's dormitory in the convent school. Fortunately, being Easter recess, the other girls have gone home. She commandeers one of the beds and lovingly runs her hands through Isobel's hair to detangle the long auburn mess. She caresses Isobel's colorless cheeks, rubbing warmth into them, then checks the girl's hands and feet for frostbite—she has suffered a considerable number of scratches and bruises, but, miraculously, she otherwise appears to be in good shape. She eases the girl onto the bed, and Isobel falls back into a deep sleep.

Sitting on the edge of the bed, Sylvie can no longer hold in her sorrow and breaks into wracking sobs. It's a wonder Isobel didn't lose all or part of her feet to frostbite. Or her long, delicate fingers, which she needs to play her cherished flute. But what of that? Gone too, like the rest of the poor girl's life.

She'll have to get new papers for her niece under a Christian name. Fortunately, Mother Superior can be counted upon to help with that. Brushing her tears away with the sleeve of her habit, she looks around the spartan room, which will now be Isobel's bedroom, to be shared with four other girls. This isn't going to be an easy transition for her privileged, rather spoiled niece. She can hardly bear to awaken the girl.

Sylvie tries to rouse her by rubbing Isobel's hand softly at first. In her sleep, Isobel moans a sharp rebuke to whoever is disturbing her and snatches her hand back, instinctively turning over and onto it, out of reach of the tormentor in her dream. Sylvie smiles, imagining the maid trying to wake her petulant niece. Well, she's going to have to get over all of that. She will, of course, help her, but Isobel has a monumental amount of work to do if she's to escape the Nazi roundup—and if she's not going to put the rest of the nuns and girls at risk. They might as well get started. She drags her niece's hand from under her and rubs harder.

Isobel awakens with a start and bolts upright. "Where…where am I?"

Sylvie smiles sadly, her stomach in a tight coil.

Isobel starts to shake. "Aunt Sylvie? I had the most horrifying dream. You were there, and I could hear my parents…" Her voice trails off as she glances around the room, shakes her head violently, and jerks her blanket up against her chest. But, evidently feeling its scratchiness, she scrunches up her nose and angrily flings it aside. "What's going on? Aunt Sylvie?"

She takes her niece by her thin shoulders, trying to calm her.

Isobel throws her hands up against her aunt. "Tell me," she screams, "I have to know."

Beginning gently, Sylvie says, "You must get a hold of yourself."

Isobel searches her aunt's tear-stricken face and wails, "It's true. They're gone—aren't they?"

"We'll try to find them, darling. I will ask Mother Superior, and we'll see—"

She gasps, "We should have left like Mama said." She cries so hard that she can barely speak, then after a while, she whimpers, "The Nazis took them, and I'm never going to see them again, am I?"

"We'll look for them, I promise."

"What happens to me, Aunt Sylvie?"

"I'm going to take care of you, my darling."

"You're a nun now. How can you take care of anyone?"

Sylvie's heart sinks as she longs to tell her niece she's not really a nun—she's only adopting that persona, that disguise, as a front for her work in the resistance. But the less her niece knows, the better. In any event, Isobel will now have to blend into the convent, where her aunt can watch over her.

"Listen to me very carefully. You can't let anyone here know you're Jewish."

"You mean I have to stay here?" She looks around, horrified.

"Until we find your parents, yes."

"That's impossible. I won't…I want to go home." She balls up her long, graceful fingers and pounds the bed with her fist.

Sylvie raises her voice, trying to impress on the girl the urgency of the situation. "I wish you could, but there's no home for you to return to—the Germans ransacked your house. Took everything."

"Everything? My dresses? My flute? Surely they'll give me back my flute?"

"We'll try to get you another one."

"I don't want another one. Papa bought that flute especially for me. It was tempered silver with an exquisite tone."

Sylvie feels her exasperation mounting. "Listen to me, Isobel. I'm sorry about your parents…and your flute." She gets up and paces the dormitory floor. "Your life is at stake here. Mine too. Everyone here is at risk." Her voice rises, "No one must know you're Jewish. Absolutely no one, do you hear me?"

Sylvie waits a moment to gauge her niece's reaction. "You've got to be very modest. Not do anything to attract attention." She brushes back her niece's thick auburn hair.

Isobel bolts upright on the narrow bed. "You're not going to make me cut my hair?"

Sylvie feels the stone floor give way. "Ah...I'm sure that won't be necessary." She quickly adds, "But you must keep it tied back and under a kerchief at all times. Do you hear me, young lady?"

Isobel nods slowly, solemnly.

"Your name, from now on...your name is..." Sylvie improvises, "Marie Josette. You are Christian, and your Catholic parents were—" she adds slowly, then in a rush, "Your father died in the war and your mother in the flu epidemic last year. That's all there is to it."

Sylvie feels a crushing sorrow for everything her niece has suffered. But the girl must get hold of herself and the situation. Isobel has a tremendous amount of growing up to do if she's going to fool everyone in the village, especially the Nazis, into thinking she's indeed the good Catholic girl, Marie Josette.

CHAPTER FORTY-TWO

Foix. Summer, 1942

FOR MONTHS NOW, Sylvie has emphatically insisted that her niece, Marie Josette, is a Catholic, despite her not knowing any of the rituals, which Sylvie shrugs off as her sister's religious neglect. She senses that the nuns in the convent suspect the girl is Jewish, but the Archbishop of Toulouse has taken a well-publicized stance against the Nazis for persecuting the Jews, so they feel obliged to shelter her, despite the risk. She's sincerely grateful to them, especially because it's quite obvious that they blame her and Isobel for Father Michel's death, although no one outwardly speaks of it.

Meanwhile, Isobel dutifully pulls her hair severely back, and covers it at all times with a kerchief. The girl has debilitating moods that vary between sullen anger and severe depression. Even bringing Isobel to the refugee camp to play with the children proves futile, as the girl only sinks deeper into despair. Formerly gregarious and lively, she can often be found sitting on the cold stone floor in her dormitory room, her knees against her chest, picking at her nails.

Adding to Sylvie's distress over her niece is that she learns the

Germans will start to move considerable numbers of their refugees by train to the east. Word reaches the camp, and a steady stream of refugees approaches Sylvie, begging her to hold their valuables—watches, jewelry, papers, and photos. She meticulously catalogs these items in her cell, astonished they managed to hide them from the guards. She's determined to find a place to bury their cherished belongings until after the war when, perhaps by some miracle, she'll be able to track them down and return their property—or if they do not survive, at least give their valuables to their next of kin, if they can be found.

Sylvie sits on the narrow iron bed in her cell, fingering a gold brooch an elderly lady entrusted to her, when Sister Paul urgently knocks.

Sister Paul says, "Sister, a train is coming. You wanted to be informed."

Rushing to join Hélène and Dr. Duchamps from the refugee camp, they cross the bridge over the river to the train station. Halfway across, Sylvie looks to her left and stops short—a string of rail cars stretches as far as she can see, marked on the sides: *limit 50 horses.* In the stifling heat, hundreds of refugees wearing yellow six-sided stars mournfully climb down from German lorries and trudge to the train, along railway tracks where the gravel is already blisteringly hot. As many of the elderly stumble on the sharp stones, Dr. Duchamps moves to assist them. He shuffles towards them, his yellow star nearly covered in dust from the tracks. Sylvie laments that he's no longer the small, dapper man with whom she and Hélène worked in Foix and at the camp, but a man who has aged decades since the outbreak of the war. She gently puts her hand on his arm. "Dr. Duchamps, as much as you want to, I don't think it's a good idea for you to be here just now."

Hélène adds, "Sylvie's right, doctor. Why don't you wait for us back at the camp?"

He looks at both the women, smiling his kindly, knowing smile. "My dears, I must help my patients until the very last."

Hélène says, "Of course, but the guards…" Her voice trails off as an SS guard, in his black uniform, briskly steps over to them. Carrying a clipboard, he turns to the doctor.

"Your name?"

"Dr. Ernst Duchamps."

"Papers?"

The doctor slowly wipes his brow with a handkerchief, looks up, and starts to say something, but then defiantly pulls them from his breast pocket and thrusts them at the guard.

"*Jeuden?* It says here."

Sylvie's pulse stops as the guard looks the doctor up and down, then consults his list.

"Not on the list." The guard pauses, staring at the doctor's yellow star. "Not yet. You may pass."

Hugely relieved at the doctor's safe passage, Sylvie rushes back with Hélène to the convent to alert the nuns and get Isobel to help them. She finds the girl sulking in the dormitory. "Isob—Ah...Marie Josette, come quickly to the kitchen. We don't have much time."

Isobel, sullen as usual, reluctantly joins her aunt in the kitchen. Hélène brings out boxes of gruel from Mother Superior's last shipment, which Sylvie has hidden in the convent away from the thieving camp guards. They are joined by four nuns in the spartan kitchen. Sylvie calls to all the women, "Quickly now, everyone. Wet down the gruel. Wrap it into small packets of paper."

Isobel hesitates, then says, with more than a little sarcasm, "Sister, I don't understand what we're trying to do."

Often exasperated when her niece tries to get out of work, Sylvie forces herself to explain in a level tone, "We need to give them something to eat for their trip."

Hélène adds, "And some water. Please, sisters, stack those tin cups into that large bucket."

The women work feverishly to prepare hundreds of food packets. Sylvie leads the procession back to the train, where she searches for whoever is in charge. One of the German soldiers points out an SS officer in a black uniform, who stands in the shade of a railway signal post, surveying the proceedings. Sylvie takes a deep breath to steady her nerves, then adopts a commanding tone. "These people must be given something to eat and drink before they leave."

Although the SS officer is already considerably taller than Sylvie, he steps onto a cement block to further assert his higher position of authority.

"Sister, how do I know what is it you give them?"

Suppressing her anger, Sylvie motions for one of the nuns with a tray of gruel packages to come over. She splits open a packet and shows it to the officer. He bends down, sniffs, and then abruptly straightens up.

"Smells like dog food." He gives her a mean smile. "*Ja*...it is suitable for them." He jerks his head towards the train.

When she reaches the first cattle car, Sylvie is confronted with pleading screams, angry yelling, whimpering and moaning, as a sea of arms surges from every slat available, grasping for the packets. She motions for Isobel to stand next to her and help her pass out the packets, while Hélène and the others pour water in tin cups onto the onslaught of desperate cupped hands.

Suddenly, a woman reaches out and presses a scrap of paper into Isobel's hand, startling her. A small voice plaintively calls to the girl from within the car. "Please, I beg you, tell my daughter I love her. I did not leave her by choice..." Isobel quickly looks around then slips the note into the waist of her skirt. Sylvie's heart heaves as she sees Isobel call out and frantically search for a face to go with the voice, but there's so much shoving in the car that the woman quickly recedes out of sight.

Sylvie is horrified to see Isobel drop her tray of packets, turn, and shout at the guards. "Don't take them. They have families." The girl's pale skin turns sheet-white, then a searing red as she continues to yell, "Why are you taking these people? What have they done to you?"

Isobel begins to stomp over to the SS officer in charge, but Sylvie drops her tray and races in front of her, grabbing her tightly.

Isobel is shrieking now over Sylvie's shoulder, "Just because they're Jews?"

Sylvie claps her hand over her niece's mouth. "Don't say another word."

The SS officer who gave Sylvie permission eyes her and Isobel with an amused look. He lifts his whip to motion to another soldier, presumably to have both the women put onto the train. Sylvie feels an icy-cold shudder but, just then, the train itself shrieks, expels a huge burst of steam, and starts rolling. Someone shouts up ahead, and the SS officer swears. As he walks briskly ahead to see what's happening, he casts an angry glance back at them.

Sylvie, shaking from fright, musters the strength to gather Isobel close and lead her, sobbing bitterly, back to the convent. She turns to watch the nuns running alongside the tracks, slipping as much food as they can into the cars before the train picks up speed—most certainly taking to their deaths all those woeful refugees Sylvie had vowed to protect.

CHAPTER FORTY-THREE

Prison Camp. November 1942

BY THE CHILL penetrating the air during the day and the light frost setting in overnight, Jean figures it must be at least late October—he hasn't known an exact calendar date for as long as he can remember. He's tried to put thoughts of Sylvie out of his mind because they create unbearable torment. This generally works, except when he's drifting off after he's found a place to sleep on the crowded concete floor; although they've moved him to a bigger cell, it's just as crowded. Perhaps, having assumed he's dead, she's found someone else. Remembering their moments together in the cave and the sweetness of their love-making stokes not only his sorrow but his hatred for the *Boches*. Every night he swears he won't think of her, but every night he can't help himself.

Meanwhile, he and Albert continue their grueling tasks—Jean disposing of bodies and Albert keeping count for the engineers. Walking back to their cell one evening, Albert whispers, "I hear a rumor. We're moving to another, larger camp. Bastards have some kind of new method of disposal."

Jean winces, "Something more efficient, I'm sure."

"Ten of us in the disposal unit are going." Albert's toothy smile broadens. "Must be our marvelous expertise."

Jean nods sullenly. *That's not the reason—it's because we've become immune to the horror of the bodies and the stench—and we work faster than if the scum had to recruit and train new prisoners.*

Albert has expanded his lottery on the number of prisoners dying in their cell to include betting on the total count of bodies disposed of each day, thereby amassing a considerable amount of contraband. At first, Jean was repulsed and refused to participate. But the lottery stash began to grow, even as Jean's hatred of himself also grew, so he gave in, figuring they might at some point be able to bribe their way to escape. Now, during the transfer, they could have their chance. The order to be moved comes down so rapidly that they're herded directly from their workstations to waiting lorries. But before they depart, Jean urgently needs to get back to their cell and retrieve their stash, hidden under a concrete slab in the corner.

As they are being shoved into the lorries, Albert stalls, joking with the kommandant, "Mein Herr, aren't you coming with us to supervise?"

The kommandant looks askance at Albert and shakes his head, the wire of his gold-rimmed spectacles glinting in the bare bulbs of the corridor. "*Ach*, where will be the lotteries without you? Who will run them with such accuracy?"

"I can give you the latest bargaining tally. They're betting on the body disposal count daily as well as for the full week now." Albert leans his substantial bulk towards him, coarsely whispering, "There's a lot of profit to be made."

The kommandant laughs out loud. "I always admire your spirit." He lowers his voice, "Get me the tally sheets."

"We'll be right back," Albert says, motioning for Jean to come with him.

They hurry back to their cell block, and Jean keeps a lookout while Albert, with his huge hands, pries up the concrete slab. They each slip some small packages under their shirts. Then Albert tears the tally sheets—large pieces of brown paper—down from the wall, rolls them up, and hands them to the kommandant on their way to join the disposal unit prisoners in the lorries.

Jean is elated to retrieve the contraband. With his bitterness deepening every day in this place, he revels in the thought that he's outsmarted his captors, if just for a moment. They tried to reduce him to no more than an animal, but he still has the will to defy his captors and secure something of his very own—something which he can use to bargain with and wield influence in the currency of the prison camp. He's exerted power, sometimes cruelly, over his fellow prisoners to get what he wanted, but didn't the others do that as well? How could anyone blame him for doing what he had to, in order to survive in this unspeakably horrible place?

The only emotional bond he's allowed himself is with Albert, who's become like a father—but not like his own weak and insufferable coward of a father. Albert showed him the ropes and how to survive. He's done everything Albert taught him—whatever it took to stay alive—atrocities and all. Survival, that's all that's important. To hell with morality.

Outside, Jean sees half-track vehicles with guns mounted and positioned front and back to escort the two lorries of prisoners. As the SS guards pass, Albert slips one guard a bribe, while Jean gives the other guard two cigarettes. Albert rolls his eyes as if to say that's too much, but Jean only shrugs. As they climb into their lorry, Jean is giddy with the prospect of getting out of the prison camp—if only for the short time it takes to transport them to another. More than that, he's keenly alert to any opportunity to escape. The two guards they've bribed get in behind them and knock on the side to signal they're ready to depart.

The convoy heads east, towards the high mountains. Although it's a bright sunny day, the weather becomes colder very fast. Clouds with darkened underbellies roll across the sky, and the road narrows through a tangled and dense forest. Just as dusk settles in, Jean hears shots coming from the surrounding trees. The vehicles come under heavy fire, and an explosion directly in front causes Jean's lorry to overturn. The guards in the cab jump clear and start firing into the thick foliage. Jean, Albert, and a couple of the other prisoners are thrown to the ground. They get up and run diagonally towards the shooting, trying to stay out of the direct line of fire. The SS guards shoot at the fleeing prisoners as well as their attackers. Jean turns to see one prisoner fall beside him. Then he sees the guard he bribed drawing down on Albert. For a moment, he thinks things will be all right— after all, this was the guard he'd bribed with the two cigarettes. But no, the guard still has Albert in his sights, so Jean dives to knock Albert to safety behind the wheel of the lorry. Despite Albert having lost considerable weight in the camp, he's much too heavy for Jean to move. Bullets riddle Albert's bulky form, catching him up and spinning him sideways.

Jean screams and kneels over Albert, ripping away his shirt, and pressing his fist down to staunch the blood. Albert's red "political prisoner" patch soaks up his crimson blood, which flows over the thin fabric into Jean's hands from gashing wounds on Albert's side and chest. Enraged, Jean pounds on Albert's chest. "Get up, you son of a bitch!" As he continues to yell, he's dimly aware of being sharply pulled up by his shoulders.

The man says, "Leave him. Come with us."

Jean shakes his head so hard that he bites his tongue, tasting blood in his mouth. As he's dragged away, he rants, "I'll kill those sons of bitches. Let me go. I'll kill them all."

The man holds him fast and shoves him ahead, deep into the forest where the towering, dense canopy provides cover from the wet-soaked twilight sky. Soon, Jean stops struggling and walks with his rescuers like someone already dead. They are a rag-tag bunch, ranging in age from teenagers to men perhaps in their sixties. In the distance behind him, he hears several more explosions, then machine gunfire. In addition to Albert, five of his fellow prisoners were mowed down by the guards.

The rest now walk, also in a daze, with their liberators. He doesn't suppose any of the guards survived, not that he cares about them. He shambles on and imagines grabbing one of their guns and turning it on the guard who shot Albert. He'd make him beg for his life, then shoot him one limb at a time, working his way up to the man's chest. He'd take his two cigarettes back and finally shoot the man in the heart. As he walks, Jean plays this scene in a loop, over and over in his head.

After perhaps an hour of walking, the men come to a rough camp in the woods, with makeshift tents. The man who grabbed Jean says, "Now we got some new machine guns, *merci*. Where were they taking you anyway?"

Still in shock over Albert's death, Jean can't get any words out of his mouth. He's handed some water.

"He was your friend?"

"He taught me..." Jean whispers, "Kept me alive in there." Jean's hands shake uncontrollably as he tries to guzzle the water. "Got anything stronger?"

Someone else hands him a flask. "Go slow. You look like you haven't eaten lately." Jean shrugs dismissively, takes a swig, then turns towards the woods and throws up. The men laugh good-naturedly, and someone gently takes the flask back.

Jean studies the man who rescued him—presumably their leader. Black beret, black leather jacket, corduroy trousers, and machine gun belts crisscrossed over his thick chest. Wide black mustache, salt and pepper hair, and face seamed with lines that Jean thinks make him look considerably older than he probably is, judging from his nimbleness and strength.

Not really posing a question, Jean says, "You're the *Maquis*."

Showing a wide swath of tobacco-stained teeth, the man smiles. "You've heard of us?"

Jean slowly nods.

CHAPTER FORTY-FOUR

Toulouse. November 1942

ONCE AGAIN, SYLVIE sits like a schoolgirl on the massive chair in front of Mother Superior's massive desk. But her anguish is far beyond anything she'd ever experienced when in school. She worries the fabric of her habit, unable to still her hands as proper nuns are trained to do. Since the deportations began, at least five train-loads of Jewish refugees have been taken away. In only a matter of months, the camp, which numbered close to five thousand refugees at its maximum, has been reduced by deportations to half that.

Mother Superior leans her substantial frame across the desk towards Sylvie. Her rotund face seems pinched into the white band supporting her veil. "What's troubling you, Sylvie?"

"Mother Superior, I don't understand how the world can stand by and let all these wretched people be sent to their deaths."

The older woman nods solemnly, then crosses herself as she speaks. "Thank God the Allies have landed in North Africa. I hear they're pushing the Germans back there."

"Yes, but the Nazis are retaliating by tightening their hold over all of France, violating their original promise to Marshal Pétain. You know as well as I, the *Boches* are about to overrun the Free Zone and occupy all of France. Damn them." Sylvie's face reddens. "Sorry, Mother."

Sylvie slumps, head down. She continues in slow, detached tones as if she can't quite believe the horror of what she's saying. "They're going to close Marseilles and all the ports along the Mediterranean. Even for those who've bribed officials to obtain their exit visas."

"Yes, it's disastrous for our work."

"Especially for smuggling the Jewish children out of the country." She looks directly into Mother Superior's kind eyes. "With your help, Hélène's managed to get dozens out through Marseilles. But now—"

Mother Superior shakes her head, her veil swishing mournfully. "We're always trying to find homes where they can hide. But I'm afraid the rest of those poor children are doomed to be sent to slave camps in the east."

"These people...their hands...clawing at me through the slats. I see them day and night." Sylvie's eyes well up. "They won't let us do any more than throw them packets of gruel. Splash them with tin cups of water. I can't bear it."

"I'm deeply...deeply sorry I can't make it easier for you. But God wants you to continue with your—"

Sylvie barks, "You aren't there to see their misery."

Mother Superior draws back, then softly adds, in her deep-throated voice, "I can't imagine how you deal with it." She rises, lumbers around her desk, and puts her arm around Sylvie, who curls into the elderly nun's embrace and sobs. Mother Superior lets her cry for a few minutes, then gently pulls up her chin. "You're washing my entire habit."

Sylvie pauses for a moment, then laughs.

"And I just got it back from the laundry." Mother Superior draws a handkerchief from her sleeve, smiles, and hands it to Sylvie. "Keep it."

Sylvie sniffles and laughs and sniffles some more. "Thank you. I'm sorry." She loudly blows her nose into the handkerchief, then stuffs it into her sleeve.

Mother Superior chuckles. "So ladylike and just like a nun."

Sylvie shrugs, smiling wanly, then turns serious. "Sometimes I just can't stop crying. I see Father Michel in that burning truck—"

Mother Superior reaches out her large, plump hands, covered with liver spots, and takes Sylvie's small hands in hers.

Mother Superior says, "You are not to blame. He was doing what was right."

"I keep telling myself that, but...and then there's my sister and Isobel."

"You saved your niece from certain death. How is she doing?"

Sylvie sighs deeply. "The first few months were the worst. She was willful and stubborn."

A broad smile makes its way across Mother Superior's spherical face. "Does that sound like anyone we know?"

Sylvie grins sheepishly. "But now...it's like a miracle. Since the first time she helped out on the train, she's become a different girl."

"How do you mean?"

"Seeing those suffering people seems to have galvanized her—made her sincerely grateful for what she has. She does everything she can for them now." Sylvie smooths out the wrinkles her worrying hands pressed into her habit. "She's gained a kind of inner peace."

"What about you?"

Sylvie turns away. A thick rasp is all she can manage. "I wake in the night, trying to scream. But I can never get a sound out."

Mother Superior takes her by the shoulders to squarely face her. "You haven't lost your faith?"

Sylvie reddens as if she'd been slapped. "No! Not at all. In fact, prayer is the only thing that helps."

"Well, in a church, prayers are a good thing."

Sylvie nods, whispering, "Father Michel once said something

similar." Then her face hardens. "Praying is the only way I can survive." She bursts out, "Mother Superior, I want to take my vows. I must take my vows. I've no right to pose as a nun. I've no right to…it's the least I can do to make up for—"

Mother Superior's deep voice booms, "For continuing to live—" She pauses, then her voice quiets to a hush. "While so many have—"

Images of her recent life in the convent flicker through Sylvie's mind—kneeling in prayer until her knees bleed, her rosary beads wound tightly around her clenched fingers as she desperately tries to expunge her guilt. "Yes, damn it." She gets up, stomps to the window, and looks out onto the Toulouse Convent's rose garden, so much grander than her garden in Foix. "I don't deserve to—"

"How many have you saved?"

Sylvie rears back, shocked. "I don't think of it that way."

Mother Superior's voice is sharp. "You only think of those you haven't?"

"I suppose so. But—"

"You must find it within yourself to continue. If taking your vows will ease your personal suffering, I will agree. But you are making a dreadful mistake."

"Why?"

Mother Superior returns to her desk and settles her habit around her. "For one thing, you'd actually have to obey orders from the Church. You've never been very good at that sort of thing."

"I can be."

"I believe you had this same argument over obedience with Father Michel. But in the end, nothing matters except whether, in your heart, you can give yourself to God."

Sylvie is resolute. "I've already decided to give myself to God." Even as she speaks, a sickening dread courses through her—Jean, bloodied and dying in the Ardennes. The man she loved and gave herself to. *I will cloak my grief behind my veil—it's the only way I can survive.*

Mother Superior seems to read her mind. "My child, if you feel you must take your vows to survive—to serve God in the way He's chosen for you—I won't stop you. But you should be running towards God, not away from your guilt."

Sylvie takes in Mother Superior's words. She exhales deeply as the fact that Mother Superior will agree to let her take her vows slowly permeates. But her heart also wrenches as an inner voice seriously questions her motives. Again, she worries her hands in the folds of her habit. Is taking her vows just a cowardly emotional escape? Will that calm her, indeed numb her enough to continue her work? But, will taking the veil in earnest be even more blasphemous than her charade, posing as a nun? And will it be so offensive to God that it will damn her soul for all eternity?

CHAPTER FORTY-FIVE

Eastern France, Voges Mountains. November 1942

JEAN FEELS UNBOUNDED gratitude to be given such luxuries as a blanket and a woolen sweater. The *Maquis* have fashioned several timber lean-tos in the forest, which provide reasonably good shelter from the icy wind. As there is plenty of wood, they've built a hearty fire and made a bubbling pot of broth. He drinks a cup, then immediately plunges into a deep and troubled sleep.

As he awakens the next morning, he rubs the grit from his eyes. Looking up, he sees tall, dark firs laden with a dazzling sprinkling of snow. Sunlight filters through the forest canopy in thin diagonal shafts so bright he has to squint, unaccustomed as he is, to natural, bright light. He's overjoyed to be out in the open, not in his overcrowded cell, sleeping cheek by jowl with scores of filthy men. He stretches languorously, savoring the space to spread his legs and arms. Then it comes rushing back. Albert gunned down. Losing his only friend. And what of Sylvie? How could he ever explain shoveling bodies—some of them not even fully dead—she would never understand—only someone like Albert knew what he was forced to do and never judged him. He turns away from the men who rescued him, silently howling with rage and shame.

He must have dozed off again, because slowly he becomes aware of low, hushed sounds penetrating the forest. The *Maquisards* are sitting in a circle before the fire, dividing up the spoils from the attack, passing around boots, guns, and parts of bullet-ridden SS uniforms. They try things on, laughing and joking about what might fit each of them and how they will draw lots for the rest of it.

Unaware that Jean is awake, they discuss what to do with him and the three other prisoners they liberated from the SS guards. Several want to turn the weaker men loose, as winter is about to slam into the mountains where they make their camp, and they've barely enough food as it is. Others insist the men should be nursed to health, then trained and made to join their resistance cell.

Jean decides to protect his interests by joining the conversation but is embarrassed that, as he tries to stand, his legs go out from under him. A large, strapping teenager comes over, helps him up like he weighed nothing, and walks him to join the others. The *Maquisards* are finishing their breakfast and begin to roll cigarettes from scraps of paper and weeds mixed with precious strands of real tobacco. He's given some chicory coffee, a chunk of black bread, and a slice of cheese. He wills his stomach not to reject this food, the most flavorful and largest amount he's eaten in more than a year.

Jean turns to the man he assumes to be the leader. "Can you tell me where we are, *monsieur*…ah?" He pauses, hoping a name will be forthcoming.

"Call me Bertrand," he says, reaching out his gnarled and calloused hand.

Jean stares at it, at first, not knowing what to do. Then he realizes it's been that long since anyone extended this simple human gesture of friendship—an offer to shake hands.

"They didn't tell you where you were?"

"Only that they brought in prisoners from a place called Drancy."

"Damned *Boches*. You're in Alsace, east of Paris, on the border with Germany. Not far from Stuttgart on the German side." He adds with a sarcastic tone, "Except it's all the German side now, isn't that right, Julien?" This last is directed at the tall teenager who helped Jean walk.

Julien jokes, "We're in the Black Forest. Can't you see how black it is?"

Bertrand says, "The *Boches* occupy all of France now. The bastards are closing the ports too."

Julien chimes in, "Because the Allies and the Free French have landed in North Africa."

The others cheer while he looked puzzled. "The Free French?"

Bertrand adds, "You haven't heard? General De Gaulle? They established a front in North Africa for the invasion, whenever that comes." Bertrand stops for a moment. "Your turn. Tell us what you know."

Jean tells them how he was in the French army, in the Ardennes, and how the Panzers broke through. Shivering and sweating at the same time, he describes waking up in the lye pit, being arrested, and the atrocities in the camp. Someone lights a cigarette and offers it to him. The *Maquisards* listen in disgust, spiking his narrative with a profusion of obscenities.

Bertrand grabs the communal flask and takes a heavy swig.

Julien cheerfully admonishes him, "Hey, it's only morning."

Jean isn't sure if he should ask but does so anyway. "What's to become of us?"

Bertrand inhales sharply on his cigarette and looks over to the other three rescued prisoners, still fast asleep. Jean follows Bertrand's glance and cringes to see the men pressed tightly to one another, cheek to jowl, sleeping as they did in their overcrowded cell, even though they're now free.

Bertrand turns back to Jean. "Let's see, shall we? When you're all more recovered."

Jean nods, goes back to his place, and lies down, wondering what his options are. He feels obliged to these men for rescuing him. Of course, he believes in having a resistance to fight the Germans. And, of course, he wants to tear their throats out, one by one. But his profound sense of rage and bitterness is mixed with a crushing feeling of absolute hopelessness. Why should he fight and risk his life? Everything he does only leads to more suffering and death. For Suzanne. The children. Albert. And anyway, what does he have to go back to, after what he's done? Sylvie would never understand—would never forgive him. She's lost to him. Together with any decent person he ever knew in Foix.

Julien comes and sits beside him. No more than eighteen, he's slim and very tall, with blue eyes, blonde hair, and strikingly handsome Aryan features. He leans close. "I got one of the SS uniforms. No one else is tall enough." He lowers his voice. "I can wash the blood off and pass for a *Boche*. And, I'm from around here, so I speak German."

Jean looks around to make sure they're not overheard, then stares at Julien, an imposing young man looking older than his teenage years. "What are you thinking?"

"I'm damned tired of this war. I want to get down to Marseilles, then to North Africa. Lots of money to be made there. On the black market."

"Why tell me?"

"You could come with me. Be my prisoner."

Scanning the area for Bertrand, Jean lowers his head. In prison, he learned to speak with his mouth virtually closed. "What makes you think I don't want to stay and fight with them."

"Tell me I'm wrong."

"Aren't they closing the ports?"

"That's why we have to leave—tonight."

It only takes Jean a moment to make up his mind.

That night, the two make their escape with some boots and extra clothes that Julien steals for Jean, which enable him to change out of his prison rags. They travel mostly by night. Jean finds walking over the precipitously steep and rocky terrain nearly impossible, but his anger and shame propel him forward. Julien is the model SS soldier in looks and swagger. When they reach their first checkpoint, he imperiously waves off the sentry's request for papers and roughly shoves along his prisoner—Jean. He sneers in German that he has orders to get his prisoner to the next town and then, for each subsequent town, makes it up as he goes along.

Jean's mind swirls. After being confined for so long and having been claustrophobic from being crammed into his overcrowded cell, he's now prone to panic attacks from open spaces. Julien, in earnest, has to shove him along, threatening to beat him if he slows down. Although this plays into their charade, it raises Jean's anxiety. Somehow, they make it to Marseilles, just before the port is about to close. Julien pawns his SS uniform, a Lugar, and some German equipment he stole and amasses enough money to bribe a ship's captain to take them to North Africa.

The voyage to Algiers is another nightmare for Jean, as the captain secrets him and Julien in an airless closet in his cabin for the rough voyage across the Mediterranean. Sweating and dizzy, Jean feels his muscles spasm. Desperate for even a tiny bit of room to stretch, Jean relives the terror of waking up in the death pit after the Panzer attack, as well as the horror of the prison camp's claustrophobic confines. He also imagines the agony Albert must have felt after being thrown into solitary, and with every panicked and labored breath, berates himself for not being strong enough to save Albert from being shot by the SS when they were being rescued by the *Maquis*.

Jean and Julien are offloaded via shipping container, which is unsealed in an alley some distance from the dock. A scalding blast of North African hot air punches Jean in the gut. Feeling like an outcast, Jean's bitterness festers, and his cynicism and self-loathing sink deep into him. With no papers, he and Julien must quickly vanish up into the Arab quarter high on the hill overlooking the harbor. They climb higher and higher, entering a filthy, deplorable city within the city of Algiers—the Casbah. It's crammed tight, rife with all manner of Algerian Arabs as well as European refugees fleeing the continent who intermingle with a kaleidoscopic array of Middle Eastern Arabs and African Blacks.

Jean and Julien penetrate deep into the tangled labyrinth of narrow winding alleys, with their never-ending stairs leading up to terraces that lead up to more narrow winding alleys that bend off to the left and right into never-ending stairs that all seem to lead nowhere. Jean feels increasingly suffocated as they bump into goats, mangy dogs, and merchants in the souqs, hawking food cooked in the sweltering heat on smoking grills. Inner courtyards with elaborate Moorish arches and tiled floorings stretch five and six stories high, every inch packed with veiled women, screaming children, and small dark Muslim men. Mosques dot the sharply inclined stairways, whose inner courtyards offer a rare but welcome sight of small patches of blue sky.

"Julien, I can't stand it here," Jean spits as they climb higher through the disgustingly grimy steps of the winding closed-in stairways.

"Just keep going up, my friend. And don't step in the sheep dip."

Jean bumps into a vendor with birdcages full of squawking parrots. "I know what sheep shit smells like—this is much worse."

The alley takes a sharp right curve upwards. Julien bends his tall frame to get under a low Moorish arch. "Only because there's no air."

Jean grinds his teeth. "Don't remind me."

Various gangs control the terraces, often with hard-bitten women in charge of their entry. It's possible to traverse the length and width of the Casbah by climbing and descending the myriad terraces without having to navigate its pinched alleys, where no one is safe from being pickpocketed at best and outright robbed with your throat slit at worst.

The French police don't dare enter the web of winding stair-cased streets, as they would be immediately overpowered by the soldiers of the illicit drug dealers, gangs of roving thieves, or swarms of women with their high-pitched, rapid-tongued screeches.

From the moment Jean climbs his first set of switch-backed stairways, he feels confined, pinned in by the chaos of hawkers touting their wares, women yelling, muezzin calling Muslims to prayer, and a cacophony of noises from the crush of people and animals. The stench is unbearable with the appalling heat and no breeze in the filthy, oppressive, tomb-like alleys. As Jean climbs, he feels his throat closing, his eyes stinging, and his knees buckling. Julien helps him up to a small apartment he's procured by bribing a prosperous-looking Arab wearing a fez and a silk cummerbund carrying a carved walking stick.

They settle into a small apartment laden with pottery and thick rugs, which only make it seem hotter and more confining. Like virtually every unit, their apartment is built up against, below and above other white mud-brick and stucco Moorish structures. It has the typical thick wooden doors secured by multiple heavy iron locks. While their outside entrance is, by Casbah standards, luxuriously appointed with brightly tiled Moorish arches, inside, the few windows that look out onto the harbor below are covered with bars against the thieves.

Julien counts the money they have left. "I need to get us some papers. What name do you want?"

Jean lifts a ceramic pot on a small charcoal burner encased with years of grime. His smile is faint. "How about Pierre Nobile?" He winces, knowing there's nothing noble left in him.

After he gets his bearings in this atmosphere of lawlessness, Jean realizes how grateful he is to Albert, who taught him how to set up lotteries using a lucrative system of bets and odds. Everyone in the Casbah gambles on the slightest pretext, and he and Julien soon build up a profitable racket, taking bets on all manner of things such as news from down below in the harbor regarding army troop movements, victories, and defeats. Julien's Franco-Germanic heritage in Alsace enables them to fence weapons, radios, and other equipment to both the Germans and the French. They pay protection to the local gangs and develop a network of enforcers, equally unscrupulous men who fled their military service, either in France or Germany.

As the money flows in, Jean and Julien order servant girls to bring them wines, grilled sheep, falafel, and spiced rum. But, in their relentlessly close quarters, Jean's claustrophobia regularly grips him. Most evenings he bribes his way to climb the many sets of winding stairs up to one of the roof terraces, just to see the sky and breathe. He turns to Julien. "How can you stand living here?"

Julien shrugs. "You have a problem with our lifestyle?"

Jean looks out to the boats down below in the harbor. Decades ago, after occupying Algeria, the French built a series of luxury hotels and massive navigation-related structures throughout the harbor. "Not when I can see the Mediterranean, and there's a cooling evening breeze."

"Look all you want. We can never go down there."

Despite his own cynical views, Jean is still amazed at how despicable other people can be, especially during wartime. His mantra becomes: No one can be trusted and everyone he ever cared about, especially Sylvie, will abhor him for the things he's done. Therefore, he'll be the first to cheat, steal and reject anyone who tries to befriend him.

He finds it ironic that General Charles de Gaulle, leading the Free French from his base in London, has inspired idealistic Frenchmen and other foreigners whose countries have been overrun by the Nazis to swarm to North Africa to join the fight. Jean wants no part of the war and recognizes that the Free French pose a serious threat to him—if he's discovered, he'll be conscripted. He and Julien skulk about in the dark shadows of the Casbah. They frequently move their apartment and their stash, lest the corrupt and brutal Arab gang members—especially those they themselves have bribed—confiscate their money and goods—and give them up, for the bounty, to the French gendarmes to be arrested and conscripted. Jean knows a prison cell in Algiers will be as horrendous as a German prison camp and certainly hotter, given the relentless and oppressive North African heat.

CHAPTER FORTY-SIX

Foix. Spring, 1943

THE ESCAPE ROUTE for downed pilots that Sylvie, Alastair, Uncle Claude, and the others have put together is now operating in full force—despite all the risks, near-disasters, and sheer terrors they've all endured. The Allies have relentlessly escalated their bombing raids, targeting industrial locations in Germany, Belgium, and France. They hope to cripple the Wehrmacht regime by striking key factories, critical transportation, and utility targets. With the mounting number of British—and now American—sorties, it's inevitable that more and more pilots and their crews will be shot down and need a way out of France.

The French begin to organize a more systematic, widespread resistance, assisted by British parachute drops of agents, couriers, and radio operators, as well as canisters of weapons, explosives, radios, money, and medicines. The resistance establishes more than a dozen "circuits" throughout the country, each with its own code name such as: *Comet, Phalanx, and Ajax*. Several *freedom lines* of escape evolve from largely ad hoc venues to established routes over the sharp and treacherous mountains to Spain—passing airmen along to various safe houses, then smuggling them out of the country. Main routes originate in Brussels and Paris and continue south to the west coast of Spain to San Sebastián, or through Sylvie's route, via Foix, to the east coast of Spain to Barcelona.

Since Sylvie took her vows in earnest last November, she feels more emotionally restored. She doesn't have to lie about masquerading as a nun and freely engages in deep, prayerful sessions that cleanse her soul. Sessions that shut out the pain of the world, if only for an hour or two, as she kneels with her rosary beads or lays prostrate, arms out and in the position of the Christ. Devoting herself fully to God also allows her—reluctantly and tearfully—to finally accept Jean's death.

She continues to be amazed as well as heartened that her once spoiled and petulant niece has become a different girl. Isobel can't do enough for the refugees—she works every train, distributing food packets and water alongside the nuns and Hélène. She also accompanies Hélène to collect any scraps of clothing the village women can spare for the refugees.

One night, Sylvie calls her niece into her cell to let her know how much she appreciates the change that's come over her. Sylvie greets Isobel with a deep and loving hug, takes her hand, and leads the girl to her iron bed. They sit, hands entwined like they used to do when the girl was growing up.

Sylvie says, "Dearest, I can't tell you how much your work here has touched me."

Isobel looks sheepishly at her aunt. "When I first arrived, I was absolutely horrid."

"I wouldn't say that, exactly." Sylvie pauses, then laughs. "Well… maybe. But I'm so proud of you now."

Isobel reflects, then says, "I suppose the turning point for me was that day, last summer. We were at the train, and I was giving out the packets. This woman…I couldn't even see her face…but she pleaded with me to get a note to her daughter telling her that she loved her." Isobel's voice wavers. "She might have been my own mother. Knowing, really being sure, she truly loved me—"

"You were the center of your mother's life. And your father's."

"I suppose I knew that. But it made me see she didn't choose to go away." Isobel's eyes blur with tears. "So how could I be angry with her for leaving me?" Sylvie opens her mouth to say something, but Isobel cuts her off. "It was irrational for me, I know, to be mad at her...that she left me. But I'm not angry anymore, knowing what horrendous things they might be going through while I'm here, safe with you." Isobel heaves her slender shoulders, barely able to get the next words out, "I feel so guilty, being here when they are—"

"Shusssh...You didn't cause the Nazis to become inhuman monsters."

"I want to get out there and help these poor people as much as I can. To show my mother and father, I'm not this spoiled little...I'm sorry about what they're all going through..." Isobel sinks her head into her aunt's lap and weeps.

Sylvie gently rubs circles around the girl's back as if she were a baby. It pains her to feel Isobel's shoulder blades so sharp in the girl's thin body.

Isobel whispers, "I don't even know if they're alive. And Joshua. What do you suppose happened to him and his family?"

"You used to play such lovely music together." Sylvie sighs. "I wish we could get you a flute."

Isobel spreads her long, graceful fingers in front of her. They're raw and chaffed, her nails brittle. "I'm not sure I'd remember how to play. And, with no music..." Isobel's voice trails off as if from a vanishing ghost.

Sylvie takes the girl's hands again, rubbing her love into every cracked pore. "You know you have nothing to feel guilty about."

Isobel shudders, expelling a sigh that wracks her frail body. "I suppose you're right."

Sylvie whispers, as much for Isobel's benefit as for herself, "No, I mean it. You've done everything humanly possible."

Sylvie is deeply gratified that discussing Isobel's feelings about her parents' plight seems to have given her even more strength of purpose. As the refugees' ranks are depleted every week with the relentless stream of deportations, Hélène and Dr. Duchamps make some decisions. With Isobel's increasingly able assistance, they organize the nuns and women volunteers from the village to take over all the refugee work. This leaves Sylvie free to focus on the growing numbers of airmen—getting them up the mountain to their hiding place in the cave, going with the *Maquis* to the parachute drops, and organizing the supplies they acquire.

Things are progressing well with the escapees. With increased numbers of airmen reaching Foix, there are at least three or four at any time, waiting to cross over to Spain in convoys. Claude personally leads most of the groups, although some of the younger *Maquisards*— especially the courageous young Jacques, with the lightning-strike scar down his face—are getting good at evading the Germans and will soon be able to guide convoys on their own. Also, with the additional guns Alastair has ordered dropped in, they're better able to defend themselves when they are, on occasion, discovered.

So far, Claude has had to shoot only one German on patrol to enable an injured airman to cross a river that had risen unexpectedly. After that, the Germans intensified their patrols along the border. Even without this extra danger, however, it's an arduous trip, and Sylvie is increasingly concerned about her uncle's age and stamina.

One evening, sitting together in the cave in front of a small fire, Sylvie cautiously approaches the topic. "Uncle Claude, don't take this the wrong way, but would you ever consider going over, maybe every other convoy."

Claude draws his chin back as if he were considering the matter. He takes his time scratching his head and patting down his few remaining wisps of white hair, then grins. "Are you saying I'm slowing down?"

Sylvie studies her worn boots, glowing in the firelight. "Not at all, but the younger men... well, it's a rough journey. With the extra patrols. And you have to move entirely at night—"

He pounds his knee. "The night belongs to the *Maquis*!" His large ruddy face darkens to a deep crimson. "They may have their dogs, but we know the way." He pauses for a moment, then puffs up his broad chest and exclaims, "They're afraid of us at night."

Sylvie smiles and repeats the phrase as if it were a mantra. "The night belongs to the *Maquis*." She grins at her dear, proud uncle, undaunted and so like her father for whom nothing was ever too hard to accomplish.

Meanwhile, Louis and the others continue a stepped-up campaign of sabotage—setting charges, first TNT then later *plastique*, on railroad switching stations and telegraph wiring centers. Constant talk of an allied invasion further energizes Sylvie, who hasn't felt this much sense of mission and well-being since the war began.

CHAPTER FORTY-SEVEN

Algiers, North Africa. Summer, 1943

IN A FEW months' time, the only place Jean feels comfortable is in the one-room flat of his favorite prostitute, Raza. It's up five flights, behind the souq, but in the shadow of a mosque, so it's in the shade. There's a tiled inner courtyard for a bit of space and a window that looks directly up to the sky when she opens the dark wooden shutters. Except for brief periods when he goes out to conduct business, he stays with her, smoking exotic drugs to help him overcome the bouts of shakes and panic attacks that continue to plague him.

Jean turns over on Raza's lushly pillowed bed, awash with sweat. He slowly opens his eyes, slits in his pounding head.

She washes his forehead with cool jasmine-scented water. *"Cheri*, you had another..." Raza's voice trails off as she turns aside to rinse the cloth.

He tries to open his eyes wider. Although the light is only a few shafts that glance between the wooden shutters, it crushes his vision. "Too bright, close," is all he can manage, as his eyeballs burn in their sockets.

"Mais, oui."

Through his limited vision and his drugged fog, he recognizes the billowy silk drapes—magentas, ochres, yellows—hanging on the sides of the tall, narrow window of her apartment. Beads and silks are everywhere, as well as towers of soft pillows. She lights a candle then softly pads barefoot across the carpet to close the shutters the rest of the way. Bracelets around her ankles jangle delicately. Her long black hair shimmers auburn in the thin shafts of light. Thick and flowing, her tresses sway slightly as she moves her ample hips. The multi-layered flowing silks she wears keep moving, even when she stops at the window. She closes off the rest of the light and turns towards him. Her olive skin glows in the candlelight and a fine line of perspiration forms just above her full upper lip. She raises her chin seductively, sways back to the bed, drops her silks onto the carpet, and offers him her nakedness.

He tries to rise to touch her but feels weak, as if he were sick with a vicious flu. Moaning, he falls back onto the bed, staring up at the ceiling fan.

She whispers, "What do you want, *Mon Cheri?*"

Nagging memories of joyful times past stir within him. But they are soon obliterated by the usual seething anger that eats away at him—his self-loathing at having been forced to commit abhorrent acts. He's lost everything and everyone he ever held dear. And now he's nothing but a coward, shivering and sweating—just like his father.

Suddenly, Jean sits up screaming, "I'll kill them all...dump them in their own ovens..."

She strokes his head. "Shussh...you are free now." She gives him a bubbling pipe, which he greedily inhales, determined to suck the mind-numbing drugs into every crevice of his brain. He welcomes the drugs that launch his mind into colorful swirls, like the patterns on her soft cushions and billowing curtains. Less and less interested in having sex with her, he prefers to spend his days drifting into drug-induced stupors. Sometimes, with a relentless pounding in his head, Raza's dark olive skin morphs into Sylvie's oval-shaped face. The voluptuous figure in front of him...Raza's? Sylvie's? He feels the room turbulently spinning and reaches out, beyond Raza, for the ghostly figure floating in his mind. She recedes then rushes back at him. He yells, "Don't look at me like that. I had to stay alive." He grasps for her, but she withdraws into a cave with towering stalactites and an indigo lake, then vanishes into the depths of his drug-crazed mind.

Raza shakes him. "Pierre. You are hot again." She drizzles cool jasmine-scented water on his forehead.

His eyes flutter, then open. "Raza, I keep seeing you, but it's really her."

Raza smiles, saying in her dusky full-throated voice, "*Cheri*, it is just me you are seeing in your dreams. No one else. Do not worry. I am right here with you."

CHAPTER FORTY-EIGHT

Foix. Spring, 1944

WHILE HE NO longer controls the refugee camp, Hélène hopes Major Spitzer will retain control of the whole of Foix, even under the new, full-scale military occupation. She fears what might happen if another, more ruthless officer were put in charge. Apart from deporting the refugees, which the major insists is a Wehrmacht central policy he can't alter, the rest of his administration of the village has been relatively tolerable.

There have been reprisals, of course, especially when the *Maquis* blew up a nearby telecom exchange and ten random men from Foix were imprisoned for a month. But elsewhere in Southern France, such reprisals would have resulted in those village men being shot, with the whole town forced to watch. Hélène is also grateful that, despite being Jewish, Dr. Duchamps is allowed to minister to the detainees in the camp—in other refugee camps in the south of France, non-German personnel are completely prohibited, and treatment suffers greatly. Hélène prays that sharing Spitzer's bed is at least partially responsible for his somewhat more humane attitude—that would make her sacrifice worthwhile for the benefit of the villagers as well as the refugees.

Even so, she remains agonizingly conflicted. Some time ago, she learned that her husband Gérard was a prisoner of war in Poland, conscripted into forced labor. Claude confided to her that the plight of such prisoners was extremely grave. When she got the news, she felt even more defiled and guilty. What would be more disastrous—if her husband returned to learn of her everlasting shame or if he didn't?

Adding to her internal turmoil, Hélène finds that, quite against her will, she's warming to the major's touch. Needing it. Staying in bed with him at night even after their love-making, instead of rushing to scrub herself and then taking to her own bed, alone.

One morning, as the soft early morning light angles through the shutters, he pulls her to him and starts to make love. He's nothing like Gérard, her big, playful ox, but he's well-muscled, if quite slender. Earnest. Serious. Respectful of her. Despite her attempts to remain emotionally distant, she feels warmth spreading through her. And in spite of everything, she responds. When they're done, he kisses her softly, curls her onto his chest, and rustles his delicate fingers through her hair.

"It is a shame that such a woman as you has not borne a child."

Suddenly Hélène feels cleaved in two. Angry that Gérard might never come back, but drawn to what she senses is the major's genuine caring. The kind of caring she's desperately missed.

Trying to be nonchalant, she slides to the side of the bed and pulls the covers between them. "Oh, well. I'm getting on in years." Making light of it, she retreats into the shell she's constructed to survive—the place inside of her where she tells herself she's only sleeping with him to get information.

He pulls her back, gently lifting her chin and turning her face towards him. His dark brown hair is close-cropped but tousled, like a boy's. His gray eyes are softer, less watery, and more honest. "Hélène, who's to say how long we will be here, in France. Do you ever think—"

She realizes that she must stop him before he goes too far—to a place that will be untenable for both of them. "My goodness, look at the time. I must get your breakfast. You can't be late to headquarters."

As she gets up, she catches sight of him in the mirror on her parents' dresser. He sinks back in bed, the blood draining from his already pale face. She feels a twinge of remorse that he's becoming attached to her—that spurning him is cruel. But she must keep her distance—after all she's still married to Gérard. Deep down, though, she knows there's little hope of Gérard ever returning. Even so, whenever she feels too close to the major, she does what she always does to stiffen her resolve—she recalls the brutality of his holding his gun on her the first day he arrived while making her bend to pick up those wretched yellow stars.

Hélène usually waits a decent interval after the major departs before she leaves the house since she doesn't want even the hint of impropriety. After all, he's billeted to her house against her wishes, so how could the villagers gossip about them? She's careful never to let anyone besides Alastair, Claude, and Sylvie know the extent of her relationship with the major. Today, however, she's late, so she leaves immediately after he does. She feels flush from the intensity of their morning love-making, as well as from racing about to get ready. Still straightening loose strands of hair into her chignon, she turns to lock her front door. She glances to the side and sees Étienne coming her way, passing right by the major, whose step seems to Hélène to be light, even jaunty. She can't see the major's face, but apparently, he makes some kind of jovial nod to Étienne.

Étienne passes by him, then jerks around to stare at his back as the major heads off. Étienne rushes to Hélène. She feels it coming—the look he always gives her. Searching deep into her eyes, never losing hope she'll return the love of his teenage crush, despite the disparity in their ages and that she is, in fact, still married. She feels for the boy as he tries to make himself older by sporting the army jacket that was Jean's, which he never takes off. But today he seems particularly distraught, as he looks back at the major, then stares intensely at her as she continues to fix herself up.

"Madame Hélène, ah...I came into town early. So we could go up to the camp together."

Embarrassed to be seen leaving her house even somewhat disheveled, and to be confronted by him, she stammers, "Well—ah—Étienne." She can't meet his gaze. "It's good of you to come. I didn't—I wasn't expecting such a handsome young man to escort me today."

His voice, having generally settled into a deeper register, rises. "Madame Hélène. Is something wrong?"

"Not at all." She looks away, fumbling with the lock and finally managing it.

"I know you think I'm very young, but I've learned a lot from Uncle Claude."

She turns to him, smiling to make light of what she knows he's driving at. "I'm sure you have."

"No, I mean, if anyone should ever bother you—" He glances back again towards the major, who has just turned the corner. Confident the major is out of sight, Étienne moves intimately close to Hélène. He bends down and whispers through rigidly clenched teeth, "I would kill him if I thought he'd ever dishonored you."

Hélène feels a shock of concern at his tone, as well as the ruthlessness of his admission. Where is Sylvie's sweet but impetuous younger brother? Who is this adolescent boy before her, teeming with jealous rage? She resolves to double her efforts to hide the truth about her and the major from Étienne, which she knows would trigger a chain reaction and a certain, violent end for this earnest, young boy.

Several weeks later, Hélène is in the infirmary at the refugee camp, wrapping an elderly woman's wrist, when Sylvie rushes in. "Hélène, I got word you wanted to see me?"

"Give me a moment." Hélène helps the woman out and washes her hands. She turns to Sylvie, and trying to control the outrage in her voice, says, "Sister, they deported Dr. Duchamps."

Sylvie gasps and crosses herself.

"From the first, he wanted to go. Be with his people. But we convinced him to stay and help." Hélène is unable to corral her anger. "All of a sudden, he was on the list. And then he was gone."

Sylvie furtively looks around. "Shussh....a guard will hear." She puts her hand on Hélène's shoulder and squeezes. "I'm so sorry. I can't imagine the strain on you."

Hélène slumps onto a stool by the corner shelving, now virtually bare of bandages and other medical supplies. "They're taking so many now. There won't be any left for me to treat. She affects a slight, sarcastic laugh, "I suppose that'll lighten my load." She looks up at Sylvie, her words turning acerbic. "If the *Boches* are so sure of an invasion, why don't they just concentrate on defending their territory? Why bother with these poor people? It's like they want to cram in as much killing—as much evil as they can—in the short time they have left."

"It's horrific, I know. But with the stepped-up Allied bombing raids, we've got a steady stream of airmen to get out. The liberation must come soon." Sylvie's excitement grows. "Even those with injuries, they're all so anxious to get back to their planes for another run."

Hélène nods mournfully. "I'll try to sneak out tonight. But it's harder. Spitzer's more diligent since they brought in their reinforcements."

"Be careful."

Hélène winces. "I make sure he sleeps soundly."

Sylvie kneels down and wraps her arms around Hélène. "I can't imagine how dreadful it is for you. But your information has been absolutely invaluable. Remember that."

Hélène feels a fierce revulsion sweeping over her. "I wouldn't mind so much, but the villagers give me such vile looks. Like I was collaborating."

"That's ridiculous." Sylvie whispers in Hélène's ear, "I'll vouch for you when the liberation comes. Everyone will know you were working with the *Maquis*. And when Gérard comes back—"

"If he comes back." A vein juts out in the milk-white of Hélène's slender neck. Her voice is hoarse. "I'm not sure I ever want him to know."

Sylvie shoots her a solemn glance. "Let's face that when the time comes."

"You know, before the end, they'll kill as many French soldiers as they can." No longer able to tamp down her grief, Hélène moans, "My God, when the liberation comes, what price will be paid?"

CHAPTER FORTY-NINE

Foix. Spring, 1944

ISOBEL IS GENUINELY proud of herself for helping Hélène collect surplus clothing from the women in the village. She waits in the downstairs parlor for the elderly woman upstairs to sort through her things
and labor down the stairs with what Isobel knows will be a meager
bundle. No silks. No bonnets with ribbons trailing. No matching para-
sols. A shiver of cold runs through her as she catches sight of herself
in the mirror over the fireplace. There are no mirrors in the convent,
which is just as well, as she can't bear to look at herself anymore. Her
aunt decided it was best always to keep her hair tied up under a kerchief so as not to attract attention, so her best feature is hidden away,
only to emphasize her worst feature—her freckles. And she's become
so thin—well, best not to look.

It's been difficult to remember her new name, but even more difficult to demonstrate that she's Catholic in order to blend in: when to
cross yourself, what to mumble over those beads, when to get up and
when to kneel. It's all too confusing, although the seriousness of the
matter weighs heavily on her at all times. And missing her mother and

father…well…she can't think of that just now, or she'll dissolve in tears, and people might notice.

Despite all this, when Isobel keeps busy at the camp with Hélène, she truly feels like she's doing something important, helping the poor refugees. And she's grateful not to have time to dwell on her past life. But now, standing in the cramped parlor waiting for the old woman upstairs, she has time to think. The room is neat and modest, with faded lace doilies covering the frayed arms of the chairs and the one small sofa. Square and oval framed photographs of the woman's family are meticulously placed just so on the mantle. There are, however, no silver trays of champagne, no candles in a gleaming chandelier, no books, no piano, and no music stand. Isobel chokes down a sob, remembering her beautiful mahogany music stand, polished to a high gloss and richly carved with G clefs and notes. Closing her eyes, she goes through the motions of assembling the three pieces of her silver flute, which her father bought for her by special order. She buries her face in her hands, her slender shoulders heaving as she struggles to hide her soft crying.

"Mademoiselle, would you please come up and help me down with these," the woman calls from above.

Wiping her tears with the sleeve of her coarse muslin blouse, she calls up, "Of course, Madame."

Isobel carries the woman's small bundle down and into the street outside the house. She's just turned into the plaza when she sees a horrifying sight—a torrent of armored vehicles rumbling into Foix—tanks, motorcycles with machine guns mounted on sidecars, and lorries filled with soldiers. Sylvie has told her that the Allied forces have made incursions in North Africa and are stepping up their bombing campaign. Everyone anticipates a massive Allied invasion, but of course, no one knows when it will come and from which direction. Since Foix is the most substantial French village near the border with Spain, the Germans have already reinforced it militarily, and now they must be adding additional strength. As the forces rumble in, the townsfolk, who've been sitting around the town's central fountain enjoying an early taste of warm spring weather, scurry to the perimeter of the plaza.

Watching the barrage of Nazi soldiers, Isobel feels a sickening grief, as she recalls the night they took her parents. Her knees weaken as she stares at the scene from the edge of the plaza. Startled, she nearly screams as Hélène comes up alongside. She wraps her arm around Isobel's shoulder and presses them both against the side of a building.

"What's going on, Madame Hélène?"

Hélène shakes her head. Isobel feels faint, seeing tremors of rage coloring Hélène's porcelain skin. Lorry after lorry arrives. Benches on both sides are filled with Wehrmacht soldiers—square-jawed, broad, and fit in their pressed gray-green uniforms. Most stare arrogantly at the villagers, although Isobel notices one boy, in particular, who stares off into a distant horizon. He's very young and seems exceedingly uncomfortable amid the brash boastfulness of his fellow soldiers.

Hélène nods at the boy, covering her mouth, so only Isobel can hear. "Look at that one. They're bringing in children now. They must be desperate."

"He doesn't look happy to be here. Not like the others."

Hélène turns sharply to Isobel. "You're not feeling sorry for him, are you?"

Isobel feels a flush that freckles her entire face. "Of course not." She turns to go, clutching her bundle of clothes. "I'll get these to the church to be sorted, Madame Hélène. I know you're eager to get back to the refugees."

Hélène's tone is bitter. "Those that are left." Hélène heads off, calling over her shoulder, "Please dear, get back to the church as soon as possible."

The lorries stop in the plaza to unload the soldiers while the villagers sullenly watch. Isobel starts to return to the church by going around the back and through the side alley but decides to stay, just for a moment, to see what's going on. The soldiers are buoyant, triumphant, as they hurl themselves down from the lorries, stretching their legs and doing calisthenics. They seem eager to display their strong physiques, especially for the benefit of the young women of the village, who eye them with varying degrees of contempt, interest, and suspicion.

The boy she noticed earlier doesn't take part. Instead, he slowly walks to the side of the fountain and splashes some water on his face. The ideal picture of the Hitler youth, he is powerfully-built, square-jawed, and blonde. Isobel ducks into a doorway to watch.

A portly older soldier with cauliflower ears and a tall, gangly soldier saunter to the fountain, take out cigarettes, laugh, and smoke. They snicker and point to the statue honoring the French soldiers from World War I that stands atop the fountain, riddled with bullet holes, the Germans having used it again and again for target practice. The young man seems to be brooding, as he steals glances at them.

Just then, one of the other soldiers in the plaza revs his motorcycle, making a loud retort. A skinny dog flees in terror across the plaza and skids into the fountain, splattering the portly one's boots before it races away.

"*Ach*," he yells, then says something in German that Isobel thinks sounds like "Mongrel."

The tall one flashes a sinister smile and kicks the young soldier's leg, motioning for him to clean the portly one's boots. The boy pretends to ignore them and turns away to polish his helmet with his sleeve. The tall one kicks him again, shouting, "Mongrel. *Dummkopf.*"

Isobel flinches. She's surprised to find that she's actually glad to see the boy drawing back his fist and preparing to take a swing. Before he can, another soldier steps between them and calls a halt to the harassment. From his gestures, he seems to be admonishing the tall one for acting up in front of the townsfolk.

Isobel continues to stare at the young soldier. Joshua was tall, but this boy is not only tall but blonde, broad, and muscular—not like most of the boys from her temple in Toulouse or the village boys in Foix. The nuns have drilled into the convent girls that they should never stare at people, although she hasn't had much occasion to stare at anyone. Even so, unconsciously, she gives a slight toss of her head. It's hard to completely forget the pride in herself that her father deeply instilled, not to mention how willfully she always sought to be the center of attention.

The church bell tolls once on the half-hour, and Isobel decides she really must go. As she turns from the young boy, their eyes meet. He quickly looks away. Embarrassed to be caught staring at a German soldier, she lowers her head and races down the side street. How mean they are, even to one of their own. What could that boy have done to engender their taunts?

CHAPTER FIFTY

Algiers. Spring, 1944

JEAN RECEDES INTO a never-ending whirlpool of hallucinations, drugs, incense, silk pillows, Raza, and more hallucinations. He cedes his business responsibilities more and more to Julien. They meet every week to divide up the profits, smoke acrid Arabic cigarettes and knock back spiced rum in a small café near the main souq in the Old Quarter. One week, however, Jean has had enough of his confinement in the tangled mass of stinking alleys. Julien has warned him against leaving the Casbah, where the French police dare not go, or they'll surely be arrested. But Jean insists on going down to the port to meet in one of the luxurious cafés along the water.

Jean sits drinking in a large wicker chair under an arbor of flowering vines. "This is whiskey, my friend. Not that piss we drink up there." Jean is sweating profusely, his shirt mournfully rumpled. It's stifling hot, with hardly a breeze off the water.

Julien chides him. "Why do you risk everything by coming down here?"

"For the view." He downs his drink and motions for the waiter to bring another. "I'm tired of living like a mole."

Julien stretches out his long limbs and adjusts his wide-brimmed fedora that covers his blonde hair. "My friend, you are much more suitable to our subterranean lifestyle than I am." He laughs and takes a swig of his whisky. "You are very mole-like. You have powerful forelimbs, well adapted for digging."

The waiter brings another drink, and Jean swirls the glass around, staring at the amber-colored whiskey before swallowing it down. "If I were a mole, I wouldn't see all the filth we live in." As he slams the empty glass down, he misses the table, and the glass crashes to the floor.

Julien looks around, alarmed. "You should lay off the whiskey...and the drugs. Especially the drugs. They are dissolving your brain." Julien waves to the waiter for the bill then turns back to Jean. "You need to keep up your end of our business."

"That's all you care about, my friend?"

Julien breaks out into a boyish grin. "You know I love you very much." He exhales a sooty puff of his cigarette and tugs at Jean's arm, exhorting him to stand. "Why else would I agree to your insane request to meet down here? We've got to get back right now."

Jean shrugs him away, impatiently motioning to the dark-skinned waiter to bring two more whiskeys. Already in the process of bringing the bill at Julien's request, the waiter looks puzzled, then hastily retreats to the bar for the extra drinks.

Jean turns to Julien, his eyes drooping as he slurs his words. "There's something in my mind, but I can't quite remember it. I thought if I came down here, I'd be able to breathe again. And I'd remember."

Julien pulls Jean's arm to get him to stand. "Not good to remember too much, my friend."

Jean starts to answer, but his chin falls against his chest. He's barely aware of Julien, who seems to be looking nervously around. He's just alert enough to appreciate Julien's concern but not sufficiently in control of himself to prevent nodding off.

Julien shakes him, urgently whispering, "Get up. The gendarmes."

Jean tries to form his words, but his tongue seems to be too big for his mouth. "Just bribe 'em. You c'n do that, can't you?"

"You want to go back to prison?"

At the mention of prison, a knife slices through Jean's consciousness. He makes a desperate attempt to pull himself together, but there's nothing he can…he's losing…losing consciousness…slipping into oblivion.

Before he's even fully awake, the familiar smell of urine assaults him. And the smell of other men. Filthy men. His eyes flash open. *Merde.* An Algerian prison.

He's slumped on a concrete floor, drenched in sweat, the heat intolerable in the narrow but towering cell of crumbling white stucco. Two vomit-green lizards race each other up the walls toward a grille about ten meters high, where the blindingly blue North African sky is just visible beyond. His pulse races. Distraught, he can't quite make his mind work. How did he get here, and what happened to Julien? Why didn't he just pay off the gendarmes like he pays off the gang members who shake them down all the time? As the horror of his situation slowly but fully dawns on him, Jean twists around and smashes his fist into the wall. If he were arrested and left to languish, Julien could keep everything they'd built together. And Raza would be too afraid to offer a bribe, lest she ends up in prison too.

Still feeling drugged, he draws himself up and goes to the cell door, which is steel with only a small barred window looking out onto myriad similar interior steel doors with similar small barred windows. "Guard…guard." No one comes. Sweating as much from the stifling heat in the airless cell as his withdrawal from the drugs saturating his veins, he lumbers to the one high window with a hint of skylight. It is rectangular with rectangular bars. His arms shaking, he lifts himself onto the ledge just below the window and looks out. He is stunned, faced with an entire square courtyard of white stucco walls, one small rectangular window per cell, hundreds of cells that he can see and more above that aren't in his range of vision. He cranes his neck to look down onto the courtyard where he sees, to his horror, a guillotine.

He jumps down from the window ledge and stumbles to the cell door. Again, he shouts, and again, no one comes. He curses and shouts until he's hoarse. Finally, he groans loudly and slumps down the wall, sliding against oblong trails of lizard shit and ending in a fetal position on the stucco floor.

He's dimly aware of three other men in the cell staring at him, ignoring his ranting with a remarkable level of indifference. Two are large, burly, and vicious-looking men of indeterminate foreign origin, probably Russian. The third is an old drunken Frenchman, who snores loudly and keeps everyone awake until one of the others takes off the old man's sandal and stuffs it in his mouth.

Jean is relieved that the guards let the poor old guy leave the next morning, so he and the Russians can get some sleep in between calls to prayers five times a day and the other prisoners' yelling in Arabic, French, and languages he's never heard. They sweat during the day and freeze at night. The guard brings some kind of turmeric-spiced slop, disgusting beyond belief. He is so hungry he's tempted to gnaw on one of the lizards that climb freely about the cell or chew on one of the many beetles crisscrossing the stucco floor. He is not amused that the Russians fight over one, especially plump water bug which skitters by. All the time, Jean is shaking from withdrawal and pleading with anyone within earshot to let him speak to someone in authority. Periodically, Jean hallucinates and drifts in and out of consciousness, dreaming about eating water bugs and lizards fashioned into kebobs and grilled outside the souq in the Casbah.

In moments of lucidity, he tries to engage one of the small, slender

Arab guards, hoping to bribe him. They patrol in twos, however, so he can't get the attention of just one and doesn't want to risk being shaken down by both. Anyway, he has no money for a bribe. His time in the prison camp taught him a bitter lesson—a man is as good as dead if he doesn't have money or something tangible to barter.

The morning of the third day, three guards come. One puts in the slop they call food, while the other two motion for Jean to come with them. One leads a German shepherd dog on a leash. They shackle his hands in front of him, and as he can barely walk, drag him through a brightly sunlit whitewashed courtyard into a low white stucco building. A preposterously obese and slovenly Algerian officer with leather skin sits behind a desk. The man uses his thumb to shovel tobacco from a dainty velvet pouch into an ornate, long-stemmed black pipe. His fingernails are tobacco-stained a putrid brown, as are his gums and teeth. He's missing alternate teeth, so when he speaks, his mouth looks like a checkerboard. There's another chair a meter or so to the side of the officer's desk with a ring on the floor just in front of it. The guard with the dog pushes Jean down onto the chair and fastens his shackles to the ring. As he does, the dog barks and snarls viciously.

The dog's barking triggers a violent reaction as Jean shakes and starts to mumble incoherently. He's back at the prison camp, shoveling corpses, hissing and moaning, into the oven with the snarling dogs nipping at his feet. The guard kicks Jean in the shin, and the fat officer orders the guard and the dog to leave. Jean manages to slow his rapid, shallow gasping and get control of the involuntary terror that invaded him.

The officer says, "Please, *monsieur*, let's talk."

Although Jean is desperate to get out of there, he wills his voice to be level. "Can you tell me why I'm here?"

"You were causing a disruption. Collapsed in a café." The officer smiles—a corpulent Cheshire cat with checkerboard teeth. "And then the papers. Ah, you see, your papers are false. Well-made but blatantly false. We arrested the poor fellow who made them last week. He got twenty lashes." As he laughs, his belly shakes. "Then we turned him loose to make more false papers, so we can arrest him all over again. We take bets on how many times he will be stupid enough to get arrested and when his back will be too flayed for him to move."

"I can explain."

"No need, Pierre. Whoever you are. You are French. As you know, there is a war on. I am paid a bounty for every conscript I deliver to the Free French." The officer moves closer to Jean, his belly flopping over the table. "I am sure you want to enlist to serve your country...don't you?" He squints, malevolently adding, "We can arrange to have you lashed until you agree to enlist."

Jean scans the immense girth of the officer, judging he can easily fit three of himself into this man's single, gross body. What does this man want most? Everyone has their price. But how should he broach the subject of a bribe? "I can see that you are a betting man. I can make it worth your while, many times over, to look the other way."

"Ah, but you see, your friend Julien has already made it worth my while."

Furious, Jean tries to stand, straining at his shackles. "What have you done with Julien?"

The officer leans away and out of Jean's reach. "He was most cooperative in handing over certain items of value."

Jean slumps back down onto the chair. "Where's Julien now?"

"He decided to serve his country, just as you will. Most patriotic. Especially since they shoot deserters." He laughs a booming, belly-shaking laugh. "The French military with their firing squads...most civilized." He sucks on his pipe. "Much more enlightened than flaying a man until he's ready for the guillotine."

Jean slams his eyes shut, trying to stop the burning throb in his forehead. The officer gets up, waddles towards him, and sits, buttons bulging, on the side of the desk. He leans down directly into Jean's face and says, through his brown smattering of teeth, "There is an Allied invasion coming. They need cannon fodder." His laughter thunders as his garlic breath diffuses into the far corners of the room.

Jean imagines leaping up to rip the man's throat out but calculates that he's just out of reach. And, if he tried, they'd shoot him on the spot. Or worse, take him for the lash, then behead him. Instead, enraged, he grits his teeth and grabs the arms of the chair, squeezing them until his knuckles whiten and throb. Meanwhile, the officer calmly heaps more tobacco from his dainty velvet pouch into his pipe and lights it. Then, with the greatest satisfaction, he blows a thick puff of putrid smoke directly into Jean's face.

CHAPTER FIFTY-ONE

Foix. Spring, 1944

ISOBEL HAS JUST finished washing clothes in the bend in the river closest to the convent. Struggling uphill with her basket, she catches sight of the young German soldier crossing the bridge. He sees her, looks around to make sure no one is watching, then tentatively walks down the riverbank towards her. She quickly tucks a loose strand of her hair underneath her kerchief.

He offers a shy smile, then says in French, "May I help you, Mademoiselle?"

She sidesteps him and heads back, fearful of being seen with a German. "No, thank you." Then she turns back and fixes him with a surprised look. "You speak French?"

"*Ja*, my parents used to speak it at home."

Isobel shoots him a quizzical look.

"They played music, and we had, well, what you call soirées. Lots of musicians."

"Really?" Isobel feels her pale face reddening, which she hates because it exaggerates her freckles. "Music? What kind of music?"

"Bach, Beethoven. Not just German composers. Handel too."

"I haven't heard that kind of music for so long—they just chant old stuff in the church." Isobel turns to go, but vivid images lodged in her memory burst through, stalling her determination. She can't resist putting the basket down and proudly announcing, "I used to play the flute."

"I started on the piano." He looks down at her, smiling sheepishly. "I had big hands. I could reach the octave when I had four years." He pockets his hands and shuffles his feet.

She feels drawn in. Fascinated by him. Suddenly, she realizes she can't be seen talking to him. "Thank you, but I...ah...I can manage."

He says, with sad resignation, "You do not like to be seen with me. But I would have wanted to help you."

"I'm fine. Thank you." She bends to pick up the basket, but her curiosity wins out—she straightens up and asks, "Why do they treat you so badly?"

A dark, ruddy color rises from under his collar and splays across his square jaw. His young face is still ever-so-slightly plump, although Isobel guesses he must be about her age.

He jerks his head towards the bridge, then turns to leave. "I cannot say."

"Wait, tell me."

His friendly tone dissolves into one of panic. "You must not be seen talking to me."

"Stay. Just one minute."

He hesitates, looks around, then whispers, "I am not one of them. That is why they call me mongrel."

"Mongrel? I thought that's what they were saying. But why?"

He looks up the bank and sees a patrol crossing the bridge. His voice is more urgent. "If you are certain you can manage, I must go. For your sake, Mademoiselle."

"Marie. Marie Josette. But you can call me Marie."

Nervously, he twists around to leave, then turns back, flashing her a broad smile. "I am Karl."

Isobel feels an odd fluttering in her stomach. All proper young women must avoid the Germans, but she feels compelled to follow him with her gaze as he takes the riverbank in a few bounding steps, then easily jumps up and onto the bridge. Just as Karl reaches the small buildings where the village begins, he looks back at her. Isobel is exceedingly pleased.

Isobel has noticed Karl in the village for some time, but he's always kept a discrete distance, and she hasn't had the courage to approach him. She's furious to see the two soldiers continuing to harass him but pleased to catch him looking her way every now and then. Why would they act that way towards him? Especially because he looks like a model German soldier, with his broad physique, rosy complexion, and blonde hair? Never deterred from discovering any secret which might remotely involve her, Isobel contrives to bump into him. She slips him a note to meet her the next afternoon before vespers, in the apple orchard on the hill behind the village.

The mild May weather sets the fields to bloom. Neat rows of lavender have suddenly spiked, providing myriad hidden paths leading up to the apple orchard, now also in full blossom. As rich soil is scarce in this rocky area of France, everything is densely planted. Isobel has thought long and hard and decided that the orchard is a perfect place for a clandestine rendezvous.

Isobel excitedly gets ready. Remembering her aunt's strict admonition about her hair, she wistfully pulls her auburn tresses straight back, although she exchanges her usual utilitarian kerchief for a long scarf she managed to keep for herself from the clothing donations. Before she leaves, there being no mirrors in the convent, she primps in the reflection of a brass water jug. Food has been in short supply for so long, she's lost weight and bemoans the fact that her willowy figure is now downright skinny. But she's determined to make the most of her looks. Smiling into the brass jug, she puffs out her cheeks to lessen the sunken look of her angular face. She checks her teeth, bites her lips to give them color, and smoothes her eyebrows. Finally, she shakes out the wrinkles in the one good skirt she's been given from the charity bin.

Isobel arrives early. A gentle breeze shakes the branches of the craggy apple trees, and a few glorious, white apple blossoms cascade to the ground. She picks them up and turns them over and over in her hands, trying to quiet her nerves. She salivates at the thought that soon there will be plump fruit hanging there instead—pure magic to a city girl from Toulouse. She hears a rustling and glances down to see Karl making his way up through the dense lavender blooms and apple trees. The trees are not very big to begin with, and against his tall, muscular frame, they appear even smaller. Feeling color rapidly migrate to her face, she turns away and vigorously fans herself with her slender hand to minimize her freckles.

As he approaches, she looks down demurely, as her mother taught her. Her whole body is trembling, but she manages to say, in a steady, clear voice, "I wasn't sure you'd come."

"I should not be here, Marie. But I did not want you to think I am ignoring your note."

Isobel knows that most of the townsfolk make sullen accommodation with the Germans and are especially proud of fleecing their occupiers in any way possible. One price for local spirits for the French, another for the *Boches*. They also sell them black-market food from neighboring farms at inflated prices. The villagers are amazed that many of the *Boches* still act as tourists on holiday, buying up local lace tablecloths at artificially high prices to ship home.

She also knows that a few of the village bar women have taken up with certain soldiers, to the utter disgust of the remainder of the townsfolk. But as the German presence wears on year after year, and in the absence of any hope of liberation, some women have formed what the convent girls euphemistically call "relationships." Apparently, these women have decided this to be preferable to entirely wasting their youth. Isobel certainly doesn't plan to stray along this path, but even so, she's extremely curious to find out just what a "relationship" might involve.

With Karl standing right in front of her, she wills herself to adopt a cool and mature tone. She starts off, "I was interested—" In a deliberate effort to appear nonchalant, she leans against the trunk of a small, craggy apple tree and positions herself so that the blossoms frame her face. "You said your parents gave soirées." She shrugs. "I thought it might be nice to hear about them."

Karl brightens, closing his eyes, she assumes, to better visualize the scenes at home. "Everyone comes dressed in fancy clothes. They bring their instruments and play into the night."

Isobel feels a thrill listening to him and looking up, through a profusion of white blossoms, at the azure sky. She might as well be hundreds of miles away from all the suffering she's endured. "That must have been wonderful. Your parents were musicians?"

"My father was first chair in a big symphony orchestra. My mother, she plays the viola."

Isobel licks her lips as if preparing to dive into a bowl of ice cream. "Tell me more about the soirées."

Karl smiles slyly, bowing his head a little, pretending to be ashamed. "I used to eat a pickle sitting on the floor. Right in front of the oboe player."

"You didn't!" Isobel's giggle wafts melodically upwards through the blossoms.

"You should have heard him go off-key!" Karl puffs his cheeks and mimics.

They laugh, their heads coming close together, like school children conspiring to play a trick on their teacher.

"Most nights I fall sleep listening to them play."

The smile vanishes from Isobel's face—all his talk of music and home triggers a searing pain. She's on stage at the auditorium in her temple, her hair coiffed in luxurious ringlets, her flute gleaming in the stage lights. Waiting for the conductor to cue her solo, she steals a glance at her proud father. In her reverie, she lets her long scarf slip down around her shoulders.

Karl continues in a rush, "Except I try to stay awake for Father Christmas. Weren't you excited about him coming down the chimney?"

Isobel shifts uncomfortably.

He briefly waits for her reply, then plows ahead with his own reminisces. "I never could see how Father Christmas fit down the chimney." Another pause for her response.

She jerks away from him.

"Marie, tell me how happy you were when—"

Isobel bursts out, "We never celebrated Christmas." She freezes, then gasps at her inadvertent outburst.

Karl looks at her in surprise.

Isobel tries to regroup. "Oh, I...I don't know...it's been so long...I don't remember." She's shaking violently.

He studies her auburn hair and angular features. "Your family is..."

"I didn't say anything, I swear." She braces herself, expecting the hillside to fall away beneath her. "Please, you mustn't tell."

Karl looks around protectively, then says with genuine assurance, "Of course not."

Trembling, she turns to leave. She fumbles with her scarf and adjusts it tight around her face. "I've got to go."

"I promise. I will not ever say a word." He reaches out to squeeze her hand. "You can trust me."

Slowly, she turns back and studies him intently. She feels the ground becoming steadier underneath. "Really?"

He nods. As he stares down at her, his open, earnest face calms her. Isobel breathes heavily for a minute to get her bearings. Now that she feels more in control, she's a bit emboldened, more like her old self. Curiosity still nags at her, and now that he knows her secret, maybe she can find out his. "You never said why they hate you."

"You will not believe me."

"What do you mean?"

"No, I am serious."

She pouts. "You know a secret about me. Tell me one about you."

He swallows hard, the muscles in his jaw setting firm. "I am not German."

"Wait a minute." She eyes him, uncertain.

Now it's Karl's turn to start to leave. "I knew you would not believe me."

Isobel stops him. "No, I want to know...really."

He takes her by the hand and walks deeper into the dense blossoming foliage. He crouches into the grass and gently pulls her to kneel beside him. "I will tell you my secret. But you must promise to keep it like I promise to keep yours."

She nods solemnly.

"I am a guinea pig...an experiment. They call it behavioral engineering."

"I...I don't know what that means." Confused and frightened, she starts to stand, but he gently tugs her back down.

"Wait, please. I saw them shoot my parents. In Warsaw."

Shocked, Isobel pauses, then blurts out, "I think they killed my parents too. But no one knows for sure."

"My God, I am sorry."

Isobel starts to weep. After a moment, she stands, tears in her eyes, and turns to rush away. But he scrambles up, blocking her path.

"Wait. We are both...alone."

Isobel is terrified by what they've shared. She shakes her head, tears still streaming.

Karl takes her by the shoulders. His face anguished, he implores her, "Wait, please."

Isobel softens under his gentle but firm touch. "All right. Tell me the rest."

He takes her hand, and they sit under a craggy tree. He continues. "This doctor. He has a school in Germany. He makes children into what he wants. They control everything you do."

"I feel like the nuns control everything I do."

Karl's tone becomes increasingly bitter. "They fill my brain with oaths to the Master Race. We train to be Hitler's finest youth. But behind the doctor's back, everyone tells me I am inferior because I am really Polish and not German. That I will never be one of them."

"What did you do?"

"I just try harder...I try harder to be accepted. To be good at sports. Rifle practice. Conjugating verbs."

Karl pauses for a moment, then starts to laugh, which triggers a mass of giggles from Isobel. "I was never good at conjugating verbs either!"

They laugh together—such a good feeling, as she hasn't truly laughed in years. He puts his arm around her. At first she's alarmed, then slowly warms to his embrace, and they sit together, in silence. Isobel feels a combination of trembling fear and elation.

The church bell tolls. She gasps. "Vespers is in an hour. I must go."

He nods and helps her up. She hurriedly brushes herself off and adjusts her scarf. She pauses to smile at him, then rushes back down towards the convent and through the blossom-laden apple trees, fairly dancing among the lavender.

CHAPTER FIFTY-TWO

Foix. 21 August 1944, Six o'clock p.m.

THE SUMMER HEAT is at its peak, and the church garden is in full bloom—with a riot of azaleas along the back wall and a profusion of roses climbing the trellises. But Sylvie barely notices them as she escorts two airmen into the garden then back out to the hidden riverside passageway. The first is broad, and sandy-haired; he's wounded in the side, and having some difficulty walking. The other is shorter with a dark complexion and dark curly hair. Sylvie is touched by the affection between them, as the shorter one offers his shoulder to the bigger one to serve as a human walking stick. She especially admires him because, through his gestures, he makes light of the situation, nodding and smiling as if nothing were wrong.

After butchering the French code phrases at the entrance to the garden, they don't try to speak as they walk. Sylvie is a bit nervous that the sandy-haired man might be a spy, given his large, impressive, and muscular physique. But the shorter one's manner towards him and their easy camaraderie doesn't fit her impression of Germans as being rigid, uptight, and always formal. By now, she's used to airmen being astonished when she pauses along the stone passageway to fling off her habit, revealing her trousers underneath. It always amuses her to see their startled looks, and these two airmen don't disappoint.

Deeper into the forest, Sylvie decides to stop and give the large wounded man a rest. The men pull out French-rolled cigarettes, obviously given to them by the *Maquis* somewhere up the freedom line. In fractured French, the small man introduces his friend as Bruce McDonald from Omaha, Nebraska, and himself as Joe Garabaldi from Brooklyn, as if that were a city and state combined. When word spread of the Allied landings on the sixth of June in Normandy, everyone in Foix was ecstatic. Now, Sylvie wants to find out more.

Bruce laughs and slaps his knee, a gesture Sylvie associates with American cowboys. "We're gonna get those damn Krauts!" He says this in English, but Sylvie gets his drift.

Joe motions for him to be quiet, and as much as Sylvie enjoys Bruce's exuberance, she has to agree—following the build-up of their military reinforcements several months earlier, the Germans have increased their patrols over the whole area.

"How long will they take to liberate all of France?" Sylvie speaks slowly in French and a bit too loudly, as people often do when speaking a foreign language to someone who can't understand.

Bruce tries to guess her meaning. "You want to know about kicking the Jerries out of France?"

Sylvie vigorously nods.

"Won't be long now. First Paris—"

Her eyes brighten and she crosses herself. "Liberate Paris? Thank the Lord."

"Wait a minute," Joe interrupts. "Hasn't happened just yet."

Bruce sits up and smiles. "But it will. Soon. Bet your bottom...oh well, Sister... I mean—" He shoots Joe an anxious look.

Sylvie, confused, looks between the two. But then catches his meaning and decides to have some fun with them—she throws them a stern look.

Joe sharply exhales, sputtering cigarette smoke. "Wait, Sister. He didn't mean—"

Sylvie laughs her mellow, throaty laugh to show she's playing along with the joke. Bruce guffaws but then grips his side and doubles over, blood seeping through his fingers.

Alarmed, Sylvie motions for him to lie down and for Joe to stay with him. She races ahead and brings back Claude and two of the younger, stronger *Maquisards* to help get Bruce to the cave. They carry him in a sling made with blankets and have almost reached the cave when he passes out. She decides to immediately go back down and ask Hélène to come up that night and tend to his wounds.

Whenever Sylvie enters the cave, she stops to deeply inhale the cold, dank air and remember. The lights from the men's lanterns and a small cook-fire bounce onto the stalactites, illuminating her cathedral. Framed by the arched sides of the cave, the lake appears to her like a massive, holy baptismal fount. She relives her time with Jean. Loving him. Grieving for him. And now she honors him by enabling so many to hide here so they might live. It's a different way for Sylvie to say her rosary—one rocky outcrop at a time. Each time she enters, once she allows herself this brief moment, she switches into high gear.

This evening, there are six airmen and one female agent waiting for the next convoy. Depending on the weather, they're scheduled to cross the mountains into Spain during the next night or two. With the female agent and two new arrivals, Claude and Jacques would be taking a total of nine. This group would be larger than normal, but with the massive increase in bombing raids in the last months leading up to the Normandy invasion, considerably more escapees have arrived than usual.

Everyone helps the unconscious Bruce settle by the fire. Sylvie is certain he won't be well enough to travel with this next group. The mountains are rugged, and there are more guards patrolling since the Germans have dug in. The streams present the greatest obstacle, especially for a wounded airman. Even with just a modest flash rainfall, the rivers can abruptly rise to torrents, fast running and treacherous. Unfortunately for their circuit, more than one healthy airman has been swept away, struggling to cross at night. Those who lose their footing survive only by managing to grasp tree limbs or rocky outcroppings of ledges, which takes unusual strength—something a severely wounded airman will undoubtedly lack.

Sylvie feels a spate of anger that an exuberant and brave fellow like Bruce might never make it back. She must get Hélène to treat him. He's everything she associates with Americans—jovial, open, warm, and somehow bigger than life itself. She needs to save every airman she can, not just for them but to honor the memory of Jean. She takes a deep breath, shoulders her duffle, and starts back down the mountain.

CHAPTER FIFTY-THREE

21 August 1944, Six-fifteen p.m.

I'T'S STILL LIGHT when Hélène returns to Foix from the refugee camp. She disembarks from the lorry by the train station. As gasoline continues to be virtually unattainable, all the lorries have been converted to charcoal for fuel, which gives off a thick smoky residue. Stepping a few feet away from the charcoal-burner fastened onto the side of the vehicle, she takes a deep breath of fresh air. As she does, she looks up the hill just outside of town, stunned to catch a glimpse of two figures emerging from the orchard. Isobel swiftly walks one way while the young German soldier, whom she'd seen when the additional troops rolled into Foix several months ago, strides in the other direction.

At first, she's furious that Isobel would sneak around with a boy—and a German boy at that—but then she feels a stab of fright at the peril the girl might be courting. Since the June landings in Normandy, all anyone thinks about is the Allied liberation and how far the troops are pushing into occupied France—this brings a different set of horrors. With villages liberated all over the North, vicious reprisals are being carried out by the French against anyone who collaborated with the *Boches*. She must warn Isobel off, not only for the girl's sake but for the sake of her dear friend Sylvie as well.

Hélène circles around behind the church and meets up with Isobel rushing up the alley. "What do you think you're doing, young lady?"

Isobel comes to an abrupt halt. Looking flustered, she lowers her eyes and says, "Excuse me, Madame Hélène. I'll be late for vespers."

"You know the Allies have landed and are pushing the *Boches* back."

"Isn't it marvelous?"

Isobel steps aside to bypass her, but Hélène blocks the girl's way. She tries to keep her voice level, despite a mixture of anger and fear. "I agree. You know what else is happening?"

"What do you mean?"

"As every village throughout France is liberated, the French are punishing people who collaborated with the Germans. It's turning quite horrible, especially for young women."

"Collaborated? I...I don't know what you—"

"I saw you with that German boy just now. Coming down the hill."

"I can explain. He's not really German."

Hélène, exasperated, leans into the girl. "Look, young lady. What would your aunt think if she knew you'd gone back to your old self-centered ways?"

"I'm not. And I'm not lying. He's not German. They murdered his parents in Warsaw. Then the Nazis took him when he was young and put him into a German school to make him into—"

"Please."

"It's the truth."

Hélène eyes the girl, who seems entirely sincere. She grabs her and ducks them both into a doorway, deciding to give her the benefit of the doubt. "Even if things are as you describe—"

"You must believe me."

"Whether I believe you or not doesn't matter. No one's going to wait to verify your claim before they attack you." Hélène glances around, then harshly whispers, "When the Free French liberate Foix, the women are going to come after the bar-women and all the others who've been with Germans. With shears."

Isobel pulls her scarf tight against her head. "Oh my God. But—"

"To shave your head. Maybe worse. Especially if you could be pregnant."

Isobel's trembling hand grabs onto Hélène's wrist as she says, "Madame Hélène, I never did anything with Karl, I promise. We only meet and talk about music. I swear."

"Even so, you'd better not have been seen."

"I'm sure we haven't."

Hélène winces. "I saw you."

Isobel starts to cry, her pale, freckled face turning a deep rust color. As angry as Hélène is, she softens and hugs the girl. She sincerely hopes no one has seen them together. How could anyone blame such a young girl, who'd lost her parents and her whole way of life, for searching out a tiny bit of warmth and comfort? Immediately, her stomach sours as she turns the question back onto herself—what about her relationship with Major Spitzer?

Hélène lets Isobel cry for a minute, then looks her in the eye. "You must never see him again. Do you understand?"

"I've got to tell him why."

She looks around to make sure they're not overheard, then raises her voice. "No you don't. It could be the end of you, do you hear?" When the girl doesn't respond, Hélène barks, "You must promise me."

Isobel sniffles and weakly nods her head.

Hélène kisses her on both cheeks. "All right then. Go back to the convent, and let's hear no more of this."

Isobel whispers, "You won't tell Aunt Sylvie?"

"Not if you do as I say."

Isobel is shaking so badly she can hardly walk. Hélène watches her navigate the cobblestone plaza and disappear, like a waif, into the side door of the church. She prays the girl will do as agreed but knows it isn't likely. Isobel has Sylvie's brave, albeit stubborn streak, which is why she admires and loves them both so much. This is also why Hélène has an overpowering dread that she and the girl will both come to a bitter end because of their involvement—in their own very different ways—with enemy soldiers.

CHAPTER FIFTY-FOUR

21 August 1944, Seven-thirty p.m.

SYLVIE HURRIES FROM the cave down the mountain, then through a forest of giant sunflowers, and finally along the passageway by the river to the church. Before entering the garden, she slips on her habit and tucks her hair underneath her veil, then rushes to her cell to hide her trousers and duffle in her trunk. She goes around the side of Hélène's house and raps softly on the kitchen window, in case the major is home. When Hélène comes out, they quickly walk up the alley, out of sight.

"Hélène, you must come up tonight. There's a new airman. A Yank, and he's badly hurt."

"The major insisted I make dinner tonight. He wants to talk about something. I'm not certain what, but they're all on edge with the Allies making such progress."

"They'll get a taste of what they deserve."

Hélène flinches.

In a whisper, Sylvie snaps, "You think because I took my vows, I don't hate them. All those innocent people they deported. My sister and her husband—"

"I'm not criticizing you. My Gérard's still a prisoner of war, remember?"

Sylvie says, more sharply than she intended, "Well then, make some excuse tonight, but come to the cave." She stops short. "I'm sorry. I didn't mean it like that. This Yank up there. He's worth twenty *Boches*."

"If only they'd push through the rest of France. Liberate us right now... tonight."

"There's talk of another landing. On the Mediterranean. They could be here sooner than we think."

Hélène morosely looks back towards her house. "What's to become of them?"

Sylvie registers surprise. "Won't you be happy to be rid of him?"

Hélène's reply is sharp. "What do you think?"

Sylvie brings her into a swift and urgent embrace. Hélène's sacrificed an unfathomable amount for the resistance. Sleeping with a Nazi officer—something Sylvie's certain she'd never be able to do. She starts to leave, then turns back. "Have you seen my niece?"

"Ah... yes, in fact, I... ah... I saw her earlier. Going to vespers."

Sylvie beams, proud of Isobel and how hard she's been working with the refugees. "The daughter I never had."

Hélène barely nods.

"Something wrong?"

She hesitates, then quickly adds, "I'm just worried about what Major Spitzer wants to talk to me about."

"Probably concerned about saving his skin. Don't forget, come up to the cave tonight. No matter how late." Sylvie kisses her on both cheeks, then rushes off.

CHAPTER FIFTY-FIVE

21 August 1944, Seven-forty-five p.m.

As she prepares dinner, Hélène hears Major Spitzer enter the house, humming. Food shortages have worsened considerably this past year, although he still manages to acquire eggs and other precious commodities. Spitzer hangs his hat on the rack by the front door, then spritely steps into the kitchen, triumphantly handing her a package wrapped in brown paper. Opening it, she gasps to find a small slab of meat, something neither of them has seen in ages. She shoots him a questioning glance.

"The Wehrmacht high command is sending whatever it can to boost morale."

She thrusts both palms down onto the kitchen table. "Morale? Whose morale?"

"Hélène, please. This isn't easy for any of us."

She sneers, "What's been so difficult for you?"

"We've been over this. I am looking for any honor possible in this situation. We are planning something big which should bring me recognition—"

"Recognition? Honor? That's what you've been looking for?"

"It has been hard to live in a country where everyone despises you. The only time any of us can relax is when we are on leave. Out of uniform. When people don't know we are German."

"You certainly do relax when you're out of uniform."

"Hélène, what's come over you? I have told you, many of us would like to make peace with your people."

"Now you talk about making peace. When the Allies are making gains all over France. Say it...you're all afraid of what's going to happen when they get here."

He slowly shakes his head. "Many of us would go back, but...to what? The Führer is completely paranoid. Forbidden anyone to retreat." He strides back and forth in the small kitchen like a caged animal, his shiny leather boots sharply clacking on the planked wooden floor. His thin lips form into a grimace. "My home...in the countryside outside Berlin...at least your house is standing."

"What do you mean?"

"Everything I had is gone...my sisters...my parents died. In a bombing raid."

Hélène eyes him with ferocious suspicion. The man she's been sleeping with for so long never mentioned any of this. Is this a ploy to get her sympathy, or is he telling the truth? It's all so awful. How could she feel anything for this...this monster? Yet, she's felt so isolated and emotionally alone, with the villagers shunning her—some even spit in the street as she passes.

"Hélène, you are correct. We may be facing the end of our time here in Foix. I want to ask you something very serious." He tries to guide her gently by the arm. At first she thrusts him aside, but as he insists, she permits him to sit her down at the kitchen table. Not exactly kneeling, but leaning on one leg against the table, he takes her hand, stroking it in both of hers. "I would like you to marry me. Perhaps we can stay in France. Maybe not here precisely, but—"

Hélène jerks her hand back as if it had been sliced by a sharp knife.

She leaps up and backs into a corner, as far away from him as possible in the small room. "I'm married. Or did you conveniently forget?"

"Hélène, I am very sorry. I have been meaning to tell you this for some time." He takes a few steps towards her, his gray eyes clouding over. "I received word that your husband...he did not...he died a few months ago."

She gasps, then slowly shakes her head from side to side, unable to comprehend what he just said. Her eyes swim with sorrow, and then, finally, a low rumble becomes a groaning howl that makes its way to her throat. Her hands clutch her stomach, she leans over and retches into the sink. Then, slumping over the faucet, she runs the water and washes out her mouth.

He comes up behind her, whispering in her ear, "I could never find the correct time to tell you." He gently offers her his handkerchief.

Hélène stares at the white linen, clean and pure. It makes her feel defiled and filthy. Then terribly alone and frightened. "I...I can't talk to you now. Please, I must go."

He grabs for her hand, but she slaps it away. His voice is strident yet pleading. "We are both suffering because of things we can not control. Could we ever, do you think, find some happiness together?"

"Happiness? Is that what you think this was all about? My sleeping with you? For my...my...happiness?"

His eyes squint down. "I thought that I gave you some comfort."

As she realizes the truth of what he says, her guilt rises inside her like a column of fire. She's furious at him—and at herself for needing this comfort. But now that she knows Gérard is dead, she can't possibly admit it to herself. And certainly not to him.

She twists her face into a hard ball of hatred. "Comfort? You people come in here and make our lives a living hell. Deport all those innocent people to some hellhole and their certain death. And you think you give me the slightest shred of comfort? You're as delusional as your Führer."

He jerks back as if punched in the face. His trim figure remains rigid, but his features turn wrathful, and she can see him kneading his fists to avoid striking her. Terrified at what he might do to her and of what secrets she might reveal to him, Hélène swiftly steps away, trying to maintain enough composure to make it to the stairs. With her mouth open in a silent howl, she grips the banister, seizes her stomach, and hoists herself up, one step at a time, then collapses onto the bed in her room. Despite the thundering in her ears, she hears his boots furiously traverse the hallway below. Then he slams the front door, shaking her small house to its core.

CHAPTER FIFTY-SIX

21 August 1944, Seven-forty-five p.m.

ISOBEL IS SO upset by Hélène's admonition, that she wanders down to the river to think things over. When she finally gets back to the convent dormitory, Isobel is still quaking from her conversation with Hélène. As it is still summer, with the other girls at home working on their farms, she has the room to herself. She sits down on her narrow iron bed and looks up at the crucifix hanging on the wall above. Why do they hate us so much? What did the Jews ever do to them? Her sorrow turns to anger at the injustice of it all—of her parents being seized from their home and taken away, most certainly to their death, and of her life upended with the loss of their warmth and love.

Restless, she wanders down the hall and decides she can't possibly make herself attend vespers, especially since her being Catholic is such a lie. How could her aunt condone such hypocrisy? It riles her to think that, while it's one thing to pose as a Catholic girl to hide from the Nazis, it's quite another to be asked to recite Latin gibberish like you were in some kind of a trance. She stands still for a moment, listening to the faint lilting voices of the nuns singing, their high-pitched tones wafting upwards towards...what? What is up there? Their heaven with clouds and angels and a man with spikes in his hands and feet? It's barbaric. Something the Nazis might dream up to interrogate the resistance. Why are these people always paying homage to a man, sad as it may be, who was tortured and died? Despite her years of going through the rituals to keep up the ruse, Isobel knows there's no way she can ever incorporate any of this into her own religious beliefs. Religion is the Torah, and reading about the law of the chosen people like her father taught her. Well, she thinks bitterly, we certainly have been chosen—for cattle cars and death camps.

Her thoughts turn to Karl. She wants to do what Hélène told her. But never seeing him, and not even telling him why? That can't be the right thing. That's too cruel. And here she is, in this place where everyone always preaches turning the other cheek and kindness.

Confused, she walks through the empty stone corridors of the convent and reaches the stairs to the roof. Climbing up, she cautiously walks to the edge. The sky at dusk is magnificent, with the striated colors of the late summer's sunset—violet at the horizon where the dense green valley meets the steep mountains—then turning orange, pink, and lighter still, up to the pale blue of the evening sky. This has always been a comforting place for her to come and think, as she tried to reconcile her past life with the one she was forced to lead. As she paces around the roof, she hears Germans singing and shouting. She tiptoes to the far side of the roof, leans over, and in the next alley over from the church garden, see the two soldiers who are the bane of Karl's existence.

She's learned from Karl that the stout, square one with the cauliflower ears is Sergeant Rolf. Now, she looks down to see his bald head lolling atop his squat body as he staggers from the bar in the alley. The tall, gangly one is Private Schmidt. He teeters against the building, finally sliding down onto the pavement. A plump barmaid rushes out of the bar and kneels beside Schmidt. Even from a street away and two stories up, Isobel hears the woman belch, then slobber kisses all over him.

Suddenly, she sees Karl walking in the distance down the alley—it looks like he's daydreaming, not looking where he's going until Rolf and Schmidt catch sight of him.

Rolf yells at Karl, something she doesn't understand.

Karl simply says, "*Ja*," and turns back down the street to avoid them.

But Rolf goes after Karl, puts his arm around him, and leads him towards the bar. Karl steps aside, shaking his head, while Schmidt laughs at Karl's reluctance. Watching from her perch above, Isobel becomes increasingly irate, as the two soldiers taunt Karl.

Schmidt's barmaid gets up, plants kisses all over Karl, and musses his hair. Isobel is angry and even a bit jealous, she hates to admit, as she watches Karl fight the barmaid off. Karl raises his voice to them, and although she can't entirely make out the language, he seems to be telling them he has an errand for Major Spitzer. Cognac. Sister. Celebration. L'Église St. Volusien.

Isobel deduces he's coming to the church to ask Sister Geneviève for cognac for some kind of celebration. She leans further over the ledge, struggling to see and hear more. Rolf pushes away Schmidt's barmaid and motions for them to grab Karl on either side. They lift him off the ground, and half goose-stepping, half staggering, march him down the street singing, *Cognac... cognac... cognac* to the tune of some kind of German drinking song. Isobel feels a wave of shame for Karl, although he seems to be controlling his anger, even smiling as he does his best to pretend it's all in good fun.

Isobel knows there's trouble coming. She runs down to find Sylvie before the drunken German soldiers can stagger over from the next alley to the church.

CHAPTER FIFTY-SEVEN

21 August 1944, Eight o'clock p.m.

SYLVIE RETURNS TO the church, having delivered her message to Hélène to make certain to attend to the wounded Yank airman that night. Too anxious to retire to her cell, she goes into the garden, where the soft glow of the light lingers after the setting sun. She bends to trim back some roses to encourage new growth, comforted to envision France also enjoying a new growth after such a long and horrific war. *God willing that day will come soon!*

Sylvie is about to go inside when she hears rustling behind the locked garden gate leading to the alley. She's struck through with terror—the airmen have been told only to arrive between six and seven, and it's already eight o'clock. She creeps to the gate and whispers, "Who's there?"

A low masculine voice comes from behind the portal, offering her the code, "Fall is coming early this year."

Despite her fear, she decides to answer, on the chance that the airman on the other side is genuine and has merely been detained. She whispers, "Winter will not be far behind."

After unlatching the gate, she brusquely motions for him to hide behind the nearest rose trellis, then secures the gate. She listens outside for a moment, then draws her veil close around her face and whispers, "You can come out. I wasn't expecting any more tonight."

He emerges from behind the trellis and limps out into the garden. He replies in a soft, coarse voice, "*Desôle,* Sister. I was delayed getting down the mountain."

She's surprised that his French is so good, even spoken in her local dialect. But there's no time to ask him about it. "I've already brought two up tonight. Come quickly." She motions him to the rear of the garden, then turns back to double-check the gate to the alley.

She hears him stumble and swings around to see him limping badly. As she rushes towards him to give him a hand, her veil brushes aside, and a streak of light from the afterglow of the setting sun passes across her face.

The man steps back, startled. He erupts in a course whisper, "Sylvie? Is that you? Sylvie?"

At the sound of her given name, she freezes, trying to process the unfathomable. She wants this person before her to be real yet fears he cannot be. She searches his face.

He whispers, "It's Jean."

The man before her slowly comes into focus. Worn corduroy trousers and a rumpled leather jacket. Dark, weather-beaten skin. Hair unruly. Cheekbones gaunt.

"*Mon Dieu!* Is it?"

He nods, solemnly.

She remains motionless, afraid to approach this apparition. "They...they told us you were dead."

"I was." He limps a step towards her. "I can explain—"

"You're hurt?"

"It's nothing."

In a daze, she has presence of mind enough to ask, "You're not bleeding?"

"No, Sylvie. I'm not."

Shock gives way to joy as she flies into his arms. She holds on tight as if she were drowning, her head nuzzled into the long-ago familiar crook of his neck. He squeezes so hard she thinks she might suffocate, except that she can't breathe anyway.

Trembling, tears welling, Sylvie says, "I...I can't believe—"

Jean holds her face in his hands. "So long—"

"It's really you? You don't know how I've prayed—" She's about to kiss him when she breaks apart. "Jean, I've got to tell you—"

"Wait." He studies her for a moment then picks up the corner of her veil. "Let me guess. Some sort of disguise?"

"In a way."

Loudly, he says, "Christ, that's a relief."

"Shush...the patrol."

He moves to kiss her. Her first instinct is to meld into him once again. To merge what's happening now with the memory of all those nights she's dreamt only of this. Lying entwined with him, their sounds of love-making rising above the soft lapping of the lake in their cave. But no, this isn't just one of her reveries: this actually seems to be real. There's so much she needs to know—and so much she needs to tell him. She inclines her head away, gently but firmly avoiding his kiss.

"What's wrong?" Then, with a wry smile, he shakes his head and shrugs playfully. "You married someone else."

"In a way." She rushes to add, "But there isn't another man."

He shoots her a confused look.

Sylvie turns away, slipping her hands into the sleeves of her habit to shield herself from his further touch. "I don't know how to say this."

Jean paces a couple of steps, then turns, his voice rasping, "Out with it!"

She slowly pivots back. "Jean, I took my vows."

He looks awestruck for a moment, then flashes the same impish grin she knows so well. "Well, take them back."

Sylvie says defiantly. "It's not that easy."

"What do you mean? I'm back. Sylvie, you can't be a nun...that doesn't make sense."

Sylvie's deep melodious voice turns to pure ice. "My name is Sister Geneviève now."

"I came back to take you away."

"Take me away?"

"I owe you an explanation. I promise I'll tell you everything." His voice rises, "But right now—"

"Be quiet, the patrol." Surely she's imagining that he's standing there asking her to come away with him—to renounce her vows. She must be cracking under all the pressure. She squints at him, having begun to forget the finer features of his chiseled face, his eyes set close together like a falcon's; she's only had a small photo hidden in her cell these past years to remember him by. She retreats into the shadows, covering her face with her veil, so he can't see her confusion. "Jean, it's not that simple." Then her anger flares. "They took my sister and her husband. So many have been killed. Father Michel. You...Taking the veil was my salvation." She stares at him, still trying to process that he's alive, there before her. She whispers, "You couldn't let us know you were alive?"

"Sylvie, I was taken prisoner." He pushes her veil aside and grabs her by the shoulders. "They left me for dead, but I made it back. All that I ask is when I tell you everything, you forgive me. Come away with me. I'll explain—"

"All we had was your jacket. Étienne never takes it off."

"I remember...I used it as a tourniquet. For this boy." He pauses. "Then all hell broke loose...Panzers everywhere."

"We didn't even have a body for your funeral."

He rolls his eyes, chortling, "You had a funeral for me?"

She nods solemnly, looking off at some painful distant scene. "Not at first, but finally. Father Michel convinced me."

"Good food? Wine? You never could hold your wine."

She smiles through the tears pooling in her eyes. "We had food then. And yes, I drank a lot of wine." She sighs deeply, remembering the grief, the blackness of the nights spent wondering if he was alive— if he was being tortured or worked to death. Wanting him to soothe her as she battled Major Spitzer, trying to get humane treatment for the refugees. Hoping he would forgive her for showing the *Maquis* their cave, their special place where they consummated...She closes her eyes and leans into him.

He takes her in his arms and moves to kiss her again, but she forces her head away, even as she remains firmly in his embrace. She wants nothing more than to kiss him, like before. Interweave her body with his, her life with his. With his touch unbearably urgent, she feels him wanting her as he once did—as she wanted him, so long ago, when she was another person. She's dizzy with conflicting emotions. She's longed for this moment. But long ago she resolved to live with the memory of him and the pain, which she's finally managed to get under some semblance of control by taking the veil. What does he mean— come away with him? How can she open herself up to the grief she would feel if she lost him again? Now that she's finally found peace? Now that her prayers—chanting when she wakes, chanting at mid-day, chanting when she drifts off to sleep—have finally enabled her to think of something else but the anguish of losing him.

Jean clenches his jaw. "Damn it, I come back, and you're...gone."

She shakes her head slowly, desperately trying to resolve the mass of conflicting emotions waging war within her. "I'm right here."

Just then, the sound of drunken singing wafts towards them amid the clacking of jackboots on the cobblestones in the alley outside the garden gate. Jean and Sylvie abruptly break apart. She heads for the gate, but he blocks her way, obviously seeking to protect her.

She looks directly at him. "Stand back. I'm in charge here."

An astonished look crosses his face before he reluctantly limps aside to hide back behind the trellis.

Sylvie looks through one of the narrow slats in the garden gate. Two older, obviously inebriated German soldiers attempt to goose-step their way towards the garden, dangling a youth between them. The older ones are singing, while the younger one struggles to free himself.

She hears the young one say, "Herr, Sergeant Rolf—" but can't catch any more.

The taller, gangly soldier staggers and falls, nearly pulling the others on top of him.

The portly one yells, "*Dummkopf,*" followed by some drunken mumblings. Then he yanks the tall one up, and they stagger back the way they came.

Sylvie watches as the younger one straightens his uniform and approaches the gate. She hears him rapping, checks to make sure Jean is hidden, smooths her habit, and opens the gate.

She's surprised that the young soldier doesn't salute with the typical snap of a *Heil Hitler.* Instead, he respectfully places his helmet underneath his arm and says, "Good evening, Sister. My name is Karl."

"Yes, private."

"I am the supply liaison for Major Spitzer. He is the kommandant of—"

"I know exactly who he is."

As Sylvie turns slightly to check the garden behind her, she catches sight of Isobel coming out from the church. She motions for the girl to stay back. Isobel stops short, then reluctantly nods and slips back into the shadows.

Karl clears his throat and says, "Kommandant Major Spitzer is making a further request."

"Doesn't he know the Allies are pushing through France? They'll be here soon enough."

Karl slips past her and comes into the garden. She senses he's looking around for someone. Does he know about Jean? Sylvie tries not to panic as she blocks him from advancing further.

"I am sorry, Sister, but he asks you for a supply of cognac."

"Everything's been given over long ago. The villagers are starving."

Karl shuffles his feet and edges back towards the gate, stopping directly in front of the trellis where Jean is hiding. Acid rises in Sylvie's throat.

"*Mein Kommandant*...he says you will know people...parishioners who are hiding such things."

Her eyes dart between him and the trellis. She snarls, "Impossible."

Although the young German looks flustered and increasingly uncomfortable, he says, "Forgive me, but the major wants the cognac tonight. He said to tell you—his exact words: *You know I can be very strict.*"

"He'd imprison more villagers if I can't find his damn cognac?"

"I am very sorry, Sister."

"And you're just the messenger. Is that right, private?"

"Please, my name is Karl."

"Tell him I'll see what I can do."

Sylvie sees relief spread over the young man's face as he replaces his helmet and sneaks another look around the garden, back towards the church.

This angers Sylvie. "And stay away from the girls in the convent."

Karl flinches, makes a small, stiff bow, and leaves.

Sylvie slams the gate shut and locks it. Pressing her back against it, she lets out a huge sigh of relief. Jean slowly emerges from the trellis.

Sylvie barks, "Damn Spitzer. That fascist pig."

"You have his cognac?"

"The last of it is hidden in the cellar. We've been saving it for the wounded airmen."

Jean looks her habit up and down. "They told me a nun was involved, but I never—" Abruptly, his face flushes with anger. "I won't have it."

"What won't you have? This is what I do now."

"But you could be killed."

Just then, the German shepherd dogs, attached to the normal patrol, bark in the next alley over. Jean tenses up, his head whipping around as he searches for the origin of the sounds. He breaks into a sweat, starts shivering. Sylvie is startled by the violence of his reaction. She holds up her palms, indicating it's all right.

Jean tries to pick up the thread of his thought. "Well…you're…you can't do this kind of work…you're—"

"A woman? That's observant."

"I…I mean, nothing must ever happen to you." As the dogs' barking becomes louder, Jean freezes.

Sylvie grabs his arm. "Jean, are you all right?"

In a daze, Jean rages, viscously, "Bastards…I'll shove them all into their—"

She's utterly confused by his reaction but knows she's got to calm him, or they'll both be in danger. "Jean, stop it. You're in Foix now."

He slowly turns to her, murmuring, "What? Yes." Then his tone turns cool and focused. "Tomorrow, the Free French…we're landing up on the mountain. To liberate Foix."

"*Mon Dieu!*"

"We'll force those Nazi bastards down to Toulouse. The Allies are landing in Marseilles and across the south. They'll be waiting for them."

"The occupation will be over!"

Jean snaps fully back to the present. "But we need help from the *Maquis*."

"We got a message on the wireless, but we didn't know how important it was." Sylvie grins. "Our men will be at the drop."

"Good. We're flying in explosives to blow the German munitions dump in the village."

"Blow the munitions dump?" she pauses, then continues, "Let me guess. You want to distract the *Boches* while your men land on the mountain?"

"Right. Then you're coming with me."

Sylvie is truly shocked. "Hold on—"

"Your work will be over."

"But my vows—"

Jean seems erratic once again as he lunges to embrace her. "Forget all that church nonsense. Sylvie, I've dreamed of this—"

"Jean, please—"

He clutches her to him. "I'll see them free the village, then my time in the army is done."

"I don't understand."

"I was captured, so they'll decommission me right away. Let me go."

Imagining what he must have suffered at the hands of the *Boches*, Sylvie allows him to hold her fast. She whispers, "It will be wonderful to have you home again."

He brushes her veil away, strokes her cheek. "I'm selling my farm. We'll make a fresh start in Algiers." She jerks back but he seizes her by her arms. "You should see North Africa. Thousands of refugees are streaming through there. If you're French and you have money, you won't be cooped up in the Arab Quarter. There's a fortune to be made."

She struggles. "You never cared about money."

"I'm not breaking my back to farm that God-forsaken pile of rocks my coward father left me."

"You're talking crazy."

"I've been in one God-forsaken prison or another for…I don't know how long. I've earned the right. We'll live like royalty. I'll buy you silks from Arabia. You should see their silks. More colors than you could imagine."

He pulls her hard to him and bends to kiss her.

"Jean. STOP IT!"

"I thought you loved me."

"I did, but—"

"That's all we need."

Sylvie is losing her bearings. He's here one moment, then talking crazy about running away together. She coils herself up and abruptly gives him a shove. "No, it isn't. We'll talk about this later. I've got to get you out of Foix. Wait down there." She motions him to the back gate, with its steps down to the passageway and the river. Then she heads back into the church—she must find Isobel and tell her about the cognac for Karl.

She halts abruptly, turning back towards him. "You weren't followed?"

"No. They dropped me in last night, up on the plateau. That's when I smashed up my knee. But I managed to bury my gear on the way to our cave before heading down here." He grins broadly, and she sees her former lover emerge. "You remember our cave? Where I wanted to make an honest woman out of you."

Sylvie tries to be annoyed but smiles despite herself. "I was already an honest woman." She motions him ahead. "Go down there and wait. I've got to tell Isobel about the cognac."

"Your niece?"

"We call her Marie now. I'll explain on the way."

Jean limps down the stairs while she rushes into the church.

Isobel is waiting for Sylvie, nervously straightening and re-straightening the missives in the first pew. She tries to sound nonchalant. "Was that Karl?"

"Listen, dear, go down to the cellar. Get six bottles of cognac out of the crypt. They're for Karl to give to—"

Isobel's face lights up. "He's coming back?"

Sylvie is surprised at the girl's reaction, but there's no time to discuss it further. "He's coming to get the cognac to give to Major Spitzer. After you give it to him, you must make that boy leave, right away. Do you hear?"

"But—"

"Something's about to happen. I can't tell you what. But you must not be seen with him."

"You mean Karl?"

"Don't even use his name. You know what's happening to girls who've been with Germans?"

"Madame Hélène told me. The women are shaving their heads."

"Often worse than that. Please, do as I say." Sylvie thrusts her keys at her niece and turns to leave. As she does so, she feels a rush of anger, seeing that, despite her harsh words regarding Karl, Isobel has removed her kerchief and is straightening her dress and primping her hair. "What are you doing, young lady?"

Isobel becomes defiant. "And where are you going?"

"I have to take someone… My darling, I love you so much, the less you know—" Sylvie kisses her on both cheeks and heads towards the garden.

Isobel calls after her. "Who is that airman I saw you with just now?" With a mocking tone, she adds, "Sister?"

Sylvie whirls around. "Don't be fresh. And Karl—"

"Honestly, he's not like the others."

Sylvie barks, "They're all alike." Then she pauses, not wanting to leave with harsh words between them. She hugs her niece very hard. "You must trust me."

Sylvie rushes back to her cell and pulls out her knapsack. She whips off her habit, slips on her trousers and cap, stows her habit in the duffle, then runs to join Jean on the back garden steps.

Jean takes one look at her and grins. "Now I recognize you!"

"Let's hope no one else does."

Sylvie runs down the rest of the steps. Jean, still limping, follows her as best he can. They hear men shouting and dogs barking loudly in the distance.

Sylvie whispers, "Hurry. It's almost curfew."

Jean freezes up again. As the river rushes past them, he leans against the stone wall, an agonized look on his face.

Sylvie nudges his shoulder. "Jean, can you hear me?"

He snaps back and nods.

"Follow me. We've got to go. Now!"

Sylvie leads him farther down the passageway by the river. The gravest of fears seeps into her. The man she yearned for, then grievously gave up for dead, has returned. But who exactly is this man who has returned?

CHAPTER FIFTY-EIGHT

TRYING TO KEEP up with Sylvie, Jean stumbles as he rushes along the ancient stone passageway that leads from the church garden, alongside the river, and then to the field beyond the village. He swears under his breath. He hates feeling incompetent and out of control, even though he knows his knee injury from the parachute drop is only temporary. Everything is riding on his mission to get with the *Maquis* and recover the drop of explosives, then lead a diversion in the village while Free French paratroopers land and liberate Foix.

Sylvie stops for a moment. "Jean, Are you all right?"

"Of course."

She shrugs and continues. Limping along, he thinks back to his arrest in Algiers, when he was handed over to the Free French army. His addiction to drugs, coupled with his constant rages and erratic behavior, got him thrown into solitary. But he managed to provide enough detail of his time in the German prison camp to enable his superiors to give him the benefit of the doubt and remove his "deserter" classification. They moved him to the infirmary, where the doctors helped him get off the drugs in his system. Another doctor talked to him at length and helped him deal with waking up in that death pit, causing the deaths of Suzanne and the children, and experiencing the prison camp and the atrocities he was forced to commit. Profound feelings of love for Sylvie and the life they shared before the war flooded back to fill the deep void created by the horrors he survived. Although his nightmares persisted, and certain events still triggered his rage, he began to focus all his energies on working with the Free French to get back to Foix and help liberate his village.

He sees Sylvie up ahead in the passageway. At last, this is his chance to redeem himself. To salvage his family's name and prove wrong all those who taunted him for being the son of a coward. In Algiers, he boasted that he was the only one for this mission—the only one who knew this territory and the only one who would be trusted by the locals. So what if he still flies off the handle every now and then? And so what if, after the liberation, the army will soon discharge him? Having been a prisoner of war, that's the least they can do. He'll show them he can control his restlessness and his erratic bouts of uncontrollable anger. He has only to think of Sylvie to have a calm warmth spread over him.

"Jean, we're almost through the passageway. We have to be especially careful of the patrols."

She's impressive. He always admired her ability to hunt, and then after her parents died, to manage her farm. He genuinely loved being a role model for her younger brother and basked in the honor her uncle bestowed on him, who privately told him he'd be overjoyed to welcome Jean as Sylvie's husband. But things have changed. He's certain he doesn't want to stay in Foix to eke out a meager living on his rock pile of a farm. As soon as he's discharged, he'll sell the farm and take her to Algiers—prove his worth to her—and himself. Go straight to the European sector down by the glittering water with the glittering hotels—not to the filthy tangle of stairs and alleys in the Casbah. Resume trading on the black market and become even wealthier than before. This time, he won't need the drugs to search for her in the recesses of his mind—she'll be right there with him. He'll have made peace with the memory of his father, having suffered the same shell shock—he'll overcome the past with a successful mission and expunge the name *coward* from his family legacy. It will all be worth it if he can make a life of luxury with the woman he loves.

He watches her ahead, dressed in her familiar trousers and cap, speeding along the passageway. They're together, just like in the life they had before. But no—she's working with the resistance now—leading it, in fact. *I can't lose her to such dangerous work. Not when I just found her again.*

The river is rushing past him below the stone quay, splashing up droplets that cool him but also make the stones slick. He slips every now and then, cursing. He swallowed his pride to let her take the lead in dealing with the young German. But damn it, this is war, and after all, she's still only a woman. And damn it to hell, she's become a nun. If she's really serious about all that nonsense, they won't have a life together. But... since when has he ever given up easily? She only took the veil thinking he was dead. *I'll make her change her mind and come with me to North Africa.* These fragments of anger, as well as hope, press into his mind as he lags farther behind.

"Jean, hurry up!"

He's still fuming as he follows Sylvie. She got so damn angry when those damn dogs barked—she doesn't understand. The doctors say he'll get over it. It's happened before and he always snaps out of it—eventually. But now, it feels like he's falling into a trance. He's back in the prison camp, where the dogs snarl viciously and nip at his heels as he shovels the bodies onto the gurney. He starts to sweat, remembering how the guards punished prisoners by letting the dogs loose on them to rip their limbs to shreds. He sees the blood and gore mixing with the dogs' saliva—not injuring the prisoners enough to kill them right away, just making them suffer horribly as they bleed to death...

These images surging back into him paralyze him, and he's vaguely aware that Sylvie has had to nudge him back to reality more than once. He can feel her growing exasperation, but he's helpless to do anything about it, which only compounds his sense of desperation at being so out of control.

Finally, they're out of the passageway and into the meadow. He feels immense relief that he's made it. Wait a minute—even the tall sunflowers at the edge of the forest menace him. Guards standing in his way. Smirking sadistically. Slapping his face as he brushes past the towering green stalks with their bright yellow collars.

As she turns back towards him, he can see her olive skin reddening with a mixture of concern and anger. Her usually soothing voice is sharp as a knife. "Jean, can you hear me?"

"Yes…I'm doing fine. Let's go."

As they climb into the forest, his anxiety diminishes, and he begins to feel the thrill of recognition. Even though it's getting dark, the sunset afterglow lingers among the purple shadows of the familiar jagged peaks. He feels a sudden, unbounded joy being with her again, seeing the craggy mountains and smelling the deep pine scent of the trees—reminders of his childhood, when he freely hiked the mountains and finally found the girl to share his life. There she is, just up ahead, charging forward, as if they'd never been apart. She'll marry him, and that will absolve him of all his sins. Then, she'll come away with him to live a luxurious life.

Sylvie stops by a ravine in the forest. She commands more than suggests, "Jean, you need to rest."

Her vexation cuts him to the quick. He wants her to be overjoyed to see him, not guarded and concerned for his health. He wonders what the years have done to her. As they settle against a tree, he searches her deep brown eyes for a hint of what she's thinking. Her broad, strong forehead is lined with concern.

As she reaches towards him, he deflects her hand. "I'm fine."

"Of course you are. I just wanted to—"

"Help the cripple?"

Sylvie leans back against the tree, exhaling a deep breath. "Even I'm exhausted. This is my second trip of the evening."

"I told you, I had a hard landing."

"I wasn't criticizing you, Jean. What's come over you? You were never so damned temperamental."

"Look, Sylvie, things aren't what I expected."

"I could say the same."

"Aren't you happy to see me?"

"Of course." She squeezes his shoulder. "Give me some time to get used to things. This is quite a shock."

"It's quite a shock to see you've become a nun." He moves closer. "If I'd been alive, would you have taken your vows?"

He watches her intently as she lifts her eyes to stare at the tall firs and the dusky sky. Flickering stars have just begun to appear.

She whispers, "I'm sure I wouldn't. I would have just remained in disguise. A cover to give the airmen a contact to meet up at the church."

Jean feels vindicated. He says, in a frenzied tone, "I knew it! Sylvie, you still love me."

She stares intently at him, quietly adding, "Jean, I will always love you."

He's nearly overwhelmed with relief, but he still needs, now more than ever, to possess her. He reaches out to caress her, but she firmly pushes him back. He can't hide his surprise. "You want to continue life as a nun?"

"It's not that simple. I can do things I couldn't if I were just...well, just a woman...just someone's wife." She leans her head against the tree, pauses, then continues softly, "I've come to view my habit as a shield...a kind of armor I use against the Nazis." She turns towards him, her voice stronger. "I've been able to save lives. Organize with the British so Uncle Claude and the others can guide the airmen over the mountains into Spain and—"

"We heard all about your legendary circuit. You and the *Maquisards* have done an incredible job—no one's denying that. But the war's ending. What'll you do after?"

"I really don't know. It's not something I honestly ever thought would happen."

He sneers, "Sylvie, you're not a nun. You're not humble. You're too proud. Stubborn. Face it—you like the power it gives you."

Sylvie jumps up. "Who are you to tell me how I feel? I don't even know who you are."

Jean struggles to stand, his knee buckling. He finally rises, grabs her, and leans her against the trunk of the tree. He kisses her deeply. Her cap falls off, and her thick black hair cascades down her back.

As he kisses her, he feels her body soften, giving him permission to caress her. He runs his fingers through her hair. "I always loved your hair." He strokes her tresses as if he were calming a wild mare. He suddenly throws his head back and laughs his old, wiley laugh. "Your hair! I knew you couldn't really be a nun...heart and soul." He looks into her surprised eyes. "You couldn't cut your hair off. You've too much pride."

She blanches and twists her hair, roughly stuffing it back under her cap. "Jean, I can explain—"

"No need, Sylvie." His joy is palpable.

"Listen to me. Mother Superior knew I'd be mixing with townspeople when working with the *Maquis*. Close-cropped hair like that would have put me under greater suspicion."

"Make what excuses you will. I love you. And you still love me. Say it."

She whispers, "Yes...you're right. I could never part with my hair because I knew you loved it." She trembles. "Some part of me, deep down, never really believed you were dead."

She leans into him, and he feels her giving in—allowing herself to be loved, once again. He feels his elation spreading to her, erasing the fears and sorrows they've both endured over the years. He lays her down on the ground and starts to make love. In his mind, he hears the faint drip of water from the stalactites, transporting him back to their cave.

"Sylvie, my love. I still want to marry you."

Her breath becomes shallow and quickens as he feels her arch into him. *Sylvie, my Sylvie. My salvation*! As she's let down her defenses, he'll make his dream complete. He whispers, "Then we can go away together."

She bolts upright. "Jean, I could never leave Foix. Everyone I love...everyone I have left is here."

Jean's voice turns sharp. "Surely you love me more. I'll make you a queen."

"Please, Jean. We've got to sort this out." She scrambles up.

"What is there to sort out? You said you loved me. Can't I trust you?"

"Trust? I need to feel some trust here too. We need time to get to know each other again."

"God damn it! You're leading me on. Enjoying your power over me like you enjoy your power over the Nazis in your nun's armor." He growls, "I hope you're satisfied."

Sylvie steps back, an anguished look on her face.

He struggles to get control. They killed Suzanne and those innocent kids. Dumped those bodies on the gurney, all those bodies, day after day, many only half dead. Waiting to be burned. To be put out of their misery. Moaning. Whimpering. And Albert—the only one he could trust. Shot as Jean tried to shield him. Doesn't she realize what he's been through? He's tempted to pull his revolver. He reaches for it. He could end this now. For both of them. His hand shakes violently. She's staring at him in pure revulsion. Staring at his hand—reaching for his gun.

Something inside of him snaps. He stops short and looks at her absolutely bewildered. Stunned at his own behavior. Someone else is occupying his body.

"Sylvie, I'm sorry. I don't know what comes over me. Forgive me."

"Jean, right now, I've got to get you to the cave. Mobilize the men for the drop. Let's just focus on that."

She's shaking, but her voice is strong and commanding. His anger flashes again, fiercely hating her for her restraint. He used to have that kind of control. She's right, they have a mission, and they can work all of this out afterward. She said she loved him. She was on the brink of making love to him again. There's still hope.

Sylvie collects her things and reaches out her hand, which he takes like a drowning man. They resume trudging up the mountain towards the cave. *I survived. I can do it again.* He keeps repeating these words, a loop in his head, over and over.

CHAPTER FIFTY-NINE

21 August 1944, Ten fifteen p.m.

ON THE LAST leg of her trip, bringing Jean up the mountain to the cave, Sylvie is at a loss to know how she feels about his return. He clearly suffered greatly and is no longer the same man. But neither is she the same woman. Now, with all their differences, could they possibly reconcile? Could he give up this crazy idea of going to North Africa? Could she give up the veil? Would she even want to? And yet, as she looks behind her to make sure he's keeping up, she fervently hopes their common cause to liberate Foix will draw them together again, perhaps with an even deeper bond.

They reach the last ridge before the entrance to the cave, which is hidden in the brambles about ten meters above them. The thistles glisten as the moon shines down. She feels a rush, remembering how they pushed the brambles aside and entered the cave so long ago. How he drew her to the edge of the lake where they consummated their love.

Jean signals that he needs to stop and rest before making the final push up to the cave. They put down in a dry ravine against some logs and fallen trees. She feels a surge of sympathy as he straightens himself up before seeing the others.

She says, gently, "They'll be overjoyed to welcome you back."

He breathes heavily. "I...I hope so."

"You were always Étienne's hero. Uncle Claude thought of you as a son."

He looks away. "Sylvie, I've done some pretty nasty things."

"We all have."

"I'm no one's hero."

"Étienne still brags how you took him hunting. He's a head taller now."

Sylvie thinks back to how they used to sit, cleaning their game, and talking like this. Now gaunt, he's still strong for his wiry frame. Same piercing dark brown eyes, although at times, they now dart erratically with menace. And his handsome, rakish smile, so quick to his lips, is virtually gone. What can she do to heal him from his torments? Get him back to his old self? She feels a sharp stab as she envisions giving up the veil: her spiritual lifeline. Mother Superior would, of course, understand. But what does she really want?

She shoves these thoughts aside and gets up. "We've got to get to the drop in time." She's pleased that, this time, he manages to rise more easily, with less pain.

As they enter the cave, Sylvie feels the warmth of a sense of belonging, a great camaraderie. Along the far wall are the two Yanks she brought up earlier that evening. Omaha Bruce lies on a straw pallet, while Brooklyn Joe sits beside him, telling a story, mostly with his hands—clearly entertaining the others gathered around. Uncle Claude laughs boisterously as he pounds his appreciation on Joe's back. François pulls on the left side of his large mustache, his lips open in a huge smile, as he alternately drags on a cigarette and translates for Joe. Louis whoops in laughter and slaps his knee.

In addition to several young *Maquisards* who've joined the group, there are also a number of British airmen and one female agent waiting for the next convoy to escort them over the mountains and down into Spain. Being British, their laughter is reserved but still appreciative. And, of course, there's Étienne, sitting next to Uncle Claude, listening intently. His smiles come a beat or two behind the others as he tries to follow Joe's story.

Sylvie watches them for a moment, then steps farther into the cave, announcing in a clear voice, "*Maquisards,* we have company." She moves aside, as a magician might, to unveil Jean.

Complete silence, except for a few drips from the stalactites and the lapping of the underground lake. From a distance, and in the dim light of the fire and the lanterns, Claude is the first to rise, slowly, as if he'd seen a ghost. He cautiously steps towards Jean.

Étienne, however, recognizes him right away and rushes over, but then comes to a halt, not sure how to act. He whispers, "Jean, is it really you?"

Reaching up to the young man, Jean clasps Étienne to him and plants a kiss on both cheeks. "Weren't you tall enough as it was?"

Claude strides over. "Jean, how can this be?" He gets Jean in a bear hug.

Sylvie blinks away her own tears as she sees Jean squinting, trying to avoid welling up himself, as he submits to Claude's rough embrace. François and Louis gather round, clap Jean on the back, and introduce him to the young *Maquisards.* Étienne takes off his wire-rimmed glasses, smiles, and charges at Jean, wrestling with him as they'd so often done before the war. Sylvie and Claude cheer them on.

Jean gets winded very quickly but tries to hold his own. "Étienne! Still fast on your feet."

Étienne gets Jean in a hold. "You're sure you're not a ghost?"

Sylvie shouts to her brother, "Watch his knee!"

Étienne pulls Jean down, and Jean surrenders, laughing and patting the teenager on the back. As they get up, Étienne turns around to show off, modeling Jean's old military jacket.

"Want it back?" He asks Jean, in a tone clearly hoping he doesn't.

"And trade this authentic Free French army surplus jacket? Not on your life."

Étienne beams. "Thanks!" The young man rushes over to his duffle, talking to Jean over his shoulder. "Want to see what I'm reading? Uncle Claude gave me these pamphlets."

Sylvie smiles as she sees Claude trying to quiet the boy, but Étienne is too excited to take the hint. "They're about a new and better society where they treat everyone as equals. Even if you've been weak and everybody made fun of you as a kid. I'm finally going to be somebody."

Sylvie turns to Jean. "Étienne's become quite idealistic."

Jean playfully elbows the boy. "You haven't gone Red, have you?"

Étienne protests, "People are going to share everything,"

Jean's tone turns vicious, cutting Étienne to the quick. "And who gets to decide who gets what? Giving men power over other men only turns them into animals."

"But, Uncle Claude says—"

"Maybe later, Étienne," Sylvie cuts in, "I'm sure Jean wants to rest before we go to the drop."

She's pleased to see Étienne dampening his disappointment at Jean's outburst, as the boy says, "I'll go with Jean. Like when we used to go hunting."

"I'm not sure I can keep up with this young fellow."

"I'll be your crutch."

"You little...I don't need a crutch!" Jean playfully punches Étienne on the shoulder.

Sylvie quiets them down and speaks to the group. "Men, this isn't just any drop." She turns to Jean, who informs them of the plan. They react with whoops and hollers, then Sylvie settles them down, and the *Maquisards* gather their things and set off for the drop. Brooklyn Joe asks to come along, but Sylvie insists he stay back and care for Bruce until Hélène arrives. She also wants the Brits to rest up, although she tells them they might not have to make the trip over the mountains after all—if the liberation goes as planned.

Sylvie can barely contain her exhilaration that the allies are so close and their misery under German occupation might soon be over. Still, she isn't sure what that will mean for her personally and for her relationship with Jean. A deep ache has worked its way through her as she considers Jean's condition—he seems only the shell of the man she loved so deeply. It's horribly unfair. She barely recognizes this angry, sullen man, at times uncharacteristically arrogant towards her, who is obsessed with running goods on the black market. His soul seems to have been sucked out and replaced, yielding someone she'd have loathed the moment they'd met. Then, suddenly, he returns to his old self—apologetic, playful, and loving— only to snap back just as fast, into a man with intolerable hatred of everything and everyone. She strains to see behind the angry façade, to find the true Jean hidden within. She shudders as it slowly dawns on her—perhaps it might have been better if he'd died after all—rather than have turned into such a callous, self-absorbed, and immoral man.

But, as she's so often had to do in recent years, Sylvie decides to suppress thoughts or emotions that might interfere with the mission at hand. She and Claude lead the *Maquisards* up to the open field, where Jean gathers the men together.

"I'm expecting ten rucksacks to be dropped, containing the explosives. Each man carries a complete unit so, if the others get lost or shot, any one of us can pick up a sack, assemble the explosives and set the charges."

They move into a straight line formation, their torches set in the direction of the wind, with Claude off to the side, prepared to signal the coded confirmation to the pilot. They listen for the low humming of the aircraft bringing the drop.

Sylvie is relieved to see Jean calm and in complete command. The night is brilliantly clear, with not a hint of a cloud to diminish the pure luminosity of the full moon. She looks at Jean's wiry silhouette against the whitened, jagged ledges that surround the small clearing. It takes her back to when they roamed these hillsides. This is still the same man...it must be. They've been under so much stress for so long. Surely she's been imagining things to be much worse than they really are?

The drop comes. They open the canisters, pry apart the wooden crates inside, and load bundles of explosive *plastique,* cord, and fuses into their rucksacks. They cut up the silk from the parachutes and bury that with the canisters. Sylvie announces she must return to Foix to make sure Isobel is safe when the young German returns for the cognac. Jean seems to understand why she has to go, but as she leaves, he catches hold of her hand, seeming to read her thoughts.

He grins broadly. "Sylvie, old times on the mountain, *n'est-ce-pas?*"

Enveloped by the old warmth she felt for him, she whispers, "Yes, it is, Jean." She gives him a fierce hug and sets off, back down the mountain to Foix.

CHAPTER SIXTY

21 August 1944, Ten thirty p.m.

WHEN THE MAJOR slams the front door, Hélène feels an icy shudder slice through her. She lies in bed, in a stupor, her eyes vacantly staring up at the ceiling. She is thoroughly chilled, despite the warm, late summer evening. Through some dim mist in her mind, she recalls Sylvie saying how important it is to go up to the cave tonight, no matter how late, to treat a Yank airman.

She doubts she can walk, so great is her agony at learning of Gérard's death. Especially learning of it from the man, a *Boche* no less, with whom she's been sleeping. Not only that, a man for whom she'd begun to have—she's thoroughly ashamed to admit—real feelings.

Hélène always assumed that when Gérard returned, she wouldn't tell him exactly, but somehow he'd come to understand and forgive her for doing what Alastair and the *Maquis* had implored. With that possibility now gone, she feels as if someone has heaped heavy stones in a huge pile onto her chest. She imagines a funeral pyre in India, where the widow flings herself onto her husband's corpse and is entirely consumed by the flames. Isn't that exactly what she deserves?

Screaming into her pillow, Hélène pounds the bed and shakes her head wildly. How could he have lied? Kept on sleeping with her, even after he knew? But she feels an even deeper fury—for allowing herself to become vulnerable to him and beginning to care about him. Yes, he'd probably been far easier on the refugees and the villagers because of her influence. But did that excuse her betrayal of her husband? She groans in agony as she's forced to acknowledge that the fault is not entirely his, nor were the feelings between them completely one-sided. This not only enrages her but makes her feel wanton, defiled, and bitterly ashamed. How can she face the others, knowing what she knows to be true about herself?

Her thoughts festering, she lays in bed for some time before she realizes she has to leave if she's going to make it to the cave that night. As Sylvie sounded so desperate for the American, she resolves to put her feelings aside and do whatever she can for him. Nursing and helping others has always been her salvation. In a daze, she laces up her boots, covers her head with a scarf, and sets out for the cave.

As it's out of curfew, Hélène has to duck under the bridge to avoid the patrol. She steps into the fast-flowing river to make sure that, if she were spotted, the dogs couldn't follow her tracks. She almost wishes she'd be discovered—so the dogs could rip her shame to a bloody end.

The only thing that keeps her going is her determination to help the Yank airman, as well as the fact that the *Maquis* know her sacrifice. Surely they won't judge her weakness too harshly since she's provided such helpful information under real peril. Stars blanket the indigo sky and the moon, so white it looks frozen, lights her way through the tall grassy field beyond the village. When she reaches the cave, she finds that the *Maquisards* have gone to the drop. She immediately goes to the airman and surveys the situation. Her mind automatically slips back into nursing mode—into saving someone's life. Her instincts take over and crowd out the horrible guilt buzzing in her head.

The Yank is a big, broad man. Big like Gérard. *Stop thinking about him. Do your job.* He is jovial, despite the pain he can't hide when she examines the wound in his side. As she tends to the large man, the female British agent translates for her so Hélène can better assess his situation. She's surprised when the English that the woman uses to talk to the Yanks turns into effortlessly Parisian French when she speaks to Hélène. The Yank's small, dark-haired friend pretends to be light-hearted as well, but even in the dim firelight, she sees his grave concern. When she asks him to get her some clean hot water, he leaps over to the fire, obviously grateful to be of any kind of help. It's touching the way the two men act with each other. Hélène finishes up by shaking some of their supply of precious sulpha power into this wound and bandaging him. She washes her hands and slumps down by the fire. Only then does she allow thoughts of Gérard and the major back into her consciousness.

Feeling the warmth of the fire, Hélène closes her eyes tight in a valiant effort to hold back tears. Meanwhile, the female agent sits down next to her. The woman's voice is calm. "They've gone to the drop. They should be back any minute." She is slender and dressed in a tweed skirt, a linen blouse, and a short professional-looking jacket. The soles of her shoes are made with wood, as are everyone's in the country—leather and rubber being wartime commodities too rare for use in footwear.

As Hélène rubs her hands to warm them in the fire, her mind returns to the altercation with the major and her shame. Staring into the fire, her eyes blur as the flames take on the shape of a woman thrusting her burning arms high, pleading to be put out of her misery. She gasps involuntarily, then shakes her head, trying to regain her composure. How she dreads having to tell Sylvie about Gérard, but she resolves never to mention to a living soul how her feelings for the major had evolved.

"Someone named Jean came up with a woman."

"Jean?" Hélène jerks her head up and turns to the British agent. "What did he look like?"

"Dark hair. Not too tall but very slender. Seemed to know Claude and the teenage boy quite well." The woman stirs the fire. "They were right glad to see him. Been in a prison camp."

"That's incredible." Hélène murmurs, "Sylvie must be...Oh my God." What astonishing news for dear Sylvie, having mourned Jean for dead all these years. So courageous to have been able to go on without him. *How will I ever go on knowing that—wait a minute—could Gérard be alive too? Did the major tell me he was dead just so I would agree to marry him?* Hélène gasps, slumping over. *That monster could easily be that cruel.* Her thoughts swirl then land on her husband. *If Gérard does return, how could I ever face him knowing how I've dishonored him?* She presses her hands hard against her temples as if she had her head in a vise.

"Are you all right?"

Hélène can barely move but manages to whisper, "Just tired."

"Well, you'll be glad to hear that the Free French are parachuting in tomorrow. To liberate Foix." The woman smiles broadly. "Isn't it brilliant?"

Hélène raises her throbbing head and stares incredulously at the woman, trying to process this information. Just then, Claude and the other *Maquisards* tramp in carrying heavy rucksacks. They are jubilant. Claude, still out of breath, sputters to Hélène that Jean has indeed returned and that Étienne and Jean, due to his hurt knee, are lagging behind them. After the drop, he explains, Sylvie went straight back to the convent to look after Isobel but will soon join them. "See here. We've got all this *plastique* to assemble. Then we go down to Foix—"

"Blow those bastards up," Louis interjects. "Like no Bastille Day you ever saw."

François, towering over Louis, grabs the small man and exuberantly lifts him off the floor of the cave. "Boom! Boom!! My friend. Your greatest explosions yet."

As François lets Louis down, Claude wraps his arms around both men and the three jig in a little circle. The young *Maquisards* sing "La Marseillaise." Even the Brits and Joe are elated, humming and mumbling words they don't know to the French national anthem. At the last refrain, everyone breaks into simultaneous laughter and tears as they march in place and sing, *"Marchons, marchons."*

François and Louis announce they're going to gather the rest of the resistance units hiding outside nearby towns like Tarascon, and bring them into Foix as reinforcements for the final battle.

Hélène is caught up in the celebration, although no one would suspect that her tears are more from rage, sorrow, and shame than from joy.

CHAPTER SIXTY-ONE

22 August 1944, One a.m.

ON THE WAY back to the cave from the drop, Jean finds it impossible to ignore the searing pain in his knee, even as he desperately tries to keep up with Étienne. They're the only ones left on the trail, as the others have gone ahead to the cave, and Sylvie has gone back down to the church to see about Isobel. Finally, Jean has to admit he needs help carrying the heavy rucksack, and Étienne offers to double up and put one over each shoulder to lighten Jean's load.

Étienne's tall, skinny form blends in with the looming fir trees. Under the glint of his glasses, his smile emerges from the darkness as he teases Jean. "Old man, I'm happy to give you a hand."

"You young buck." At first, Étienne's offer riles Jean, and he feels enraged and ready to shout at the boy. Then he catches himself and loosens up, especially since the drop of canisters and supplies has gone without a hitch. Jean reluctantly hands him his sack, joking, "You'll be sorry."

"Only if we don't blast those *Boches* to hell and back."

"We will, I promise."

"Louis always assembled our explosives. Didn't want anyone else getting hurt." Étienne purses his lips, "At least that's what he said."

"He can't always have all the fun. I'll teach you myself."

Étienne smiles and quickens his pace.

Jean is limping badly now. Although he knows Étienne is anxious to get to the cave and start work on the *plastique*, he's compelled to stop. He finds a log and sits down hard while Étienne grudgingly joins him.

Jean says, "You go on ahead. I know the way."

"I promised Sylvie I'd look after you."

Jean smirks and curses some more.

Étienne turns to look at him. "I'm really glad you're alive. Tell me what happened."

Jean stares at Étienne's expectant face—the teenager, wearing his old military jacket, looking at him like he was a hero.

"Some things are better left unsaid." He rubs his knee, wincing. "Tell me, why did Sylvie become a nun?"

Étienne grins. "So she could boss people around. More than usual." He sighs like a man with years of experience. "Oh, you know women."

"I thought I did. Not anymore."

"I've got a secret. I'm in love with someone."

"Who's the lucky girl?"

"I can't tell. She's married."

"That's tough."

"But he's been away at the war. Nobody really thinks he's coming back."

Jean's tone is fatherly, although he hopes it isn't patronizing, as the boy seems deadly serious. "If he comes back, you'll find another. If he doesn't, she'll be in mourning, so you'll have to give her time."

"I don't have time." Abruptly he rises and paces in front of the log, wildly wielding his rifle. "Sylvie still treats me like a child. After all I've done at the refugee camp…and at the cave. But Madame Hélène appreciates me. She does, I know."

"Watch that rifle."

"That *Boche* major at Hélène's house. I'm gonna kill him! With the liberation, I've got an excuse." Étienne points the rifle at the nearby tree and pantomimes shooting.

"Hold on, Étienne. If that goes off, we're dead."

Jean is stunned at Étienne's erratic behavior and violent outburst. Still, he sees his reflection in the anxious boy, who desperately needs to prove himself to the unattainable woman he loves.

CHAPTER SIXTY-TWO

22 August 1944, One-thirty a.m.

ALONE IN HER dormitory room, Isobel pulls out the brass jug that serves as her only mirror in the convent. She checks her reflection and smooths out her skirt. She feels dispirited, remembering the silk dresses she took for granted growing up. Her eyes burn as she recalls her mother lovingly curling her long auburn hair. She sighs heavily at the prospect of not seeing Karl again. Impetuously, she decides to defy her aunt for once, so she loosens her hair and piles it up with just a few strands falling for effect. Then she picks up the cognac bottles from the crypt and brings them into the garden to wait for Karl.

She fusses about placing herself on a bench and leaning this way and that, giving her best profile to an imaginary Karl sitting beside her. Time drags on, bitter disappointment sets in, and she catches herself dozing. After several hours she falls asleep and awakens, startled, to an urgent rapping on the garden gate. At first she races to open it, but as she gets closer, she slows down and primps so as not to seem too anxious to receive her guest. As she opens the gate, Karl darts inside, his face beet red.

"Where is Sister?"

Isobel struggles to suppress her joy at seeing him. As Sylvie instructed, she knows she must adopt a stern and resolved attitude, turning him away as soon as she's handed over the cognac. Still, she feels compelled to detain him and coquettishly says, "I thought you were coming earlier."

"I couldn't get away. I must speak—"

Isobel motions to the cognac. "I'm supposed to give you these. Then you have to leave right away."

"But—"

"If the villagers saw us. I'm sorry." Her lip quivers. "Sister…sister made me promise." This is much harder than she thought. She forces herself to start back into the church.

Karl heads her off. "We have a meeting. So I am late. There will be a raid. On the partisans."

"That's horrible. When?"

"Early in the morning. But, for security, they wait to tell where it is."

"I'll tell Sister. She'll be back any minute." Reluctantly, she turns towards the church.

"Wait. I may not see you again."

She stops, panic rising. She knows she shouldn't prolong their time together, but she can't bear to lose him like all those she's ever cared for. She reaches out to take his arm, but he stiffens and nods, gently deflecting her.

"You are right. We must not be seen together."

As he starts for the gate, she finds the words to stop him. "This raid," she pauses to meet his gaze, "will be dangerous?"

"I do not know. But the war cannot last much longer."

"You think your side's going to lose?"

He seems genuinely sad. "They are not my side." He pauses for a moment, then looks directly at her. "I want them to lose."

He leans down to kiss her. No one's ever kissed her on the mouth. Isobel feels her stomach flutter.

Just then Sylvie, dressed in her trousers and cap, rushes up from the river and into the garden. Aghast at seeing a *Boche* soldier kissing her dear niece, she barks, "You there, private. Take your cognac and go."

Karl breaks from Isobel.

Isobel interjects, "We were just—"

"I know what you were just—"

Karl's face turns scarlet. "Forgive me, Sister. I must tell you—"

"I said get out of here!"

The boy sighs deeply. He picks up the cognac and starts to leave.

Isobel turns to her aunt. "Please, he says there's going to be a raid."

Sylvie eyes Karl suspiciously. She whispers to Isobel, "What were you thinking...kissing him?"

"You should listen to what—"

Sylvie seethes. "I saw them cart your parents away. My very own sister. Screaming as they threw her into the back of a van."

"I know, I know. But I'm sure he's telling the truth."

Incredulous, Sylvie stares at her niece for a moment then says, "What if he's lying just to get close to you?"

"I trust him."

"Well I don't." Sylvie thinks back to all the times she's seen her niece flirt with the boys at her parents' temple. How much has she really matured since then? Just as she maneuvered her flirtatious way around those boys, this boy could be manipulating her, except to a much deadlier end. As Isobel doesn't blink or divert her gaze from her aunt, Sylvie recalls that her niece may have been frivolous, but she never lied to her. She decides to hear the boy out and turns to him. "A raid you say? Who's leading it?"

"Major Spitzer. That is why he wants the cognac. To celebrate destroying the resistance."

"Where will this so-called raid take place?"

Karl's voice is hushed, even as he meets Sylvie's harsh stare. "Early in the morning. I am sorry. That is all I know."

Sylvie searches Karl's face trying to size him up and evaluate his information. Suddenly she bursts out, *"Mon Dieu,* I've got to go."

Karl turns to Isobel. "I must go also. I wish I did not." He casts a loving look at Isobel and leaves the garden.

Sylvie scoops up the trembling Isobel in her arms. "My darling, you must stay inside the church, no matter what." Her heart melts as she watches her niece turn, then stumble on her way back inside. Sylvie races down the steps to the river.

CHAPTER SIXTY-THREE

22 August 1944, Three a.m.

IN THE BRIGHT moonlight, Jean moves through the forest as fast as he's able, propelled by the vision of liberating Foix and recapturing Sylvie's love. He sees her everywhere—up ahead of him, then by his side, then following him, their leather pouches crammed full of pheasant. Her olive skin is flushed with exertion, but her deep brown eyes are alight with the joy of being with him. Then they are children, and her father is taking them hunting, crisscrossing the narrow, ancient trails of the Pyrénées and traversing their craggy passes. He loved that man, especially when he'd laugh, telling them how these very trails had been navigated for eons by goat herders and smugglers alike. "Sylvie and Jean," her father chuckled, "you're their modern counterparts." If only he knew!

Étienne ahead, calls back to Jean, "How're you doing, old man?"

He nods and waves the boy on, watching with a mixture of pride and envy as Étienne, now shouldering both packs, scales the ledge above. He fondly recalls taking the boy hunting. But then, one day, he realized that this naïve, almost otherworldly boy didn't relish shooting anything; Étienne only went hunting to be with him.

Jean admires how Étienne has flourished in this wartime environment. Claude's been a good influence in many ways. But the boy is much too quick to blow things out of proportion, and Jean worries about those communist pamphlets. It's disturbing how the boy talks about a "new" society and how much fairer things will be when everyone is "equal." Jean's natural mistrust of authority has ballooned into outright hatred of any kind of governmental organization. After his experiences in Spain, he regards the communists as especially duplicitous—in the guise of being equitable to all, he's seen, first hand, how a select few exert brutal control. He worries that Étienne will explode unexpectedly when his idealistic view of the world comes up against reality and is eventually shattered.

But Jean keeps trudging, sweating, and wiping his brow. "You know, young man, you're stronger than you look."

Étienne turns back, beaming. "Just let me know when you need another rest."

Jean smirks, once more reluctantly admiring the boy.

Sylvie climbs through the forest and up onto the mountain. She must get to the cave in time to warn the others of the raid, or it will be a horrific bloodbath. Nausea slams into her as she imagines Jean dying a second time. She pauses to catch her breath and comes to a decision: no matter how erratic Jean seems, she still loves him, will always love him. She will find a way to keep him in Foix with her. If that means renouncing her vows, so be it. People will understand. What's more, she doesn't care if they do or not.

As she scrambles higher, she catches a glimpse in the moonlight of her beloved Foix below. As it is well after curfew, the village is largely in darkness, with the only ones about likely to be *Boches* on patrol or off-duty soldiers coming and going from the village bar. She tries to make her way as quietly as possible, in case the patrols have expanded their coverage in anticipation of the raid she feels certain will be targeted on the cave.

But in her haste, she stumbles, and a large dry branch cracks beneath her, which sets off ferocious barking from dogs on the mountain. Sylvie wrenches in fear, as this signifies a patrol between her and the cave above. *Merde.* She's got to double back and come up the longer way around. She prays she'll make it in time to warn the others.

CHAPTER SIXTY-FOUR

22 August 1944, Five a.m.

HÉLÈNE, STILL REELING from her mixture of feelings about Gérard and her confrontation with Spitzer, channels her hatred of the major into helping the *Maquisards* arrange the fuses and cords to assemble the *plastique* explosives. Despite her distraction, though, ever alert for changes in her patients, she hears the large Yank airman groan. She hands her work off to one of the others, moves next to him by the fire, and feels his forehead, feverish. She quietly seeks out Joe, who is happily cutting cord and handing it to Claude. Using sign language to underscore her words, Hélène says, "You need to help me give him more sulpha powder."

At first he doesn't understand but then says, "Yeah, sure thing."

After they treat Bruce and she tends to the other wounded airmen, Hélène goes to the underground lake and draws some water for cold compresses. The dim light of early morning filters through the brambles at the opening of the cave. She wonders where Sylvie is and hopes that Isobel is all right. She tries to imagine what Jean might look like now, how he was treated, and whether Gérard shared any of his experiences.

She desperately needs to know how her husband died—if indeed he died at all. Perhaps when the fighting is over, they will discover the truth, and if he is dead, records that might give her some measure of comfort that he didn't suffer terribly. Focusing on her nursing to keep these thoughts at bay, she squeezes the excess water from the compresses and starts back to the wounded men.

Suddenly she hears a noise at the entrance to the cave. The *Maquis* always post a lookout. Quickly searching inside the cave, she realizes that in their haste to assemble the explosives, the man assigned as lookout has left his post and come inside the cave to join the work crew.

Hélène turns to see that Claude has also caught the sound, as he quickly signals for the men to be quiet and get their Sten guns. Turning back towards the entrance to the cave, she lets out a blood-curdling scream. There are *Boches* dismembering the branches to the entrance, clearing a path with lightning speed—a blitzkrieg—and rushing into the cave. A dozen or more in their coal shuttle helmets bend down, cram themselves inside the cave, then straighten bolt upright, rifles and submachine guns pointed directly at Hélène, as she stands in front of Claude, the young *Maquisards*, and the British and Yanks waiting to escape.

A soft, pale pink light filters over the peaks of the jagged mountains, signaling the beginning of sunrise. With every agonizing step, Jean's head pounds as if someone were holding his head in a vise, operating on his skull without an anesthetic. It takes every ounce of his resolve to keep slogging behind Étienne. Finally, they come to a ravine with a clump of fallen trees.

Exhausted, Jean says, "I've lost my sense of direction. How much farther to the cave?"

"Just over this ravine and up the slope. We can rest here."

Jean collapses behind some fallen logs.

Étienne offloads the two heavy rucksacks and sits next to Jean. "You all right?"

Jean furiously rubs his temples. Then, as much to calm himself as to reassure the boy, he turns to Étienne and says, "I'm proud of you."

Étienne adjusts his wire-rimmed glasses. "Hélène would be too, wouldn't she?"

"I remember when she left Foix to become a nurse in Toulouse." Jean nudges him. "She's quite a bit older, isn't she?"

"I work with her. I know what she needs right away."

"She's still married."

The boy winces. "But no one knows if her husband is —"

"Slow down. You need to get your head clear."

"Is your head clear? About Sylvie, I mean."

Jean leans back and imagines his life with her in North Africa—how her thick black hair and olive skin will look against a profusion of yellow, orange, and red silks. "Never clearer."

"I liked her better before she became a nun."

Jean grins. "So did I."

Suddenly, Jean hears muffled sounds of breaking branches and men walking in the forest. Alarmed, he pushes Étienne's head down, then checks his rifle. He leans over the ravine barrier and sees them: there must be forty *Boches*, fanned out in the surrounding forest, down the ridge, and up to the entrance to the cave. Despite their gray-green uniforms that offer some camouflage, an occasional blinding glint of sunrise exposes them through the trees. They move slowly, deliberately. Jean carefully eases back down, blood pumping furiously through the veins in his neck.

Étienne raises up. "What is it?"

"Just outside the cave. A whole unit."

"Hélène's in there!"

"My damn knee. We would've been there by now."

"Sylvie too—"

As Étienne jumps up to scale the ravine where they're hiding, Jean reaches out with all his strength to grab the boy and hold him back.

Hélène squints against the shafts of sunlight which, with the brambles now completely cleared, pierce the mouth of the cave. She hears a roaring in her ears. Her terror squeezes down on her, troubling her breathing, and causing everything to happen in agonizingly slow motion. Major Spitzer marches triumphantly into the cave. She shudders as he stares at her with those unblinking eyes of his, pure hatred spreading over his face. He waves his gloved hand around to indicate to the cave and its inhabitants. "You did not think you could keep such as thing as this from me, did you?"

His words are like hammers. *How long has he known?*

Claude and the others, rifles drawn, stand rigidly still, facing off against the Germans.

Spitzer calls to the British and Yanks in the back, "You there, stand up so I can see you."

Some of the British airmen and the female agent stand, but one or two of them are too wounded, and the American, Bruce, is barely conscious. Joe moves cautiously in front of him.

Whether because of her rage at the major or her instinctive need to protect her patients, Hélène moves between Spitzer and the wounded men. She says, with venom in her voice, "They can't stand. They're wounded, can't you see?"

Spitzer jerks his head, motioning for some of his men to go to the back of the cave. Roving his eyes over Hélène, he growls to the soldiers, "*Schießen Sie.* Shoot them."

Hélène feels her knees buckling. She hears herself say, from somewhere outside of her, "Major, I implore you."

A square, portly soldier is quick to respond to Spitzer's command.

He stomps around the lake towards the back, taking with him a very tall and lanky soldier. As they leave their position next to the major, Hélène recognizes the young soldier, whom she saw with Isobel. He slips stealthily to the entrance of the cave and vanishes. Claude and the others move in front of the advancing two soldiers, blocking their way to the wounded. Although the *Maquisards* are vastly outnumbered, they remain steadfast, rifles aimed at the Germans.

Hélène's hatred for Spitzer overrides her fear. She shrieks, "Leave them alone! What kind of monsters would shoot wounded men?"

Spitzer sets his jaw, curling the side of his mouth into what passes for a smile.

"You tried to play me all along, didn't you?" His sarcasm is vicious as he adds, "Madame Hélène? Our pure and noble nurse. Working for the resistance all this time, but all too happy to share food and my—"

"You've been lying to me all this time about Gérard. That makes us even." Hélène burns with shame and searches Claude's face for his understanding. Would he forgive her if he knew how she'd come to care for the major? Claude takes his eyes off the major for a fleeting second to give her a single fierce nod—his affirmation. Profoundly relieved, she feels emboldened to make one last anguished appeal to stop the *Boches* who have their rifles drawn. "Please, Major, don't take your hatred for me out on these wounded men."

Jean can barely keep hold of Étienne, so determined is the boy to scramble over the side of the ravine and race up to the cave.

"Christ, Étienne. If they know we're here, we can't help anyone."

"I've got to save Hélène."

"Getting us killed won't do that."

"You don't really care about Sylvie!"

Jean glowers at Étienne. His mind flashes, imagining how, if he saves Sylvie and the *Maquisards*, he'll redeem himself and regain her love. He relaxes his hold, just for a moment. Étienne takes advantage, kicks him in his bad knee, grabs his rifle, and starts up the side. Despite the pain, Jean manages to claw up the slope, desperately trying to reclaim his gun.

Suddenly, Étienne jerks his head away from the entrance to the cave. Jean follows his gaze and sees a young German soldier with blonde hair sprinting away from the cave. The soldier stops, bends over, and vomits against a tree.

Étienne comes to a rapid halt on the slope and attempts to steady his footing, even as Jean grabs his leg, trying to drag him down.

"Damn it, Jean. Let go. I'm gonna kill that bastard."

"Don't shoot. They'll be down on us in a second."

"I don't care." Étienne kicks Jean's hand away and takes aim. "This is for Hélène."

"No!" Just as Étienne takes the shot, Jean rises up and throws himself against the boy. Étienne shouts a blood-curdling curse as he misses the young soldier who bounds down the mountain towards Foix.

Inside the cave, Hélène's terror mounts as Spitzer snarls to the portly German who threatens the wounded men, "*Schießen Sie! Schießen Sie!* Shoot! Shoot them all!"

Hélène swiftly moves between the portly German and the wounded men, slowly raising her hands and challenging him as if to say: *you'll have to shoot me first.* The *Maquisards* take their cue from her, lower their rifles and also raise their hands in surrender. The German soldiers flanking Major Spitzer stand waiting, their rifles at the ready. They nervously stare back and forth between Hélène and the major.

The portly one turns back to the others and takes up the major's command, *"Schießen Sie!"* But none of the soldiers move. Everyone in the cave stands frozen, waiting.

Spitzer's face contorts in fury. "Kill them all!"

Hélène flinches, startled to hear not only the major's crazed order but also a shot. A shot that rings out from somewhere outside the cave. A shot that precipitates the chaos that lets loose as submachine gunfire from the Germans fills the cave. She covers her ears against the shattering noise as bullets ricochet off the ancient striated walls of the cave. Stalactites are shorn in two, pockmarked from bullets slamming into the gently flowing streams of water that slide down and feed into the lake. Chunks of rock and bullets, sharp and cutting, fly about as clouds of hot dust rise, burning Hélène's flesh. She sees it all happen in terrifyingly slow motion. Everything is bright yellow. No, it's bright orange. No, it's bright white. The last thing Hélène remembers is Spitzer's unblinking gaze, his eyes, the blackest of pearls, boring into her as she plummets into a soft, black void.

Jean grabs the rifle from Étienne and knocks him out with the butt. Then he hears a volley of submachine gunfire deep in the cave. Men screaming. Smoke pouring from the cave.

Fury surges through him as he envisions the carnage within. Sylvie falling. Her long black hair flying through gunfire, guts, blood, and debris. All his efforts for naught. Like his time with the Republicans in the Spanish civil war—nothing but a lost cause. If only he'd gotten there in time. But what could he have done against all of them?

He pulls the unconscious Étienne down from the crest of the ravine back into the ditch, just as the *Boches* stream out of the cave. He hears muffled grenade blasts from within the cave that shake the ground around him.

Jean looks over at Étienne, his skinny, awkward frame lying splayed

THE NIGHT BELONGS TO THE MAQUIS

out in the ditch. Sylvie's brother. A gawky, head-strong kid—all that's left of Sylvie. He crawls through the dust to Étienne, takes the boy in his arms, rocking him back and forth—and sobs.

▄▄▄

Sylvie finally makes her way around the *Boches* up to the cliff above the cave. From where she crouches, she hears the brutal stuttering of submachine gunfire, then grenade blasts. As black smoke billows, she wrenches back in a silent scream. *I've lost Jean. I'd hardly found him, and now he's gone.* She slowly kneels onto the jagged rocks, making the sign of the cross. *Pray for us sinners now and at the hour of our death.* Uncle Claude. Étienne. All those men. Now there will be no liberation. Her cherished Foix will remain imprisoned.

She silently wails. Her cap flies off in the wind. Her long black hair whips wildly, wisps plastered over her tear-stricken face. She thrusts her arms out on either side, like the Christ, imploring God for mercy on their souls. She looks up to the heavens to let the sun, now fully risen and bright, burn into her face. But it cannot dry her tears, as they come so fast. The sunrise, every day a redemption? *Not this sunrise!*

She kneels there, paralyzed, her mind racing with thoughts of everything that should have happened that day. They should have all gone back and assembled the explosives. She and Jean and the *Maquisards* should have crept down to Foix that evening and blown up the munitions dump, while the Free French, having parachuted onto the mountain, should have done battle and liberated Foix. She rolls over and curls into a ball, never wanting to move again.

▄▄▄

Jean is curled over Étienne, holding him like a child. In his mind, he sees Sylvie by his side. The munitions dump in Foix blown to

394

smithereens. The French paratroopers landing up on the mountain, then streaming down to free his village from the *Boches'* tyrannical hold.

Through the haze of his grief, Jean thinks back. Why was he so hard on her—taunting her for taking her vows and for wanting to be in control. That was who she was, and he's always loved her for her indomitable spirit. Why did he try to crush it? He only wanted to make her love him again. To forgive what he'd done.

Now he knows firsthand how his father suffered from agonizing bouts of shell shock— constant noises of war in his head that triggered terrors at night and emotional paralysis during the day. He's suffered these too and become what he never, ever wanted to be—his father. If he'd succeeded in his mission, he would have overcome the stigma of being labeled a coward's son. Instead, he'll carry an even greater stigma—failing in the most important mission possible. And he will never have earned back Sylvie's love and admiration.

Étienne stirs then jerks up.

As the *Boches* have left, Jean lets him rant. And cry. And moan. And yell at him, "Why didn't you let me go?"

"So you'd be dead too?" Anger and desperation propel Jean to focus on how to salvage at least part of the mission. "At least we have two rucksacks of *plastique*. We can create some kind of diversion."

Étienne searches for his glasses in the dust, recovers them, and straightens out their bent wireframe. Before Jean can stop him, the boy scrambles up the slope and into the clearing leading up to the cave. "I've got to see if anyone's still alive."

Jean understands the boy's need, but his memories of the prison camp flood back into him—bodies hardly cold, brains leaking onto indistinguishable gore, and the sweet smell of blood he could never get out of his nostrils. He wants to shield Étienne from those horrors that will rob him of sleep for the rest of his life. Except that he knows he must go too—to face what might be left of his beloved Sylvie.

The two make their way inside the cave. Jean feels a strange quietness, as the scene around him seems far away. With leaden steps, they cross the hot embers of still-burning rubble and debris. Smoke and acrid dust billow with each step. Gnarled chunks of stalactites cling to the vaulted ceiling above, and remnants of once-proud stalagmites lie shattered on the floor. Rubble fills the lake. The carnage is beyond anything he could have imagined.

He searches among the bodies and finds the large, red-faced Claude, barely recognizable. Jean shakes his head, a searing agony spreading within. *He treated me like a son.* Further on, at the back of the cave on what had been his bedding, the big Yank is riddled with bullets. Gore and intestines lie across abdomens everywhere. Several bodies lie where they fought, arms and legs stiffly akimbo. He's startled to hear a gunshot but realizes it's just a piece of stalactite, pulverized by bullets, falling haphazardly. He shouts for Étienne to watch out as another large chunk breaks off and smashes the head of a young, dead *Maquisard.* Jean howls a silent curse.

Étienne spots Hélène's body, pierced with dozens of bullets, her arm severed from the rest of her body and her legs bloody and askew, like a broken rag doll. His slow moan grows into a plaintive wail. He reaches under her and clutches her to him, kissing her passionately while he runs his fingers through her wavy blonde hair, now covered in dust and drying blood.

Jean, transfixed by the boy's grief, tries to steel himself for the moment he will find Sylvie's body. Searching some more, he hears rocks crunching outside the entrance to the cave and motions for Étienne to be quiet and hide. The boy can't hear him for his own moaning, so Jean creeps behind a remaining portion of rock and takes aim with his rifle.

Backlit by shafts of sunlight pouring into the cratered open mouth of the cave, a figure emerges, stirring up a cloud of hot dust that lingers in the air. Jean blinks to clear his eyes, certain his mind is playing tricks on him. "*Mon Dieu.*" Jean charges through the rubble and reaches

Sylvie at the mouth of the cave before she can enter. He flings down his rifle and takes her in his arms.

Sylvie's voice is thickened by smoke. "Jean, thank the Lord."

They stand together, holding tight. Breathless. He strokes her face, reassuring himself that she's real. He whispers coarsely, "I thought I'd lost you for good this time. I'm sorry. So sorry."

"I did what I had to. But I never stopped loving you."

"Can we ever go back to the way it was before the war?"

He feels the ground give way underneath him as he watches her hold back a moment, intently searching his face. Then she nods.

Both are trembling now as they kiss deeply. Urgently.

Sylvie slowly breaks apart from him and starts to enter the cave. "I heard—"

"It's best you not go in." He moves to shield her, but she insists on entering. He accompanies each step she takes, watching her shake so hard she can barely walk.

She keeps murmuring, "No. Oh no. Look what they've done. Ohhhhhh, *Mon Dieu*. My dear Uncle Claude. And the rest of them." She kneels and makes the sign of the cross before each barely recognizable body.

Spying Étienne with Hélène's body, Sylvie slowly steps through the debris to her brother, who rises and fiercely hugs her. "Sylvie, we thought they killed you too."

Looking up to him, she pulls him tight and wipes tears from his sooty face. "I got delayed. I had to circle around. I'm so sorry. I should have been here to warn them."

Jean says, "It wasn't your fault." Then he turns to Étienne. "My boy, there was nothing any of us could have done. There were just too many of them."

Étienne looks daggers at Jean. He opens his mouth to say something, and Jean flinches, thinking the boy means to explode with accusations. Instead, he silently shifts his focus back to Hélène's body and stands over her as if to keep a vigil.

Sylvie says, "Poor, poor Hélène. An angel. I'm so sorry, Étienne."

Étienne breaks into a fresh round of sobs.

Sylvie puts her arms around her brother. "You meant so much to her. She'd often say—"

"What did she say? Did she love me? I loved her, you know."

Jean watches as Sylvie pauses to gather her thoughts. He admires how tender she is with her brother.

"Of course, she loved you. You meant the world to her."

Seeing that Sylvie is safe, Jean reminds them of their mission. "We've still got two sacks of *plastique*."

She looks at him, puzzled. "You want to blow the munitions dump with only two bags of explosives?"

"It'll be enough if we set the charges right. But we've got to get the packs down to Foix. Is there somewhere safe we can assemble them?"

"There's a secret room in the church. Through the panel to the right of the confessional. In emergencies, I hide an airman there until I can move him." She turns to her brother. "Étienne, you know where it is and how to get in."

Jean is unnerved that Étienne doesn't seem to hear her or understand what's going on. She tries again. "Étienne, listen to me. You've got to get hold. Do this one last thing for Hélène."

Étienne blinks a few times, as if coming out of a trance.

Jean reinforces Sylvie's urging. "Come on, Étienne. You go ahead and take one of the sacks. Sylvie and I can manage the other.

Sylvie adds, "We'll be there as soon as we can. You must go right now. Clear the tables downstairs in the church. Start laying things out."

Étienne suddenly bursts into a fury. "I'll kill them all. Every last one deserves to die for what they did to her." He stomps back and forth, kicking up clouds of burnt powder. "I'll kill that major myself. Promise me, Jean, you'll let me have him."

Jean barks, "I know how upset you are. But, we've got to set the charges by sunset."

Étienne continues to stare at Hélène's mutilated form.

Jean shouts, "Otherwise, Foix doesn't get liberated, and you can't avenge her death." He grabs the boy by the shoulders. "Do you understand?"

Étienne jerks away, whispering, "We can't leave her like this. We've got to bury her."

Sylvie says, "Étienne, we'll come back for her. I promise."

Jean yells, "Étienne, the room in the church. Can you do that? For Hélène?"

Étienne nods mechanically, and the three somberly prepare to leave. When she reaches the rubble of what was the entrance to the cave, Sylvie turns back to the horror inside, kneels, crosses herself, and murmurs a prayer.

Jean watches her deeply reverent gestures with mixed feelings. She just said she loved him, but when the time comes, will she really give up the veil to be with him? He's lost her twice now—he could never survive losing her a third time.

CHAPTER SIXTY-FIVE

22 August 1944, Ten thirty a.m.

HER NERVES TAUT, Isobel paces in front of the altar in the church. The traditional white and gold cloth covering is streaked with various shades of red, blue, and purple, cast by the sun through the stained glass window. To keep up the pretense of being Catholic, she knows she should be kneeling and crossing herself each time she passes in front of the Christ hanging in the center of the apse. But she's too distracted. Her hair, carefully coiffed for Karl last night, is a mess of falling strands, but she doesn't notice as she tries to imagine what might have happened to her aunt, Jean, and Karl.

She's startled by a noise from the rear of the church and whips around to see Karl, disheveled, lurching into the back pew. As he collapses, she runs to him, alarmed to see his face blotched red and bathed in sweat, his uniform torn in several places.

Gasping for breath, he manages to say, "I could not do it. And I could not stop them by myself. So I ran. I ran away."

Isobel looks around to make sure no one else is in the church, then slides into the pew next to him, grabs his arm, and ducks them both down and out of sight. She whispers, "Tell me what happened."

"They should have taken them as prisoners. Not shoot them like dogs."

"What are you talking about?"

He shudders and looks away. "They will kill me. They will consider me a coward. And a traitor."

"What?"

"The cave. I could not kill those people. The nurse. Those wounded men."

"Hélène?" Isobel recoils. "They killed Hélène? And what about my... I mean Sister. Did they kill her too?"

"*Nein*, I do not think she was there."

"Thank God."

Karl raises up to look around and beyond the pew, then quickly crouches back down. "She must give me sanctuary. I beg you to ask her. Otherwise, I am dead."

Wide-eyed with terror, Isobel stares at him, pauses, then shakes her head. "If they find you here, they'll shoot her. And the rest of us in the convent." Isobel shudders at the thought of Hélène's death and is utterly confused about what to do about Karl. He's one of them, but he isn't. Doesn't his refusal to take part in the killing spree prove that? Or is her aunt right—the *Boches* are duplicitous and will say and do anything to get what they want? But didn't they kill his parents just like they killed hers? Or did they?

Her mind a blur, she watches as he stands up in the pew, takes his handkerchief out and rubs the sweat from his face, then straightens his uniform. Stepping around her and out into the aisle, he adopts a razor-backed position of resolve.

"You are right. I must go. I cannot ask this of Sister. Or you."

Just then, Étienne appears at the front of the church. He steps from behind a pillar between the altar and the side entrance. He drops his pack, raises his rifle, and aims at Karl, shouting, "What can't you ask, you goddamned Nazi?"

Isobel feels her stomach lurch. She wants more than anything to run and hide, but her innate stubbornness takes over. With calm but forceful determination—she has no idea where it comes from—Isobel steps from the pew and stands directly in front of Karl. "Étienne? What are you doing?"

Étienne screams at Karl, "You bastard. You killed Hélène." He steps to the side to avoid Isobel and give himself a clear shot at Karl, but he's up against the pillar, and Isobel remains squarely in his sights.

Karl calls out, "I did not kill anyone, I swear."

Isobel sets her shoulders and takes a firm step towards Étienne. "He's not like them."

"You stupid, pampered girl. They're all alike. They killed your parents, for God's sake." His hands shake as he slips the safety off the rifle. "Isobel, get out of my way."

Karl glances at her, shocked. "He called you Isobel?"

She whispers, "Trust me. I will explain." She turns and takes a few more steps towards Étienne. Her voice is steady and commanding, "Cousin Étienne, you don't want to shoot."

"Why not?"

"Aunt Sylvie would—"

"I don't give a damn about Sylvie."

"You'd be killing someone in cold blood. You'd be just as bad as them."

His hands shaking violently now, Étienne tries to steady the rifle.

"Besides, everyone will hear," she says.

Stealthily, Jean comes up behind Étienne and says, "She's right. It'll bring the *Boches* down on all of us."

Isobel gasps—it happens so quickly! Jean reaches up to the taller Étienne, grabs him in a chokehold, and, using his elbow, knocks the rifle from Étienne's hands. She cringes, waiting for the gun to go off, but miraculously, it doesn't.

Étienne wrestles against Jean's hold, breaks free, and starts to come after him when a nun steps between them. Isobel fears it's one of the other nuns but then recognizes her Aunt Sylvie, who's changed from her trousers back into her habit.

Sylvie says, "Étienne, stop it."

Imploring, whining, Étienne shouts to Jean, "You promised I could kill them."

Sylvie hisses, "Shut up. Someone will hear."

Isobel shudders to see Étienne wholly unhinged as he threatens Karl, but she's relieved to see her aunt forcefully interceding to prevent bloodshed. Does that mean she'll listen to Karl? To the reason he fled the *Boches* in the cave? Her mind races to shape the arguments she'll use to beseech her aunt to give Karl sanctuary. Surely she will—she's been in love too, hasn't she?

Even though she's very much awake, Sylvie is certain she's having a nightmare—seeing Étienne go wild, lunge at Jean, and then at her. After losing Hélène, she can understand his hatred of the young German— she still doesn't entirely trust him herself—but her brother is acting crazy, jeopardizing all of them as well as what's left of the mission.

Étienne shrieks, "I knew I couldn't trust you to let me avenge Hélène."

Sylvie desperately tries to quiet him, but he continues to rant until Jean, shaking his head in exasperation, pulls back his fist and knocks him out. As Étienne falls, Jean grabs him and sets him down on the stone floor behind the pillar.

Jean looks up at Sylvie. "Sorry. Had to be done."

Much as she hates to see her brother injured, Sylvie agrees there was nothing else Jean could do. He takes some rope from his pack, and they tie

Étienne's hands in front. Then Jean raises the rifle he took from Étienne and aims it at Karl, standing with Isobel at the back of the church.

Out of the side of his mouth, Jean asks Sylvie, "What do we do with him?'

Sylvie struggles to contain her growing sense of panic. "First, we've got to hide Étienne." She rushes to the far side of the confessional and slides back a panel, revealing a secret, heavy stone door. She heaves against one side to open it, then calls to Isobel and Karl, "You two, come here, with us."

As Isobel approaches, her eyes widen. "Jean? Is that really you? I thought—"

Sylvie interrupts. "Yes. I'll explain. But now—" She turns to Karl and motions to her brother on the stone floor. "Pick him up."

Jean wields the rifle around, butt end towards Karl. "This won't make a sound if I bash your head in. Understand?"

Sylvie is relieved to see Karl nod and lift Étienne, easily slinging him over his shoulder. She collects her brother's glasses and slips them into her habit. She motions for Isobel to take one of the heavy packs of explosives while she takes the other. The girl has to grip hers with both hands, but she manages.

Sylvie lugs her bag down a stone staircase leading to a landing, then down another staircase to a chamber with a low, vaulted ceiling. The air is chilly and dank. Sealed off from the church above, it is soundless and dark. She feels her way to light two lanterns, revealing straw bedding in pallets along one wall and piles of extra men's clothes in the far corner. There are some wooden chairs and a large rough-hewn table that looks like it's been there since medieval times. Jugs of water, some rope, links of chain, and various tools are scattered about.

Jean holds the rifle on Karl, who carries Étienne down the stairs and lays him on a straw pallet. As Karl straightens up, Jean orders him, quietly but forcefully, to raise his hands.

Jean whispers to Sylvie, "We've got to unload the packs and separate this stuff into piles. Assemble the explosives." He nods towards Karl. "Any suggestions what to do with him?"

Sylvie thinks back to the carnage in the cave. "Send him back. I don't trust any of them."

Isobel jumps in, "Please, he's the one who warned us about the raid."

Through gritted teeth, Sylvie says, "Maybe he was just trying to get on our good side. He knows we're winning."

Karl lowers his hands and takes a step forward.

Jean says, "Not so fast. Keep them up."

Karl raises his hands again but turns to Sylvie. "Sister, *Ja,* I was at the raid. Major Spitzer gives the order to shoot them all. Even the wounded. Our soldiers are standing there with their guns aimed. But I cannot do it. I am going to be sick, so I run outside. Then I hear—"

Jean interrupts, "It's true, I saw him running away. Étienne tried to shoot him. Right after that, I heard guns firing inside the cave." Jean lowers his rifle. "So he wasn't there. And he's telling the truth about being sick."

Exhaling sharply, Karl lowers his hands.

Still, Sylvie is reluctant to let him off. "Maybe he was just afraid. Being a German coward doesn't exonerate him."

"Please, Sister," Karl implores, "I would not lie to you in the house of God."

Sylvie whispers sharply to Isobel, "If I give him sanctuary and they find him, you know what they'll do to us?"

"Aunt Sylvie. He's not a killer. There's something you need to know—"

"He's a Nazi. They took your parents."

Karl starts to leave. "Sister is right. I must go. I cannot put you all in danger."

Sylvie says, "That's right. Go!"

"I don't know if I believe him or not," Jean says. "But we can't just let him leave. He could go straight back and tell the others."

Isobel says, "No! I've been trying to tell you. He's not one of them."

Jean's tone is bitter, sarcastic. "That's odd…he looks just like one of them."

As Karl starts to ascend the stairs to the church, Isobel blocks his way. "We've got to let him stay. If we don't believe Karl, where does this end?"

Sylvie snorts, "You're too young to know—"

"Then we might as well all live in convents. Shut away from the world." Isobel takes Karl's hand. "I'm going with you."

Jean barks, "You'll both be killed out there."

Karl gently but firmly shakes off Isobel's hand. "Please, you must stay here."

Although Sylvie is desperate to protect Isobel, there must be something that her niece knows about Karl to make her believe in him so fervently. "Isobel, how can you even look at him after what they've done to us all these years?"

Isobel vehemently shakes her head, strands of her hair falling haphazardly around her face. She angrily brushes them aside. "If we live for revenge, they'll live for revenge, and we'll live for revenge, and on and on. It's got to stop. Here. With us."

Sylvie is taken aback at her niece's retort—her Jewish niece, whom she taught the teachings of Christ, is now living those teachings in ways she isn't. "You're willing to risk your life?"

Isobel gravely nods.

Sylvie looks between Karl and Isobel. Each seems so earnest. With her faith in the Lord, how can she refuse to show mercy to these innocents? She softens, saying quietly to Karl, "I will give you sanctuary."

Karl makes a slight bow. "Thank you, Sister."

Isobel presses her eyes shut in relief.

Sylvie wonders if she's just agreed to the most charitable thing in her life or whether it's the stupidest, most dangerous thing she's ever done.

CHAPTER SIXTY-SIX

22 August 1944, Eleven o'clock a.m.

SYLVIE FEELS A hush descend on the room as the enormity of her decision dawns on everyone, virtually sucking the air out of the ancient stone chamber beneath the church.

Finally, Jean breaks the stillness. "All right. We've still got a mission." He turns to Karl. "I'm warning you. These women might believe you, but as far as I'm concerned, you're only here because we can't let you go."

Karl makes a slight bow. "I will not betray Sister's trust. You have my word."

Jean brusquely engages the safety and sets the rifle against the wall. "Let's start then. Karl—that's your name? You help Isobel and ah—the Sister here prepare the *plastique* to blow the munitions dump."

They pull chairs up to the table, and he directs them: "Open those bags, remove the straw packing. There's a tube of salve. Rub it on your hands, or you'll get a violent headache."

"Right," Relieved they're now underway, Sylvie takes some salve and hands the tube to Isobel and Karl.

Jean continues, "Unwrap that yellow stuff and knead it to soften it."

Isobel's hands tremble as she takes hold of the *plastique* material. "Smells like almonds."

Jean says, "That just means it's fresh. Don't worry, it's not going to blow until we put the detonator in."

Even with this assurance, Sylvie feels pounding in her temples. "It's soft, now what?"

Jean surveys their work on the first batch. "Good. Now roll it into sausages."

Sylvie catches Jean narrowing his eyes as he scrutinizes Karl. Seemingly satisfied, Jean continues with the assembly, pulling out something that looks like a pencil.

"Sylvie, when we get there, this is very important. Press the copper, see here? That breaks open the vial of acid, which melts this wire here. That drops the plunger that strikes the detonator. The color we use determines how long we have. This one...the red one...gives us three minutes to get clear. Then BOOM!"

Sylvie says, "Understood."

Jean nods to Isobel and Karl. "Wrap them in packs of four. Hurry, we've got all these to do."

After they work for several hours, Étienne moans, slowly regains consciousness, and looks around, confused. He spies Karl. "That Nazi bastard! What's he—"

Jean calls to him, "Shut up. We know for sure he didn't shoot Hélène or anyone else."

Sylvie says, "Jean's right. We need him to help us get the *plastique* ready."

Étienne struggles to free his hands, then deflated, leans back and watches them work. After a few minutes, he whispers to Sylvie, "Let me help—"

"How could we ever trust you now?"

"I swear to God."

Sylvie is firm. "No."

"I swear on Hélène's life."

Sylvie sincerely wants to believe her brother but turns to Jean. "What do you think?"

"I don't know. It's late, and we need the help." He hesitates, then says to Sylvie, "Watch him like a hawk." Then to Étienne, "I'm warning you."

Étienne nods, prompting Sylvie to reach in her sleeve and return his glasses. As she kneels to untie him, reining in the long folds of her habit, a deep apprehension floods her—if they're successful in liberating Foix, she's promised to give up the veil to be with Jean. But she's found unbounded solace within the church in her greatest times of need. Her trials under German occupation might soon be over, but if they are, does she truly want to renounce her vows for another, worldlier, set of marriage vows? Her nun's spiritual veil for a secular bridal veil? Years ago, that's what she dreamt of. But now? No matter how much she loves Jean, it's unthinkable to renounce her vows and leave the church. Adjusting her habit as she tends to her brother, she shoves these unnerving feelings aside.

Jean hisses at Étienne, "Sit at the end, where we can keep an eye on you." He tosses the boy some cord and a knife. "Wrap these in bundles of two. Use this cordex—this white cable here—to join the bundles."

Slumping like a whipped puppy, Étienne takes his place at the end of the table.

Karl continues to mold the soft yellow *plastique*, then stops. "You know where is the ammo?"

Jean says, "I have a pretty good idea."

"I can take you to it. A stone house where they keep the munitions. We should make single bundles too."

"Why?"

"There is motor pool…armored cars, jeeps. Next to the stone house. Big bundles for munitions. Small to blow up vehicles."

Sylvie shoots Jean an uneasy glance.

Jean nods to her then sharply puts a question to Karl. "How do we get past the guard?"

"I will tell the guard Major Spitzer wants to see him right now."

Sylvie can't hide her concern. "Jean, does this make sense to you?"

"I'll be training my rifle on him the whole time." He turns to Karl. "You'd better make good on your promise."

Karl whispers, "Sister has already treated me with more respect than they ever did."

Étienne goes red in the face. "How come he gets to play hero?"

Sylvie has deeply unsettled feelings about Étienne, who continues to bristle. She catches him stealing malicious glances at Karl. But they must finish as fast as possible—perhaps she's reading too much into this? She returns to her work—intently practicing the sequence she'll have to execute perfectly to ignite the charges—in the dark and under the most extreme time pressure imaginable.

Jean studies Karl as he works, then says, "All right. It's settled." He turns to Sylvie, "We've got to get him cleaned up. To fool the guard."

"If he's wearing their uniform," Isobel protests, "He could be shot by the resistance. Or the paratroopers."

Sylvie says, "It's a risk. But, we'll be with him."

Jean turns to Karl. "Are you willing?"

Karl nods and takes Isobel's hand to reassure her.

Jean says, "Karl, stay close to us. We all come right back here, understood?"

"Then what?" Isobel clings to Karl.

Sylvie turns to survey the extra clothes she keeps in the corner. "We'll have to get him something else to wear."

Jean says, "Isobel, will you tend to that? I need to check the radio. If the landing's on schedule, they'll broadcast a special message: *the chickens are coming home to roost.*" He and Sylvie share a smile. "Where's the radio, Sylvie."

"Hidden under the altar. The antenna runs up inside the bell tower."

Jean grins. "Clever."

While Jean sees to the wireless, Sylvie feels a flush of warmth towards him. Surely he's back to his old self—the man she's loved her whole life. They're working seamlessly together again, as they did hunting in the mountains for so many years. As he climbs the stairs up to the church, Sylvie is alarmed to see him still limping, although clearly trying to minimize his incapacity.

As Karl continues his work on the explosives, Isobel searches through the pile of clothes in the corner. Meanwhile, out of the corner of her eye, Sylvie notices Étienne, slowly jerking a length of cord back and forth in his hands. Again, she puts it out of her mind, focusing instead on Karl's situation.

"Karl, even if we take back Foix, both sides have reason to kill you. You'll have to go into hiding."

"Sister, you are right. But where?"

She thinks for a moment. "The only safe place I can think of is my farm."

Isobel brightens. "We'll go together."

"I don't know about that." Sylvie hesitates, then adds, "Yes, my dear. I'm afraid you'll need to go into hiding as well. People may have seen you together."

Suddenly, Étienne stops work. "Hélène's Nazi murderer? Not in my house!"

Sylvie snaps, "Étienne, he's risking his life to help us. It's only right."

Étienne screams, "Bastard!" He lunges at Karl's throat with his knife but misses, piercing his right shoulder instead. A thin trail of blood oozes from the wound. Stunned, Karl raises his hands to staunch the bleeding.

Isobel shouts, "No!"

Sylvie grabs the rifle that Jean had held on Karl as they descended the stairs, then set in the corner. She aims it at her brother. "Stop right now." *This can't be happening, not after he promised.*

Karl seems disoriented as he looks down at the blood running between his fingers. Étienne takes advantage and throws himself against Karl. He knocks him down and jumps on him, knife in hand. Isobel tries to pull Étienne off while Karl heaves up, but with Isobel virtually on top of Étienne, he can't dislodge Étienne.

Still aiming the rifle at her brother, Sylvie shrieks, "Étienne! Stop right now!"

Étienne, his face twisted with venom, starts a downward thrust with his knife, this time aiming directly at Karl's neck. But Karl manages to get his knee up and shoves him off. Isobel goes flying and knocks into Sylvie. The rifle goes off, hitting Étienne in the chest. He crumples to the floor.

Sylvie stands horror-struck, rifle poised in mid-air. Isobel scrambles up and stares down at Étienne. Blood trickles from his mouth. His eyes turn glassy, unbelieving, as he squeezes his chest over his heart, where the bullet entered. Sylvie screams and throws the rifle down. Meanwhile, Jean opens the door from above, slams it tight, and rushes down the stairs.

"What the hell? Étienne?"

Isobel rips some cloth from her skirt to press against Karl's shoulder. Her voice trembling, she calls to Jean, "Étienne was trying to kill Karl. I tried to stop him. Aunt Sylvie warned him. She did—"

Sylvie slowly kneels, her habit billowing around her. Awash in grief, she takes Étienne in her arms. His breath is shallow. She rocks him like a baby, moaning softly, "God forgive me. God forgive you. Pray for us sinners now, and..." Sylvie's pitiful sob finishes the prayer.

Jean kneels beside Étienne to examine him, then shakes his head. Étienne jerks from side to side, gasping for breath, his terrified eyes darting around. He opens his mouth, looks up at his sister, pleading, "Sylvie?" Suddenly, his hands go limp, and his body slackens in Sylvie's arms. His breath rushes out all at once, and his eyes fasten on some distant object, then open wide before they go still.

Sylvie feels all the blood draining from her. Her hand shakes erratically as she makes a feeble sign of the cross over her brother's body.

Jean bows his head and whispers, "God have mercy on his soul." He bends down, presses his hand over Étienne's eyes, and shuts them.

After a moment, Jean goes to Karl and quietly asks, "Are you all right?"

Karl slowly nods.

Jean turns to Isobel, "See what more you can do about the bleeding. Then bandage him up."

Isobel takes Karl's tunic jacket off and tears more cloth from her skirt for his bandage. Jean moves back to Sylvie and kneels by her side.

Sylvie wails, "He wouldn't stop. I told him. Jean, he wouldn't—"

"I know, Sylvie."

"I never meant to—"

"Of course not." He gently lifts her chin. "Sylvie, we've got to go. It won't be long now."

Sylvie murmurs, "He was so young. He just wanted a better world—"

"The *Boches* will be gone for good. You and I can live our lives—"

She tenses up, causing him to stop mid-sentence. She stares at him, unbelieving. "What did you say?"

"You and I—"

She whips her face away from him. "I must make this right with God."

Jean reaches out to her. "You had no choice. God understands."

She strikes his hand away. "How would you know?"

Jean abruptly stands. "*Merde.*" He turns to the others. "Isobel, get Karl cleaned up." Then he turns back to Sylvie, "You can see to Étienne after the attack. We need you now."

Dazed, Sylvie barely hears Jean.

He repeats—this time, it's a command. "Now."

Sylvie mechanically rises as if she doesn't inhabit her own body.

She hesitates, looks down at her brother, and then slips her habit over her head, revealing her trousers underneath. She kneels, and using her habit as a shroud, covers Étienne's body, making the sign of the cross over him.

Jean watches her in silence, then turns to Isobel, who's just finished bandaging Karl's wound and cleaning up his German uniform. "Is he ready?"

Isobel nods as Karl brushes himself off. She rises to kiss Karl, and he leans down, taking her in an awkward but fierce embrace.

Through her misery, Sylvie sees Jean staring longingly at the young couple who seem so much in love. She can never imagine feeling love ever again. Or anything else.

Jean says to Isobel, "Wait in the church, but keep out of sight." Then to Karl and Sylvie, "It's time."

Sylvie can scarcely hear him for the screaming in her head. She's screaming her rage...her agony...her sorrow...but no sound emerges. Her grief has shredded her voice. In a daze, she helps them bring the packs of assembled *plastique* up to the church. At the top of the stairs, she turns and looks down at her habit, now covering Étienne's body as a funereal shroud. Blood seeps from beneath the folds of the cloth. She crosses herself, murmurs a prayer, then shuts the heavy stone door behind her.

CHAPTER SIXTY-SEVEN

22 August 1944, Five o'clock p.m.

J EAN FOLLOWS SYLVIE and Karl through the back alleys of the village on the way to blow up the munitions dump. Each has a rifle, and Jean has a pistol as well, jammed into the small of his back. Despite his aching knee, he struggles to keep up, all the while constantly eying Karl in case he bolts. The two men lug the bags of explosives while Sylvie carries another sack with additional ammunition for their rifles. But the exuberance he might have felt at the prospect of liberating Foix is diminished by Sylvie's change of heart. True, she's devastated by her brother's death, but how could she break her promise that they would go back to the way they were before the war?

Suddenly, he hears dogs viciously barking in the next alley over. He freezes, breaking into a sweat as images flood his mind. *Albert. The dogs. Suzanne. The children.* He struggles to fight off his demons and make his way back to the present.

Sylvie turns back. "Jean, what's wrong?"

He snaps to. *Fine, when I'm done here, my father's name will be cleared. The army will be done with me, and I'll head back to North*

Africa. More dogs bark. He stumbles as a wave of nausea crests over him. *So much for trusting Sylvie. Or anyone.*

He grits his teeth and carries on. From the lengthening shadows in the narrow cobblestone streets, he sees that it's already very late in the afternoon. To coordinate with the forces landing on the mountain, they must create their diversion no later than six o'clock, which means they probably have about half an hour.

Sylvie puts her arm around his waist, walking him along. "You can do this."

Her touch is like a salve. *I loved her. I know she loved me.* But then he recoils. *She's no longer the same woman.* He takes a ragged breath. *I survived before. I will survive again.*

As they round the next corner, they run into François, Louis, and some of the other *Maquisards.* Jean is relieved to see these reinforcements for the attack. He always thought of Louis as hot-headed, and true to form, Louis immediately pulls his pistol on Karl. Jean swiftly moves in front of the young German to protect him.

Sylvie urgently whispers to Louis, "Don't shoot. He's helping us."

François, tall and lumbering, turns to her. "I don't understand."

"You must trust us," Sylvie shoots back.

François cocks his head questioningly. Jean nods his confirmation, then François motions to the others to let them pass. As they do, François whispers to Sylvie, "Where's Claude? The others?"

Jean watches Sylvie's reaction with dread, hoping she can hold together. Her lip quavers. "Killed. There was a raid. We're all that's left."

Louis pauses for a moment to take this in, then hammers his fist into the wall. *"Merde. Non, Mon Dieu."*

A large man, François seems to deflate to half his size. "Claude? Jacques? All of them?"

Jean musters all the resilience he can. "We're it now." Motioning towards Karl, "He's helping us get into the munitions dump to set the

416

charges. You and your men, be ready behind their headquarters. The paratroopers should have already started down the mountain."

François trudges over to Sylvie, puts his arm around her, and gives her a swift, powerful squeeze. "For Claude. This night will belong to the *Maquis*, I swear." François and the others take off.

Jean hears the sharp retort of jackboots on the cobblestones. "A patrol."

Sylvie grabs Jean's arm and pulls him back into an arched doorway. "Quickly, back through here."

Karl checks the street behind and slips in, following them.

They race along a small alley that leads to the end of the street. Sylvie jumps over a low garden fence, with Jean and Karl bringing up the rear. They crouch down, listening for the patrol.

Jean whispers to Karl, "Is there another way in?"

Karl nods and leads them down yet another alley. When they finally reach the munitions dump, he keenly watches Sylvie brush off Karl's uniform.

She briskly kisses him on both cheeks. "God protect you."

Karl hands Sylvie the French Sten gun he was carrying, crosses himself, adjusts his uniform, and gives her a small but respectful bow from the waist. Jean claps Karl on his good shoulder. Karl takes a breath and strides to the gatehouse.

Jean anxiously watches as Karl speaks to the German munitions guard. He trains his rifle on Karl, just in case. Karl continues to talk to the guard. *Merde, this is taking too long. Why did I ever trust Isobel?* Jean is just about ready to shoot when Karl points in another direction, the guard gives a *Sieg Heil*, thrusts his rifle into Karl's hands, and runs off. Karl takes up the man's position and waves to them.

Inhaling sharply, Jean signals Sylvie. They run into the facility, each carrying a bag of *plastique*. Jean sets the bundles under munitions crates. He waits for a sign from Sylvie, so they can push down their copper detonators simultaneously, giving them three minutes to get away. She works on the vehicles, setting single charges in the steel treads and axles and near the fuel tanks.

Exhilarated, Jean will finally have his revenge. For Suzanne and the children. For Albert. And this will be his redemption too. He can hardly wait for Sylvie's signal. What's taking her so long? Yes, she's working with single bundles but—just then, she waves to him that she's ready. They coordinate, push down their copper detonators and run, taking Karl with them.

As the place blows, Jean shouts, "THE NIGHT BELONGS TO THE *MAQUIS*!!!

Shocks from the blasts throw the three to the cobblestones. Vehicles burst into the air like toys. Smoke surges and blankets the area. Jean hears shouts in German, whistles blowing, and an air raid siren. He strains to see up, onto the mountain, to make sure the Free French have landed. But billowing black smoke against the orange and scarlet evening sky, as well as flying debris, block his view.

Shooting begins near Nazi headquarters a few blocks away. Jean hears German machine guns stuttering and prays the *Maquisards* can hold out in Foix until the paratroopers make it down into the village. Jean's natural instinct is to join the fighting, but he resists, knowing he needs to help Sylvie get Karl back to the church in one piece.

As they duck into narrow alleyways, Jean hears the German volley returned with a fierce retort. *The Free French have entered the village!* Ecstatic, he rushes with Sylvie and Karl back towards the church.

Jean sees François coming around an alley, this time with three young *Maquisards*. They have two German prisoners in tow, hands tied behind them. One is portly, square, and balding, the other tall and lanky.

Jean feels Karl jerk his arm to stop him. The boy motions towards the portly one who takes one look at Karl and struggles violently, attempting to break free to attack the young German.

The portly one snarls, "Traitor! Mongrel!"

The tall one also tries to lunge at Karl, but François keeps a tight grip.

Karl lurches out of reach and shouts to Jean and the others, "In the cave! This is Sargent Herr Rolf. Major Spitzer gives him the order to shoot."

Sylvie screams at Rolf, "You bastard."

Jean grabs Rolf, takes his pistol from the small of his back, and shoves it into the portly German's mouth.

"Stop!" François shouts. "We take all prisoners to the cells then to Command in Toulouse. They will deal with them according to law."

In Jean's rage, everything turns blindingly white. He ignores François and cocks his pistol, ready to shoot. Rolf gags on the barrel of Jean's gun.

Carefully, Sylvie comes right up to Jean. She says, in a low and urgent voice, "Jean, stop. Let François have him."

His hand shaking badly, Jean bores the depth of his hatred into the German's eyes, then slowly extracts his pistol from Rolf's mouth and shoves him onto the cobblestones. Meanwhile, Louis has come from another direction. He creeps behind Rolf, and with his knife, slashes the fat German's throat. The big man gurgles, lifts up, and for an agonizing moment, seems suspended in air, then falls like a large pig onto his side.

Sylvie shouts, "Louis. No!"

Louis wipes his knife off on the prone German's sleeve, then boots him in the back. A diabolical smile crosses his face. "He's all yours, François."

François grunts and shakes his head. He steps over Rolf, signals for the other *Maquisards* to follow him and bring the tall prisoner, who howls and tries to reach Karl to batter him. The others pull him away, but not before he spits at Karl, who deftly dodges the spittle, which lands on Rolf's lifeless body.

Karl and Sylvie continue back to the church, with Jean following. He briefly stops against a shopkeeper's door to rest his knee. He takes a last look back as Louis kicks Rolf's body over. A knife falls from the top of Rolf's boot, which Louis picks up, kisses as a trophy, and pockets. Jean sneers, pleased that at least one of them has met a swift and violent death for the atrocity in the cave. He turns to catch up with Sylvie and Karl.

The Free French paratroopers have fanned out in full force in the village, and the fighting, although fierce, is largely confined to pockets. Now that they've liberated Foix and ended German occupation, Jean anxiously waits for Sylvie to come to her senses.

CHAPTER SIXTY-EIGHT

22 August 1944, Nine thirty p.m.

SYLVIE HAS EXERTED every ounce of willpower to suspend her remorse over her brother's death and focus on the mission. Arriving back at the church, she only wants to kneel before the altar, light votive candles in every side chapel, and hide in the empty confessional—do anything but descend the stairs to the chamber below where her brother's enshrouded corpse lies on the cold stones.

As she stares down at Étienne, her fury rises up, overtaking her grief. How could he be so irresponsible, self-centered, and immature? He jeopardized their desperate efforts to throw off the yoke of occupation. They've all made unfathomable sacrifices—he wasn't the only one to have lost someone he loved. Still, Sylvie mourns that she was the one to end his life—whether she meant to or not.

Sylvie finds herself sinking to the floor next to Étienne's body. She reverently smooths her habit that lays upon him—his shroud. As if to comfort him. As if he can feel her loving hands. She slowly lifts the fabric covering Étienne's face and pats his hair into place. She wipes his cheeks and kisses each, in turn, feeling the full, crushing weight of her grief.

Somewhere behind her, she becomes aware of Isobel rushing to Karl, checking his shoulder. Somehow she has the presence of mind to say to them, "Get ready. You two must leave right away."

Isobel gives Karl some clothes from the pile in the corner. "I found these. I think they will fit." She turns to her aunt. "Aunt Sylvie, I'm really sorry. I couldn't find a jacket. So I took the one Étienne was wearing. I...I managed to scrub off most of the blood."

Karl shakes his head, takes Étienne's jacket, kneels down, and solemnly offers it to Sylvie. "Sister, you must keep this."

Sylvie feels her lungs collapsing in her chest. She stares at the jacket—once Jean's, which he used to tourniquet a young soldier, who in turn, gave it to her in the hospital. Refusing to admit that Jean was dead, she gave it to Étienne, who never took it off. She can't find the breath to speak—instead, she quietly pushes the jacket back at Karl, then squeezes his hand to indicate he's done well and deserves it. Karl nods, clasps the jacket to his chest, and rises.

Jean says to Karl, "Take good care of that. And—you should know—we're grateful for what you did." He turns to Isobel. "Help him get cleaned up." He clears his throat. "Will you give Sylvie and me a moment?" He takes Sylvie to the corner of the room.

She feels his presence but is unable to look at him.

Jean takes her by the shoulders. "Sylvie, the war's finally over for us."

She jerks away, rasping, "Yes, the fighting's over."

"We talked about going back to the way it was. You agreed."

"That was before—"

"I'll be out of the army soon. We can—"

"Jean, we can't speak of such things." She growls through clenched teeth, "I just killed my own brother."

"An accident. You had to stop him." Jean reaches out, trying to get her to look at him. "We liberated Foix. You deserve some happiness."

She deflects him. "Not in this life. Or in the next."

Jean recoils. "What about me?"

"I'm sorry, Jean. I can't feel anything right now."

"You'll feel things again. In time. I promise."

"I don't want to feel things again, Jean. Nothing. Ever again."

"Damn it, the war's over! We've got a right to live."

"And ignore those who died?"

Jean reaches to clasp her hands, but she shoves him away. He shouts at her, "You're not the only one grieving. What about the men in my unit? The private I gave my jacket to? The prisoners tortured and killed in that prison camp."

Her voice barely audible, Sylvie adds, "I'm grieving too...for my sister and her husband. For Father Michel. For all those innocent refugees. And now for my brother. But his blood is on my hands."

"He forced you into it, Sylvie. If we don't go on living, why did they all die?"

"You're asking me? If it weren't a sin in the eyes of the church, I'd...I wouldn't go on living."

"You of all people must survive." He swallows hard. "Don't you love me?"

Sylvie bites her cheek so hard she can feel the sickly taste of blood mingling with the bile surging from her stomach. She turns away, unable to meet his stare. "God help me. I do love you. But Jean...I'm sorry. I can't be with you now...not ever."

"That's it, then?"

Sylvie feels like all the ancient stones in the church above have smashed into this chamber and buried her alive. "Forgive me."

Jean works his lower lip, then spits it out, "All right. I'll drop them at your farm, then head back to North Africa."

She throws him a confused look.

"I'll arrange to sell my farm from there. Get my army discharge from there as well. There's nothing left for me here."

Sylvie absorbs Jean's words as if they were blows—blows that are just the beginning of her life-long penance for killing her brother.

Isobel finishes helping Karl into French clothes, and they gingerly approach Sylvie. Isobel is trembling, but even so, Sylvie detects her excitement. The girl says, in a rush, "We're ready."

Sylvie hugs her fiercely. "I'll get word to you up there when it's safe to return. I love you." Then to Karl, "Be careful."

Jean silently leads them out. He turns at the top of the stairs for a last look. Sylvie can see his face twisted in anguish. As they exit the heavy door to the church, she slumps next to her brother's body. A silent scream courses through her entire body like a powerful and deadly electric current. This opens the flood of tears she valiantly struggled to hold back during the mission. Finally, drained of all emotion, she makes the sign of the cross and arranges herself in the Christ-like position of ultimate penance, face down, arms stretched out. She remains there, innate, on the cold stone floor.

CHAPTER SIXTY-NINE

Leaving the church, Jean walks into the night air filled with smoke, people shouting, and gunfire. The villagers, the Free French, and the *Maquisards* are celebrating and shooting their guns into the air. The jubilant villagers crowd the narrow streets and spill into the plaza. Someone is up in the belfry, tolling the church bells. Everyone is laughing, screaming, singing *La Marseillaise,* hugging and kissing each other. French tricolors materialize out of nowhere as the townsfolk tear down and stomp the Nazi flags that had, for so long, flown over the Town Hall and hung from every building throughout the village.

Karl is dressed in worn French clothes and boots from the spare pile in the corner, but Jean fears that his height and broad physique could give him away. Isobel tried to darken his blonde hair by rubbing dirt from the spare boots into it, but he's still unmistakably Aryan. Jean deems it best to avoid the plaza in front of the church where the celebrations are underway, so he leads them out the church's back garden gate, along the stone passageway by the river and into the sunflower fields beyond Foix.

He looks back at the village, aglow with the celebration. He yearns to share in the joy, but he's exhausted, emotionally and physically. Karl also walks silently, apparently feeling similar battle fatigue, although Isobel twitters with excitement. Jean envies the young girl's resilience as she chatters on about a new life. In stark contrast, he dreads seeing his old farm next to Sylvie's—the farm he'll soon put up for sale and renounce for good. At least he can now make peace with his father's legacy—knowing that suffering shell shock, as he did as well, does not make someone a coward. And, having successfully completed his mission despite overwhelming odds, he's finally proved his family's worth to himself and the village.

As they arrive at the fork, which leads either to his farm on the right or to hers on the left, he halts, ostensibly to rest his knee. The night sky is a deep midnight blue, brilliant with an array of stars sweeping across a seamless Milky Way of white glistening particles. As a child, he often climbed up here. Away from the dim, flickering lights of Foix, he'd marvel at the vastness of unknown galaxies—where he imagined he might one day travel. So far, his journeys have brought only the greatest anguish. But he's determined to move on to a new life by himself. She wouldn't take him back—so much for her church's canon of forgiveness. *Merde.*

He resolves to see the young people in hiding at Sylvie's farm, then return to the exotic color of the bazaar, but especially the color of money changing hands on the black market. He knows his way around—this time, it will be in the luxury of the European sector down by the waterfront.

He takes the fork to Sylvie's farm—best not to take even a quick look at his farm. Have a lawyer arrange the sale—leave it all behind—just go.

Jean pulls Sylvie's barn door open. He didn't expect to see any livestock, as they were undoubtedly seized by the *Boches*. But he's pleased to see that the farm tools are in order, hanging between closely set nails hammered into the walls. He takes a pitchfork and tosses it to Karl, motioning for him to pitch some hay down from the loft. "Make yourself something comfortable down here. Then go up and lay out a place for Isobel. If you hear anything—anything at all—both of you get up there immediately. Then pull the ladder up behind you." The two young people set up the barn. A melancholy smile crosses Jean's face—it looks like they're playing house, dazed but happy and preparing for the first stage of their young lives together.

Jean turns to them. "I'll be right back. I'll get whatever food's available in the farmhouse. Meanwhile, stay here. Keep this door boarded, except for my knock." He raps three times.

Leaving the barn, Jean thinks back to the life he and Sylvie could have shared together. He stumbles, not from the ache in his knee but because of the deep sorrow coursing through him.

As soon as Jean has left the barn, Isobel feels overcome by acute nervousness. She's extremely shy being alone with Karl—really, with any boy—for the first time. She watches him, bracing his arm to protect his shoulder, as he pitches hay down from the loft gracefully, rhythmically. He's so unlike any of the boys at the temple. They wouldn't have known how to use a pitchfork—they were all so intense, furrowing their brows as they debated the finer points of the Torah, just like her father.

Isobel feels a wave of sorrow—will she ever know if her parents are dead or alive? She flushes, certain that her father would never have approved of someone outside their chosen faith. How could she not despise Karl and everything he appears to represent? Yet, he was chosen too—by them after they killed his parents, most probably just like they killed hers. He doesn't act anything like the *Boches*—arrogant and cruel to the bone—and he risked his life to help Aunt Sylvie and Jean. She smiles as he goes aloft and straightens things up for her, then bounds down, several rungs at a time. He holds the ladder for her, beaming his warm, ruddy-faced smile and bowing slightly. She climbs up to the loft, and he follows, holding a lantern. The loft has an upper slatted window that he's opened, enabling her to see the full moon as well as the starry night sky. It's all very romantic, being unchaperoned, up here with him.

Amused at his stiff and proper demeanor, she starts to tease him about it, like she might have teased the boys at the temple but stops—that was so long ago, and so many horrible things have happened. Still, she enjoys how this earnest young man arranges then rearranges the same pile of hay to make her comfortable.

Karl scoots back to let her try the bedding. "It is all right for you, Marie?"

She blushes, her hand flying to her cheek in the knowledge that her freckles must be multiplying manifold—she's glad it's dark up here. "Isobel. Remember? My name's Isobel."

He jolts upright, knocking his head on a rafter. "Of course. You will pardon. I forget."

Isobel smiles sweetly. "It's really not important. I actually got used to Marie in the convent." She nervously babbles on. "But really, I do prefer Isobel. I was raised with that name. I mean, I only used Marie for—"

Jean knocks on the barn door below, and Karl races down the ladder, straightening himself up. She looks down from the loft smiling, as he appears to be standing at attention in front of Jean, ready to salute.

Karl stammers. "We were...I mean, I was—"

Jean grins. "At ease, private. You proved your worth."

Karl reflexively clicks his heels although, in the hay and his French boots, there's no sound.

"I wouldn't go around doing that. And you're going to have to slouch quite a bit to pass as a Frenchman." Jean playfully punches him in the stomach. "Maybe lose some of that muscle too."

Isobel giggles from above.

Jean calls up to her, "And you, young lady. I'm expecting you to behave yourself." He takes out some food from a sack. "It's not much.

But I did find some cans, a knife to open them and some bread. I'm afraid it's rather stale, but you can scrape off the moldy parts. Or feed them to the mice."

Isobel screeches, "Mice?"

Jean laughs. "Don't worry. I'm sure they were starved out long ago."

Karl looks at Jean. "How is it we can thank you?"

Jean says, "Just stay away from the villagers. Tonight, I'll sleep in the farmhouse. In the morning, I'll head out before sunrise."

Jean kisses Karl on both cheeks. "Take good care of her."

Isobel comes down the ladder and embraces Jean. "I'm really sorry about...well, you know...about my Aunt Sylvie."

Jean turns his head, ostensibly to check the barn door. But Isobel is saddened to see him working his jaw, obviously holding back tears as he nods to her, exits quickly, and slides the barn door shut.

He calls to them from outside, "Put an extra plank in the slats. Don't open it for anyone but Sylvie."

Karl finds a large shaft of wood and firmly places it across the door. Then he turns to Isobel and shrugs as if not knowing exactly what to do. She shrugs as well, leaning against the ladder and pulling on some strands of hay. They both stand there for a moment, looking around the barn, pretending to examine all manner of hoes, pitchforks, hammers, and axes.

Finally, Isobel focuses on the sack of food. They sit on some barrels and share some of it then it's time to prepare for bed.

Karl's fair skin turns pink. He clears his throat and says, "We must get everything in order for the night."

Isobel smiles shyly as she climbs back up the ladder. Lying down in the loft, she says, "Good night."

He calls up, "Good night."

After about ten minutes of looking up at the night sky through the loft window, she calls down, "Are you comfortable down there?"

"*Ja,* well....maybe this floor is...maybe a bit hard."

Isobel can't resist. "It's pretty hard up here too. But I think it might be softer than the floor."

"Are you...are you certain?"

"You did such a good job with the straw."

Trembling, she closes her eyes in anticipation as she hears him get up and brush himself off. She sneaks a look to see him climbing up the ladder, his muscular frame rising towards her in the moonlight. He lies down—but not too close—and stiffly straightens himself out.

Isobel feels her pulse fluttering. Her mouth goes dry. Softly, she says, "Karl, would you put your arm around me?"

"Is it all right that we do this?"

She nods, and he holds her. She sighs, then starts to cry.

He bolts up, "Something I did?"

She settles him back down. "No, no. I'm just glad it's over."

He gently strokes her face. She lets out another sigh, this one very deep.

Karl says, "Now, something I did?"

She squeezes his hand, then puts her head against his shoulder. "Oh yes."

She tousles his blonde hair, then looks over at him. Fast asleep. She smiles, snuggles up, and drifts off.

CHAPTER SEVENTY

23 August 1944, Seven a.m.

AFTER SPENDING ALL night in her penitent position on the stone floor, Sylvie attempts to get up. At first, a mist of dull aching enshrouds her, then a wave of searing pain crashes over her—so intense that it literally pins her back down to the floor as if she were a butterfly mounted on the stone slabs. This is where she should remain, prone, next to the prone body of her brother. Perhaps they won't find her until...no...the church forbids her from taking her own life. In any case, that would be the coward's way out.

She knows full well that the sin of killing, anathema to the Church, means she must give up the veil as the first step in her new life of penance. She must also see to Étienne's funeral. She struggles to her feet, wearing a close-fitting mantel of sorrow in place of her habit. *If only he hadn't been so irrational...so obsessed.* She should have seen it coming and protected him from himself, as she did for so many years.

Gathering her thoughts about how to handle her brother's burial, she slowly climbs the stairs and makes her way to the church garden outside. Smoke lingers in the air, and ashes from smoldering debris drift into the alleyway. Looking up, however, she's comforted to see the reassuring silhouette of the Château, the indomitable symbol of her village, now firmly back in French hands—Foix is once again victorious against the marauding invaders she once so mightily feared.

Suddenly, she hears screaming from the plaza in front of the church and rushes to investigate. Dozens of women from Foix have formed a ring around the three village women who worked in the bar, which the Germans frequented. The oldest is a hefty blonde, flanked by two slender, younger dark-haired women. The male villagers and some of the Free French soldiers have encircled the ring of village women, allowing them free reign to taunt the three bar women in the middle. Sylvie senses that something awful is about to happen and fights to get through the crowd to stop it, but the men in the outer ring hold her back.

Sylvie is horrified to see the village women lifting knives and pairs of scissors into the air. One skinny woman from Foix wields a length of pipe while the throng screams, "Get them. Bitches. Collaborators."

Although the three women in the middle clutch each other, when the mob surges, they're separated and attacked by three individual swarms.

Sylvie screams, "Stop! You can't do this!"

One French soldier turns to her, smirking, "We couldn't stop those women with a tank. Even if we wanted to."

"It's not right. It's as brutal as they were to us."

"Be glad you're not in there."

Sylvie recoils, seeing the swarms of women pulsing. Reams of long hair are flung into the air, then set upon as trophies, as the village women fight over the bar women's tresses. Jumping up to see over the crowds, Sylvie catches sight of bloody scalps, where scissors had shorn their hair too close. But the most horrifying thing happens when the skinny village woman with the pipe goes over to the first swarm and yells for the others to hold down the hefty blonde woman. The crowd goes silent.

Sylvie struggles to get through but is again rebuffed. Meanwhile, the village women pull up the blonde woman's skirt and rip off her black lace panties, which another woman grabs, swirling them in circles over her head. The skinny woman plunges the pipe into the blonde woman. Her screams are blood-curdling. The crowd cheers, closes in on the woman, and stomps her bloody, until the soldiers finally tear them off and drag her away, limp and bleeding.

The other two young French women watch in terror, begging, "We were only tending bar. Please."

"We wouldn't have served them, but we had to."

The skinny woman with the pipe yells as she approaches the first one. "Let's make sure she doesn't give birth to a Hun bastard."

The first one pleads, "I just served them beer."

"You served them more than that. Didn't you?"

The crowd screams and chants.

Sylvie can't bear to look as shrieks penetrate the plaza, each one followed by a roar of the crowd. She crosses herself and runs back to the church to light a candle and fervently pray that Isobel and Karl are, by now, safely hidden on her farm.

CHAPTER SEVENTY-ONE

IN THE MORNING, Jean awakens in Sylvie's bed in the farmhouse, longing for her to be lying next to him. After a fitful night's sleep, his whole body aches. He goes to the window and gazes up at the familiar craggy limestone peaks. They are shrouded by the darkened shadows that appear just before the sun touches the rocky cliffs above. He's transported back to the times he and Sylvie hunted pheasant together. To the times he watched her prepare Sunday supper in her mother's ceramic pots that she loved so well. *How could I have lost my quest to reclaim her love?*

He collects his rucksack and heads south to the border with Spain—towards the highest peaks dusted with snow even in August. As he hikes, he feels a comradery with Claude and the other guides, as they followed this same route to get, by their count, more than five hundred airmen safely out of France. An astounding accomplishment.

Trudging further along, however, he feels desolately alone. He's certain that Sylvie loved him before the war and that she only took on the guise of a nun to fight the Nazis. Receiving word that he was dead, she must have suffered horribly to take her vows for solace. She's always been devout, but she was also earthy and passionate, not fundamentally suited to the life of a nun. Still, she must have found enough comfort within the church to turn her back on her independent character and instincts. But…she never cut her hair. That was her last holdout to totally giving herself to the church. Proof she'd always clung to the hope he was alive. Would she have so completely embraced the church had he been there to embrace her?

Coming to a riverbed that is mercifully dry under the August sun, he sees a scraggly tree, breaks off a limb to act as a staff, then sits exhausted in the tree's meager shade. He thinks about Étienne. That damn impetuous boy who looked up to him—would never take his jacket off. Jean knocks his staff against a rock. The boy would have made a good teacher if he'd been less judgmental and listened to others. He was smart but stubborn. In many ways, like Sylvie, although she was infinitely more temperate. How will she ever cope with having shot him, even though the boy brought it on himself? It was an accident, but her guilt will never allow her to accept that—he fears it will forever close her off from him and everyone else.

He pushes on—scrambling up the narrow, steep goat trails, his knee buckling. He slides down in the dust, then catches the limb of a tree and pulls himself up again. Above the tree line, the wind is hot and filled with clouds of fine dust. But the higher he goes, the more he finds himself looking back. He was the one to plan and execute the diversion that led to the successful liberation of Foix. She has to recognize how he redeemed himself. Isn't forgiveness and redemption part of her faith? Couldn't she forgive him? In time? And, even if she never did, would it be enough for him just to live on the next farm, even if they never married?

He swigs a sip of water and pours a few drops into his hands to wash his face and wipe away the dust. How many drops to wash away how many sins? He stares at his hands—hands that have sinned but also hands that have liberated. He makes a decision. *She knows I've always loved her and that I love her still. I will accept whatever comes.*

Gathering his things, Jean starts back down the mountain trail. He decides to look in on Isobel and Karl before continuing down to Foix to find Sylvie. He's a different man now, different from the one she abhorred when he returned. She must see that—and forgive him—eventually. Energized, he slides down the steep terrain, immune to the pain in his knee and to the pain from the burrs and small sharp stones that pierce the palms of his hands.

When he gets to Sylvie's farm, he sees that someone has slid the barn door open. Acid rises in his throat. He runs inside to find everything in disarray. "Isobel? Karl? Where are you?"

Straw bedding from the hayloft is scattered onto the floor. His eyes dart to the jacket lying at the foot of the ladder leading up to the hayloft. His jacket—Étienne's jacket—then Karl's jacket. Karl would never have willingly left it behind.

He goes to the farmhouse but finds it empty as well. *Merde.* The *Maquis* must have taken them. He rushes back down the mountain to Foix.

CHAPTER SEVENTY-TWO

DESPITE RETREATING TO the church to get away from the ferocious crowd, their vicious harangues still burn in Sylvie's ears. She must see to her brother, but not while the crowd is raging outside. She paces in front of the altar, mortified that her neighbors, people she's known all her life, could be so brutal. Yes, they were subjected to terrible privation during the war, everyone was. And Jean, what had he suffered? Was it so surprising he was angry, shell-shocked, and desperate to have her back? Given what tortures he survived, is it so unthinkable that he might want to live in comfort and provide them a few luxuries?

She strides through the nave, then kneels and crosses herself and slips into one of the pews to pray. She takes out her rosary and fingers the loop of beads in her hands... ten smaller beads, one larger bead, ten smaller beads... one *Our Father,* ten *Hail Marys,* then again and again. She wants to put herself into a trance and shut out the horrors outside. But she can't shut out what's burning inside, as she remembers when she and Jean were growing up, how encouraging he always was. *Full of grace...* When he could have been competitive for her father's attentions, he was proud of her hunting skills. *Our Father...* He was there for her after her parents died, risking his life smuggling supplies into Spain to keep their farms afloat. *Holy Mary...* And, hadn't he loved her enough to ask her to marry him? *I must get back to this damn rosary...one Our Father, ten Hail Marys.* But then, they took him and tried to break him. Don't we both deserve some happiness, just for surviving?

Groaning, she leans over the pew in front of her, clenching the loop of her beads tightly in her hands. *Hail Mary...* Poor, poor Étienne. So foolish. Idealistic. Stubborn. She trusted him. He gave her his word. *Give us this day...* She tried to stop him, no one could say she didn't. Jean's right, it was an accident. *Pray for us sinners...* So why this terrible, searing guilt for living while he died? And living while all the others died as well? Her tears land on the beads, a waterfall of anguish. But, as she wipes them from the rosary and prepares to begin the loop again, she pauses as a bitter thought abruptly surfaces: *Who is God to judge us so? And why did He allow all this suffering to happen in the first place?*

Just then, Jean races into the church.

Sylvie catches sight of him and rises. "Jean?"

He swiftly comes to her pew. "Sylvie, they took them."

"What?"

"Isobel and Karl. They took them."

"That can't be." She pockets the damp rosary and exits the pew. "We've got to get to François. He's in charge."

They rush out of the church and across the plaza, dodging the angry crowds still milling about. The bar women have been dragged off, and the townsfolk are shouting, calling for more collaborators to be brought out of the Town Hall jail and punished. The putrid smell of vengeance is thick in the air. Sylvie and Jean rapidly take the steps up to the Town Hall, where François and the *Maquis*, together with the Free French military, have set up a temporary local government in the Mayor's office. Paratroopers, with their rifles at the ready, stand guard outside the open door to the office. Inside, Sylvie sees army men scurrying about the room, listening to radios, consulting maps splayed out on various tables, and bringing papers back and forth for signature. François leans against a table, smoking and conferring with an army captain. Louis stands by, grinning and nodding his approval.

Sylvie pauses at the door, gasping for breath. She calls inside, "François, we must speak with you."

He motions for the guards to let her and Jean pass.

She rushes to him. "They took my niece and the young German, Karl. Where are they?"

Drawing deeply on his cigarette, François looks askance. "Downstairs. Right now, the females are in the jail for their own safety." He shrugs. "But we have to let them out sometime."

Looking like a bulldog, Louis barks, "For the crowd…better to punish them here—"

Sylvie interjects, "You can't be serious."

François adds, "Better than to take them to command in Toulouse where they'll be locked up for who knows how long."

Sylvie says, "That's not fair. My niece—"

François clears his throat. "She was found with him. That makes her—"

Sylvie tries to keep her voice level. "François, don't you remember, he's the one who helped us blow up the munitions dump? You ran into us, Jean and me, on the way there, with him."

A French paratrooper dashes in with some papers on a clipboard for François to sign. He slowly looks them over, ashes from his cigarette falling on the top paper. He brushes the ashes aside and signs the document. As the soldier races out, François turns to Louis. "They've commandeered *Boche* trucks to transport those bastard soldiers."

Louis slams his fist on the map table. "Too bad we can't deal with all of them here."

Sylvie watches with gnawing anxiety. The large heavy-jowled François, who had been Claude's closest friend, must be prevailed upon to be fair-minded. Surely he will help, although the smaller Louis is his usual bombastic self, quick to anger. She continues to press her case. "What about Karl? You must remember him with Jean and me."

Louis turns to Sylvie and says, with a malicious grin, "Not so fast. How do we know he wasn't a deserter who only pretended to help you?"

Jean steps up. "Louis, you listen to me. He showed us the back entrance to the armory. Risked his own life to divert the guard."

Sylvie adds, "We couldn't have blown up the munitions dump without him." She turns to François. "And it was my niece who was with him. You know her as Marie, from the convent. I swear, on my Uncle Claude's life, she's not a collaborator. You can't let that ferocious crowd have her."

Jean shouts, "Enough. Where is Karl?"

Louis smirks. "They're loading the *Boches* in trucks. Sending them to the prison in Toulouse."

Sylvie is incredulous. "You put him in with them? They'll kill him."

François thinks for a moment, then, in his deep sonorous voice, says to Louis, "I suppose if they try to kill him, he really was helping us."

Louis sneers, "Maybe they save us the trouble of taking care of one more."

Another paratrooper enters, jostling Sylvie, who knocks him aside, firmly standing her ground. She shouts, "We're wasting time. Louis, you've got to take Jean to the loading area to find Karl. François, please, you must bring me down to free my niece."

François sighs deeply through the cigarette dangling in his mouth. "All right, Sylvie. We'll do it for your uncle's sake. And because we owe you so much."

Sylvie follows François down the corridor of the Town Hall. It's jammed with paratroopers and villagers. A roar goes up in the plaza outside, and Sylvie shudders. "François, how can you let them have these women? It's barbaric."

He shrugs. "The soldiers are under orders not to let the women kill them, just punish them. Then they're free to go."

"What about a trial? Haven't we fought for fairness? Decency?" Again, he shrugs. Sylvie fumes, but there's no time to debate François— she must save Isobel. They descend the stairs to the jail on the ground floor of the Town Hall. Sylvie practically knocks him over as she searches for her niece. There are cells on either side of the corridor. About a dozen women are heaped together in one cell, which has a small window that looks out onto the plaza. A few women stare out the window, tears streaming. Just then, a roar from the crowd outside wafts into the cell, and Sylvie feels a wave of nausea. How horrible that the jailed women can see what's happening and the fate awaiting them. Some of them appear sullen, others softly moan, while still others scream and cry hysterically. She finally sees Isobel scrunched against the front bars in the far corner, as far as possible from the window and the noise. The girl is shaking and crying.

Isobel's voice breaks as she calls out, "Aunt Sylvie. Here! I'm here."

Several women in the cell mutter, mimicking her.

Sylvie frantically grabs hold of her niece's hands through the bars. "My darling, you're going to be all right." She turns, impatiently waiting for François to shamble over with the keys.

"François, unlock this right now. She doesn't belong in there. And you know it."

He grudgingly unlocks the cell, and Isobel rushes into her aunt's arms.

CHAPTER SEVENTY-THREE

JEAN FOLLOWS LOUIS down a set of stairs to a side entrance of the Town Hall. He's enraged at the injustice of arresting Karl, who was as good as his word, risking his life to help them. He feels a rush of nausea when he sees the long line of German soldiers, hands tied in front, shuffling forward as he once did. Some slump, looking defeated, while others stubbornly remain upright, defiant and proud. Several large German lorries commandeered by the Free French await the line of prisoners, which is flanked by French paratroopers, alert with rifles poised. One lorry is just about full, and the French soldiers are loading the next one.

Louis nudges Jean. "See him?"

Jean anxiously searches the queue getting ready to board the second lorry. His eyes rest on the tall, gangly German who was with Rolf and who shot up the cave. The tall man is staring at him, grinning.

Jean stomps over to him. "Where's Karl?"

The tall German sneers and shrugs.

Jean is about to punch him when he notices Karl shuffling out of the side door with another group of German soldiers. As Jean hastens to him, he's shocked to see Karl leaning over, holding his stomach, his face bruised and blood streaming from his nose.

Jean unties Karl and helps him straighten up. He snarls at Louis, "I told you, he was working with us." Jean uses his sleeve to wipe away some of Karl's blood. "Are you all right?"

Karl winces but nods. Then he quickly adds, "Isobel? You must save her."

Jean says, "Sylvie is taking care of her."

Just then, Sylvie and Isobel appear at the side of the building, and Isobel sprints to Karl.

Karl manages a coarse whisper, "They try to kill me. For what I did to help Sister."

Jean turns to Louis. "You bastard. You saw this boy with us last night."

Louis spits out, "If you'd been here to see what they did to us, you wouldn't be so quick to excuse any of them."

"I saw what they did. To me and so many of us. You'll never know the whole of it." He turns back to help Karl.

Isobel reaches down and tears more from her skirt to stop Karl's bleeding. She teases him. "Please don't get hurt again. I'm running out of fabric."

Karl laughs, then looks over her shoulder, back at the queue of Germans boarding the lorries. He calls to Jean. "On the first lorry. Major Spitzer. He is the one who orders the attack in the cave."

Jean searches the faces of the prisoners, finally locating an officer smugly sitting on the side bench at the back of the first lorry. His hair is a dark brown, causing him to stand out among the largely blonde *Boches* in captivity. He stares at Jean unblinking, holding his head high in defiance.

Sylvie recognizes him as well. "That bastard." She yells to Louis, "Take him off that lorry. He's responsible for the massacre in the cave." As the truck starts its engine, she shrieks, "Stop. He killed Uncle Claude, Hélène, and the others."

Louis sprints, trying to reach the cab and alert the Free French soldier who is driving, but the lorry has already started to pull away. Louis shouts and runs after it but is unable to catch it.

Sylvie shakes her head. "We can't let him get away with what he did."

Jean clenches his teeth. "We'll get word to Toulouse. So they can segregate him and put him on trial."

Sylvie says, "Jean, you can't imagine what he put Hélène through. And killing my uncle and all those wounded men. They were wounded, Jean. He deserves to die right here. Right now."

"Sylvie, you're right."

She balls her fists and shakes them at the departing lorry. "They just take him away? Maybe they'll charge him, and maybe they won't." Sylvie's voice rises. "There are so many to hold to account. You know he'll get better treatment than they ever gave you."

Jean takes her fists and presses them against his chest, trying to calm her. "You're right. I'm sorry. But he's gone now." Jean holds her fast, encouraged that she's allowing him to comfort her, to be there for her once again.

Sylvie looks directly at him. "I think Mother Superior was right. I don't have the temperament to be a nun. Right now, I just want revenge. I want him dead."

She tries to pull away, but Jean holds her fast. This time, he's not going to let go—not ever again. He'll win her over—he will. He stares into her face, framed by strands of her thick black hair flying loose. A formidable woman. The woman he loves more than anything. "Sylvie, you had exactly the temperament you needed. For everything you did." She slowly nods as he continues, "We've all done things we wish we hadn't. But we survived...triumphed even. We need to appreciate what we accomplished and move on from there."

Sylvie stands with Jean holding onto her amid the throng of Free French paratroopers loading the German prisoners and the jostling villagers, who've gathered to taunt the prisoners as they leave. She sees Isobel ministering to Karl, ushering him to safety, back behind the phalanx of paratroopers. She turns back to search Jean's face, trying to determine which version of him now stands before her—the erratic and crazed Jean or the caring man she fell in love with long ago? Would that he were her old Jean, fully returned to her. She searches his gaunt face, chiseled with lines of fatigue and suffering. His piercing eyes, even with their traces of profound sorrow, still twinkle with the glimmer of the man she once knew and loved.

She thinks back to how they were with each other before the war. How she insisted on bonding with him by making love, rather than going through a church ceremony that would not have afforded them time to consummate their marriage. Back then, she was so secure in her faith and her love of God that she didn't need the formality of her marriage vows. She could make peace with the Church and still find it within herself to carry on her life. Why can't she do the same now?

Sylvie knows that everything she did was for her beloved Foix. And for the airmen, the Brits and Yanks, who trusted her with their lives. She knows that Jean is proud of her, probably in the same way that she's proud of him—for surviving and ultimately not losing his humanity. She admires him for leading the liberation of the village and is touched by how earnestly he fought to protect her niece and Karl instead of leaving to indulge his pursuits in North Africa. But most of all, she's elated to decide that it is indeed the same Jean she knew and loved who stands before her now, saying he loves her still. She moves closer, allowing him to put his arm around her.

He looks at her, silently inquiring with a slight, mischievous shrug of his shoulders, "Do you think we can ever be together?"

She bows her head for a moment to remember Étienne, then raises her eyes to hold Jean's earnest, expectant gaze. At first her smile is tentative—then it grows, full force, across her face.

-The End-

AUTHOR'S NOTE

THE NIGHT BELONGS to the Maquis is a work of fiction, although it is inspired by real people and true events. I have long wanted to tell the story of three members of the French Resistance (*Maquisards*) whom I was fortunate to have met in 1988. At that time, I had become fascinated by an important aspect of French Resistance efforts, involving how the *Maquis* saved the lives of allied pilots who had been shot down by the Germans, as well as French officers and other agents needing to escape France. A "Freedom Line" grew up as the French guided these pilots and other "evaders" in convoys over the Pyrénées in Southern France into Spain, where the RAF smuggled them into North Africa. By sheer coincidence, an article appeared in the June 26, 1988 *New York Times* entitled "Journeys in the South of France." It prominently featured a small village in southern France named Foix, which was the jumping off point for many of these evader convoys. That article sealed my interest and lead me to travel there in November of 1988, hoping to get more information.

Shortly after getting off the train in Foix, I met Monsieur René Staad at the Foix Chamber of Commerce, who had been a guide in one of the very first convoys over the mountains. After his initial trip safely guiding his charges into the hands of the British in Spain, the RAF asked him to relocate to an airbase in Scotland. There he was asked to work with pilots who might eventually be shot down and teach them ways to disguise themselves and blend in with the French citizenry (by holding cigarettes differently, walking with more of a slouch and less of a military bearing, etc.). From his time in Scotland, the English he spoke was with a Scottish accent!

When M. Staad learned of my interest in this aspect of World War II, he enthusiastically introduced me to the head of the *Grimaud* French Resistance Circuit, Monsieur Ernest Gouazé, who was kind enough to invite me to have lunch with him and his wife. He recounted some of his astoundingly brave exploits. He established his circuit early in 1942 and operated it until he was captured by the Gestapo in December of 1943. He was tortured by Klaus Barbie and personally gave me his deposition in the Barbie trial (rendered to Le Juge D'Instruction Chargé de L'Affaire: BARBIE, PALAIS De JUSTICE, 1969, Lyon) which I used in writing the torture scene in the novel, as well as for other aspects of resistance activity in the region. He also showed me the many medals and citations he was given for his bravery (which he kept in a chocolate box in his study). These included: from the U.S., the Citation for Medal of Freedom With Bronze Palm, September 21, 1946; and from the U.K., the King's Medal for Courage in the Cause of Freedom. This latter citation indicated, in part, that Monsieur Gouazé was charged with initiating and organizing an escape route in the Ariège region of France on the border with Spain. Quoting directly from the British document:

> After recruiting other helpers and establishing numerous important contacts, Monsieur Gouaze was finally successful in preparing a base of evasion activities in Arege (SIC), and operating an escape line across the Pyreneean sector. This line was responsible for passing both Allied evaders and French officers who were endeavouring to escape from France and regain the Free Forces in

Allied territory. The principal centre for assembling and equipping evaders was at Foix (Ariege)....the line operated with maximum efficiency until the date of Monsieur Gouaze's arrest in December 1943.

I supplemented this information with another trip to Foix in October of 2016, where I met Monsieur Bruno Manuguerra, Directeur du Centre d'Histoire de la Résistance et de la Déportation en Ariège. He kindly dug into his archives and scanned numerous documents for me. In an email, he directed me to a monument in the village of Ax-les-Thermes, which memorializes that this escape route, operating even after M. Gouazé's arrest, was responsible for getting approximately 500 evaders out of France.

During my first trip to Foix in 1988, M. Gouazé insisted I meet a third *Maquisard*—another guide in his circuit who lived in the mountains on the route to Spain. As M. Staad drove me up there, we joked about having to fasten our seat belts so many decades later when in times past he and his pilot evaders were on foot, walking through this steep and treacherous terrain. M. Staad introduced me to a small, wizened guide who invited us into his farm house. We promptly began drinking shots to the *Maquis* of something I think was home-made Armagnac (which partially explains why I can't recall this courageous Frenchman's name). As he had made many trips leading convoys of pilots and evaders, I asked him if he had been afraid of the Germans at night with their dogs. So many years after the war, he proudly slammed his shot glass down and said: "They were afraid of us at night. The night belonged to the *Maquis*." This became the title of the novel I was eventually to write.

Here, I must pause to reiterate, in the strongest possible terms, that my novel is fiction, my characters are imagined solely to achieve dramatic effect, and my story deviates substantially from the lives of these courageous men, even as I drew on some of their exploits. I would not want anyone to think that some of the less desirable actions and unsavory characteristics of my Jean Galliard character in any way resembled those of the three *Maquisards* whom I met.

By coincidence, I found another important source of information. It came from a dear friend of mine, Harriet Marple Plehn, whose aunt was named Harriet Marple and who was involved in refugee work in Toulouse, from the fall of 1940 until January 1942. My friend Harriet told me of a valuable memoir which provides detailed accounts of this time and place and which mentions her aunt: the book is *Over the Highest Mountains: A Memoir of Unexpected Heroism in France during World War II* written by a Norwegian nurse named Alice Resch Synnestvedt.

Alice was among the numerous aid workers from the Societies of Friends, including the English Quakers and the American Friends Service Committee who cared for massive numbers of refugees streaming into the Toulouse area of Southern France as the Germans descended upon Paris in June of 1940. Alice had been a nurse serving under Dr. Lawrence Fuller, Director of the famed American Hospital of Paris. With his encouragement, she worked with others to establish an aid center in Toulouse, just north of Foix. Meanwhile, having done aid work and raised funds for refugees during World War I, Harriet Marple came to Alice's group via the same Dr. Fuller, who advised her that the best way she could help the current war effort was to buy a car and bring supplies to Alice's group. Alice describes her as a stylish American woman who used her own money to buy a car to transport supplies for the refugees across zones in France and who was also a tireless worker organizing sewing machine workshops to help clothe the refugees. The United States entered the war in December 1941, and as an American, she was saddened to feel compelled to leave France in January 1942, while she could still get out of the country. (Citations to her work and photographs appear on pages 47, 84, 105-6 and 111 of Alice Resch Synnestvedt's memoir.)

The memoir also proved a valuable reference for creating the refugee camp in my novel—Darcet—which is an amalgam of the camps Alice describes including Gurs, Darcet and Aspet. Alice and her workers valiantly struggled in these camps to care for, as well as hide, the persecuted from the dreadful deportations. The book also chronicles relief efforts by the Catholic Church in Toulouse to hide refugees, especially Jewish adults and children whom they smuggled to Marseilles and onto boats out of France before the borders were closed. Members of the church also collected and buried in church yards valuables from deportees, hoping later to repatriate them to their owners or, in the worst case, to their survivors.

My character Father Michel was inspired by Alice's account of the invaluable work done by the modest Archbishop of Toulouse, Jules-Gèrard Salière, who "was not afraid to speak up against the persecution of the Jews. Both the convent and monastery opened their doors and filled their homes with frightened, persecuted people who sought a place to hide." (page 118) Finally, my character Mother Superior was inspired by Alice's account of the Mother Superior in the convent La Motte in Muret, a small town just west of Toulouse. Born Dolores Salazar in Argentina, she is described as having a great sense of humor and was widely read, spoke several languages and played the piano. Having married an English aristocrat, she was widowed early and took the veil. She sheltered Alice and a colleague who couldn't find accommodations because all the beds in Muret were taken by German occupation troops. The real Mother Superior, who had been playing and singing for some small children in an empty warehouse, regaled Alice and her colleague with a lively South American tango. (page 207)

The cave in my novel is an amalgam of two real places. The first was the "cave des larmes" or the cave of tears, in the eastern part of France, which I found in one of my reference books on the resistance. It was used as a make-shift hospital for wounded *Maquisards*. The Germans stormed it, killing the wounded men. The second real place is an underground cave just outside Foix called the Rivière Souterraine de Labouiche. I reimagined this cave, replacing its underground rushing river with a quiet lake near the entrance which then disappears into a river, but only at the far end.

Although I have taken some liberties for dramatic effect, I have generally been true to the terrain and layout of the medieval village of Foix, having refreshed my memory with a trip in 2016. Foix's river Ariège flows by the town, there is one bridge from the town to the train station, and the cobblestone streets are laid out in labyrinthine fashion. The Château Des Comtes de Foix dates from the 11-14th centuries and still towers over Foix, keeping watch against past and future mauraders. The Church of St. Volusien, the Abbatiale Saint-Volusien de Foix, was originally founded in the year 849, although very little of the original structure remains, following destruction during the many secular and religious wars. Reconstruction was undertaken from 1609 and completed in 1670. The church, with its famous organ, sits on a plaza where there is a wrought-iron farmers market structure and inviting cafés. The hidden quay and passage along the river, however, exist only in my imagination.

The war in North Africa and the incidents in Algiers, which I fictionalized in my novel, are based on actual places in the Casbah of Algiers and in what was then the notorious Barberousse Prison, since renamed the Serkadji Prison, with its infamous guillotine in the inner courtyard.

I have utilized more historical non-fiction books than I can count to achieve as much accuracy as possible in describing how the war progressed, when the German occupations took hold in various parts of France and when Foix and other villages in the Ariège were liberated—although I did take fictional liberties with the actual liberation of Foix itself. And, for the sake of the drama of the story, I have embellished some historical events and neglected others, for which I apologize profusely to any true historian who might happen upon my novel.

ACKNOWLEDGMENTS

ALTHOUGH I FIRST became interested in this story in 1988, I finally started writing it in novel form in 2015. During the intervening years, I was fortunate to have had an immensely satisfying career as an economist for a global non-profit organization, while also working as much as time permitted in theatre as a director/choreographer and playwright. But the story would never leave me.

In addition to the invaluable sources I mention in my Author's Note, I would like to express my gratitude for their continuing support to the following: Chris Ceraso, Casandra Medley, Jon and Rosemary Masters, Peter Firestein, Andrew Tank, Christopher Castellani and my fellow seminar attendees at the Key West Writer's seminar, Tim Weed at Grub Street, Regis Donovan, Christina Ivaldi and her late husband Jacques, and June Kelly. There never would have been a novel had not been for Diane O'Connell, her editorial acumen and her unfailingly positive but rigorous approach to writing. I also must thank the production team at Station Square Media, including: cover and interior designer Steven Plummer, copyeditor and proofreader James King, and post-production manager Janet Spencer King.

Finally, I wish to thank my husband, Howard Greenhalgh, for his expert advice on weaponry and war-time logistics, as well as his willingness to read and discuss revisions too numerous to count. I could not be more grateful for his deeply committed emotional support all these years, but especially during the pandemic, which enabled me to make the last rewrite leading to this publication.

ABOUT THE AUTHOR

CAROLYN KAY BRANCATO fuses her extensive research background with her lifelong involvement in theatre to create unique and vibrant characters in compelling historical settings.

Her debut novel, *The Circus Pig & the Kaiser*, was published in 2019. It received rave reviews as a "fast-paced drama of wit and humor amid politically charged circumstances...an authentic, charming and heart-felt portrayal of a band of circus performers."

She has written two nonfiction investment books, *Getting Listed on Wall Street* and *Institutional Investors and Corporate Governance*, published by Business One Irwin.

Carolyn has been a director, choreographer and playwright. Her plays have been produced at such venues as Steppenwolf in Chicago and the John Houseman Theatre in N.Y.C. as well as at the Church Street Theatre in D.C. She created the play *Censored* to celebrate the First Amendment—bringing to life banned books, art and other cultural institutions that have been repressed in the United States.

She earned her B.A. from Barnard College, Columbia University and her Ph.D. from New York University. She lives in the Berkshires with her husband.

Carolyn would love to hear from you! Please follow her on her Facebook Page and on her website at www.carolynbrancato.com, where you can also read her blog about World War II and the French Resistance. And please consider posting your thoughts about *The Night Belongs to the Maquis* on your own social media site and leaving a review wherever you purchased her book.